PRAISE FOR
AN ACRE OF FOOLS

"Scott MacLellan is one of the very few authors who truly understand and authentically capture the reality of addiction, the mind and motivations of the addict, and the splintering effects of addiction on the family. *An Acre of Fools* is intensely honest, personally revealing, and captivating from start to finish—a remarkable read."

—**NANCY ALCORN**, founder and president of Mercy Multiplied

"With raw vulnerability, MacLellan unfolds a gripping tale that explores the questions: How far will one man go to save his daughter, and at what cost? The answers you'll find are messy, like real life, but certainly more intense than most of us will ever face. *An Acre of Fools* is a must-read, with twists and turns that reveal the protagonist in his sincere and flawed humanity—embodying the classic and conflicted hero. Put *An Acre of Fools* by Scott MacLellan at the very top of your reading list!"

—**MARK TILGHMAN**, co-CEO of Dandelion Media and producer of *An Acre of Fools* TV series

"*An Acre of Fools* is the rare novel that authentically captures the pain, power, and desperation of addiction. Scott understands that it is not only the addict who suffers but everyone close to the illness. He reminds us that it is never too late to fight for those suffering. We can never give up."

—**CHRIS GRANT**, Emmy Award–winning producer and managing director at Charlotte Street Studios

"*An Acre of Fools* is a profound family saga that slams the reader smack into the ragged, full-frontal face of evil, like a page-turning mystery thriller! This mature, hard-souled family narrative is filled with enigmatic paradoxes—along with plot twists that are never predictable! It never fails to surprise, keeping the reader more on the question than on the solution side of events. It's a powerful page-turner!"

—**GEORGE WATKINS**, producer, director,
and partner at Synergy Films

"A riveting story of unimaginable events. Scott MacLellan reminds us there are times when life brings us to 'the darkest night of the soul,' so that 'God can finally have His way.' You cannot read this book and be the same."

—**CHERYL BACHELDER**, former CEO of Popeyes
Louisiana Kitchen and author of *Dare to Serve*

"Scott MacLellan has done the near impossible. He's taken the most raw and personal elements of his family's tumultuous story and turned them into a gripping, evocative, and entertaining book. The theme of addiction is all too resonant in our world today, and Scott's novel manages to lead the reader right into the epicenter of the issue while providing a fresh and personal take."

—**SHARON PAUL**, co-CEO of Dandelion Media
and producer of *An Acre of Fools* TV series

AN ACRE OF FOOLS

A Novel

SCOTT MACLELLAN

GREENLEAF
BOOK GROUP PRESS

Published by Greenleaf Book Group Press
Austin, Texas
www.gbgpress.com

Distributed by Greenleaf Book Group

For ordering information or special discounts for bulk purchases, please contact Greenleaf Book Group at PO Box 91869, Austin, TX 78709, 512.891.6100.

Design and composition by Greenleaf Book Group
Cover design by Greenleaf Book Group
Cover images used under license from ©Adobestock.com

Publisher's Cataloging-in-Publication data is available.

Print ISBN: 979-8-88645-351-5

eBook ISBN: 979-8-88645-352-2

To offset the number of trees consumed in the printing of our books, Greenleaf donates a portion of the proceeds from each printing to the Arbor Day Foundation. Greenleaf Book Group has replaced over 50,000 trees since 2007.

Printed in the United States of America on acid-free paper

25 26 27 28 29 30 31 32 10 9 8 7 6 5 4 3 2 1

First Edition

This book is dedicated to the Austins of the world. We are all lost. We just show it in different ways. This book is about all of us and the mistakes each of us makes along the way.

Everything will be okay in the end.
If it's not okay, it's not the end.

—**FERNANDO SABINO**, *O Tabuleiro de Damas*

CONTENTS

AUTHOR'S NOTE

Okatie (pronounced oh-kuh-tee) is a city in between Beaufort and Bluffton, South Carolina. The city was named after the river that runs through it. Meaning "quiet waters," or just "quiet," Okatie is a phonetic spelling from the original Native American word that was spelled many different ways. In modern times, the city settled on Okatie, while the river retained its original spelling, Okatee.

PROLOGUE

AUSTIN

To almost everyone in this small town, it was a beautiful fall day. The normal stifling heat had given way to a cool 55° temperature that felt wonderful in comparison. Shoppers strolled casually through the markets and sat outside sidewalk cafés sipping tea while outdoor fire pits sent the aroma of burning hickory into the gentle coastal breeze.

Austin remembered that smell from her childhood in Chicago. It reminded her of Christmas, when her father would insist on lighting a fire and playing carols in the background before she and her sister could come down the stairs into the living room.

But today was not Christmas, and this certainly was not Chicago. Nor was it a cozy living room filled with gifts and a loving family. She was alone, tucked back in an alley by the dumpster of the local grocery store. She liked this place as she could sometimes find good food only partially eaten, and there were plenty of cigarette butts she could still smoke before the filter ruined the burn.

Although the day was not bitter cold, it was the kind of chill that numbed the bones after a couple of hours of wearing only a lightweight short-sleeve shirt and a thin, worn-out pair of jeans. She could not get warm no matter where she went or what she did. Of course, it didn't help that her five-foot-six frame only weighed ninety-two pounds.

Although this was her favorite place, she wasn't quite sure how she got here; nor did she remember much about the night before. After finishing off a fifth of vodka, she had somehow made her way to this spot. She was always looking for a place to stay and was willing to do pretty much anything to sleep in a bed rather than outside on the street, even if that meant she had to do unspeakable things to get there.

She stared at the wall on the opposite side of the alley, contemplating how the bricks came together and where the mortar had cracked and fallen apart. She would have used a different mix to get a better, longer-lasting result. She had learned a lot about building from her dad, who was pretty handy around the house. She prided herself on having the skills of a man and the body of an attractive young woman, at least until the drugs ravaged her once-muscular frame and left her scabbed all over her face. She wasn't worth much anymore. But she did what she had to do to survive.

As her mind settled into the maze of bricks, she remembered something important and raced to look inside the plastic bag that now served as her purse. "Ah, perfect!" She reached down into the bag and pulled out a needle that had served as the god of her own making for longer than she could remember. She had saved some of the heroin she scored late last evening for an occasion such as this. She had learned not to be too greedy with her dosage. It was no longer about feeling good. Now, it was only about not feeling bad.

She pulled out the tourniquet she used to get her tired veins to pop and injected the needle into one of the few places that no longer had tracks. Soon she would have to move to her neck to find any vein at all, which was no problem, since that would be a quicker and better high anyway. As the drug coursed through her veins, she could feel her entire body relax. It wouldn't be long before she passed out for the next few hours, which would be just enough to help her make it through the day until the creeps came out from their parents' basements to trade drugs for sex.

Austin was a long way from her family and a long way from the person she had once dreamed she'd be.

PETER

Peter looked at himself in the mirror and found it hard to believe what he saw staring back. The water he had just used to wash the vomit out of his goatee was still dripping off his face. He reached up and traced the droplets as they fell off his cheekbones and down into the facial hair he had grown just a few months before.

His hair was as long as it had ever been in his life, well past his ears now and flowing down toward his shoulders. What would his military father think of him now?

The light in the bathroom was terrible, and it was hard to see much of anything. This house had only the bare necessities and had been run down since it was repossessed. The financial crash had left so many of these properties abandoned all over the country, but especially here in Florida.

He looked down at his shirt and could see blood, freshly stained. He touched it, somehow trying to see if it would change his mind at all about what he was about to do. It did, and then it did not. Then it did again, and then it did not again. Damn this double-mindedness. It was a weakness, plain and simple, and he was tired of being weak.

He pulled the shirt up over his head and threw it down on the floor. He avoided eye contact with the mirror because he knew what he'd see, and that would only stop him in his tracks and change his mind once more. He both wanted to stop and did not want to stop. He knew that what he chose to do in the next five minutes had eternal consequences, both for him and the young man tied up to a chair in the other room.

Peter opened the door, and his prey looked up with pleading eyes. He had been very defiant earlier in the day but quickly became humbler as the reality of his situation hit him hard. The man in front of the captive was older but very muscular and strong. He knew the man could fight because he'd been beaten severely by him, both when he was taken from his car and then again since he'd been tied up in the chair.

With Peter's shirt off now, the captive could see a huge Christian cross tattooed on the man's chest. It took up almost all the space on his left pectoral muscle, just over his heart, and stood in stark contrast to the angry warrior himself.

"Dude, I don't even know you. What do you want from me?"

Peter, in the darkest parts of his mind, had fantasized about this moment for years. He pictured all the things he would do to this deadbeat and so many others like him. Peter's list had seven people on it, and this young man was on the top, number one, the worst of them all.

"You know me, but I meant nothing to you at the time. You had your sights set on something else—something very precious to me."

The young man searched his memory quickly and intensely. He could not place him. "Dude, I swear to you, I don't know you. You have me confused with someone else."

Peter looked down and took great comfort in his captive's fear. This boy had destroyed Peter's family, and now, finally, the pain and confusion were placed where they should be, in the mind of those who do evil. The scales of justice had finally tipped toward Peter. He pulled out the hunting knife he had strapped to his belt and moved closer to the chair.

This was it, the moment Peter had both feared and craved for years. Peter had wondered how he would respond when the time came. His first glimpse into the dark side had come when he'd kidnapped the boy, and later, when he'd strapped him down. It was easier than he thought. Each step toward violence made it easier for him to take another. His conscience was being seared, and he was grateful for it.

The boy screamed, "Help, somebody, please help me!"

"No one can hear you, boy."

Something about the word "boy" jarred the captive's memory. The past lunged forward and, for a brief moment, terrified him. He knew what he had done to Peter. But seeing the cross tattoo assured him that there was still hope. He was a clever boy, after all. He hadn't made it this far without being quick on his feet.

He looked up at Peter and said the only thing that could have stopped him from what he was about to do. "I know no one else can hear me. But you can."

MIMI

Mimi was perched on a windowsill, looking out from one tall building to the next. She couldn't be farther away from where she wanted to be, and yet she knew she was where she was supposed to be. She gazed out at the snow and watched as it blew around the glass and settled onto the brick just outside the window.

She turned and gazed down at Austin, lying in her hospital bed. Mimi wondered if there would ever be an end to the torture. Although her child now slept most of the day, there was no rest to the sleep. Austin groaned and cried out throughout the night, never even aware of her unconscious pleas for a life different from the one she was living.

Even during the worst of Austin's childhood illness, Mimi had some sense of understanding about her circumstances. Sometimes people just get sick, and there's nothing you can do about it. Cancer, transplants, and one surgery after the next had all blended together into one big mess. Yet there was a small place in her mind that could accept that nature can be cruel. Cancer happens, and it's nobody's fault, even when it happens to children. But this, now, was a choice Austin had made—a purposeful decision to die slowly, enslaved to her body.

The last thirteen years had been like a car crash viewed in slow motion, spread out over more than a decade, with each day advancing one frame at a time. The rest of the Stewart family watched from the viewpoint of their sober lives, seeing Austin's recklessness and wondering if the airbag would deploy to save her, to help her survive the wreck.

So they watched, totally fixated and obsessed with what the next frame would bring, even while Austin seemed oblivious to the danger and annoyed that anyone would think she was in the middle of a crisis. They observed the horror day by day, unable to think about anything else. Her life consumed them. Austin, however, lived completely unconcerned about her personal well-being or what she was doing to the rest of the family.

Austin no longer looked like the beautiful child she once was. Her face was pocked and dripping with bloody scabs. The weight loss had changed the contours of her face, and over time, her teeth had rotted and turned almost black. Lying there without makeup, she was unrecognizable as the daughter who had once been so naturally beautiful.

Yet Mimi was the only one who could see the old Austin. The vision in her mind was stronger than the vision in her eyes. She could still see her running on the sandbar, chasing the birds away from their lazy perch on the only dry land in the middle of the half-mile wide Chechessee River. Those were better days, even if it hadn't felt like it at the time.

Years ago, Mimi had been the first to give up the vision of a healthy and whole Austin. But she also was the only one who could coax it back, here, at the end—when it mattered the most. She would be the last one to hold Austin in her arms, and then she would be gone to the only place that brought rest to her soul.

GRACE ELIZABETH

Gracie had lived with the devil for over ten years, but nobody knew it except her. She had tried to make them see the evil for all that it was, but evil has a way of masquerading as innocence and pity. If people are not sure if evil is truly evil, they will hesitate to judge for fear of seeming unjust. To thrive, evil counts on uncertainty, and so it plays with its prey before devouring it.

But the truth will always come out eventually, and now the devil was on full display for all to see. There was no hiding it anymore. Evil degrades and rots from the inside out. Sooner or later, it hits the outside, and no amount of makeup or tearful apologies can cover the sins spread out over an entire decade.

Yet there was an incredible miracle that had come out of all the pain, and that blessing was sitting right behind her in the back seat. Two years old, but nothing terrible about him, little Grayson was smiling at her in the rearview mirror. She waved and said, "Hi," and he said it back with a giggle that was so sweet she couldn't stand it.

Gracie was not so sure where their next stop would be. They'd been driving for almost seven hours, and it was well past Grayson's bedtime. She opened a sack next to her, exposing about $10,000 in cash. She grabbed a couple of $100 bills, closed the zipper back up, and put a baby blanket over it.

She saw a sign for a few budget hotels and got off the exit. The first had a police car in the parking lot, and so she drove past it and checked out the next one. It seemed dark and unremarkable, so she pulled in and began to unpack their things.

She started to move toward the lobby before remembering something important. She returned to the car and got a baseball cap to cover her face. She put a hoodie on Grayson and pulled it up over his head. She pretended to play peek-a-boo with him to keep him interested in keeping it up over his face.

As they got settled into their room after this first day of traveling, Grayson eventually fell into a deep sleep. Gracie just stared at him and rubbed his back. As she sat there on the floor, reaching down into his playpen to stroke him, the gravity of what she had done began to set in, and she started to cry quietly.

Heroism always starts with great strength and clarity. But if the moment lasts too long, fears and doubts start to take hold. Questions about the validity of her valor seeped in, and she wondered if what she had done was so "right" after all. Gracie thought about turning back. This was not a small commitment she was making. It hadn't even been twelve hours, but she was already tired. *What had she done?*

ACT I

YEAR 66:
THE END OF OUR STORY

Our family's story started simply enough but soon wrapped itself around a web of complexity and deceit that suffocated and hardened the hearts of even the most faithful among us. Yet it prepared me well for the life I lead today, in which a simplistic view of good and evil is mocked, and people glorify the games of manipulation and degradation.

I'm the only one left to tell the story, and I'm the reason they're all gone. I come to this place now to remember them. We were happy here, and the little bit of love we had that was untainted flourished in this house. It was the only time we laughed and prayed and wept together as a family in a way that I imagine other families do. We spent only a week a year here, but it was enough to get us through the other fifty-one.

We called this house "River Soul," in part because it sat on the marshy banks of the Okatee River but mostly because it was the only place where we all felt ourselves—our real selves. Here, we were the people we thought God intended us to be. It was a place without pretense or malice, and it taught us to be different people, first to ourselves and then to each other.

Like the tides that rose and fell through the Port Royal Sound, we, too, could feel our souls rise and fall in a rhythmic pace that pleased the heart and helped our minds settle into a calm we rarely felt. It was in that place of rest that all the complexity would gradually subside.

My dad would say that this is how he imagined Jesus worked: filling us up with God's love and then, bit by bit, washing away our sins. But the rest of us just knew this place had a way of healing our family, if only for a week. Our desperate need to understand why we were trapped in such horrible circumstances would simply subside into a knowing that there was no decent reply. If there are no reasonable answers, why bother asking difficult questions?

When you stop asking "why," life becomes simpler. You stop judging each other, and you stop judging yourself. Dad would say you even stop judging God. If you accept what you have, you can become grateful for even the supposedly bad things in life.

But our life was filled with judgment: bad life, bad parents, bad children, bad siblings, evil people who worshipped a cruel God who showed no mercy to any of us. Judging each other was good sport in our family, and we became experts at tearing each other apart. Each of us acted as a god of our own creation, certain that only we knew what was right and what was wrong for everyone but ourselves.

It is said that the Original Sin was the thought that we could be independent of God, and it is that constant fight for independence that causes all the grief in our lives. If that be true, then we are all fools because we fight for control every minute of every day. In that way, we all fall short of what God hopes for us. At least that's what Dad thought—that is, until he didn't know what to think anymore.

And that is when our story turned the darkest—when Dad lost his faith. Though none of us had much religion, we counted on Dad's faith to cover us all. As long as he was right with God, then all of us were. But when he fell, we all fell. He always said that if we looked to him as our source of truth, he would disappoint us eventually. And he was right. He did.

But I'm way ahead of myself. I can't start at the end. We must go back to where it all started, when Mimi and Dad first found what was to become our annual, week-long getaway: River Soul. You will see the entire mess, as this story must be told. I hold our family out to you so that others might learn from our brokenness and the destruction we caused along the way.

I will narrate, but I cannot tell the story in the first person, at least not here in this particular house. There is too much pain in the story, and this place does not serve as a safe harbor for the hard things in life. And so I will tell it as though it happened to someone else, to some other family in some other time. I will hide among the details of a fictional cast who represent the essence of what we were to ourselves and to each other.

I take comfort in the distance I will place between this family and our own, for it allows me to think about where it all went wrong. It's easier to see the truth when we are not wrapped up in the mess of it all. For truth is not what we feel or say or do. Truth is a constant. We spin around it as though we know what it is, but truth is elusive, maybe even unknowable in this life.

And so I will tell the story as though I know what really happened. The way I saw it and heard it. Because who can really know what happened, or what people were really thinking along the way? Only they know for sure, but even that may be untrue because if they knew themselves, none of this ever would have happened in the first place.

Dad used to say that the Spirit knows all things, even the deep things of God. But I just can't see how that can be true. Because if God really knew us, He would not claim to be our God. He would look the other way and make it as though we had never been born at all. Sometimes, I wish that were the case. That none of us had ever been born. But Dad said we are all brought to this earth for a reason, for a purpose. Perhaps mine is to testify to the fools I call my family.

YEAR 1:
THE BEGINNING OF OUR STORY

Dad used to say that nothing calmed him more quickly than entering the gates of River Soul. It seemed that all of the stress of the world parked itself on the South Carolina state line when he'd cross over on his trips to Okatie. He knew the burdens of the world would be waiting for him back there, but he also knew that they had no power over him here.

We all felt that way about this part of the world, eventually. There were other places that were more dramatically beautiful at first glance. And, taken at low tide in particular, this place could seem like a wasteland of dried-up reeds, mud, and dilapidated shrimp boats abandoned for insurance money.

The Lowcountry seemed unexciting at best and boring at worst. At the very beginning, before we all were even born, Dad had found nothing appealing about it, and he couldn't understand why Mimi had brought him here to look for a house on the river. It was not what he expected, and he wasn't sure it was living up to her romanticized view of what she had read about either. But Dad thought she was staying positive merely to counteract him being so negative.

He had promised Mimi a place in the South ever since he moved her to Chicago. Mimi hated Chicago equally as much as Dad loved Chicago, which was a lot on each side of the love-hate equation. A Southern girl had no business in below-zero weather, let alone being trapped inside a house for more than half the year. Even when the warm weather came, it was so gray and gloomy that being outside left her as empty as being inside.

She tried to convince herself that she should be happy regardless of the weather. But a girl meant for sun was never meant to survive in the snow and rain. She came to realize that no matter how much she tried to think positively, this was just not who she was. She could no more be a woman of the North than Dad could be a househusband. He was made for business, and she was made for sand and water.

So, as they turned off the main road at the "For Sale" sign on the Okatie Highway so many years ago, Dad settled into the promise he had made her, and he stopped complaining so she could enjoy whatever it was that this trip meant to her. The dirt and gravel road kicked up enough dust to make it hard to see, but even Dad was a bit taken aback at the beauty of the oak trees lining each side of the road leading to the house.

The trees created a canopy above them, and only flickers of sun were visible through the Spanish moss that draped around and fell from expansive and crooked branches, giving the moss the appearance of hanging lanterns. It almost felt as though it were sunset even though it was just barely after 3 p.m.

The house came into view after a few minutes, and it was as rundown as everything else he had seen on the drive down from Charleston. It was old, broken, and deserted. Clearly, no one had done a thing for this house in the last twenty years, and Dad had no interest in being the first to try. He turned to express his displeasure to Mimi when she looked over to him and said, "Oh, Peter, it's just as I pictured it."

The house had different levels that terraced to match the landscape. It was clear certain parts of the home had been added after the original construction, as very little matched from one section to the next. It had the feel of a compound, since the garage was detached and a dilapidated shed leaned toward the right side of the house. It was a disaster through and through.

Still, Dad knew then it wouldn't matter what else he had to say; this was going to be a house he would own, and this was going to be a place he would have to spend the rest of his life fixing. With all the hours he spent at work, the thought of hard labor while on vacation proved to be a daunting vision of the next sixty-something years.

But Mimi was persistent. She envisioned children and grandchildren running all over that land as clearly as she saw the actual house that stood before her. She had a way of seeing things that none of us could ever see—especially when it came to her family.

"Mimi, really? This place?"

"Yes, Peter, this place. This is it. Call the agent and tell her we'll take it. And don't argue about the price. I don't want to jeopardize this deal. Just say the words 'We'll take it, as is.'"

Dad kept his gaze fixed on the house without giving her eye contact.

"Peter, say the words."

It's wise not to fight when you know you've already lost the battle. You only prolong the pain and take everyone down with you. So Dad relented and said the words, "We'll take it, as is." He hung his head and looked around at nothing at all.

"Now, there's a good boy," Mimi said with some playfulness. "Good boy! Now you go make the call, and I'll look around just a bit. We have some work to do."

Peter turned the car around to head back to the gas station after Mimi got out to walk the land. He had seen a payphone there and would use it to negotiate a better deal out of earshot. Although he dreaded everything about that place, he loved to see Mimi happy and would do almost anything to see the spark lit by something she loved.

He was not an outwardly emotional man, but he felt love deeply inside him with certain people. Mimi was on the top of that list and always would be.

As Peter drove out of sight, leaving only a dust trail behind him, Mimi turned her attention to the river. There was a deepwater dock at the end of a very long pier that had seen much better days. The wood was splintered and twisted with time and was contorted into a wave design like you might have to walk at a carnival fun house. Several boards were loose, and it took some careful attention to avoid crashing through or falling off as she made her way down to the dock.

Deepwater access was a prized possession on the Okatee. With a tidal shift of ten feet, the river went from lapping at its banks to hundreds of yards away in a matter of hours. At low tide, access to the river could only be had across a vast expanse of gooey tidal mud called plough (shortened to pluff). Even with the river in view, anyone attempting to reach it would be sucked knee-deep into the exposed mud of the riverbed before making it more than three feet from shore.

But as impossible as it was for a human to cross the pluff, it was alive with all matter of creatures from shrimp to oysters to crabs. While shrimp hunted, they created a gentle popping sound as their hammer claws shot water—water that could reach speeds of more than sixty miles an hour—at their prey. Pools of water trapped on land as the tide receded captured sea life of all kinds who had to wait for the water to return when the earth rotated another quarter cycle in relation to the moon.

As Mimi got halfway down the walkway, the sound of the marsh came into her awareness, and she stopped to let it wash over her. She had been so focused on not falling off the pier that she had completely missed what lay only a few feet below her. She watched and listened and felt something she had not known before.

Even the sulfur smell of low tide had an element that she would later call her Southern perfume, much like a farmer finds the smell of manure to be a marker of home life. This was nothing a city boy from Chicago could understand, at least not at first. She knew and saw instantly what it would take most of us years to see and then appreciate.

As she continued down toward the dock, she could hear another sound, one she could not identify. By the time she got to the ramp leading down toward the water, she saw something she had only seen in pictures. In the part of the water still deep enough to hold them, two adult dolphins and their calves were circling near the dock. Mimi watched as they bobbed and weaved within reach of her outstretched arm. Unsure why they were so close, she finally realized they were feeding, taking advantage of the low tide where their prey had less room to roam.

It was a spiritual experience for a woman who rarely thought of such things. She had very little thought of the Spirit or anything of the sort, yet this made her think, if only for a moment, that maybe there was a God. She let gratitude wash over her and closed her eyes to let it reach the deepest parts within her.

Refocusing on the dolphin family in front of her, she thought of a day when she, too, would have children of her own. She dreamed of two boys who, with surfboards in tow, would follow her down the beach. For whatever reason, she always pictured them around eight or nine years old. Just old enough to be independent, but young enough to still look up to her and want to be with her always.

She was the cool mom in her dreams, the outdoors mom who was more interested in experiencing life than books and homework. They would love her for her love of nature and her love of life. Too much beyond the simplicity of love itself would be overthinking it all.

She was very comfortable updating her dream to now include this dock. Once Peter got hold of it, it would be safe again. She could see her boys running the length of the pier to descend down to a boat they didn't yet own or even know how to pay for. They would swim and fish and do all the things that boys love to do.

By the time Mimi started the trek back to the house, the sun had started its descent and was already dipping behind the line of oak trees on the lot, creating a silhouette that Mimi would study for decades to come. The trees looked even more stunning from this angle, with the sun behind them, than they did on the approach to the house.

She loved this time of day, as well as early morning. The angle of the light somehow accentuated the natural beauty of the landscape, creating an even more radiant image in her mind. Mimi was an artist, but not the kind who paints. She just had a way of holding onto things in her consciousness that would come out later in the way she cooked, the way she decorated, or simply in the way she loved us.

And that is how our story started, with so much potential, so many dreams yet to fulfill, and a couple in love with each other and the life they had just begun together. Beginnings have a way about them that are so innocent, so pure. Endings can be so tragic and so corrupted. Somewhere in between is the mystery of life, the crooked journey that captures hearts and souls along the way.

YEAR 3

The "plan," as it would later come to be called, was set off course early as Mimi got pregnant with a girl they would call Grace. The pregnancy and delivery went well. Mimi was not one for pain, but on a very cold day in Chicago, she bore her first through natural childbirth. She and Peter introduced Grace Elizabeth Stewart to the world. Mimi's plan for two boys in the South began with one girl in the North. Peter had no such plan and was delighted to have a Chicago girl as his first.

Peter was not one to live in the past, but this particular day would be a memory he would hold on to right up until the end. Gracie was born at 5:32 a.m., after Mimi had endured a full night of labor. That evening, after napping off and on, Peter awoke to the sound of soft voices. Next to Mimi's bed stood a nurse looking over Grace, who was sound asleep in Mimi's arms.

The nurse and Mimi were talking about something, but Peter could not hear, and he was grateful. If he could hear, his mind would engage. Instead, he was able to enjoy one of those rare moments when Peter thought just with his heart. The sight of Mimi holding their child, and the safety and security of knowing people were there to care for them both, gave him a sense of peace and joy he would rarely duplicate for the rest of his life.

But the calm moment in the hospital quickly gave way to the panic all parents feel when taking home their first child. Can we care for this dependent creature safely? Can we keep her from harm? Can we raise her properly? It would turn out that they need not ask any of these questions, as Gracie would grow up to be a dependable, responsible child who brought much joy to their lives. It also would turn out that they asked none of these questions when their second child was born.

They should have.

But now, here in this early part of their story, Gracie was making her first visit to the banks of the Okatee, to a house that had yet to have a name. Peter and Mimi rode up the drive that now included the gravel Peter had spread the year before. And, while the house had a fresh coat of paint, most things were still dangling every which way. Peter had finished most of the work on the inside of the house so as to make it livable during their weeklong visits. The house was nothing fancy, but at least there were no holes in the walls and no more family of raccoons living in the attic.

"Peter, the house looks fantastic."

Peter knew the house did not look good, let alone fantastic. And he knew that Mimi knew the house didn't look good. And he knew she was only throwing him some positive reinforcement so he would be energetic about more repairs this trip. And yet he would have been disappointed if she hadn't sent this compliment his way.

"Thanks. It's livable now."

"Oh, it's more than that. It's perfect."

"Let's not get carried away. It's a start."

"Okay, then, it's a perfect start."

Peter smiled at the little ways she had of blending them together. His business life was dominated by win-lose thinking. Mimi was driven to find something in the middle—not quite a compromise but more of a union. A compromise seemed something unsatisfactory. It still had an element of loss to it, with each side having to give up something. But a union took in all that there was to be had, and no one lost, or at least no one felt like they lost. He could learn from that.

"I'm going to tackle the pier this trip. By the time we get back here next year, it should be ready."

Peter had already contracted to have the pylons and posts checked for structural integrity and also to have the old pier deconstructed and hauled away. He had seen the crane barges needed to work on a pier, and he knew he did not have capacity to do that himself during either high or low tide.

Mimi switched from Southern belle to field commander and turned to Peter with instructions. "You pull in here and get Gracie out for me. I'll unpack after you get me the bags. I know you want to get to work."

Peter looked over and saw the beautiful woman he had married. She had lost all her baby weight and was once again back to her athletic self. She was strong in body and strong in spirit. Her blonde hair would soon be accentuated against the tan skin she'd have by tomorrow. "Actually, I thought this was my time away from work."

Mimi looked at Peter and smiled and patted him on the knee.

"I swear, if you call me a good boy again, I'll just camp out on the porch all week."

Mimi smiled and realized she had set the wheels in motion.

Peter pulled up to the front of the house and hopped out to get Grace. He liked to call her Grace, not Gracie. Grace Elizabeth had an air of royalty. Gracie sounded like a dog's name. But it became so common for everyone else to use Gracie that he eventually gave up and joined the crowd. Mimi was a pet name for Mary, after all, so why not Gracie for Grace.

His girls were the fun in his life. He had always been a serious fellow, but his family had become his source of joy. Watching Gracie and watching Mimi watch Gracie were his favorite pastimes. He had roll after roll after roll of film, with most pictures being completely useless. But to him, there always was one special picture out of a hundred that he carried in his wallet until the paper fell apart into shreds of faded images once so clear and colorful.

Peter reached into the back to pull his daughter from the car seat that had taken two hours to install. Peter thought that car seats were torturous devices made by people who didn't have kids and didn't have to install car seats. He worked the various clasps and buckles until he finally had Gracie in his hands and then gently pulled her into his arms.

Mimi came over and shared the moment. She made a grand gesture with her hand and said, "One day, little girl, all this will be yours!" She meant it back then, but it would turn out to be an untruth. Like so many other plans, it was not so much a lie, but something else that wouldn't turn out the way she had hoped.

Peter walked around the house, and as he turned the corner, he could see that there was a pile of wood planks stacked so high it blocked the view of the river. He was both pleased that the delivery had been made as requested and overwhelmed at the thought of having to install every plank. He moved down farther to see that the weathered pier had been properly removed and the posts all looked level. He had a good foundation to work with, and that would make the task go a bit easier.

The dock off in the distance seemed very far away to him now. It too would need to be replaced eventually, but that would be a project for another week. Docks in the Lowcountry had to float because of the massive tidal shifts. A dock at high tide sat so high in the water that walking the plank to the dock was like little more than stepping off a curb. At low tide, the plank was so steep that getting down to the boat could be a dangerous proposition. But there was no boat yet in the Stewart family, so all this work was merely cosmetic now.

He grabbed a single plank and placed it down to make sure the measurements were correct. The board fit perfectly, which gave him some satisfaction. A man needs his projects, and this was a big one. No room for variability if it was all going to get done this trip. This confidence that things were working out gave him the chance to take in the scenery for the first time since his arrival that day. The tide was turning, and the water was rushing out of the river. He was always amazed at how aggressive the currents were in this part of the country.

He had not spent much time in the backyard, as most of his projects had been inside so far. The few times he was outside were spent talking with Mimi, and that was where his concentration lay. She, however, had spent countless hours outdoors. It was his habit to watch her from the window during breaks in his work, when she didn't know he was looking. She would simply stare out at the marsh and let the tidal breezes remind her that she was in the South once again.

"What do you think about?" he finally asked her later that night when Gracie was asleep.

"I try not to think," she said quite simply, as though his question were silly. "I see what I see. The thinking comes later."

"So, what do you think about later?"

She looked up at the ceiling to process the question in her mind and was suddenly shy. "I think about why you ask so many questions."

The classic non-answer. He went to dig further but decided not to. He didn't need to know everything about her. Women have thoughts where men should allow distance. A woman wants to be known, but there are some places that are her own. She may bring you in, but it will be on her own terms, at her time.

She came to him and wrapped herself around him. She was always so cold at home, usually looking to retreat into a pile of blankets and wooly socks. Here, with her bare feet and tank top, she felt open and attractive. There was something about sun-touched skin that felt different and smelled different. She wanted to be with him. She placed her hand around the back of his head and stroked his hair while she buried her face into his neck.

The following morning, it was too early to fire up the nail gun, so Peter organized his boards and tools to get ready to begin. He sat for a moment in a dime-store folding chair Mimi had placed for him to rest in. The sun had already breached the trees and was reflecting off the water. The storks and herons that roosted in nearby branches had already made their way to their own private hunting grounds throughout the marsh. They were in the water ankle-deep (if herons and storks have ankles), waiting frozen in place for unsuspecting prey to cross their paths. Every few minutes, one of them would strike, eat, and go back to frozen form once more.

It all seemed so peaceful and beautiful until he realized that it was not so wonderful for the fish that were being eaten for breakfast. It had always bothered Peter that God had set up such a violent system. One creature ate another creature that ate another. Peter had never taken to fishing because it seemed so cruel, and he certainly never hunted. He could not imagine how anyone could shoot something as helpless as a dove or deer. It all seemed so barbaric.

It occurred to him that he was in this incredible setting, but his thoughts had somehow gravitated to the macabre. Surely Mimi's mind never went there. But then again, according to her, her mind never went anywhere out here. She just took it all in for what was placed before her. He wasn't sure how she did that. She saw beauty where he saw pain. He'd have to work on that. He'd have to fix that.

After enough time passed, he got up from his chair and began his work. His mind settled into the task at hand, which seemed to make the world right again. Mimi saw this forward progress from the kitchen and knocked on the window to give the thumbs-up sign. She was pleased that he had taken a few moments to appreciate the view and was equally as pleased that he was now at work.

Dad would often say that a prayer is only good if it motivates you to action, but for Mimi, a dream was only good if it eventually came into view. Otherwise, it was all nonsense, leading to frustration. And here in this house, her dream was slowly coming into view. It was three years better than when they had found it.

By lunchtime, the pier was far enough along that they set chairs out on the planks that smelled of freshly cut wood. Gracie was strapped in a chair with an umbrella attached to keep her shaded from the very hot South Carolina sun. Mimi eventually stretched out on a blanket to get as much of the sun as she could, while Peter was doing whatever he could to share the shade with his daughter.

It was in that moment that Peter first came to appreciate this place. Here, with the woman he loved and the daughter who would eventually become his greatest source of comfort. It was then that he decided Mimi was right to bring him here—to bring all of them here. There was something about this place that was special, although he couldn't yet put into words what that was exactly.

Later that night, he wanted to make some gesture of acknowledgment that maybe this place wasn't so bad, but it just seemed too soon. He had made such a stink about the South, the expense and the hard work of it all, that he wanted to be slow in his praise so as to put some distance between his complaints and compliments.

They sat at the dinner table quietly at first. Not a distant quiet; more of a content quiet. But by the end of the meal, there was laughter and the silliness that went along with a small child at the table. Gracie was a joy and a perfect combination between the two. Somehow Mimi had managed to find that union she was so good at creating, now in a human being. It wasn't Peter, or Mimi, or Gracie. It was all of them.

As they moved out onto the porch, a thunderstorm, which seemed to make an appearance almost every summer night by the water in South Carolina, rolled off in the distance. Sometimes, the storms made it to where they were. Other times, they just passed by in the distance offshore. But most every night's activities revolved around when the storm would come.

Tonight, they sat and enjoyed the breeze that the rain kicked up off the ocean about five miles to the east. The palmetto tree branches rustled in such a way as to give the feel of living in the islands, where the trade winds were constant and almost reassuring.

Peter came to realize that there was no other place he'd rather be. There were many places he had traveled to with his work, and they were nice, but this was as nice as he ever needed. He would go on later in life to travel the world, but his heart would eventually journey back to Mimi's precious Okatie.

YEAR 7

The flight from Chicago O'Hare to Charleston's airport was particularly crazy on this trip. Now, with two children in tow, it was tough to manage the number of bags, car seats, playpens, and toys necessary for a family of four. Peter was grateful when it all fit—albeit just barely—into the van they set aside for families such as his.

But I'm way ahead of myself. I failed to introduce Austin Leigh Stewart, born two years earlier. Austin came into the world with some excitement, seeing as the Stewarts almost didn't make it to the hospital in time thanks to the snow and ice that had accumulated during one of the most brutal storms on record.

Along the drive, Mimi silently burned to herself that the trek to the hospital would have been a lot easier in South Carolina. Even Gracie complained of the cold as they got her dressed in a snowsuit for the ride to the emergency room.

They did make it to the hospital in time, and the delivery went well, although there was a bit more drama with this baby girl. Austin was born blue, and she was moved immediately to the Neonatal Intensive Care Unit, where she spent the next seven days. Her first week on this planet was spent in the hands of strangers. Caring strangers but strangers, nonetheless.

The week was a blur as the medical team offered this or that scenario, along with a range of prognoses that went from all-clear to certain and sudden death. While emotional swings went from very high to very low, Peter and Mimi knew they had to keep steady for Gracie's sake because she was always at the hospital with them, with no other family living within a thousand miles. They sat and slept for days on waiting room floors and in the lobby where there was a little more room for Gracie to play.

By week's end, the doctors chalked everything up to an unexplained virus and discharged Austin to the care of her parents, who could not stop holding her for the next two weeks. That first week of separation had created a physical distance they worked very hard to close when they had free access to their little girl. Gracie was excited to be a big sister, and the family moved on to a more normal existence, if life with two children can ever be considered normal.

Now, with two girls in the North, Mimi had to concede that large parts of "the plan" required adjusting. She was willing to accommodate acts of nature into a revised plan that kept the family vision mostly intact. It was the man-made things that made her angry, like choosing to live in the North when there were so many jobs to be had in the South.

But now, here at the airport, they were in the South once again, and Mimi was ready to soak it all in as best she could. She had only one week's worth of time to restore her soul with enough Southern air to last her for another eleven months and three weeks. She looked forward to this moment all year, and now it was here. But there was so much to be done yet just to make it to Okatie. Getting the girls settled into the car and to the house before dark required both precision and luck.

The drive down Highway 17 toward Beaufort, where they would stop for groceries, was more tense than usual. The normal chance to decompress from the flight was made more stressful because twenty minutes into the trip, Gracie had to use the bathroom. There was only one gas station along 17, and they were nowhere near it. After five minutes of "holding it," Gracie was at a full squirm. Peter eventually pulled over to get Gracie outside.

"What are you doing?" Mimi asked.

"I'm pulling over so she can pee."

"She's not a boy, Peter. She can't just go around the car and do her thing on a tire."

"So she can squat."

"Here? Out in the open? This is the most dangerous stretch of highway in America. Do you know how many people are killed on this road each year?"

Peter looked at Grace, who had stopped squirming, thinking relief was in sight. "Do you have to go?" She nodded yes aggressively. "So then go already."

Mimi let out a huff and unbuckled her seatbelt. She got out of the car and got Grace out of her car seat. The slamming of the door startled Austin, who started to cry in her car seat. Gracie, embarrassed by having to pull down her pants on the open highway, started to cry while trying to do her business.

"Lovely," murmured Peter under his breath. Catching himself, he looked in the rearview mirror at Austin and smiled, waving his hand as if to say hello. Austin was unimpressed and continued her rant. Mimi opened the door with a screaming Gracie in tow and got her into the car seat. Mimi walked around and got in the car and, with a very aggravated motion, ripped the seatbelt around her, never actually looking at Peter.

Distracted by the scene of three angry women, Peter did not look before starting to pull back onto the highway. Suddenly, a truck slammed on his horn as it blew past their van at seventy miles per hour. Mimi yelped in fear, which caused the girls to scream all the more. Mimi joined the chorus and broke down into a full sobbing cry as well.

They all sat by the side of the road for a time until Peter pulled the car back onto 17, this time, after ensuring there were no more cars or trucks coming his way. After a few more moments of gradually diminishing sobs, they drove in silence for another half hour or so when the scenery finally caught their attention. The sun had begun to set, and it was now reflecting off the water of the marshy grasslands while also dodging behind clumps of trees that would block its light. As the car moved along, it created a strobe-like effect that calmed everyone into a hypnotic trance.

When they finally arrived at the house, they went about their business of unpacking and moving in for the week. They were silent at first, but that silence soon gave way to the verbal teamwork required to get the girls settled and all the bags and boxes into the right place. Before long, it was as though nothing upsetting had happened at all.

"When you're ready, I have something to show you and the girls," Peter said with a grin.

"What is it?" Mimi asked with a bit of anticipation and a smile of her own.

"Let's take a walk out back."

As they moved toward the water, it was hard not to recognize just how far the house had come in the last seven years. The backyard was now beautifully landscaped, and Peter had installed wooden decks and tabby terraces where Adirondack chairs now lined up and faced out to the river. A fire pit was his latest bit of work, and that would soon be ablaze to cook the groceries they had collected on the last leg of their trip into Okatie.

The sun had already set, but there was still plenty of light to see as Peter carried Austin down the pier. Mimi held Gracie's hand. "Look at the sky, Mommy," Gracie said with a manner of awe that only children can express. The sky was streaked with pastel colors of all kinds as the sun still reflected off a variety of the taller rain clouds above.

"It is beautiful, isn't it?" Mimi responded. "Do you think this is what Daddy wanted to show us?"

"That too," Peter said, "but I also have something else you might like to see."

As they reached the end of the pier, they could finally see down to the dock. There, tied up, was a canoe and four life jackets.

"Peter, where did you find that?"

"I saw it for sale in the classifieds of the *Island Gazette*. I thought it might be fun, and I asked them to deliver it here last week."

"I love it!" Gracie squealed. "Can we go out in it now?"

"No, it's too dark, but we'll head out tomorrow. All four of us."

"It's terrific, Peter. Thank you."

"Not quite surfboards on the beach just yet." Although Peter rarely spoke of Mimi's plan, it was written on his heart to fulfill every last detail of the vision she had for their family.

The lights Peter had installed the year before on the pier railings turned on automatically as the grays of dusk gave way to the black of night. This latest new feature distracted all of them away from the canoe and turned their attention to the house. They strolled back as the last of the dusk descended into a darkness one can only experience in a place where homes are spread far apart and very little artificial light disrupts the night sky.

The house looked so inviting from this distance, in this light. It was still not exactly a lovely house, but just as candlelight can bring out the radiant beauty of a woman, so too can some soft lighting make the house seem elegant somehow.

"You're doing an amazing job," Mimi said in a soft, reflective tone of voice that made her appreciation seem genuine, with no agenda or pat-on-the-back intended. It was just her expression of gratitude that they had this place to come to, and that her husband cared about what she needed and wanted.

"Thanks." His tone was just as sincere. He wanted to hear her appreciation, but he seldom felt worthy of receiving it. Tonight, he felt worthy, and he received her praise without any self-deprecating humor that usually appeared in their loving banter.

As they reached the backyard, Mimi turned to him. "If you and Gracie will start the fire, Austin and I will get the food ready."

"That sounds like a plan." Peter turned to Gracie. "Grace Elizabeth, would you help me get the fire started?"

"Of course, Daddy. I'll go get the wood."

"How about we do that together?"

"Sounds like a plan," Gracie mimicked as she ran off into the darkness toward the woodpile.

As mother and daughter moved up to the house, Austin rested her head on her mother's shoulder. Mimi stopped for a second to enjoy the feeling of her young daughter so cozy in her arms. Yet she also knew what this moment meant, and it was not a cozy feeling at all. Austin had been spiking fevers for most of the past year, and this was usually how it started. Austin would get very quiet, then move in close to one of her parents for physical attention, and then get very sick for most of the night.

They had spent most of the last year in a doctor's office, hoping for some medical explanation. Her fevers would often reach 105°, and yet no one could determine a cause. She looked sickly most of the time and lacked the energy most children her age would exhibit.

Mimi knew, here and now, that there was more to the story that would yet unfold. But there was not much she could do about it tonight. She kissed her daughter's forehead to check her temperature. "Looks like you've got another one coming on, my sweet. Let's get you fed and off to bed."

When dawn finally arrived, Austin's fever had broken. Peter and Mimi had been up most of the night doing what they did almost every night—sitting on the floor, watching Austin's every move in case she needed them. There was not much to be done while she went through cycles of fever throughout the night. It would rise and fall about five times over eight hours. Eventually, she would break into a huge sweat, which was frightening at first but soon became an encouraging sign that the fever was about to break its hold on their little girl.

Peter emerged from their bedroom first, exhausted as usual. He had always been a light sleeper and Austin's situation had made him an outright insomniac. He slept on average about two hours a night and would sometimes go three or four days without ever falling completely asleep. The only rest he ever got was when his body just shut down from exhaustion.

As he walked out into the kitchen he had renovated two years before, he grabbed a diet soda out of the fridge. He'd never been a coffee drinker but now needed the caffeine each morning just to function. Since he never slept, he was at work most mornings by 5 a.m. He might as well be at work while the rest of the world relaxed in the comfort of knowing they had healthy children.

Mimi emerged a couple of hours later and went right into conversation without the slightest hint of pretending that it was a good morning. "There has to be something wrong with her. I'm not willing to believe any longer that this is just a normal childhood virus. Something's wrong, Peter. We have to figure this out."

"And we will, but just not today. Can we sit for a moment, and just enjoy our time away?"

Mimi relaxed. She was so caught up in Austin that she had forgotten who she was when she was in this place. She moved in next to Peter and leaned into him, closing her eyes since she was still so tired. Then in a sleepy tone of voice she asked, "So, what's on tap for this week?"

Peter never told her his plans. It was a game they played. In the early years, he would listen to subtle comments that Mimi would make and write them down. He'd determine what he felt she wanted most and then tackle that project the following year. Of course, as the years went by, the comments from Mimi were no longer subtle. They had an agenda attached, and she would now carefully drop hints about what she wanted done. Still, Mimi never knew for sure what the project would be.

"I thought I'd take a break this year," Peter teased.

Mimi opened her eyes, sat up, and in good fun, gave him a gentle pretend slap on the shoulder.

"Okay, okay, I'll do something."

Mimi settled back and placed her head on his shoulder to await his news.

"I was thinking about fixing up the outside aesthetics since we have the inside far enough along to make it livable. The place still has a haunted mansion feel to it. I'll focus on the front of the house, so it looks a bit better on approach. The siding needs work, and I'm going to replace all the doors."

Mimi smiled, as this was exactly what she was hoping. "And what about the girls today? It is the Fourth of July, after all."

"Let's try out the canoe later. We'll have a picnic somewhere along the way."

"That would be awesome."

They sat on the couch for another hour before the girls woke up and needed attention. Mimi treasured these moments. Peter had become increasingly more successful at work, and with each promotion, he seemed to get that much busier, and the travel seemed to keep him away from home more and more. But here, he was the man she married. He was relaxed and attentive. Mostly, he was present. And that was enough for now.

After lunch and naptime, the four of them packed up for the first Stewart family canoe trip. With both girls in the canoe, and with Mimi firmly in place between them, Peter gently pushed away from his position on the dock and jumped into the canoe.

Although Peter had been gentle in getting into the boat, it tipped heavily to one side, almost capsizing and sending everyone overboard. In trying to keep the boat from tipping over, Peter overcorrected and tipped too far in the other direction, which sent him over the other side of the boat and into the water.

After ensuring that both girls were still inside the canoe, Mimi looked over to see Peter bobbing in the water with a sheepish look, peering out from below his floppy hat, water still flowing down from the top and over the brim. It was the silliest thing that she had ever seen, and she broke out hysterically in laughter, as did both the girls.

"Smooth move. Now, how do you plan to get back in the canoe?"

It was a good question. Peter had yet to install a ladder on the dock, and the tide was still not low enough to touch bottom. So eventually, he pulled and pushed the canoe over to the marsh, thinking he could stand up to get inside. But as he put his weight down on the bottom to jump inside, his feet sunk into the mud. In the process of extracting himself, both shoes came off and quickly disappeared into a blackish ooze, never to be found again.

Now what? Peter knew that the ground below him was either gooey mud or razor-sharp oyster beds that would slice his feet to shreds if he stepped incorrectly. So he gingerly inched his way over to some clumps of marsh grass about twenty yards away, where, after several attempts, he got enough solid surface to flop into the canoe like a seal galumphing onto dry land.

He tried to collect himself, but there was no recovering from this misadventure. The outright laughter of his three girls had subsided into quiet giggles between them. Peter was drenched, very muddy, and more than a bit exhausted.

"Well, now. Shall we?" Peter attempted to speak with some shred of dignity left in his voice, but his poor attempt at recovery caused all three to burst out laughing again. Even Peter allowed himself a smile as he began paddling out into the middle of the river with an exaggerated motion to keep the joke going.

Mimi reached over and pulled off his hat, which at this point looked ridiculous, and threw it back at him into his lap. "All right, captain, where to?"

Peter motioned with his head. "Over yonder, mates. Over yonder."

Soon, the tide was at its lowest point with a slack tide and no current, making it very easy to paddle. The water was so low that they felt as though they were making their way through the Grand Canyon on the Colorado River. The reeds and marshy grass that normally stuck out just above the water at high tide were now towering over them, making them feel as though they were insignificant in the landscape.

All manner of birds flew around and over them. Some were very large, like mature blue herons and wood storks, while others were small shore birds darting across the sandbars that were now exposed with the water so low. The fowl on the ground seemed busy gathering food during low tide, while the larger birds seemed a bit lazier as they hunted mostly at their convenience.

The sound of the paddle gently moving from side to side created a rhythm that felt very peaceful, even to excited young ladies on their first-ever water adventure. Their excitement about all the wildlife was subdued by the grandeur of it all. They each found themselves rendered silent by the beauty and novelty of it. There was nothing like this in Chicago.

Peter noticed for the first time that the river had several inlets running through it as the water made its way through the marshlands, carving out secret passageways that curved through the grass. It almost felt that this big river had many mini rivers running through it, which he could see later, even at high tide given his new eye for what lay below the surface.

Intrigued, Peter moved toward the marsh and paddled his way into one of the carved-out sections. Just feet inside the marsh, they were completely surrounded on all sides by very tall grass. As the water curved back and forth, they could no longer see back out to the river, and they felt as though they were in another world. It was surreal. They knew that civilization was not far away, and yet they felt as though they were in one of the most remote places on earth.

As they continued deeper into the marsh, they paddled around another bend and found themselves face to face with a four-foot-high blue heron. He didn't move, as one might expect, but rather just gazed at them as if to wonder what these odd creatures were doing back here in his hunting grounds. They all froze and contemplated each other until Peter moved in very gently to see how close he could get.

Within about five feet, the heron crouched to get some jump for flight. When he opened his wings, it seemed as though he might swallow the entire canoe with his body. He took off over them, sending a message that this was his territory. But rather than scaring them, all he did was thrill the four city-dwelling tourists who found him to be the most amazing thing they'd ever seen.

"All this excitement has made me hungry," Peter finally said. "Let's have a snack over there," he said pointing to a mini patch of hard-packed sand off to the side.

They carefully got out of the canoe and into the water, which was only inches high after Peter pulled up and ran aground. The four of them ate and talked and played in the river. The silty sand and warm water felt marvelous on their bare feet as they splashed about.

"It's getting to be time to head back for our Fourth of July barbecue," Mimi said after a couple of hours.

As they got back in and began the journey back out of the maze of grass, it was clear the tide was coming back in. It made the trip all the more fun as the fish made their way back into the inlets with the rising tide. They saw all kinds of aquatic life darting about as their canoe made its way back into the open water.

"See how different this place looks after only a couple of hours of the rising tide? It has an entirely different feel to it," Mimi observed. "This is so cool."

Peter did notice, but he was starting to notice something else too. It was getting harder to paddle against the tide. *No problem*, he thought to himself. *It will just make for a great workout before dinner.*

But as Peter made the final turn out into the open water, the full force of the tide hit the canoe, and Peter found himself thrashing about with the paddle. Although he was working very hard, the canoe had hardly advanced. They had traveled over an hour to get to this point in the slack tide, and Peter had not thought about the changing tide for the return trip. By now, he had been paddling for about ten minutes and had gone virtually nowhere.

Mimi was focused on the girls behind her, but noticed their lack of progress and joked with Peter, "What's happening back there, sailor?" Peter smiled and said nothing, which caught Mimi's attention. She noticed how hard he was working and that they hadn't made much progress. "You okay, skipper?"

Peter did not respond. He just paddled even harder. He had heard the stories from the locals about how you had never really been boating in the Lowcountry until you found trouble with the tide and had to wait as much as twelve hours for high tide to return.

He had already gone through that in his head. Worst case, he thought, was that they only needed to wait six hours, because he didn't need high tide, per se. What he needed was the next slack tide. He hadn't run aground. He just needed calmer waters.

The tide had been coming in for two hours, so he only needed four more hours. Four hours would put him at 9 p.m. If it were just him and Mimi, no problem. But he had two little girls, and one of them would be cranking a fever before long. They had no protection, and now, also had no food and water. And if the rains came, they'd be exposed to the elements and were sitting in a metallic canoe that now also doubled as a lightning rod.

Mimi looked directly at Peter now. Even though the girls were talking to her, she never took her eyes off of her husband. At times like these, Mimi took her strength from Peter. She could tell he was concerned, and she knew he was working a plan in his head. He was good that way, and he'd think of something.

Peter knew that Mimi was relying on him to get them back, but he also knew, at this point, they would not make it back—at least not right now. His muscles were in failure, and they were still at least a half mile from home. As near as he could tell, they had only gone about two hundred yards in the last twenty minutes.

"Ladies," Peter said, "I think we've had so much fun today that we are going to stay out here on the river. What do you say?"

"Yeah," said Gracie. Austin smiled just because Gracie seemed so happy.

Although he had been humiliated earlier in the day when he fell off the boat back at the dock, it just seemed silly now in comparison. He had been stupid and careless with his family. Mimi didn't need to say anything to convey that she agreed. She only had to turn from his gaze, and that communicated it all.

"Let's go find another place to hide away," Peter said to Gracie, who was the only one paying attention to him at this point.

Peter turned into another inlet carved out of the grass. He found an area that was relatively tight and paddled in between two sections of tall grass. The canoe slid into the tight spot, which served as a kind of dock for the time being.

After getting the girls out, Peter started to roll out the plan for the next few hours. "Let's stay over there until the water gets too high."

They made the best of things for the next hour, but soon the tide was too high to sit on dry ground any longer. They stood and played in ankle-deep water until that became knee-deep water. Eventually, Peter moved them back into the canoe, still wedged between the sections of tall grass.

As dusk began to settle in, the bugs came out and found the family of four rather tasty. At first, it was just particularly annoying. But that annoyance soon gave way to actual panic as bite after bite made them all crazy beyond their ability to take it any longer. Eventually, Peter and Mimi both took off their clothes and wrapped them around the girls. And when that wasn't enough, they each took a child and covered them with their bodies.

It was torture. Nearly naked and covered in mosquitoes, and without the ability to use their hands to swat them off or smack them into a bloody mess, the children were now cold, tired, and frightened. They cried somewhat quietly at first, but the tears flowed quicker and the screams grew louder as time elapsed. Peter was just waiting for Austin to crank a fever, and when that happened, he didn't know what he'd do. He was afraid for his family, and he was desperately angry at himself for being so unwise.

As the night progressed, he became more and more fearful. He was not afraid for himself, but for his daughters, and more specifically for Austin. If she grew feverish in the open elements, it could become very serious for her. They had no medicine, no blankets, and no path to an emergency room.

And yet it was this very fear that would change the course of his life forever. For in this moment, he found himself praying for the very first time. *God, protect my family. Keep Austin from being sick tonight. And keep the rains from coming because I just don't know that we could take that right now. Find us a way home into the safety of our bedrooms and away from the dangers that exist out here on the water.*

At the very moment he prayed his prayer, he heard booms in the distance. His heart sunk. It seemed his prayers would go unanswered tonight. And to put an exclamation mark on it, God was going to bring the rain. He pictured what he would do with his family when the worst of the lightning came. He figured he would have to get them into the water and away from the metallic canoe. He could only imagine the cold and the fear that would come when he'd tell them they would need to abandon ship in the middle of a lightning storm and wade out into the marsh where all kinds of creatures lived.

As his mind raced through all the horrible possible outcomes, Peter felt something brush against his back. He picked his head up for the first time in over an hour and realized that what he was feeling was the grass brushing against him as the canoe rose with the tide. Their boat had lifted them to the top of the grassy marsh, and they were gradually lifted into the open air, about eight feet above where they were when they first wedged the canoe into the brush.

As they were lifted out into the open, a gentle breeze found its way through, and the bugs were carried away along with it. Without the torture of biting bugs, both Peter and Mimi sat up and allowed the girls to experience the breeze as well. There was just enough light left to see each other. They made eye contact for the first time since the ordeal began, and relief came across their faces. They looked down on the girls who were now asleep and resting comfortably.

As Peter watched them rest, very bright flashes of light darted across the sky, and loud booms followed. Assuming the storms were close, Peter decided to head out into the river once more. Although the tide was still coming in, he could face the currents and make some progress.

Once he made his way out into the middle of the river, he discovered something wonderful as the flashes of light turned into different colors. The light and sound were not from a storm at all. They were from distant fireworks set off by towns like Bluffton, Beaufort, and Ridgeland. Even Parris Island, the Marine training base, started sending off streams of beauty across the sky.

Both Austin and Grace Elizabeth awoke to the splendor of the show all around them. For the first time in hours, the whole family beamed with enjoyment and wonder until the finale of each show created so much light and sound it was hard to absorb it all. Sound and fury created an odd peace in comparison to what they had just endured.

As the last of the shows came to an end, the family sat in stillness, except for Peter who had to keep rowing just to keep them moving slowly forward. Mimi started talking with the girls, and Peter set his mind on getting them back and safe. The automated lights he had installed on their dock served as a lighthouse to get them home in the darkness. Without it, Peter was not sure how he would have found their way.

As they pulled next to the dock, Mimi tied them to the cleats. Once settled on the dock, she reached out to both Gracie and Austin, who allowed her to pull them to dry land. She grabbed their hands and walked them down to the dock while Peter secured the canoe and gathered their belongings.

By the time Peter got to the house, the girls were in bed and Mimi was whispering softly to them. He walked into the room and sat down on the floor just to be present now that his family was safe. He had already forgotten in this moment that he had prayed for this very thing, and so while he was grateful, he did not yet know to whom he was grateful. He didn't even notice that for the first time in the past two weeks, Austin did not spike a fever that night.

He would remember the next morning as he recalled their ordeal that he had prayed when things seemed the bleakest. He assumed it was all coincidence that things worked out, and he wouldn't think about it seriously for many years. And yet, eventually, that very night would go down as the beginning of a faith that would flourish and diminish many times as his family matured over the decades. It was a seed planted in the soil of his soul that would grow within him whether he liked it or not.

The Stewarts would eventually head back to Chicago, scarred all over their bodies from the bugs that ate them alive that challenging evening. They were painful scars at first as they scabbed and bled. But back in Chicago, they would become a source of laughter, as they remembered Peter's floppy hat bobbing on his head in the water or the fantastic light show on the Okatee River.

But perhaps most of all, they remembered the lights on the dock that called them back home to the comfort of precious River Soul.

YEAR 10

As the plane unloaded in Charleston that July, it was oddly quiet while people marched off the jet in silence. Even as friends and relatives greeted each other at the gate, those arriving from Chicago seemed muted as they forced a smile to say hello. Gradually, families were pulled off to baggage claim where the real story eventually unfolded.

When it seemed that all had disembarked, the gate agents went to close the door to get ready for the next flight. But there, at the end of the jetway, the Stewart family emerged from the plane and started making their way up the ramp. Gracie held on to Mimi's hand, clearly having been crying just moments before. Peter held on to Austin who was, in effect, draped in his arms with her head back and legs dangling, not unlike a man holding out his dead child to anyone who was willing to mourn with him.

As they headed toward the terminal, it was clear to those at the gate why there had been such a pause since the last of the passengers had arrived. Austin was bald, very pale, and scary thin. With the movement walking down the jetway, Austin leaned off to the side to vomit all over the floor. Some of it hit Peter's shoes, and Austin began to cry for having messed her father's new sneakers. But at this point, Peter's shoes were the only things that had escaped the vomit, so it all seemed fitting to finish out his wardrobe.

Peter's blue eyes looked down at his daughter. His loving gaze was the only peaceful thing about this moment. He had resigned himself to times like this. Vomit, sickness, and chaos had become ordinary. "Don't worry about it, baby. It will wash right out when we make it to Okatie."

Gracie ran to the restroom to grab some towels, and Mimi took some bags off his shoulders to give him a free arm to wipe himself down with one hand. Gracie cleaned up the floor as best she could, and they continued on to baggage claim.

By the time they got there, almost everyone had heard the story of how this child had become very ill on board. Her bald head was an obvious sign that she had been on chemotherapy for some time, and people were unsure what to do or say. As the Stewarts turned the corner to belt 2, all talking stopped. It was a painful silence that made people unsure of what to do with their hands or with their eyes. People wanted to look but felt awkward doing so. They would cast quick glances in their direction, hoping to avoid eye contact and yet still catch a glimpse of this very sick child.

Mimi wanted to scream, "Stop staring at her. Yes, she has cancer, and she has had it since she was born. It's rare. They don't know what to do about it, and she's not responding to chemotherapy. And yet they keep pumping poison into her three times a week. They discovered it too late, and now we're not sure if she's going to make it. Is that what you want to see, the pending death of an innocent?"

But as she looked out in the crowd, they all looked away. Only a few mothers kept their gaze on her long enough to convey, "I'm with you. God bless you. I'm so sorry." It was enough to calm her down just for this moment, and she went about her business. She looked at Peter, who was a mess, and said, "You go get the car. I'll collect the bags. Meet us out front."

Peter took in her instruction and paused, she thought, to process it for logic and details. But it was so much more than that in this moment for a man who was already tired, annoyed, and a bit nauseous himself from the vomit all over him. It was logical. "Go get the car, Peter." And yet it just set him off inside.

The anger at her comment caught him by surprise. It was not so much what she said or how she said it, but what it represented to him. Their relationship had become a series of commands about how to deal with the latest crisis as best they could. He wasn't upset that she had told him to do something because he did that with her as well. It just hit him, here on vacation, that this was the sum total of their marriage now.

They were no longer a couple. They were joint owners of a nasty problem that drained every bit of energy, every bit of love, and every bit of spontaneity out of their married lives. By the time they cared for Gracie and Austin, there was nothing left. They were simply two separate people who had been tasked with a particularly cruel situation, and now they needed to survive it. And so they moved from one moment to the next, never sure of what the next minute would bring.

Peter was no longer the husband—he was the provider of the health insurance that kept Austin alive and the producer of income that kept their family just barely out of bankruptcy. Mimi was no longer the wife—she was the one who got Gracie to school and Austin to one hospital visit after the next. They no longer were either themselves or a team. They were just blended into one pile of scraps left over from the people they used to be.

They were shell-shocked, always in a daze. When they spoke, they did so in monotones that conveyed the spirit of someone who was beaten. When spoken to, especially with each other, they listened as someone who hears your voice but isn't connecting with whatever you have to say. They were always somewhere else in their heads, as though darkness followed them even on the brightest of days. They were just waiting for a demon to grab them toward the day's latest form of torture. But Peter screamed only on the inside. On the outside, he said, "Okay, I'll get the car. Gracie, you help your mom."

"I got it, Daddy." As Peter walked away, she said, "Daddy?" Peter turned back to look at her. "I'm sorry about your new shoes."

He smiled. "Thank you, Gracie. They're only shoes after all."

"I know, Daddy. But it's more than the shoes, isn't it?"

Peter looked at her as if to wonder how someone so small could be so wise. "Yes, Grace. It's more than the shoes. I love you." Peter heard his voice crack a little at the end but caught himself and stopped talking.

"Love you, Daddy."

On the drive down to Okatie, there was nothing but exhausted silence. Peter and Austin stayed in the car as Mimi and Gracie went in to get the groceries. Austin remained in her car seat, not quite asleep, but not exactly awake either. Peter rested his head against the car window. He was used to being tired from his insomnia, but this was another kind of tired altogether.

A slight rain began, and he watched as droplets of water slowly made their way down the window. It was a momentary distraction, and he found himself putting his finger up to the window and tracing the droplets down to the bottom where they disappeared from view.

"That's silly, Daddy," came a soft voice from the back seat.

Peter was brought back into the real world, and he sat up and looked behind his seat. "Can't daddies be silly?"

"If daddies were silly, they wouldn't be daddies."

"Well, then, I'm going to be the first silly daddy in the whole world."

"Yeah," Austin said, trying unsuccessfully to muster up some enthusiasm.

Peter dreaded asking this question, but he did anyway. "How are you feeling, little one?"

"Not so good."

"What can I do for you?"

"Nothing."

And there it was, the statement that haunted him over the whole situation. He knew how she felt. He didn't need to ask to know that. But it was knowing that there was nothing he could do about it that killed him. He lay awake at night thinking that there was something he needed to do. Surely daddies are supposed to protect their children. How could he be so helpless?

"I'm sorry you're sick, Austin. And I don't just mean today."

"I know, Daddy. It's okay."

"No, it's not, Austin. It's not okay. But we'll make it work, little one. It *will* all be okay."

Austin was quiet, clearly processing his comment. "Maybe," came her pensive reply.

"No, I mean it, Austin. It will all be okay."

"Okay, Daddy. If you say so."

"I say so."

Austin became thoughtful again until she asked, "Daddy, do you believe in God?"

Peter was taken aback. He wasn't prepared for such a big question at this moment. "Why do you ask that?" was his only response.

"My friend Lisa says that when we die, we go to heaven and live with God. Her mommy is there, and she says that's where I'm going."

Peter was incredulous. "She said that about you now?"

Austin giggled. "No, silly. When I'm old like Grandma and Grandpa. Maybe daddies are silly after all."

"Silliest in the world. I'm telling you!"

Peter paused for a moment. He was so proud of the way Austin handled this illness. Even as young as she was, she never complained and never felt sorry for herself. She was an amazing old person in the body of a five-year-old.

He caught her eyes in the rearview mirror. "Austin?"

"Yes, Daddy."

"When I grow up, I want to be just like you."

She paused to think. "I don't think that would be a good idea. If you were me, then you'd be sick. You just be the daddy."

The next morning, the rain had passed and so had Austin's nausea. She would need to get one more round of chemo at the Savannah Children's Hospital during their week in Okatie. It was a compromise Mimi had made with Austin's pediatricians, who were dead set against this trip.

"You are putting your child's well-being at risk," they had yelled at her. "You're exposing her to germs while her immune system is compromised. And you're not going to have access to the best care if she goes septic on you while you're gone."

Mimi was not one to shrink from a fight. "My child is more than her cancer. She is more than your blasted chemotherapy. And her spirit is more important than what's happening to her body right now. She'll be healthier when she comes home. Not sicker. You wait and see!"

If Mimi was honest with herself, she worried about all of what they had said, and she wondered if taking this trip was indeed a mistake. The trip down on the plane had been horrible, and it had taken a terrible toll on her daughter. Was she really that selfish? Was this place more important than her daughter's well-being? How could she?

Peter watched her from across the room and could see she was in deep thought. "What are you thinking?"

"Oh, just about making contact with the doctors down here."

"I thought so. How about you come over here and sit with me for a second before the girls wake up."

As she walked over to him, she wanted to relax but could not. "You know, they say her liver is failing now, and she'll need a transplant before the year is up."

"Yes."

"And they don't think one will come available before she needs it."

"Yes. I told you, let me handle it."

"And exactly how do you think you'll handle it?"

"I'll figure something out, Mimi. I always do."

"Well, that would be just freaking awesome. When do you think you'll get to that?"

Her sarcasm cut him down. She was never a sarcastic person before, but then again, she was no longer who she was before. Neither was he.

"Nice. Very nice," he responded.

"I'm sorry. I'm just so upset by all of this. We shouldn't have come here."

"We needed to come here. You needed to come here."

"You may be right." She paused. "What are you working on this week?"

Mimi knew there was nothing on this trip that Peter could work on, but she was asking to see just how bad things were. They no longer had money to do even the smallest of projects. The insurance deductibles alone were killing them financially. But when you added onto that all the things the insurance would not cover, they were deep underwater.

Peter spent virtually all of his non-working hours shuffling bills from one side of his desk to another, all while waiting on hold with the insurance companies to plead his appeal to one person or the next. He'd pore over pages and pages of hospital bills looking for discrepancies that would buy him another week or two while they reprocessed the paperwork.

He had gone through all of their savings and had borrowed most of his 401(k) money to keep both mortgages going. He made a very nice living, and yet they were on the brink of insolvency. At some point, they were going to have to sell one house or the other. And yet he could not imagine taking this place away from Mimi. It would be the end of whatever they had left together.

"I think I'll just putz around the garden some this trip. Make the place look a bit more civilized."

Mimi understood his answer, and she cringed for a moment knowing what that meant in the bigger scheme of things. They were in deeper trouble than she thought.

"I think that sounds great."

Peter appreciated the lack of criticism. "Maybe we could just spend some more time with the girls, together?"

"That would be nice." She walked closer to him, debating about whether to ask her next question. After a long pause, she finally worked up the courage to inquire. "Peter?"

"Yes?"

"Are we going to make it through this?"

Peter went to give his pat answer, "Of course," but instead, he thought for a moment. He realized that he didn't know what she meant by the question. Financially? Emotionally? As a couple? As a family? Will Austin live or die? The real answer was that he didn't know any more about any of it. So, instead, he maneuvered around it.

"People ask me all the time at work if Austin is going to be okay. But they don't really want to know the answer. Their question is more like a statement, 'She's going to be okay, right?' There isn't a yes or no answer to that question. And since they don't really want the answer, I just smile and nod. They seem relieved to not go any deeper."

"It's so unreal, Peter. If I say that she's going to be fine, it sounds like denial. If I say she's going to die, it feels like I'm giving up. Anything in between gets so muddled and complex that people can't even comprehend the answer. Even I don't understand it, and I'm living it."

"It's an impossible situation."

Mimi kept going. "She's only five, and she's already had eleven surgeries, and that doesn't even count all the exams, the biopsies, the poking and prodding. Every moment for her is either physical torture or emotional torture. I can't watch it anymore. I just can't watch her die a death of a thousand cuts. And if I have to hold her down for one more painful procedure, I think I'm going to go insane."

"I know."

"Not completely. You're there for most of it. But not all of it. At least you get away from it every now and again. You travel. You have dinners and meetings. You talk to healthy adults, men and women with normal children. All I talk to are sick children and other shell-shocked mothers. I live pain all the time."

She was right, and yet she was not right. Although Peter did get away, Austin's illness was always with him. And not just in his head but deeper, in his soul. Even as he'd laugh with his coworkers, he was never laughing on the inside. He never, ever had a moment of freedom from the pain. In his mind, at least Mimi had the fun moments with Austin, the times when she could be just a kid. While traveling, Peter was always wondering if this were the moment he would get a call that Austin was back in the hospital—or worse.

There were times when he would be speaking, sometimes in front of hundreds of people, and her illness was deep inside him, moving around and making itself known. There were even moments when he didn't know what he was saying because his mind was so wrapped up in what was happening back home. It became a kind of superpower he developed—the ability to carry on a conversation without being engaged in it.

But for now, in this moment, he wanted to tell Mimi that he was hurting more deeply than she could possibly imagine. That she seemed to forget the hundreds of times that he was right there with her, holding Austin down, or cleaning up the blood or poop or vomit. He wanted to say that he was doing all that he possibly could do. But, of course, he did not.

"I'm sorry, Mimi. I'm sorry this has happened. I'm sorry that you have to go through it so vividly every day. I'm sorry that I'm not there for you when you need me."

Mimi didn't say anything in response. She walked closer to Peter and sat next to him. She leaned into him, and he put his arm around her.

Gracie giggled on the stairs.

Peter and Mimi both looked up, startled by her presence and worried that she had just heard too much.

"Good morning, glory," Peter said overenthusiastically, trying to break the mood in the room. "You know I get to hug your mommy every now and again, don't you?"

"Yes, but please don't do it in front of the kids," she said like a grown up.

"Where's Austin?" Mimi asked.

"She's coming. She's moving more slowly than usual today."

"Would you like to fly your kites before breakfast?"

"Absolutely!"

Peter knew that was his cue to go do dad stuff while Mimi got them organized for the day. He grabbed Gracie and ran out back while she giggled all the way.

Austin eventually came down the stairs but was so quiet that Mimi didn't even notice her presence. She moved through the living area and watched Peter and Gracie run around the backyard laughing and playing as they worked to get the kite in the air. She debated in her head if she'd even go out there. She had no energy for that but wanted to be with them.

Finally, Austin opened the back sliding door, which got Mimi's attention. "Oh, hey. I didn't even see you. Want to go fly a kite?"

"I guess," she said without looking back at her mother. "What's for breakfast?"

"I'm making pancakes and bacon."

"Don't make too many for me, please. I'll just take one."

"Still not well?"

"No, I'm fine. Just not hungry."

With that, she walked into the backyard where she was greeted enthusiastically by her father and sister. Peter left Gracie to get Austin her kite.

"Ready, kiddo?"

"Would you get it started for me, Daddy?"

"Sure." Peter hoisted the kite in the air, and after it got high enough to find the breeze, he handed the string to Austin, who by then had found a place on the grass to sit down.

"Here you go, sweetie. You may need to move around a little bit to keep it from flying into the trees."

"I'll be fine here, Daddy."

"Suit yourself."

Mimi watched Austin as she watched the kite fly around the backyard. As she turned to follow it, her face was in the sun, so her eyes closed. A bit more breeze kicked up and Austin leaned her face into it, enjoying the sensation of the warm sun and the gentle breeze. Mimi took it all in, as she so often did, never sure if this would be her last memory of her daughter.

As the breeze increased just a bit, Austin's kite moved toward the mighty oaks.

Although they lived on an acre of land here in Okatie, very little of it was open space. Most of it was covered in beautiful trees. It was breathtaking, but not great for kite flying, so Peter and Grace moved out onto the pier to keep the kite from getting caught in the branches.

Austin, however, did not. She just sat there with the breeze in her face, holding onto a string that she cared little about. Her kite wrapped itself around a large branch, making quite a bit of noise in the process. Peter and Gracie turned around, but Austin never even looked up. She had lost much of her hearing because of her illness.

Peter and Mimi, each from their own vantage point, watched as Austin just sat there, completely unaware of what was happening around her. When she finally broke her trance to examine the kite, a look of deep disappointment covered her face. But as with so many things in her life, she resigned herself to the disappointment.

She didn't cry; she didn't complain; she just got up and walked back through the kitchen door. She looked at Mimi briefly and walked toward the stairs. "I'm sorry about the kite," she said in a tone of voice that was sorrowful, but not so much about the kite. "I'm going to go back to bed."

"Don't you want your pancake?"

"No, thanks. Please save it for later, Mommy. I love you."

Mimi watched her five-year-old child pull herself up the stairs, never looking back. After a few moments, Mimi realized that she hadn't responded. "Love you," she called back, not knowing if Austin heard or cared.

It was hard not to cry at a young life so lost in pain. As tears began to come down Mimi's cheek, she turned to find Peter standing at the sliding door, mourning along with her the loss of innocence and joy.

YEAR 12

Peter's house plans this year centered on a myriad of time-sucking small projects. Although he felt a bit overwhelmed with the larger projects, they at least challenged him. This common work—playing catch-up on those things that had deteriorated over the years—did not. It felt like a waste of time to redo the things he had already done.

He was grateful, though, that they were now in a financial position to start reinvesting in the house, even if only on a small scale. A couple of very good years at work had allowed him to pay off all their debt and get their heads just barely above water. The insurance company had finally started covering some of the experimental treatments Austin required, which made a huge difference in their financial outlook. It was still tough to cover all the co-pays and out-of-pocket expenses, but at least they were no longer drowning.

As he put some protective tape up on the banister to repaint the railings on the stairs, he heard a tremendous commotion coming from the upper bedrooms. He stepped up to see where it was coming from, and before he could get out of the way, both Austin and Gracie came running from their room toward Peter, who they passed without even a glance. Gracie was chasing Austin, who was heading down the stairs at breakneck speed.

As she made her way down the first section of stairs, Peter called after her to stop. But Austin was far too distracted either to hear his command or to notice the pan of paint that sat at the bottom of the stairs.

"Daddy, Austin took my shirt!" Grace shouted out in protest without looking back so as not to lose track of the chase.

"But she's not using it!" Austin screamed back while still running away from her sister.

"Girls, stop it this instant," Peter screamed out in one last attempt to avoid disaster.

With that, Austin hit the landing, and her bare foot hit the paint pan, which shot directly up in the air. Most of the paint came down onto Austin, although plenty of it also splashed onto the wood floors, the walls, and her sister.

Gracie, shocked at first, broke down laughing, with a "serves you right" look for added measure. Austin, not sure whether to laugh or cry, turned to see her father's expression as he came down the stairs to assess the damage. It was one of those parental moments where you could either make a scene or laugh it off. Knowing what his daughter had been through, Peter did what he always did now: He started to laugh—and he let Austin off the hook.

After catching their breath, Peter leaned into his girls and gave them a wet, beige hug.

"Want your shirt back?" Austin teasingly asked Gracie.

"Nope, you can have it now."

After a few moments of enjoying the fun, Peter leaned down to start cleaning up their mess. Covered in paint himself, Peter took off his old T-shirt to use as a rag. As the shirt came up over his body, he was reminded of the Mercedes Benz logo–shaped scar that made its home on his abdomen.

Knowing they had bathing suits on underneath, he gently pulled off Gracie's shirt and then Austin's. As Austin's shirt came off, the same scar became visible between the two pieces of her bathing suit. Peter turned his shirt inside out, wiped them down as best he could, and then sent them outside to wash off.

Peter noticed the natural contours of Austin's face being restored as she was backing off the heavy doses of steroids from all the surgeries, which had caused her face to swell. And Gracie was starting to look more like her mother every day. They were beautiful, each in their own way. And their joy in this moment only served to heighten his awareness of just how precious they were.

Before running away with her sister, Austin stared at her father's scar and then looked down at her own. She gently rubbed her stomach and then reached up to touch her father's belly in a similar fashion. A wispy smile came across her face and then she took off out the back door to catch up with Grace.

Peter tried to focus on the mess, but his eyes were drawn back to his stomach. It was a joyful reminder that the Stewart family had shared in something very special a couple of years earlier. With no cadaver liver available for Austin in time to save her life, their family became an experiment in living-related liver donation. Peter and Austin were among the first family members to utilize a procedure where the left lobe of Peter's liver was extracted and given to his daughter.

Peter had fought hard to be accepted into the program, and they were all glad he did. The procedure was an early success in the clinical trials. Austin's health improved dramatically, and she had more energy than ever before.

Austin seemed completely healthy again, even though the cancer that caused the faulty liver was still a threat. She ran, she played, and she participated in family activities until the last of them dropped from exhaustion. The girl who formerly spent very little time outside could not be dragged inside now. She played until dark and, even then, was known to turn on the outside floodlights to keep the fun alive. It gave Mimi and Peter a new lease on life to see their daughter love life and be a kid.

Although she was still on chemotherapy for the cancer, their family had managed the routine, and her doses were now minimized to maintenance mode. While their life was by no means normal, they had grown accustomed to this reality.

They were learning who Austin was when she was somewhat healthy, and they loved her even more. She was fun, she was engaged, and she was alive. Peter had never been more grateful in his life. He had always been thankful for what he had, but to have lost something for a time made the getting-back all the sweeter and all the more vivid. His gratitude felt tangible.

After a few moments of watching his girls through the window as they sprayed each other with the garden hose, he looked back down at this mess around him and chuckled. Somehow this mess was now a lovely creation as it held a memory this house would carry forever. Cleaning it up and making these steps beautiful once more no longer felt like a chore.

The time he spent on this project would be something he remembered fondly each time he walked these stairs. He would hear the laughter, and he would see Austin's smile as she reached up to touch his stomach.

Mimi was uncharacteristically unavailable as dinnertime approached, so Peter collected some wood and placed it in the fire pit. Within a half hour, the fire was blazing, and Peter prepared for a barbecue. He was not a talented chef, but he enjoyed learning how to cook in the pit.

Austin and Grace were still napping, and Peter wasn't altogether sure where Mimi had been for most of the day. She had grown distant over the past few months. He assumed it was her usual distaste for the North, but coming to Okatie hadn't seemed to change her mood.

As he wrapped the corncobs and placed them off to the side of the fire to cook, he noticed Mimi walking on the pier up from the dock. It was dusk and so she was mostly in silhouette, but her walk was distinctive. It was one of those things about his wife that he still found very attractive, even all these years later.

As Mimi approached the fire, she let out one of her first smiles of the week.

"Thank you for getting dinner started," she said softly. "I could see the fire from down by the water and it drew me back to the house. Moths to the flame and all."

"It's nice to have you here," Peter said, trying not to communicate what he had been thinking all day: *Where the heck have you been?* But he was not successful. She knew what he was saying.

"I'm sorry I've been a bit distant. I've just got a lot on my mind."

"I would have thought that you'd be more relaxed than ever with Austin doing so well and now being here in your favorite place. What's up?"

She relaxed a little because she wanted to talk about it, and she was glad that Peter wanted to talk about it also. She sat down next to him. "I don't know what's up, and that's part of the problem. I should be happy, but I'm not. I actually feel sadder now than I did when Austin was so sick."

"Maybe it's just battle fatigue. You've been through a lot. And now that your adrenaline is dropping, you're just plain exhausted. You haven't had time to process your emotions because you've been in a fight for her life."

"That's part of it," she said, implying there was more.

He could sense that he needed to dig. "So, what's all of it?"

She hesitated, not sure if she wanted to say what she had so desperately wanted to say for a long while. She knew that once she said it, there was no turning back.

She was hoping he'd break the silence, that he'd let her off the hook, but he did not. Sometimes silence and a long pause allowed people the space to say what needed to be said. This was a moment for quiet.

She looked him in the eye, and he noticed her eyes starting to glisten. She was beautiful and intense, and that's what he focused on in the moment. He could sense that something profound was about to be said, and he waited for it, completely locked into what she was forming in her mind.

"Peter. I'm not happy . . . with us."

"Well, I wasn't expecting that."

"You should have been."

"And how should I have been? We've been so focused on Austin that we haven't had time even to speak."

"There's been time. You've just been focused on other things."

"You mean like working to catch up from all the time away? I'm exhausted when I come off the road."

"I'm not saying that what you are doing is not important. It's just that I'd like to be important too."

"Of course you're important."

"I'd like to hear that with your actions, not with your words. You travel five days a week, sometimes six. I'm left with the children in snowy Chicago, which I hate, but you travel all over the world to warm, fun locations and talk to adults all day. When you come home, you just want downtime. I'm waiting to actually have some up time once in a while."

Peter was quiet for a moment, collecting himself. In the space between their verbal banter, he became aware of the crackling of the fire and how the sparks were rising up into the night air. It was strange to him that in this brief pause, he was so aware of the visual stimulation around him.

He continued, "People marvel all the time how our marriage survived the stress of Austin's illness, and I agree. We should be better than ever."

"Peter, we didn't survive in spite of her illness. We survived because of her illness. When she was so sick, we did what needed to be done. You were either on the road or at the hospital while I cared for Gracie. We were never together."

"Well, that's the problem, Mimi. We were never together. All of our marriage has been packed in between illnesses. It's natural for things to come to the surface when we finally have time to be together. But now we will be together. We'll have more time now."

"Will we, Peter? Really?"

"I'll make more time."

"It may be too late."

"It's never too late."

"Actually, it is. I'm moving to Atlanta."

Peter was taken aback. "What does that mean?"

"I have friends there. I can be happy there."

"Happiness is an internal thing, Mimi. It's not dependent on where you are."

"That may be true for you. But it's not true for me." Mimi stood up to walk toward the house.

"Mimi, wait. Give me some time. Let me figure out a way to get us all to Atlanta. But don't move now. Give me some time to fix it. Give me some time to fix everything."

Mimi paused to think for a moment. "We'll talk about it later. Let's get dinner ready and get the girls up."

With that, the conversation was over. Peter watched her prepare the dining room table for dinner. He was about to get up to try to finish what they had started when he saw Gracie and Austin walk into the kitchen from their naps. Mimi put a big smile on her face and wrapped her arms around them. As she stood up, she looked out to the back where Peter was now standing and looking on. Her smile faded, and she went back to setting the table.

The dynamic changed a bit over dinner as things returned to normal family friendly banter while the children were present. Peter reenacted the stairway scene for Mimi, and the entire family laughed so much and so hard they could not finish dinner. If someone had been looking in from outside of the house, he would have been fooled into thinking this family was a loving model of what every family should be.

As dinner wound down, Peter cleared the dishes and offered up a sunset canoe ride, which was met with great enthusiasm by all. The girls ran upstairs to get ready, and Mimi put away the last of the dishes. Thinking the dynamic had changed, Peter engaged in regular conversation. "I'll run down to the dock and get the canoe ready. Do you want to bring a few things for the trip?"

Mimi's upbeat attitude during dinner turned cold immediately as the girls were no longer in the room. "Whatever."

Peter had hoped the tension had gone away, but he could see that things were still as bad as they seemed prior to dinner. "Mimi, look, I just . . ."

"Just go get the canoe ready. That's all the *just* I want to get from you." With that, Mimi grabbed a bottle of wine and poured herself a very large glass.

"Don't you think you've had enough of that?"

"I haven't even come close to enough of this," came her quick and sharp reply.

"You're not the same woman when you drink."

"I stopped worrying about what kind of woman I am long ago."

"I am not sure you realize that when you drink, you become bitter and sorry for yourself."

"Maybe that's because I actually am sorry for myself."

"Mimi, I love you. But this is not you. The you I married is the most upbeat person I know."

"Well, you're not the man I married."

"So now this is about me, is it?"

"No, it's not about you. Just don't make it about me either." She stared at him for a while and said, "Now, go get the canoe ready. I'll stumble down with the girls if I can walk that far."

Her sarcasm was a clear end to the conversation. Peter simply stood there for a minute and then turned to walk out the back door. Their conversations used to linger, unhurried, one soul reaching out to another. They listened to each other without agenda, without bias.

They would talk late into the night with no particular purpose or goal in mind. Now, their talks were to the point, and only long enough to accomplish their most immediate needs.

It wasn't hard to understand how that change had come about. Peter and Mimi were always in different places. Peter would land at O'Hare airport every Friday night and then would travel downtown to the hospital for a weekend visit with Austin. By the time he got there, he and Mimi would discuss the latest in Austin's care before Mimi had to rush off to retrieve Gracie from daycare. At most, they were able to share only a few minutes with each other.

Sometimes their interaction was so quick that Mimi would leave without even a kiss from Peter. Both would be settled into their new routines before they realized that they had parted without the least bit of affection between them. At first, Peter would call from the hallway payphone, and both he and Mimi would laugh about how they'd forgotten each other in the hurry. But before long, there was no more laughter, and then there were no more calls. It would be Sunday night before Mimi would return to send Peter back home to care for Gracie.

By the end, if Austin was napping Sunday afternoon, Peter would leave a few minutes early to get just a few more moments at home to do laundry, pay bills, and get ready to leave again first thing Monday morning. At one point, he didn't see Mimi for almost a month. The distance just happened.

In their own way, both of them missed that time when they had no cares for finances, sick children, and a life that had become more of a burden than a joy. They would both fantasize about escaping it all, stealing away in the middle of the night, away from a life they never wanted and had no part in creating. While most people dream of exciting adventures or making it big, their dreams were elementary, more fundamental. Their dreams were of nothingness, of simplicity.

But now, here at this moment, Peter knew there was no escape. Letting their marriage fail was not the answer to finding whatever it was they were meant to find in this life. Their lives were complex and that was no one's fault but God's. They'd been dealt a bad hand, but Peter was not the kind of man to fold.

He turned back around before leaving for the dock and Mimi looked up at him. "I love you, Mimi. I love every part of you. I need you in my life. I want you in my life. And I'll do whatever I have to do to make that happen."

Mimi softened just enough to let a relieved smile come across her lips. Peter asked in a way that conveyed a deep longing for connection, "Will you give me time to figure it out?"

She looked at him with contemplation. If she were honest, no matter what she felt in this moment, Peter always did have a way of figuring things out.

"You go get the canoe, and I'll go get the girls." Her tone was changed, more inviting, and yet she didn't answer the question.

"Mimi?"

She liked the fact that she was in control. It wasn't often that she felt she had the upper hand. And she was embarrassed to feel that in his weakness, in his need. "I said, go on now."

Her tone had changed enough that Peter decided to let it pass. He turned to head out the back door and Mimi could not resist. "That's a good boy," she said playfully.

He turned and smiled, making a mock gesture of pretend anger, and walked out the back. There, in front of him, was one of the most beautiful sunsets he'd ever seen. Although the sun was behind him, it had created the most incredible combination of colors. The light was dispersed into visible rays emanating from the horizon. But soon the light would fade, and only darkness would remain.

YEAR 13

In all the history of our family at River Soul, this thirteenth year was the only time that no Stewart set foot on the property. Even in the most wild and worrisome visions of what the future might bring, no one could have dreamed up the nightmare that was that year.

Upon arriving home from the previous trip, Austin headed back to the doctor for her routine liver scans. After films revealed a very large tumor filling most of her chest cavity, an immediate surgery to remove it proved unsuccessful because unseen tentacles had branched out and could not be removed without threatening Austin's life.

For the next three months, Austin lay in the hospital as one infection after another ravaged her weakened young body. At least three times, bacterial infections challenged the strength of her immune system while the cancer tried to finish the job on its own. Each time, Peter and Mimi sat by her hospital bed, whispering words of encouragement and hope to a child who had lost any trust in what her body would—or could—do to save her.

After a brief period of retreat, the cancer had returned with a vengeance. In less than a month, not only had the tumor grown back, but it had birthed three more tumors into her belly and now completely surrounded her heart. The tumor's tentacles had penetrated through her heart and grown three more tumors inside the heart, flapping in the blood flow.

Doing something and doing nothing each offered its own demons. If any of the new chemotherapies proved effective, the tumors inside her heart could break off and block the blood flow, causing a fatal heart attack. But without any treatment at all, Austin was given little time to live, perhaps no more than a few days. Not wanting to give up, the doctors approached Mimi and Peter with their plan.

"We'd like to flood her with five different ultra-aggressive chemotherapy cocktails. While none of these would be effective on their own, we think, in combination, they could be effective."

"You think?" Peter asked incredulously.

"Yes, we think. We're in uncharted territory. Austin is the only person in the world to have survived her very unique condition."

Mimi chuckled under her breath in a patronizing sort of way. She refused even to give them eye contact.

Peter continued, "And what will the chemo cocktail do to her?"

"It could kill her too."

Peter looked to Mimi, who looked to Peter. They had heard all these last-gasp treatment speeches a dozen times before. Their dead, tired eyes communicated little external emotion. And yet, as they looked to each other, they both knew what each was thinking. Mimi gave a gentle nod to Peter, and he looked back to the group of doctors.

"We're taking her home."

Her primary care physician stood up quickly. "Peter, now wait a second. You can't give up." He turned to Mimi. "Please don't give up. She's been through too much to walk away now."

Mimi stood up. "You heard him. We'd like her discharged."

Peter also stood up. He knew they genuinely cared for Austin and so he softened his tone. "Please. We'd like to take her home."

"We'll be forced to put into her records that you are taking her out of here against our strong advice . . . that her death is imminent."

Mimi rifled through her purse and pulled out a pen. "Well then, I hope red ink is okay."

Peter and Mimi lay in their bed, staring at the ceiling. Realizing she was also awake, Peter reached over to hold Mimi's hand. For the first time in a very long time, she held his hand back.

Her long blonde hair was splayed across the pillow, and the moonlight revealed her slender and toned body. He was reminded how attracted he was toward her. If their lives had any sense of normalcy, he would reach over to be with her. But their lives were not normal. Thoughts of softness and intimacy were distant, almost unthinkable now.

"What time is it?" she asked.

"Two-twenty-two a.m."

"I feel like we should be up there, soaking in every minute."

"She needs some rest. And so do we. We have a long few weeks ahead."

"I've been thinking about her funeral. Who will do the eulogy?"

"I will. I've already written it."

Mimi hesitated for a moment, surprised Peter was that far down the path. She thought he was in denial over the whole thing. He was always so positive, even at the expense of reality. He was always holding out hope. Always telling people not to give up. She was actually pleased he had finally seen things for what they were. "I thought we'd make it a small service. Just family." She squeezed his hand gently as she said it.

"Sounds right."

"Thank you, Peter."

"For what?"

"For doing what needed to be done today. For taking her home."

"You would have done the same. I just spoke first."

"Maybe. You're stronger than I am. You always have been."

"I don't believe that for a second."

"I put on a good show."

"A very good show!" They both laughed lightly, breaking some of the tension, but the seriousness of the situation returned quickly.

"Why do you think this happened to us?" Mimi asked.

"Who can say?"

"No, really, I want to know what you think."

"I don't know, Mimi. I don't have a good answer for that. But I pray about it all the time."

"Wait. What? When did you start praying?"

"A few years ago. This whole thing has sent me on a search for answers."

"And are you finding any?"

"Some. God has brought us through so much. He's saved our girl so many times."

"And yet not this time."

Peter wanted to ignore this painful fact. She was right, and he wasn't completely sure how to reconcile what was happening with what he had come to believe. After a long pause, he asked, "Did you ever pray at meals as a child?"

"Yes, we usually did."

"Do you remember the prayer, 'God is great, God is good, and we thank Him for this food'?"

"Sure."

"Well, I'm not sure why, but that silly prayer keeps playing over and over in my head. I think that's what we're supposed to learn. That God is great. He controls all things. And He's also good. He never cannot be great, and He never cannot be good. He has to be both at all times."

"So He caused her illness?"

"Caused it or allowed it. Haven't figured that out yet."

"Why would He do either?"

"I don't know. Maybe a test or something. I just have to wonder if there might be some good plan we don't understand, even though this looks so bad to us right now, in this moment."

"How could this possibly be good?"

"Faith is not required if we have everything we want. Faith is only needed when things are bad. If they're a little bad, we need a little faith. If they're really bad, we need a lot of faith. Maybe those who suffer the most are the people God trusts to deal with it."

"Well, if I were God, I definitely would not handle it that way."

"No. Me neither."

With that, they could hear some commotion coming from the upstairs bedroom. And then they heard the cry they had come to dread—Gracie calling out, "Mommy, Daddy, Austin needs help."

Peter and Mimi raced upstairs, where they found Austin in Gracie's arms, gasping for breath.

Gracie was crying. "She told me she couldn't breathe, and then she started shaking."

Peter looked down at Austin. Over the years, he had seen his daughter near death at least a dozen times. And yet something was different this time. There was something surrounding him that told him this would be the last time he would see her alive.

He got down on his knees and gently removed Austin from Gracie's embrace. He pulled Austin into his chest and leaned up against the wall. Mimi got down on the floor next to him, and Gracie came to the other side. They stayed there for a few minutes while Austin's gasping breath turned into more labored, inconsistent breathing. Then it slowed to hardly any breath at all.

Peter held her even tighter. "Go home, little one. You've done everything you were meant to do here on this earth. God is waiting for you. We love you."

Austin looked up and then took one more labored breath. She leaned back, closed her eyes, and let the air go in a sound the Stewart family would remember all their lives. She was still. Peter pulled her to his face. Mimi grabbed Gracie and left the room. Peter, alone with Austin, looked up to heaven and gave himself over to a God he didn't understand or even like at the moment. But he had nowhere else to turn.

At that very hour, the waters of the Okatee River rose gently to meet the banks of River Soul. The fish swam. The birds slept in their roosts. The mosquitoes swarmed, and the eyes of the alligators reflected in the moonlight as they rested on the surface of the nearby lakes.

From a distance, it was as though nothing important had happened at all. The Okatee still flowed, and the house still stood on the land Mimi first saw in her mind on a cold day in Chicago.

ACT II

YEAR 16

Peter took two long strokes with his paddle and leaned back in his new kayak to let the current take him downriver. It was 1 a.m., and there was no one crazy enough to be on the river at that hour of the morning.

Peter's insomnia had reached a ridiculous state. If he slept at all, it was a mere three hours or so a night. But more common were the nights when sleep never came. He was in a constant sleep-deprived fog, but all the waking hours made him one of the most productive people around. By the time the rest of the world pulled off their blankets to start the day, Peter had exercised, done chores, worked a couple of hours, and spent time in prayer and Bible study.

But this voyage was not about productivity or accomplishment. It was more about appreciation. It was hard to be in this beautiful place and not experience some sense of gratitude for the life they all had been given, even considering the tough times. The last three years had put some distance between the most painful parts and the relative peace they were experiencing now.

He glanced to the horizon to see if the moon had yet risen, but it had not. He was grateful for the moments of darkness because it felt like a blank slate, a fresh start. Anything was possible. Before the world was created, the Spirit hovered over the darkness of the waters, just as he now hovered over the river.

Timing a nighttime cruise on the water required the convergence of a remarkable combination of events. The moon had to be out during the night, and it had to be full enough to provide light. The tides had to change mid-cruise, and the weather had to be clear. And, of course, he needed to be in Okatie for that special time when all these things came together at once. Tonight was one of those rare nights.

He loved the solitude of the water where he was able to contemplate what they had been through without the distractions of the often-painful facts. In the darkness, he could think more with his soul than with his overly analytical mind.

He figured it must be the calm of vacation that allowed him to relax enough before the stress of work sent his mind racing into a frenzy of ideas. Peter was now the president of a struggling mid-sized company that he had been hired to turn around. He had become known for fixing problem companies, and this was one big problem to fix. It was a hard job, but a good job. More importantly, the company was in Atlanta. Although Austin's terrible situation a few years earlier had sent his family off course, he managed to get his family, intact, to the South.

Peter had promised that he would get Mimi out of Chicago, and he did. But if he was honest, Chicago held too many painful memories anyway, and it was time for the Stewart family to start fresh. He was glad to be somewhere else, anywhere else. And Mimi was now in the South, so she was as happy as he'd seen her in a long time.

The trip to Okatie was now much easier as it was only a five-hour drive from their new home. Traveling by car afforded the family the ease of packing whatever they needed for their trip, including this very kayak, which he had tied down to the roof of their new SUV. It was a boring trip across Interstate 16, but it was so much better than flying young children across the country.

Peter figured that people would travel from around the world to enjoy what he had right now, and he was grateful for it. He rested in his thoughts and simply allowed the river to carry him along. The moon was scheduled to rise soon, and it had already provided enough light just below the tree line to help him see where he was going.

He knew these waters now and could navigate them even in the relative darkness. As he floated downstream, Peter rested the paddle on his legs. He passed other homes that were made just barely visible by dim lights in the distance. For the first time, Peter reflected on who these people might be. Since the Stewarts were here for only a week at a time, they had not met any of their neighbors or shared anything more than a friendly wave of hello, which is a necessary Southern custom.

He wondered how many of these homes were filled with full-time residents and how many sat vacant most of the year—like his own. It seemed to him to be a dream too distant to imagine that he could ever afford to pack up and move everything to this place where he could escape the real world and run from the deceitfulness of riches.

Life was good here, even when it wasn't back home. It was simpler, somehow purer. He wondered how it could be that a place so near his new Atlanta home could feel a thousand miles away. It was only a short drive, but he was a completely different man here. His personality changed when he was here. He liked himself here.

Peter wondered, he supposed as all men eventually do, who he really was deep down where it mattered. Was he the man here on the river, or was he the successful business executive back home? Surely, he was not the same man in both places. Back home, especially at work, Peter had become an intense man who made people uncomfortable. He jokingly blamed his intensity on his mother's German roots, but the fact of the matter was that he strove for complete perfection, making his family and coworkers feel less-than in comparison.

He tried everything he could to soften his countenance, but nothing worked. He wanted to attract people to a higher calling, but instead, all he managed to do was create a tension so tangible that people would shut down in front of him. And this bothered him immensely. That Peter was not the man he wanted to be.

He wondered if he was the way he was because of all that had happened to his family and his marriage, or if what happened to his family and marriage was because he was the man he was. Had Austin paid for the sins of her father? The question haunted him.

Maybe if he lived here full time, his intensity would fade. With nothing to strive for, there would be no need for perfection. With no business and no employees, there would be no conflict. Surely God would rather he be a simple man here, rather than a complex man back home. And so his mind raced with all the possibilities about what life would be like as a man with no commitments and no platform on which to perform.

With his mind so focused on self, Peter had failed to notice the rising full moon that had now crested over Pinckney Colony. It wasn't until he saw the light reflected on his metallic paddles that he raised his head to see the large yellow moon make itself known to the wildlife that moved only at night. And just as bold as the moon itself was its reflection on the river.

It was stunning, and Peter made a slight gasping sound at the sight of the scene there in front of him. The moon itself was crisp and clear, and its reflection had an impressionist feel to it as the water rippled gently with the current, dispersing the light into intriguing patterns. Both the moon and its reflection were striking, and he found it hard to know where to focus his attention.

For several minutes Peter used his paddle to maneuver the kayak to stay pointed at the moon, but soon he found himself fighting too hard against the tide. He realized it was time to turn and make his way back to the dock. Although he had just passed all this same scenery, it was so much different with the moonlight now making it appear as though snow had fallen on this summer landscape.

The sound of the paddles entering the water created a rhythmic beat for the better part of a half hour before stopping abruptly. Peter heard something beyond the noise of his own paddling.

His concern about what might be lurking nearby quickly turned to delight as he realized that a dolphin had come to claim his attention. He could see it surface in the moonlight, first at a distance but then approaching ever closer with every circle. Before long, he was so close to the kayak that Peter drew his paddle in and laid it down longwise to keep it from interfering with the dolphin's path.

Peter grew very still as the strong but sleek mammal turned on its side to swim past the kayak, revealing about a third of its body. The moonlight reflected off his silvery skin, and Peter could see every detail each time it swam by. The dolphin allowed Peter to touch his side a few times before disappearing once more into the darkness below the surface.

Eventually, the circling stopped, and Peter thought their encounter had ended. But then, without even a sound, the dolphin surfaced head-first right next to the kayak, not more than a foot from where Peter was sitting. The two gazed at each other, both almost afraid to move and ruin the moment. After a few minutes, Peter reached out to touch his elongated face, but that proved too much. The animal pulled back and then leaned to the side to submerge once more.

Peter waited for a few minutes to see if he would return. He did not. Soon, Peter began paddling back home again, but his mind stayed fixed on the gift he had just claimed. He would recount this story many times to friends and family, although no one ever believed it happened quite that way. Yet Peter knew in his heart that he had had an encounter that night with a part of the river and a part of himself that could never be properly understood by those who would listen only with their ears.

By the time Peter got close to the dock, the sun was starting to make itself known. Its first rays reflected from below the horizon onto the cirrus clouds that were spread thin and wispy across the sky. Soon, he would see both the rising sun and the full moon in the same panorama, each on the opposite horizon. It was still dark enough that the illuminated clouds painted a deep contrast with the blackish water he was moving across.

As he positioned himself toward his dock, he could see a figure silhouetted just at the top of the ramp. Usually, at that hour, no one was awake. He waved, and the shadowy figure waved back. He paddled closer, but still could not determine which face remained in the darkness. He finally gave up trying to guess and paddled the kayak into the notched section of the dock, which he had cut out after the canoe debacle years earlier. This was the way that river natives made their docks, so that smaller watercraft could be launched and docked without incident.

Regardless of the dock improvement, though, it was still hard work getting out of the craft, and it required his full attention. Peter got his kayak up in his arms and into the rack before turning around to say good morning to his mystery guest. He looked up and said, "Are you going to keep me guessing, or are you going to come out of the shadows?"

The figure giggled and then walked out onto the ramp. As soon as she cleared the shadow of the gazebo, her face came into view.

"Austin?"

"Silly Daddy, you know it's me."

With the words "silly Daddy," Peter flashed back to her childhood and all they had been through together. In an instant, he saw the surgeries, the late-night vigils by her bed, and all the bad news the doctors had given them over the years. And finally, he remembered that fateful night just three years earlier when things had gotten so very bad that they took her home to die. He could still feel her in his arms on the floor, and he marveled at how she could be standing here before him now.

"Did you have a nice morning?" she asked.

He took a breath and thanked God that she was standing there with him. "It was amazing!" Her entire body looked healthy, like any young woman her age should look.

"Nice." She motioned to the sky. "And so is this. What's it called when the sun and the moon rise and set at the same time?"

"I don't know. But I love it." He looked at her, taking in every part of her face. "Come, sit with me."

They sat down together with their legs dangling off the dock.

"Daddy, will you teach me to fish?"

"I guess, but I'll have to learn myself first."

Austin chuckled. "Always the softie. Are you afraid you'll hurt the fish?"

"I just know I wouldn't want someone hooking my face and yanking me into the water. Just seems fair to me to leave everyone as is."

"But even Jesus fished."

"I suppose."

They sat together in silence. The sun had already come up over the horizon but was not yet visible past the trees on the other side of the river.

Austin looked at her father. "What are you thinking?"

"Just how amazing it is that you're here with me."

"That's nice. I'm glad to be here with you too."

Peter had so much to say and so much to ask. Three years ago, he thought he had seen the last of his daughter. And now she was here, with him, on this beautiful morning. How was this even possible? After a few moments of just staring at her, he settled for what he wanted to say the most. "I'm so sorry you had the life that you had."

"Dad, you always say that. It's fine."

"And you always say that it's fine."

"Because it is."

The sun rose to just beyond the tips of the trees, shining warmth down on them. It wasn't until he felt the sun that he realized just how cold he was from spending so many hours out on the water. Peter looked around behind him where the moon was full. Surely this was a special morning.

He lay down on the dock and let out a sigh.

Austin turned to him. "Did you sleep at all?"

"Maybe an hour."

"Why don't you sleep now?"

Peter chuckled. "I wish."

"Seriously. Sleep. It's easier than you think." With that, Austin reached over and touched his forehead. "Sleep, silly Daddy."

For the first time, and also for the last, Peter fell asleep during daylight hours. He slept deeply, and he dreamed vividly. When Peter's eyes opened, he was still on his back, on the dock, but he was alone. He lay there for a few moments and wondered how much he had dreamed and how much was real. He even looked at the kayak to see if there was water on it. He laughed to himself about how silly he really was, and he marched himself up the ramp and made the long walk back to the house, where Mimi was waiting on the back deck with a cup of tea in hand.

"How was it?"

Peter thought for a moment. "It was nice, I think."

"I think?"

"Long story." Peter sat down beside her and grasped the oversized mug in his hand. It felt warm to the touch.

"You look good," she said to him. "Better than you've looked in a while. You must be a river soul."

"River soul?"

"You know, someone whose heart is only at peace on the river."

"Sounds more like you than like me."

"Well, that's true too. But I think you're more like that than you want to admit."

"Rumi once said that when you do things from your soul, a river flows within you."

"Okay, Mr. Mystic, I was thinking Huckleberry Finn. That's the Southern version."

Peter smiled. He looked over at Mimi and said what was overflowing from his heart. "I love you, Mimi."

"It's a bit early for that, captain."

"No, Mimi, I love you." Peter emphasized the word "love."

She knew what he meant the first time, but she loved the way he said it the second time. She reached over and held his hand.

"I've never felt so much at peace. Everything is just perfect," he continued.

They both rested in their chairs, never letting go of each other in the process. They closed their eyes and pointed their faces at the sun.

Near as anyone can remember, this was the first time this place came to be known as River Soul. Mimi had first claimed the name as her own during that year on the river. But Peter protested that she first called him a river soul, so the name was really his. Mimi later thought it best to give the name away to the place, to the house, so they both could claim it together. And so the home that went by many names before was christened on a morning in Okatie when both the moon and sun gave light to the union below.

YEAR 20

Peter and Matt sat in awkward silence, alone together in the living room. When Peter had offered to let friends come to River Soul, he was not thinking of boyfriends. He protested that it was too soon for his daughter to have a boyfriend, period, let alone to have one come here on a family vacation. But once he had made the offer, there was no turning back. The genie was out of the bottle, and his daughter would only sulk through the entire trip if he didn't agree.

Matt was almost eighteen, which was way too old to be dating his daughter. But more than that, Matt was nothing like the man he wanted for his child. His haircut bordered on a mohawk, and he was always dressed in tattered jeans and a dirty, crumpled T-shirt. He was not going to school; nor did he have a job.

"So, Matt, do you play any sports?"

"Well, I used to play some hockey, but I got injured a few years ago. The doctors said I couldn't play anymore."

"That's too bad. Did you develop any other interests?"

"Not really. I helped my dad out in his business for a while, but that didn't really work out."

"Tell me about your parents."

"They got divorced when I was eight. I live with my mom. Anyway, what do you think she's doing up there?"

Peter didn't know what was happening either. They were both desperately hoping his daughter would make an appearance downstairs as quickly as possible. This forced dialogue had gone on for hours. It was almost noon, and she was still in bed.

"I'll go see," Peter said, pretending to be helpful.

He walked upstairs and knocked on the door. No response. He knocked again. No response. He knocked again and entered slowly. The blinds were all drawn, and the room was almost dark despite the bright sunshine outside. Finally, he saw movement from under the covers.

"Dad, what do you want? Why are you in here?"

"Matt is downstairs waiting for you. We both are. We've all been awake for a very long time."

"Let him wait."

"Honey, it's rude to let him be downstairs by himself."

"He's not by himself, he's with you and Mom."

"Yes, but he's not my guest. He's your guest. He didn't come here to talk to me. He came here to be with you. And besides, I've got some projects to get done. I had planned to be working on them early this morning, but I've been entertaining instead."

"Whatever," came the reply. She finally sat up with a groan and swung her legs around the bed. Her body was skeletal-like, and her eyes were dark. There was no life either in her face or in her spirit. "I need another one," she said.

Peter looked over at the nightstand and could see that the two hydrocodone tablets he had left on her nightstand the night before were gone. "You're not scheduled for another one until later today. And you've taken too many on this trip anyway."

She snapped back harshly. "Look, the doctor said I should take these *as needed*. Well, I need one. You and Mom insisted on keeping the bottle, so I can't get them myself."

"It also says that you should not take more than four a day. And we've pushed that to five as it is."

His daughter reached underneath her shirt and pulled out two bags attached to tubes that went into her abdomen. "Do you know how much this hurts? Do you have tubes sticking out of your body?"

"No, I don't. And I'm sorry about that. But—"

"Stop giving me reasons why I can't have one. Just give it to me!"

"I can't."

"Fine, then, I'll just kill myself. I hate this life. Why didn't you just let me die anyway?"

Peter went over and sat next to his daughter on the bed. She moved farther away from him as he sat down. She had said, "Why didn't you let me die?" many times before, but Peter had ignored the comment as normal teenage hysterics. But he felt it was finally time to say what he'd wanted to say for years. "Austin, we did let you die. But you chose life."

"What? What does that even mean?"

Austin had virtually been in a coma for most of her experience seven years ago, so she had no recollection of what had happened. They did not plan to tell her unless she asked, and now seemed to be the moment to finally have the conversation.

He reached over to grab her hand, but she pulled it back. He continued patiently so as not to ruin the moment with anger over her constant rebellious attitude. "On that night we brought you back from the hospital, we did it so you could die in peace at home. And you actually stopped breathing in my arms on the floor of your room. We all saw it, and we thought you were gone. But a few minutes later, as I held you, you sat upright as though someone had shocked you back to life.

"Then the same thing happened, and then it happened again, and then it happened again. Each time, we thought you were gone. And each time, you came back to life. After the last time, when you started breathing normally again, you fell asleep and looked as peaceful as we'd ever seen you.

"Mom and I talked through the night and decided that if you had that much fight in you, then so did we. We took you back for treatment. It was very hard on you, but you kept fighting. Every scan showed things were getting just a little bit better, and within thirty days, you were cancer-free. The doctors had never seen anything like it. You're a miracle, young lady."

"Well, look at me now, with a failing liver once again. I'm not feeling like a miracle—tubes sticking out of me to drain the pus and bile from my rotting insides, and my entire body failing along with it. Why do we even bother?"

"You must still be here for a reason, kiddo, because God keeps pulling you through."

"Ugh. Stop saying things like that. God hates me. I have no room for your God thing."

"He's saved you over and over again."

"What kind of God would do this to me?" she spewed, holding up the bags for effect. "A loving one? Stop talking to me about your God."

"I don't know how to explain your pain, Austin. But I do know He's a loving God, to everyone."

"Says you, Mr. Perfect Liver, perfect life."

Peter knew there was no use pursuing the conversation when she was like this.

"Just get dressed and come downstairs. Eat breakfast or lunch or whatever it is you eat at this time of day. And we can talk about something for your pain later. I'll see you downstairs."

Peter left her room and closed the door. He sat down on a chair in the hallway. He had enjoyed only three years with a healthy Austin. After the cancer had gone away and the chemo stopped, Austin thrived. But the telltale signs of illness had returned, and slowly she started to withdraw. Her first liver transplant, having been experimental, was not as successful as they thought. She had experienced more than twenty surgeries in one year to save the transplanted liver, but it was beyond repair. She would need a second transplant.

It seemed more than any one person—or any family—could bear. Austin was right; they had suffered more than anyone should. And if he were honest, he was becoming hardened more than he cared to admit. But he knew he had to be strong for Austin, strong for his family.

He heard some rustling downstairs, and he came down to find Mimi and Gracie returning from the store, both clearly in a great mood. They had become very close and loved spending time together. With Gracie off to college, these summer months together were especially treasured.

Gracie had become such a beautiful young woman. Here features were maturing such that he no longer thought of her as a child. Her countenance was almost that of elegant royalty and yet casual and authentic. She did not require makeup to highlight her beauty; nor did she require expensive clothes. She was strong and beautiful just as she was.

Mimi looked up at Peter and could see his expression. She knew what the look on his face meant, and her expression grew more serious. Things had gotten to the point where any conversation with Austin drained the life out of a person's countenance. "Where is she?" Mimi asked.

"She'll be down sometime today, I guess."

Mimi looked over at Matt. "Why don't you go out and enjoy the scenery, Matt? I'll get some lunch ready, and you and Austin can have a picnic down on the dock."

"Okay, Mrs. Stewart," Matt replied with some energy in his voice. He was happy to be let out of any more conversation with Peter.

Mimi smiled as Matt went out the back door. "You making a new friend?" she asked sarcastically.

"Another winner," Peter replied. "I swear that girl has dated enough fools to fill this entire acre. One right after the other. And each one worse than the last."

Gracie chimed in. "I know him from high school. He's a pothead. But then again, so is that daughter of yours."

Mimi and Peter looked at each other. They had their suspicions, but to hear Gracie be that bold to say it to the two of them was painful confirmation.

"What do you mean 'that daughter of yours'? Do you mean your sister?" Peter asked.

"That person up there stopped being my sister a long time ago. I can't even begin to tell you how thankful I am to be out of the house. Being here together and sharing a room with her again . . . painful. Poor sick little Austin, always needing to be protected."

Peter interrupted. "Hey, none of us has been through what she's been through."

"Really? You, Mom, and I haven't suffered through this as well?"

Mimi came to Gracie's defense. "Of course you have. We all have."

Peter held his ground, "Yes, we've suffered too, but none of us has been tortured the way she has."

Gracie looked at her mother. She was so tired of her father always taking Austin's side. And at this point, so was Mimi. Austin had become very hard to live with, and Peter was not at home as much as she was. She bore the brunt of Austin's harsh moods.

"Dad, you don't see it. She's not the girl you think she is."

"She's my daughter, and that should stand for something."

"And what am I?"

"You're my sweet little Gracie," Peter said, putting on a smile to charm his way out of this conversation.

Gracie was not going to let her dad out of this conversation. He tried to joke his way out every time they'd get serious about Austin's condition, and that made her even angrier. This was no laughing matter, and it needed to be addressed. But Gracie looked up to see Austin walking down the stairs, and she stopped herself to address her sister instead.

"Well, now, here's my happy little sister gracing us with her presence just in time for lunch. Can I finally get access to our room now so I can get properly dressed in the light of day?"

Austin ignored her as Gracie made her way up the stairs. "Where's Matt?"

"He's out by the dock," Mimi replied. "And good morning to you, missy." Austin looked at her sharply but then softened a bit after realizing that Peter was in the room. The best she could muster was "Hello." She made her way out the door, leaving Peter and Mimi alone in the kitchen. When he saw that Austin was walking down the pier, Peter pulled a cookie jar off the top shelf and picked out her pain medicine.

"She was asking for more this morning."

Mimi started to unpack the groceries but talked while she did. "You know she's addicted at this point."

Peter bowed his head a bit in defeat. "I know. They just want to keep her comfortable until the transplant. Lesser of two evils and all that."

Mimi quipped, "Do they have something to make us comfortable while we live with her?"

Peter ignored her comment and poured the pills out onto the counter.

"Hmm."

"What?"

"That's strange," Peter thought out loud. "I thought there were twelve of these when I got her two last night. There should be ten. But now there are eight. Did you give her any?"

"No, I can't reach up there."

"Maybe there were ten and then I gave her two to make it eight. I had the number ten in my mind. I just thought it was ten left, not ten when I started. I guess I got it wrong."

"I guess."

Peter turned to look out to the dock, and he could see two figures sitting in the covered section at the end of the pier. What he could not see was Austin reaching into her pocket and pulling out two pills. One for her and one for Matt.

Mimi walked down the pier, and as she got to the end, she started making loud noises so as not to walk in on an awkward moment.

"Helloooo," she said loudly.

"It's fine, Mom. Nothing's happening."

Mimi approached them with the lunch she had prepared. They were facing outward toward the water, slumped a bit together. They never moved. She put the two trays down and walked around them so as to have a face-to-face conversation. Since neither one of them even looked up at her, Mimi started the conversation. "We thought maybe later we could go out on the boat."

"You and Dad always scream on the boat."

Mimi smiled. "Not so much screaming as talking loudly about navigation."

"And docking?"

"Well, you have me there. That's just screaming." Mimi looked at Matt. "We're first-time boat owners and docking this thing on a windy day with aggressive tidal currents . . . well, not the easiest thing to do. And I'm not the most compliant first mate. We've had our fair share of crash landings in this general area," she said, making a circular motion with her hands around the dock. Neither was responding to her question about the trip, so she tried again. "Well, yes or no?"

"About what?" Austin said, almost clueless.

"The boat trip," Mimi said, annoyed. "Are you in or not?"

Austin said, "Okay," but in a way that Mimi knew meant she would back out at the last minute. Austin had become a master at manipulating where and when she would engage with the family.

"Okay, then," she replied to Austin. "I'm going to hold you to it. Plan to leave around three o'clock. We're going out to the sandbar, and we want to time it just right—or we'll miss it. The sandbar is only out for a few hours. So three o'clock. Got it?"

"Okay, Mom."

Mimi walked away without a single thank-you for the lunch. Peter always said, "If you do something to receive thanks, you shouldn't do it in the first place." But to Mimi, it was a matter of respect, both from her daughter and from the bevy of boyfriends she brought around. This lack of basic manners, along with so many other things, started to burn inside Mimi. She had a very bad feeling now about most everything her daughter was becoming.

Mimi spent the afternoon hours getting ready for dinner on the sandbar while Peter readied the boat. The sandbar had become one of their favorite family activities ever since they got a boat three years earlier.

The Stewarts had found this gem a few years before, when, wanting to avoid another family canoe catastrophe, Peter and Mimi decided to take the boat out to explore the waterways. They left Gracie and Austin behind, on their own for the first time since Austin had been so sick a couple of years before. She was well enough back then to leave her safely.

Mimi encouraged Peter to plan their trip, and to Peter's credit, he actually consulted a map to get a sense of the best route to Hilton Head. What he didn't do, though, is review a navigational chart that would have shown the actual path over to the island. Peter assumed that all waterways were like the waters near River Soul where you get out in the middle and stay there. Sadly, that was not the case at all.

With uninformed optimism, Peter maneuvered the boat into the middle of the Okatee River and headed toward the ocean. He accelerated to get the boat to plane on top of the water, and it felt amazing to have man-made headwinds for the first time ever. At that speed, they quickly moved past all the familiar waters around their home.

As they moved into new territory of the Okatee River, thinking they were now in the clear, Peter started to accelerate even more. But as he moved into the middle of the river, the depth went from twelve feet to two feet in less than five seconds. The boat tugged hard and almost came to a complete stop. And just as people without a seatbelt fly through the windshield if they hit a brick wall, both Peter and Mimi flew forward once the boat plowed directly into the sand just below the surface.

Peter hit the console, bruising some ribs and nearly fracturing his elbow. Mimi went flying from the center of the boat all the way to the front, and then almost up and over the bow. The boat itself stalled, but through natural momentum, it plowed through the tiny sandy section and continued forward, floating away from danger.

Both Mimi and Peter assessed their injuries. In the shock of it all, they said little to one another other than checking that each was alive. Peter made his way forward and sat next to his wife.

"You okay?" he asked.

"I think so. I've hurt my knee, but I think it's just banged up."

He tried to start the boat, but the engine was flooded from the stall. He looked around to see if anyone was near, and he realized that there were no boats, no people, and no homes as far as the eye could see. All he could see was water, marsh, and palmetto trees lining the banks of the river.

"This is amazing," he said as he walked back toward Mimi. "Can you hear that?"

"What?" she asked.

"Nothing. Nothing at all. Just the sound of the water licking against the boat. This is what this place had to be like hundreds of years ago."

"Thanks for the history lesson," she quipped. "How about some ice for this knee?"

Peter went to one of the three coolers they had packed and got a bag of ice. Ever since the canoe trip, they never left the dock again without adequate supplies. "Here you go." He placed the bag of ice down gently on her knee. "So should we head back?"

"Not yet," Mimi said. "I just need a minute."

They let the tide, which was now receding, pull their boat out toward the Port Royal Sound. For the next ten minutes, they simply drifted and became a part of the landscape.

Mimi looked up from icing her knee and settled back into Peter's arms. "I feel like I'm in the islands. This place is so beautiful, so untouched."

"Uh, didn't I just say that?"

"Yeah, but now I've said it, so it matters."

Peter smiled. It was a joke, but he knew it was half true. "What are we going to name this boat?" he asked.

"How about *Mistake*?" Mimi quipped.

"Very funny. How about *River Soul*?"

"No, that name's taken."

He stood up and headed back toward the console. "You keep thinking, and I'll get the boat started again. Shall we head home or keep on exploring?"

Mimi looked at her knee. "I think it's all good. Let's keep going."

"That's it!" Peter exclaimed.

"What's it?"

"The name of our boat. *It's All Good*."

"We'll see if it's all good if we make it home tonight."

Peter stood up and walked toward the console, doing a little dance and singing, "It's all good. You know it's all good." For effect, he added a little hip action until he felt a tug at his ribs. He stopped and held his hand to his side, but he continued singing more quietly under his breath.

He turned the key and was grateful when the boat started up again. They headed farther down into the Colleton River where some houses started to appear in the distance, growing gradually more extravagant until there were mansions lined up one after the other.

Each home had its own very large, upscale boat sitting in an extravagant deepwater dock. Peter slowed down and got as close to the docks as he could without having the wake disturb these yachting luxuries. A tinge of jealousy entered them both as they wondered what life would be like in such a place.

Just as quickly as the homes had come into view, they disappeared at the point where the Colleton poured into the Chechessee. Multiple inlets converged into this one section, and Peter had to remind himself what the map had showed him. He motored out until he was in the center of that very wide, undeveloped section and turned into the widest part of the river. He looked down at his depth finder and was in the deepest water yet—fifty feet.

He looked straight ahead, and up a few miles in the distance, he could see the north end of Hilton Head. The island had gotten its name in 1663 when Captain William Hilton was sailing near the Port Royal Sound. He saw the headland of the island and named it after himself. While now a resort town, it once had served the cotton trade, the lumber markets, and even as a point of blockade for the Union troops trying to starve Southern ports during the Civil War.

Peter painted a diagonal line in his mind between where he was now and the tip of the island. After encouraging Mimi to sit, he got the boat up on plane and took off, this time keeping his eye on the depth finder. They traveled for a few minutes before the depth went quickly from fifty feet to five feet, and the depth alarm started to sound.

Peter looked to the right and to the left. They were hundreds of yards away from either bank of the river. He wasn't sure how they could be in shallow water. He thought maybe the depth finder was broken, but once again, he soon enough found they were kicking up sand and mud. Both of them got the paddles out, but it didn't seem to matter which direction they pushed. The water was getting more and more shallow.

The alarm sounded for more than ten minutes, and Peter and Mimi found themselves screaming at each other.

"Head this way."

"No, that way!"

"Push, quickly, we're running out of time." But soon there was no push maneuver that would help. The boat was at a complete stop. They both sat stunned as the alarm continued to blare the obvious fact that they were in deep trouble.

"Can you turn that thing off?" Mimi asked angrily.

Peter walked back and turned off the alarm and the battery to conserve power. They sat there quietly in defeat. They knew what this meant and what they were in for now. Mimi finally broke the silence and said, "You still think this is all good?"

"Not so much," he replied.

They sat a few moments more until the boat started listing to one side. Peter looked down and could see the sand starting to peak above the water line. There was no longer enough water on each side to keep the boat upright, and so it started tilting until it was at a forty-five-degree angle, resting completely on one side.

By the time it reached that state, they had long since abandoned ship. With all their supplies now on the sandbar, they sat on top of two coolers that were not originally intended to be beach chairs.

After a very long period of quiet, Peter said cryptically, "A three-hour tour."

Mimi looked over at him with disgust. She knew where he was going with it and did not find it humorous.

Seeing that she was not going to "bite," Peter started singing playfully, a bit softly. "Just sit right back and you'll hear a tale, a tale of a fateful trip. That started from our River Soul aboard this tiny ship."

Peter continued. "The mate was a mighty sailing Mimi, the skipper brave and sure. Two passengers set sail that day for a . . ." Peter paused and extended his arm to Mimi with a gesture for her to take it from there.

She scowled. He repeated, "Set sail that day for a . . ." Again, he extended his hand.

Mimi turned away but said softly, almost under her breath, "A three-hour tour."

Peter took that as a good sign and stood up to sing with more energy. "The shallows started getting rough, the tiny ship was beached. If not for the courage of the fearless crew, this island would not be reached . . ." Peter signaled to Mimi once again, and this time she played along and repeated the chorus.

"This island would not be reached."

"The ship set ground on the shore of this uncharted desert isle, with Mimi . . . and Peter, too, the millionaires who live nearby . . ."

As that afternoon unfolded, it proved to be one of the fondest memories Peter and Mimi would have of their beloved Lowcountry. They walked from one end of the long sandy surprise to the other while chasing away shorebirds that had come to feast on the crabs and fish left behind as the water receded. At one tip of the sandbar, they were so close to Hilton Head they could see dogs running on Dolphin Head Beach.

As time faded away, they ate dinner while the sun started to set off to the west, where River Soul awaited their return. They knew their girls would be worried, but in the days prior to portable cell phones, there was no way to communicate their predicament. And so they made the best of it, together.

Although they had been there for the better part of six hours, it came as a surprise to them when they noticed the island gradually disappearing as the tide rose to reclaim it. They didn't even get into the boat until the water was well past their ankles. To anyone watching, it would have appeared as though they were walking on water. They stood on the last patch of their fading hideaway, holding hands and watching as the sun painted the most glorious skyscape they had ever seen.

After getting back inside, they felt the boat release from the bottom. Soon, the rear of the boat swung around, and the bow faced into the rising tide. Mimi, without being asked, grabbed a paddle and pushed the rear of the boat back away from the shallow water to give the propeller a bit deeper water. She looked over at Peter who was very impressed with her newly developed instinct.

"Boo-ya," she said with some mock pride.

They motored back into the sunset that had grown even more beautiful, if that was possible. Here, with the open water and nothing but the palms, it seemed like a magical place only seen in movies.

By the time they got back to the dock, Gracie and Austin were frantic and crying. They were happy to see their parents, but angry they had put them through such worry.

As the four of them walked back toward the house, Peter thanked the God he had come to know for giving them that day, which had turned into such a treasured gift wrapped up in the guise of difficulty and confusion.

It was a quarter past three o'clock, and Mimi was steaming. She had been ready since two-thirty but decided not to press the point since she had told Austin to be ready by three. But now, here she was with Peter and Gracie sitting on the boat, waiting for their daughter to show up.

"I'm going to kill her," Mimi said.

Peter knew how much stress had come between them since his daughter had morphed not only into a typical teenager but also into an addicted one. He felt a constant struggle to keep the peace.

"I'll go get her," he said calmly.

"Don't you dare! I told her to be here by three. We've waited long enough. Let's leave without her."

Peter protested. "And leave her alone with Matt? Are you kidding me? We can't leave part of the family behind."

"I vote we leave her behind," Gracie chimed in.

Mimi pointed at Gracie, feeling validated. "See, I'm not the only one. Let's go."

Peter didn't know who to let down—his wife and oldest daughter or his youngest daughter. He just knew in his heart that Austin would be so disappointed if she missed this trip.

He slowly moved away from the dock, looking behind him repeatedly to see if Austin and Matt were on their way. When he was sufficiently far away, such that Mimi knew he was not turning back, she grabbed Gracie and moved to the front of the boat where they set up towels and started to talk. Peter continued to putter slowly until Mimi looked back and said, "Peter?"

With that, Peter pushed down on the throttle. The sound of the wind and roaring motor made it impossible to hear exactly what Mimi and Gracie were saying up in the front, but Peter guessed they were talking about him, or Austin, or about both Austin and him. So Peter settled back into his chair and sulked in silence.

It was a perfect boating day. The temperature was not too hot, the waters were flat as a lake, and there was not a cloud in the sky. And yet for the next several hours, all Peter could picture was Austin walking down to the dock, incredibly disappointed and hurt once she saw that they had left. Austin was sick and moved slowly. Now they were punishing her for being sick and slow. How cruel that seemed to him.

When they reached the sandbar, there was not even another boat in the area, let alone any trespassers on their private, salty land. They had the place to themselves. Gracie and Mimi took off to collect shells and starfish, leaving Peter behind to set up camp. He watched as his wife and daughter walked off hand in hand, and he was so thankful for their relationship. Mimi needed a friend, and she missed Gracie terribly when she was gone.

But even then, in the midst of his gratitude, he had a sinking, sad feeling about the daughter they had left behind. He could not be happy with one-fourth of the family standing at the dock, wondering why they had left without her.

As the afternoon progressed, Peter claimed to be tired and asked repeatedly to head back home. When Gracie went to take a swim, Mimi sat down beside him. "Austin doesn't care that we're gone, Peter. In fact, she probably hasn't even noticed."

Peter didn't want to ruin the moment, but he was angry at being forced to choose between his daughters. "You have two daughters, Mimi. Not just one. I'm not sure how you can be so cold as to just leave her and never give her a second thought."

Mimi stood up slowly and looked down at her husband. "You have two daughters, Peter. And I'm not sure why your mind is on Austin when Gracie is right in front of you."

She walked down toward where Gracie was swimming and got into the water up to her ankles where she watched her daughter swim playfully.

By the time they got back to the dock, it was almost dark. Peter pretended not to hurry, but he was almost desperate to see his daughter and apologize for their actions. He grabbed a cooler and walked out in front of Mimi and Gracie. They understood his rush, but they were equally as committed to making these last few moments of peace last. They knew the stress that would define the rest of the night.

Peter got to the house, and it was dark. Not even one light on. What was going on? Where were Austin and Matt? He got inside the house, and there was not a sound to be heard. He called for them, but no answer. He went into a panic. Had there been trouble? Did Austin need to go to the hospital while they'd been off playing? He knew leaving her behind was a terrible mistake.

He started frantically going through the house, turning on lights along the way. Finally, he went into Austin's room and turned on the light. There on the bed were Austin and Matt, fully dressed, on top of the bedspread, sleeping.

"Austin," Peter said in a very sharp tone. Neither moved.

"Austin!" he yelled.

Matt finally started to move, and Austin eventually looked up, pushing herself up on her elbows with bleary, sleepy eyes.

"Dad?"

"What have you two been doing all this time?"

"Nothing, just taking a nap. Is it time to go out on the boat?"

"Are you for real? It's eight o'clock at night. We've already been and come back."

Austin simply dropped to her back and closed her eyes. "Whatever."

Peter was too furious to speak. He turned around, and Mimi was standing at the door behind him. She ached for Peter, who constantly, desperately searched for the best in a child who, to her, had become so predictably disappointing. Mimi had stopped expecting good things long ago to avoid the pain of Austin's complete disregard for anyone's feelings but her own. But Peter still believed in someone who no longer even believed in herself.

As he stormed past Mimi, she reached out to put a loving hand on his shoulder. But he pulled away and ran down the stairs and outside. He knew he needed distance, perspective. But what he didn't know is that he would wish for the days when this was as bad as it got.

YEAR 21

On the drive down I-75 toward Macon, Peter looked to his side and into the back seat through his rearview mirror. All three of his girls were asleep. Peter liked to get on the road early to get the maximum amount of vacation time possible.

Peter was grateful, and it felt good. It had been at least a couple of years since he had felt anything even approaching gratitude. Austin's second liver transplant a year ago had proved successful, and she was given the "all clear" just a few weeks before. It felt good to have all that behind them.

The procedure itself had been touch-and-go. It took two years to get her to the top of the transplant list and another six months to find the right donor. The surgery took thirteen hours and, afterward, the surgeon said it might have been the most complicated transplant he'd ever done.

Austin's surgery took so long that her body had swelled to the point where they could not close her up. A thin, paper-like mesh was sewn into her flesh to keep her organs from protruding out of her belly. Her abdominal muscles were about two inches thick, like a hunk of meat on a plate that had been cut open to test whether it had been properly cooked.

Austin was mostly unconscious for the first few days. When she came to and realized that her belly was still open, she panicked. They had to sedate her heavily until they could sew her shut, but that procedure, too, proved to be so painful that they kept her in a drug-induced coma for the next few days.

When she finally awoke, Austin begged Peter to take the pain away, to make her life finally come to an end. She reached out her arm slowly, as if reaching for something in a vision, and grabbed hold to pull him closer.

She told him to pull all the tubes out, turn all the machines off, and "just walk away." Peter thought about all the times she said she wished they had just let her die. This was the first time he felt she really meant it.

Austin regained some sanity once the doctors finally backed off the meds. But this was the only positive outcome of the lessened regimen. Her addiction soon kicked in, and Austin began demanding more pain meds. Peter tried to explain to the medical team that she was an addict and questioned whether or not she actually needed the meds. The doctors reminded Peter how much pain he had experienced when he was the donor the first time around. They were right, so Peter backed off.

By the time she left the hospital six weeks later, Austin was given only oral pain meds and within a few weeks, the doctors backed off even that. Austin would call her father at work, crying about how much pain she was in, knowing that Peter would call the doctors for more prescriptions. But soon, even that dried up, and both Peter and Mimi continually had to calm down an irrational Austin, who paced the house and yelled at anyone who got near her.

The doctors had moved on, leaving the Stewarts to fend for themselves. The only guidance they could offer was to distract her, but that was like telling a two-year-old child to distract a charging bull. There was absolutely nothing that would get her mind off her need for more medication.

Finally, Peter and Mimi were able to convince Austin to do something other than pace around the house, and she eventually called some old friends. As Austin reconnected, it seemed to them that her interest in pain meds went away, almost overnight. Before long, they couldn't keep Austin at home. She started to hang out with her friends all the time, usually overnight. Peter and Mimi had no idea that this was actually the beginning of Austin's criminal drug use. They were both naive to that world and were relieved that Austin seemingly had found a distraction from her addiction.

Peter reflected on all of it during his drive, and he was especially joyful that his family was back together. He smiled spontaneously, until he looked in his rearview mirror and saw the car driving up next to him on the highway. Warren, Austin's latest boyfriend, pulled up beside the car and waved to alert Peter that they were now driving together. Peter forced a smile and waved back.

Warren had worked the night before and didn't think he'd make it in time for the Stewart's early departure, and Peter was grateful for it. Warren said he would drive down on his own and meet up with them along the way. Now, here he was, only a couple of hours into the trip, already in position to disrupt the family's private time.

By the time they reached Dublin, Georgia, his three girls started to wake up and move around. Warren could see they were awake from his car. He started honking his horn so that Austin would see him following behind. "Dad, pull over. I want to drive with Warren."

"You'll have plenty of time to visit with him. How about we spend a few moments just as the Stewarts?"

"Dad, pull over. I want to get out."

Mimi looked over at Peter. "Look, we need gas anyway. Let's pull off here and grab some lunch."

As they pulled into the gas station, Austin ran out and met Warren with a hug and kiss.

"Do we really need to see that?" Gracie asked, making a gagging motion with her finger in her mouth.

Peter walked over to be polite and say hello. "You must have made good time from work."

"I got off early so I wouldn't miss anything."

"Terrific," said Peter, who looked up to see Mimi smirking off to the side.

Austin looked at Warren and said, "Ask him."

Warren said, "Not now."

"Ask me what?" Peter followed.

"Well, Austin might be going to school in Florida next year, and we thought, well, you know, if we could take a drive down and see the place," Warren said.

"Nice thought, but she hasn't even been accepted yet. And besides, you couldn't make it there and back in a day," Peter countered.

"Yeah, but I've got a couple of friends in the area, and we could stay there overnight."

Peter was very quick to answer. "Not going to happen, Warren."

Sensing the conversation going wrong, Austin took over. "Dad, come on. I'm going to be a senior in high school. I should be able to do whatever I want."

"And I can do whatever *I* want, Austin. And this is not something I'm going to allow."

"Well, don't expect us to have fun at your stupid house," Austin screamed as she grabbed Warren and stomped off to the bathroom.

Mimi looked over to Peter. "Well, that went well. Looks like we're off to a great start this trip."

"So much fun, so little time. Let's get back in the car and head to our 'stupid house,'" he said while making air quotes and using a whining tone.

Gracie asked, "What about the princess?" as she nodded her head at the restroom.

"She's almost a senior in high school," he said mockingly. "I'm sure she can figure out how to get there. Let's get moving."

Mimi and Gracie looked at each other in amazement. As they got in the car to pull away, Gracie kept waiting for him to hesitate. But Peter pulled away and never looked back.

By the next morning, some of the tension had subsided. It had taken Austin and Warren almost six hours to find the place. Warren had directions but seemed too obtuse to be able to follow them, and Austin had never paid any attention to directions, much like she didn't pay attention to anything these days.

The two walked in embarrassed and a bit humbled, yet neither had the guts to ask if there was anything left to eat. They disappeared for the rest of the evening but were grateful to have breakfast with the rest of the family the next morning.

Warren shoveled in food without even looking up, and the rest of the family watched partly in disgust and partly in amazement. Not able to look on any longer, Peter started the morning's conversation. "How about we go fishing today?"

Everyone but Warren spun around to look at Peter.

"We can fish now, can we?" Mimi asked sarcastically.

Austin interrupted. "Dad, you don't fish."

"I do now." Peter got up and went behind the door where he had hidden four fishing poles and a tackle box.

"I took some lessons back home. I can do this. I got the fishing licenses and everything else."

Gracie looked at him with a question in her expression. "Now, wait a minute. You've caught a fish, an actual fish?"

"All right, maybe not an actual fish. But I have learned how to tie the knots and how to cast."

Austin chimed in, "This I have to see."

Mimi stood up to clear some plates and on her way to the kitchen leaned back toward Peter. "You're really stepping up, big boy." He nodded, partly embarrassed and partly proud.

Peter started handing out the rods once he got the boat positioned off Palm Island.

"Get comfortable with these and practice the casting I showed you back at River Soul. I've got to go catch some bait. I'll be back in twenty."

Peter jumped off the boat with a net and bucket in hand. He swam to shore with a sidestroke, dragging his items behind. As he reached standing depth, he put his feet down onto the slimy pluff mud at the bottom.

He got to the shoreline and prepared to cast his new shrimp net. He had seen his instructor demonstrate how to work with a net, but watching someone else do it in a store was very different than doing it himself for real here in the water. He got in position and rehearsed in his mind what he'd seen in the store.

He wound up to give it a first attempt, but as he threw it out toward the river, he didn't let it go in time, and the net ended up wrapping around his body and falling unceremoniously to the sand. He looked over to the boat, and all three of his girls were watching, giggling. Warren, on the other hand, was smoking with his legs dangling over the side in the opposite direction.

"Smooth, Dad," Gracie chided, cupping her hands over her mouth to amplify her voice.

"You just practice your casting," he called back.

After a few more tries, he finally got the hang of it. In the first few throws, he came up with little more than a few minnows. But when he gave it some time to sink, it came back filled with shrimp.

He quickly filled his bucket with water and placed the shrimp inside. After getting his net settled on the beach, he looked down into the bucket where the shrimp were swimming around in a state of panic. He knew what he had to do but struggled with taking the next step. Finally, he reached down into the bucket and pulled one out.

He looked at it, somewhat repulsed by what it looked like, but also aghast at the knowledge of what he had to do next. He held it in his hands for a while and said a prayer, thanking the shrimp for serving as bait today. After a few moments of reflection, he reached down with his other hand, grabbed its head, and twisted it off.

He looked down at his hands. One held the head and the other the body. While the actual ripping motion was easy enough, Peter was appalled at what he had just done. He kept looking back and forth between the head and the body for what seemed like an eternity. He didn't like anything about this experience and didn't understand why people did this for fun.

He realized how long he'd been staring down at his hands and finally looked up to see his three girls now standing on the boat looking at him. Gracie was the first to break the silence. "You okay?"

Peter simply lifted his hand in acknowledgment and looked down into the bucket. He had to do that at least nineteen more times and was thinking of backing out, but his family was waiting expectantly. He wondered if the rest of the shrimp knew that their counterparts were returning headless and whether that made the slow wait for death that much more anxious.

After completing his task, Peter grabbed the bucket, the net, and his male dignity and swam back to the boat as though this was no big deal. Upon reaching the boat, he handed the bucket and net to Mimi and climbed back on board. All three of his girls stood there, just looking at him. He placed his hands and arms off to the side with an exaggerated motion as if to say, *What are you looking at?*

Gracie smiled and decided to break the tension after looking in the bucket. "Remind me not to piss you off this trip."

Austin stuck her hands into the slimy mess. "This is awesome."

They all got their lines out after a few misplaced casts, and Mimi caught the first fish. As she got it near the boat, Peter grabbed a net and pulled it in. After the excitement of landing the first fish faded, he explained that they were going to release their catch back into the wild that day. But as he tried to extract the hook from a healthy redfish, he found himself ripping the fish's mouth to pieces. It took him about five minutes to get it out, and by then, the fish was nearly dead.

Peter put the fish back in the net and then placed it down in the water to see if it would spring back to life. But there was no movement. Peter moved the net around to create more water flow, but to no avail.

"Dad, it's dead," Gracie said caringly.

He sat there for a minute and pulled the fish back up into the boat.

"Sorry, Dad," Austin added.

Suddenly, Peter sat up, grabbed the fish, and jumped into the water. He held the fish in his right hand and started moving it through the water in a circular motion around his body.

Warren was finally interested in what was happening. "What's your dad doing?"

Mimi leaned over the boat. "Peter, what are you doing?"

"I'm getting water to go through its gills. Maybe that will bring it back to life."

"Dude, it's dead," Warren said with a stoner laugh in his voice.

Mimi was starting to be embarrassed for Peter. "Honey, you've done everything you could possibly do. Let the fish go."

Peter kept circling the fish around his body while his family looked on for the next five minutes. Peter kept praying silently for the fish to come back, but he could feel that nothing new was happening to the little lifeless body.

"Daddy, come back in the boat," Gracie pleaded.

"Your dad's a strange dude," Warren said to Austin.

Mimi finally started speaking in a commanding voice. "Peter, enough!" But Peter did not give up. He circled and circled. As he grew tired from using his left arm to paddle himself around, he switched it to the right and started circling in the opposite direction.

One more time, Mimi said, "Peter!"

Peter finally stopped circling and gave the fish a push in one last effort to give it life. The fish moved forward a foot or so from the momentum of the push and then slowly floated to the surface. Peter looked at it, totally defeated. He glanced up at the boat, and all four of them were leaning toward him.

Mimi spoke more compassionately. "Come on back into the boat, honey."

Peter wasn't sure how to recover from the spectacle. Finally, he pushed the fish aside, swam over to the boat, and climbed back in. He wanted to regroup, but he'd already gone so far off-kilter that he just decided to let it all hang out. He took the bucket of shrimp and heaved the headless crustaceans off the side, letting the bucket drop back into the boat. It bounced, making a very loud noise that penetrated the silence of his shipmates.

"At least some fish will get a free meal today," he blurted out. "The shrimp didn't die in vain."

Mimi turned on some music, and everyone went back to conversation except Peter, who grabbed some food and went off to the bow to eat by himself. He wasn't hungry. He just wanted to be by himself. In a cruel twist of fate, the fish never sank to the bottom. It just floated near the boat for the next hour or so, as if to remind him of his sin.

There was no more fishing for the Stewart family that year in Okatie, and no one dared make light of the story as the week progressed. It was one of those events that stood on its own, and no storytelling could ever properly express Peter's emotions displayed on the river. Although Peter felt the fool, it was one of those things that made Peter Peter.

That day would be remembered in the hearts of his family in the years to come as they thought about the man who would not give up, even on a fish.

Austin came out from her room after a nap and found her father laying new wood flooring in the upstairs study. The house had turned into a virtual showplace now that Peter had the money to tackle expensive projects each year.

"Hi, Dad."

"Hey there, sleepyhead. Where's Warren?"

"I'm not sure, maybe taking a walk."

"Want to learn how to lay wood flooring? You always used to work on these projects with me."

"Sure."

"Great. Grab me a couple of wooden slats over there."

Austin did as she was asked.

Peter instructed, "See how this side has a tongue and that side has a groove?"

"Yes."

"We'll it's real easy. You simply slot them together and then softly hammer them so as not to indent the wood."

"I can do that!"

"You can do anything," he assured her. He stopped for a moment and looked up at her. "Are you excited about applying to college?"

"Yes," she replied a little too enthusiastically.

He chuckled. "I know you've been anxious to get out on your own. Now that time is close. It will be your chance to make your mark. It's all on you at that point, and that's exciting!"

They put some more flooring down, and Peter went back and forth in his mind about what he wanted to say next. He wanted to give advice, but this subject was so touchy, and he always felt like he was walking on eggshells.

"Austin, you know you need to take good care of your body, right?"

"Yes, Dad," she said, rolling her eyes.

"You'll be exposed to a lot of bad things when you go off on your own."

"Dad, stop," she said with more eye rolling. "That's why I want out of here. You and Mom are so strict."

"We're strict because we love you, because you've been through so much."

"I just can't wait to get away from all your rules. I need to make my own decisions."

"Yes, you do. And that time has come. But everyone lives under rules, including myself. Some of those rules are made for me, some of those rules I make myself."

"Why would you make rules for yourself?"

"A rule is nothing more than a decision a person makes in advance. If I choose to live a certain way, then I've already made my decision before anyone encourages me to live another way. That way, I don't have to think about it when it happens. I've already made the decision in my head beforehand. Most decisions you make in the heat of the moment are based on what this wants to do"—he pointed at her body—"but the decisions you make beforehand you make with your mind"—he pointed at her head—"and preferably with your spirit and the Spirit"—he pointed to her heart. "So you need to make a bunch of decisions now, while you're still in the safety of your home. Who do you want to be? And how do you want to become that person?"

Austin nodded her head in the affirmative. The moment had been going so well, he thought about stopping there but continued. "Austin?"

"Yes?"

"You know you've had a drug problem before."

"Dad, stop."

"Honey, college is hard enough for a normal person. You have to decide not to do drugs now. You'll never make it in college as an addict. You'll never make it anywhere as an addict. Take advantage of this time and let us help you."

"Dad, that's it. This is why I never talk to you. I'm fine. Always have been!" Austin stormed back into her room.

"I think she doth protest too much," Mimi said from the stairwell, where she'd been listening to the conversation.

"Maybe, maybe not. She's been acting fine lately," Peter stated, a bit annoyed that she'd been listening in.

"Peter, come downstairs, I want to show you something."

Peter walked down to where Mimi was rifling through a drawer. She pulled out a tissue and handed it to Peter.

"What's this?" He unfolded the tissue and exposed about ten pills.

"There are ten more where that came from that are still in her purse. I didn't want to take them all and let her know that I know. Peter, you don't see her clearly. You only see your little girl, a girl who's been through so much. You don't even notice what she's become. You still see her as the person she used to be."

"And what has she become, *Mimi*?"

"She's addicted, *Peter*. She never got off the stuff. She must be getting this from her friends."

Peter burned silently for a moment. Austin had made a fool of him one more time for having given her the benefit of the doubt. He grabbed the tissue and ran upstairs. He burst into Austin's room and slammed the tissue down on her bedside table. "What is this? Where did you get these?"

"Where did you find them?"

"In your purse. Now where did you get them?"

"You went through my purse? How dare you!"

"How dare me? *Me?*"

"What kind of parents would go through their daughter's purse? You and Mom are terrible people!"

"You are missing the point, young lady. I asked you where you got them. Where we found them makes no difference."

Austin went quiet, thinking. "That's an old purse. I brought it back out for vacation. I haven't used that purse for a year. I always bring out an old purse for these trips so I don't ruin the good ones in the sand."

Now Peter was the one to go quiet. It was a legitimate explanation. His tone softened. "So you're not using now?"

"Dad, no."

Peter searched his mind aggressively, wondering what he should do next. He was either being scammed or he had just made a very big mistake. He walked over to her purse and threw it on the bed. "Go through it now and tell me if there are any more in there." He figured this would be a good test.

Austin started going through her purse slowly and deliberately. The last section she opened had an old prescription bottle that was in her name from back during the transplant days. She looked at him and said, "I stopped using and didn't need these anymore. I must have forgotten." She started to cry. "I can't believe you'd accuse me of such a thing."

Peter went over to the bed and apologized. He gave her a hug and then reached down and grabbed the bottle. "Well then, I guess you won't be needing these."

Austin whimpered through some tears, "No, Dad. I won't be needing those."

Peter hugged her again and got up to leave the room. Mimi had been watching and listening from a distance. When he walked out to see her there, he held up the bottle and said, "See, it's not a problem." Mimi simply dropped her head and turned around, exasperated.

Inside her room, Austin stopped crying, and a sly smile came across her face. She quietly got up and went into her closet where she lifted up a loose floorboard and pulled out a small bag. She looked around, listened, and then poured two pills out into her hand, which she swallowed without water. She lay back down and fell asleep until dinner.

YEAR 22

The twenty-second year was the first Thanksgiving ever held at River Soul, since both girls were in college and living closer to Okatie than Atlanta. Gracie and Austin were scheduled to arrive that Wednesday, and Mimi got there two days early to make the house extra special for her babies.

Gracie was the first of the girls to arrive, and Peter met her at the door to hug her tightly.

"How was the drive? How is school? How are you?"

"Dad, can I put my bags down first?"

"So tell me, how are things?"

"Good. School is good. Life is good."

"Still getting all As?"

"I've got it under control."

"You always do."

"Thanks, Dad."

With that, Mimi turned the corner. "My girl is here!"

Peter protested. "Well, that was short. Nice knowing you, Gracie."

"We'll catch up later."

"Yes, we will. Mimi has a surprise for you when you head upstairs."

"What is it?"

"I turned the loft into a bedroom for you so you could have your own space."

"Well, that's just awesome," Gracie exclaimed. "Maybe some peace will exist in this family after all."

As Mimi and Gracie headed upstairs, Peter went back to work installing some bookshelves in an office he had been working on for the last couple of years. The only way he could take a vacation anymore was to bring his job with him, and he needed a place where he could work while his family slept. He was deep into the project when the phone rang.

"Hello?"

"Dad?"

"Austin?"

"Yeah, it's me."

"Where are you, honey?"

"I'm at school."

"Why are you there? You should be here already."

"Well, that's why I'm calling. I'm not coming."

"What? What do you mean you're not coming?"

"I have a lot of work to do with finals coming up and all."

"Yes, and so does Gracie. She's here. You can study here if you need to."

"I just don't think I'm going to make it."

"Austin, you are coming here for Thanksgiving. It's been almost a month since you last checked in with us. You haven't answered your phone or responded to emails or texts. I don't even know how you're doing in school."

"Not so good."

"And how bad is not so good?"

"I'm failing . . . everything. So I need to stay here to study."

"Why are you just telling us that now? You need to come here, and we need to talk this through."

"I need to study. I can only do that here."

"Get in your car now, Austin."

"Ugh. All right."

"Bring your books with you. We'll talk through this when you get here. I love you."

Austin hung up the phone without saying anything further. Peter put down the phone and debated when he'd give Mimi the news. She was having so much fun with Gracie, and he didn't want to ruin the moment. But the moment was going to be ruined. The only question was when.

Peter, Mimi, and Gracie caught up over dinner while sitting on the back deck overlooking the river. They had finished their meal, talked, had dessert, and cleaned up before they got a text that Austin was nearby.

"What has taken her so long?" Mimi asked.

"I'm not sure. If she left when I spoke with her, she should have been here three hours ago."

"What's her status?" Gracie inquired.

Mimi chimed right in. "Who can say? She called us every day for the first two weeks after we dropped her off, and then every couple of days for the next two weeks. But then she stopped reaching out altogether."

"And Warren?"

"That broke off in the first week of school. She's with some other boy now."

"Lovely," Gracie said sarcastically. "Another fool, Dad?"

"I'm sure. But we don't know if she's even dating him still. We don't know anything."

Just then, Austin's car pulled up the drive. As he walked out the front door, it was very dark, but he could see a figure getting things out of the back of the car. Assuming it was Austin, he walked toward the car but soon heard from the other side of the front porch, in a tone that was very hesitant, "Hey, Dad."

Peter turned, confused as to how she could be behind him when there was someone over there by the car. But his confusion quickly turned to concern as he saw his daughter for the first time in three months. She was scary thin. He guessed that she had lost about twenty pounds off her already very lean frame. She was dressed in dirty sweatpants and a hoodie that was lifted up over her head.

Peter didn't want her to see his shock and so he regrouped.

"Where have you been? It's taken forever for you to get here."

"We got a little delayed."

The word "we" reminded him that there was someone else with her. The shock of her condition had caused him to forget there was a shadowy figure by the car. He turned around to see Austin's latest walking toward them with a bag in each arm and a cigarette hanging out of his mouth. As he approached, Peter could see that he was also very thin and dressed equally as messy as his daughter. As he got to Peter, he gave a head nod and said, "Wassup."

Peter just looked at him, hard.

"Dad," Austin said sharply. "Say something. This is my friend, Jack."

Peter looked at his daughter. "We weren't expecting company, Austin."

"Well, I wasn't coming here without him."

"And why is that?"

"Dad, he's my friend. And you're being rude."

Peter turned to Jack. Resigned to the situation, he extended his hand. "Hello, Jack."

Jack dropped one bag and extended a hand. "Nice to meet you, Mr. Stewart." As he said that, the cigarette fell out of his mouth and onto the ground, spilling ashes all over him on the way down. Without hesitating, Jack reached down and picked up the cigarette, placed it back in his mouth, and then wiped the ashes from his chest and stomach.

Peter looked back at the house, knowing how all this was going to go over with the rest of the family. He reached down to grab the bag Jack had just dropped and motioned toward the house.

"You'll need to put that out before coming inside," he said to Jack.

"Oh, okay, cool. I'll just stay out here and finish it off."

Peter grabbed the other bag and made his way to the front door. Austin went into the house first, but even from outside in the dark, Peter could see Mimi's expression as she saw her daughter—complete disbelief.

When Peter walked in, there was little conversation. He knew the same thing was happening to them that had just happened to him. They were so shocked by what they were seeing that they weren't even aware of the silence.

Peter came into the kitchen and made some commotion with the bags just to give them something to talk about. "I'll take this upstairs," he said.

"And, um, Gracie, you're going to need to move in with Austin."

"Why?"

"We have some additional company."

"What?" Mimi asked. "What company?"

"Jack," Peter said as he walked up the stairs.

"Jack, who?"

"You'll like him, Mom. He's really nice."

"I'm sure he is, Austin, but I didn't plan on another person for Thanksgiving dinner. I didn't plan on having another guest in the house at all. This is family time."

"Mom, it will be fine."

"I'm sure it will be fine, but a little warning would have been helpful," Mimi replied.

Grace burned silently.

Mimi looked at Austin. "Dressed comfortably, I see. You used to dress so nicely."

"Well, I'm busy, with school and all."

"Okay, well, how about you at least take the hoodie off?"

Austin hesitated, but ultimately reached up and pulled it off. Her hair was a tangled mess. But more than that, with the hoodie off, Mimi could see better how her face had broken out in the worst acne and scabbing she had ever seen.

"What happened to you?" Gracie finally said in a way that conveyed what everyone else had wanted to say up until that point.

"I know, my acne is terrible."

"Have you seen a doctor for that?"

"I'm too busy with school."

Mimi walked over to her daughter and started to straighten Austin's hair from out of the hoodie. "You go upstairs and get a good shower. Then you and I will go to work on this . . . hair."

Austin knew she was being judged from the moment her father saw her outside, and especially now with her mother and sister. She was grateful that the initial meeting was over and happy to have an excuse to exit.

With Austin out of sight, Gracie looked at her mother, dropped her jaw to make an exaggerated expression, and then mouthed the words *Oh, my gosh.*

Peter came back down the stairs, having just seen Austin out of the hoodie. He looked at Mimi and shook his head. He went to speak, but Jack opened the front door and walked into the house.

Peter just barely made eye contact. "Jack, this is Austin's mother, Mimi, and her sister, Grace."

"Hey," was his only reply. "Uh, where do you want me to go?"

Mimi was about to tell him where to go, but Peter spoke first, "You'll be in the loft at the top of the stairs, and Austin is getting cleaned up. I think it would be helpful if you did the same. There's an outdoor shower around the side of the house. There's a towel in a covered section right next to it."

Jack looked up the stairs. He did not want to be separated from Austin for very long, but he knew there was no immediate path to make that happen. So he turned around and put on his best agreeable voice. "Outdoor shower? Sounds cool. Can I use the bathroom first?"

"Sure, it's down the hall. The door outside is right next to it."

As Jack turned the corner around the hall, Gracie was the first to speak. "What the heck was that? What a creep. Both of them. They look like the walking dead. And what is that smell?"

"Cigarettes, I guess."

"And Austin smoking, with her history." Mimi was angry, and her tone reflected it. "But the smell is something altogether different."

"Let's keep our voices down," Peter recommended.

"So what? Because they might hear the truth?"

"I just don't want Thanksgiving to be one confrontation after another."

Gracie asked, "So you want us to pretend that this isn't happening?"

Peter looked despondent. "I don't know. I'm not sure what I want to do. Let's just make the best of this. It's Thanksgiving after all."

Peter left to go collect himself, using the excuse that he was going to finish a project in the office. His head was down, and he was walking aggressively, deep in thought both about Austin's appearance and about the additional knowledge that she was failing out of school. So it was startling when he turned the corner and plowed headlong into Jack, who was standing just around the bend in the hallway.

"Oh, Jack. Excuse me. I didn't know you were here. I thought you'd be outside in the shower."

"I must have gotten turned around," he said. "Which way to the outside?"

Peter walked him to the proper door and watched him as he walked out and around the house. His stoner introduction had convinced Peter this was just another of Austin's misfits. But there was something else with this one that needed more attention.

With a shower, some food, a good night's sleep, and a little makeup, Austin looked a lot better. She seemed to perk up some, even showing up for breakfast while Jack slept upstairs.

"Happy Thanksgiving," Peter said in his best welcoming voice.

"Happy Thanksgiving. Where's Mom?"

"She's out on a walk with Gracie. They waited for you."

"Not too long, I would imagine."

"Enough. It is nine thirty, after all. Don't you have eight a.m. classes you need to be up early for?"

Austin hesitated. "I guess."

"Are you even going to your classes?"

"Can I eat my breakfast before you jump into this?"

"I haven't said anything to your mother yet. And Jack never leaves your side. This may be our only shot to speak."

"Whatever."

"Are you going to class?"

"When I can."

"When you can?"

"There's a lot that goes on at school, Dad."

"School goes on at school, Austin. Everything else is secondary. Have you spoken with your advisor?"

"No."

"Well, I have," Peter said pulling out a piece of paper. "I spoke to him yesterday after you called." He started to read: "'Has missed more than half her classes, does not participate when she's in class, fails to complete assignments, was placed on academic probation in October, was placed on disciplinary probation two weeks ago, unlikely to pass a single class.' Does that sound about right?"

"What are you doing checking up on me like that?"

"Austin, I gave you three months of total freedom. You were free to do what you wanted to do, how you wanted to do it, when you wanted to do it. I didn't meddle once, even when you disappeared on us."

"I'm not Gracie."

"I never asked you to be Gracie. I don't want you to be Gracie. But I do expect you to do your best."

"I *am* doing my best."

"Really, you call not showing up to class and breaking school rules your best?"

"This is why I didn't want to come home. I didn't want to listen to your shit."

"Watch your mouth. You know I don't tolerate that kind of language."

A voice came from up in the loft. "Dude, give her a break."

Peter was furious. "What did you say, young man?"

"Dude, you're being too hard on her."

Peter started screaming up the stairs. "Who do you think you are? I don't even know you, and now you're giving me advice?"

The voice from above continued. "She's doing everything she can. Stop being so hard on her."

"Thank you, Jack," Austin said with tears in her eyes and a crack in her voice.

Peter went to shout a comment up the stairs, but decided he was not going to have this conversation with a stranger, let alone while talking to a disembodied voice. He looked over at his daughter.

"I know how smart and talented you are. I'm not buying that you're giving it your best. And look at you. Something very wrong is going on."

"That's it! I'm fucking out of here," Austin screamed as she ran upstairs. "I hate you. I hate you all."

"Do not run away from me, young lady. We're the ones paying for school. We're the ones paying for your expenses. We have a right to know what's going on."

Austin responded only with a slam of her door. Peter moved over to the dining room table and slouched into his seat. How was he going to tell Mimi? How could he save his family? How could he save his daughter?

"Told you to back off, dude," came the voice from the loft. "Told you to back off."

Even though the long weekend away had started so horribly wrong, Peter was determined to find a way to gather a few coveted moments with his family.

"So, what's the update from upstairs?" Mimi asked.

"No idea," Peter replied. "They've been up there all day." He went to the base of the stairs and called up. "Are you two going to join us for Thanksgiving dinner?"

Twenty minutes later, Jack came down after emerging from Austin's room. Peter was carving the turkey when Jack started the conversation. "She's calmed down a bit. I convinced her to stay."

Gracie said, "What makes you think we want her to stay?"

Peter looked over at Grace. "Now, now, let's be grateful that our family will be together on this special day."

"Whatev," is all Gracie could say, but in a way that was still respectful to her father. She looked over to Jack. She had no problem disrespecting him. "So, what's your deal?"

"About what?"

"About anything."

Jack directed his answer to Peter, who was now placing a serving dish of turkey down on the table. "Before you go look me up behind my back, school's hard for me too."

"Too?" Mimi interjected. "Too?"

"I'll fill you in later," Peter said.

Jack continued, "Look, I'm really in love with your daughter. That's all that matters."

"You and a whole bevy of winners," Gracie said sarcastically.

"No, really, I am," Jack insisted.

Peter had been trying to be polite, but he went up to Jack and got in his face. "If you love her, why does she look like death warmed over?"

"Dude, your aggressive tone would sound a bit more convincing if you weren't wearing that apron."

Peter looked down. It was Mimi's apron, and it did look a bit girly. He took it off and threw it down on the counter. He went to tear into Jack, but Jack spoke first. "Her idea of a good life is different from yours. Get off her case. Let her have some fun. She can do what she wants."

Peter was screaming now. "Not when what she wants is killing her!"

"Then talk to her. I don't tell her what to do."

"But you clearly have influence over her. I know what she looked like before she met you. And I know what she looks like now that she's known you for only a few months. I can't even compare the two."

"Dude, you always want to blame people. She can make her own decisions. The reason she doesn't want to be here, around you, is because you try to make her decisions for her."

Peter went to lash out at him, but Austin appeared on the steps, and the conversation ended. "What?" she asked when everyone stopped to look up at her.

"Nothing," Peter replied. "Let's sit down. Dinner's ready."

Austin spoke in an authoritative tone. "We're leaving right after dinner."

Peter looked at Jack. "I thought you said you were staying?"

"We are, dude, until dinner's over. We need to eat somewhere."

Peter looked over at Mimi and Gracie, who were waiting for his reaction. "Whatever," he said, exasperated.

They sat down, and Jack immediately dove in to serve himself, until he looked up to see everyone, even Austin, looking at him. Austin held her hands out to give him a clue as to what was supposed to come next. Each person reached out to grab the hands on either side, including Peter and Jack, who ended up holding hands together.

Peter had to calm himself down. Only minutes earlier, he had been screaming at the boy now holding his hand. He was so angry that he didn't know how to make the transition inside his head to gratitude, let alone express it to others in a prayer. He finally formed the words, but his heart was still fixated on the fight. And so the blessing felt hollow and insincere.

After the prayer, Peter and Jack were the first to release their hands, and Jack dug right back into the food. His plate was full before most people had even reached for their first dish. As Peter leaned over for some turkey, Jack looked up at Peter and said, "So Austin tells me you're some super Christian guy."

Gracie and Mimi looked at each other, and then over at Peter, who decided to stay calm given the nature of the question. "I love the Lord, if that's what you mean. Do you follow Jesus?"

"My parents took me to church."

"Do you still attend church?"

"Oh, hell no. Too many hypocrites there." Peter went to reply, when Jack looked him directly in the eye and said, "Like you."

Gracie and Mimi stopped eating and sat back in shock. Even Austin said quietly, "Jack, stop."

"I'm not going to stop. From the moment we showed up to this house, he's been judging me. He's been judging you, Austin," he said before directing his attention to Mimi and Gracie. "And you two? How does Austin fit into your little clique?"

Peter had it. He looked at Austin, ignoring Jack altogether. "Is this who you have chosen over your family? Is this what you value now? Is this what you've placed your hopes and trust in? This . . . thing?"

Jack stood up. "See? See what I mean? You can keep your Jesus. And I can keep my Austin. Let's go, baby. I'll go get our things."

Everyone else just sat at the table, quiet, until Peter broke the silence.

"Austin, this is an important decision you're about to make. Are you going to stay here with your family or go with Jack?"

"What do you mean, 'decision'?" Mimi shouted. "There is no decision to be made here. She's not going back to school with him."

Austin stood up. "Yes, yes, I am. None of you understands. None of you knows me. Only Jack gets who I am." She walked away from the table and moved upstairs, stomping her feet as she went.

"You're going to let her walk out of here?" Mimi asked. "Stop her, Peter. She needs help."

"You think I don't know that? But what do you want me to do? Physically stop her? Hold her down? She's going to go back to school in a couple of days anyway. Even if she stays here, she'll be back with him by Sunday."

"But if you let her go, it will be the end of her."

"Let's not be dramatic. Austin has to make her own decisions now."

"She's incapable of making a decision, Peter. She can't even see what's happening to her."

Jack and Austin walked down the stairs with bags in hand. Peter got up to walk toward them.

"Dad, don't try to stop us."

"I'm not trying to stop you. I just want to ask you one more time. Are you sure this is what you want to do?"

"Yes. But you know it doesn't have to be one way or the other. I can be with Jack and still be a part of this family. Why are you making me choose?"

"You're the one who is leaving, Austin."

"Dad, I will be okay. I'll figure it out. I'll be fine."

Peter hugged his daughter and ushered them out the door. He helped them get packed and then watched them drive down the dark, tree-lined gravel road.

When he returned, Mimi and Gracie were still at the table, and he sat down to finish his meal. He took a bite and began to chew slowly, deliberately. His wife and daughter just stared at him, waiting for him to say something. But words never came.

Eventually, Mimi pushed herself back from the table, got up, poured herself a glass of wine, and walked outside. Gracie sat still at the table, not knowing where to look or what to do. Finally, Peter just looked at her and said somewhat sharply. "Go!"

Gracie asked, "Dad, what just happened?"

Peter looked back at his meal and took another bite, never looking back at Grace Elizabeth. "Go," he said more softly.

Gracie sat still for a few more moments, holding back tears, until she got up from the table and followed her mother outside. Peter dropped his fork and pushed back from the Thanksgiving table, still barely even touched by a family that was now fractured and resentful. They were as far from thankful as a family could be.

Peter had almost finished cleaning up the mess from dinner when Gracie came in from outside. She walked directly upstairs without stopping and said in a somewhat sterile tone, "Good night, Dad. Oh, and by the way, Mom's drunk again."

"Lovely," Peter said softly under his breath. "Good night, Gracie. I'm sorry I snapped at you earlier."

Gracie never broke stride. "That's okay," he heard as the door to her room closed behind her.

He put the last of the dishes in the cabinets. Mimi opened the outside door and came in to get more wine. She was about to head back outside when Peter said, "Do you think that's going to help?"

"Oh, it already has helped." She turned to walk back outside but then spun around to grab the entire bottle. "You're a real tough guy with me. I wish you'd be half that man with your daughter."

"Nice," Peter said. "You're such a great example for our girls."

Mimi spun around hard, causing the wine to spill over the edge of the glass. "Jack was right; you do like to place blame."

"You know what, Mimi, maybe Jack was right. Maybe we are judging Austin."

"Of course we are! There's so much to judge. Should we talk about her drug use, her foul language, her appearance, her choice in men, her lazy butt that does nothing to help around here, her disrespect for her parents, her disrespect for her sister, her constant requests for money that goes God knows where, her total lack of communication, the constant flow of lies that comes out of her mouth, her never-ending sleeping, the fact that she loses everything of value we give her, the way she ruins every family moment we ever try to create, or the fact that she's killing herself after we spent our entire lives trying to save her? Shall I go on? I've got plenty more."

Peter hung his head and spoke in a softer tone. "We're called to love people unconditionally, even when they are unlovable. Especially when they are unlovable. Everything you just said is a condition of her receiving our love. We're driving her away from God. We're driving her away from our family."

"Holy crap. You're going to get spiritual about this?"

"The fact of the matter is, Mimi, that if Jesus came back to earth today, He wouldn't come to visit you and me. He'd throw a party for Austin and Jack."

"Well, perfect, He can have them. But I am telling you right now. You better man up on this thing. Wake up from your little Christian fantasy world. Your daughter's a drug addict."

"That's the problem. You see her as a drug addict."

"No, the problem is that you don't. You can hope, you can pray, but it's not going to change what is."

"Actually, that does change what is."

"And you're doing such a wonderful job of it, Peter. How is prayer working so far?"

"I won't give up on believing in her."

"That will look great on her tombstone. 'Here lies Austin. Her dad never gave up.'"

"At least I believe in something. You've become a bitter woman who believes in nothing."

"And you've become a scared little boy. Won't take on a skinny punk, even while he's leading your daughter astray."

"God loves him, too, as much as He loves me and as much as He loves you."

"Oh, my God. *Stop!* Stop it, Peter. Look, either you get her in a program by the New Year, or I'm out."

"Out of what?"

"Out of all of it."

"How convenient. Can't deal with the problem, so you choose to escape it."

"The only person who has been escaping it is you. You run to your work, you run to your Bible, you run to your office, you run from confrontation, you run to your sappy platitudes. How about looking the problem in the eye and dealing with it for a change?"

Peter stopped. She was hitting at the heart of his internal dialogue. He was just standing by while this horrible little "man" dragged his daughter deeper into the pit.

But he continued. "People say you need to let addicts hit bottom. You can't save them from themselves. Only they can save themselves."

"That must give you great comfort, Mr. Christian. It gives you every excuse to hide behind people who don't know a thing about our daughter, to hide behind your prayer life. You sit cozy in your fantasy world while that creep is doing who knows what to our baby."

"All right!"

"All right, what?"

"We'll get her in a program. We'll try it your way."

"How? We'll have to pull her out of school."

"Oh, so now you're not so sure how to do it either. Are you?"

"No, Peter, I'm not so sure how to do it. You were the first thing I had to figure out."

"I'll fix it."

"So fix it already!"

Mimi and Peter sat on the porch of River Soul waiting for Austin to pull up after driving from school. It was Christmas, but this was going to be a rough holiday season. Peace, love, joy, and hope were not words they would use to describe this Advent. They weren't sure if this would be the last time they would ever see Austin alive. Even if things went well with what they were about to do, she would hate them for it.

Peter and Austin's advisor secretly devised a plan whereby Austin would leave school for a semester and then come back again in the fall to retake her freshman year. Then they tricked Austin into thinking that they were having Christmas in Okatie and that all was forgiven from Thanksgiving. They told her it was okay to bring Jack with her but that they needed just a couple of days together as a family. He could join them after Christmas and stay until they went back to school in January. Austin seemed very pleased.

If, in the next couple of hours, all went according to plan, Austin would be coming back with them to Atlanta. They had arranged for her to join a rehab program back home, which had taken the better part of a month to arrange.

The only way to guarantee a bed was a $5,000 down payment. But the one place with a possible open spot still made no promises that they would accept her after talking to her. "If she's not ready," the counselor said, "then there's no use for her to be here."

"What?" Mimi shouted while sitting in the director's office. "We are finally to the point where our family is willing to do this, and now you're saying you might not take her after we go through the pain of confronting her?"

"If she's going to be a negative influence on the rest of the kids, then we can't keep her in the program."

"How in the world could she be a negative influence on them?" Mimi retorted, pointing her chin to the crowd outside. A pack of teenagers shivered in the cold outside the window while they smoked with the counselors, all of whom were former addicts.

"Don't judge them by their appearance. Some of them are ready to make a change in their life."

Mimi's comment gave Peter the courage to say what he had been embarrassed to admit ever since he pulled up. "I'm trying to give my daughter an example of what normal people look and act like. How's that going to happen when she is hanging around people like that?"

"Your daughter no longer relates to what you call *normal* people." He turned around and opened the shutters wider to make a point. "These are the kind of people she now resonates with. That is what your daughter feels like on the inside. And however ugly or outlandish you think it looks, it's ten times worse inside her head."

Mimi and Peter both went quiet. That group was the "bad crowd," the people other parents try to keep their children away from. Yes, Austin was not herself right now, but surely she was not like that. Even Mimi felt that Austin had not gone that far.

"Look, our daughter had medical issues. It's not like she chose this for recreational purposes, like they did," Mimi continued as she stared out the window.

The director smiled gently. He'd seen one parent after the other try to justify their child's addiction. "Get her here, and we'll see if we can help your daughter. But just know that eventually she's going to have to help herself."

As difficult as it was to find a place for her, nothing compared to the tension they were feeling here now at River Soul. There would be no escaping an inevitable confrontation. They had talked about it a hundred times on the way down, what to say, how to orchestrate their moves. Now, it was go-time.

When her car pulled into the drive, Peter started second-guessing all they had planned up until this point. His daughter had missed out on everything childhood was meant to offer, and now he was about to steal from her the one thing that had kept her alive during the worst of her second transplant—a path toward the normal life that all teenagers dream of. She had a right to experience one normal thing in her life and college was that thing. Now he was taking it away.

Mimi looked over and knew what he was thinking. "She brought this on herself, Peter."

"I know."

Austin pulled up and waved out the window. When she got out of the car, she was smiling for the first time since they could remember. "Hey there, what are you two doing out here?"

Peter went over and hugged her. "We were just anxious to see you. It's Christmas after all."

Austin walked over to hug her mother. She looked even worse than when they had seen her just four weeks earlier. She was thinner, if that was even possible, and her face was covered with even more scabs than before. Her teeth were turning black, and her clothes were dirty and reeked of a terrible smell—a combination of cigarettes, homelessness, and turpentine.

Peter called over, "Hey, throw me the keys. I need to move this. We're expecting a delivery later."

Austin tossed him the keys. Mimi pretended to pat herself down and asked Austin to borrow her phone. "I promised Gracie I'd text her when you got here. Could I use your phone?"

Austin deleted a few things first. "Here."

"Thanks."

Peter went to get some bags out of the car and handed them to Austin. "Grab these. I'll get the rest." Austin put her purse down for a second, and Mimi leaned over to snatch it.

"Hey, what are you doing with my purse?"

"I just want to hold it for a moment," Mimi said, realizing how ridiculous that sounded.

"Mom, give me my purse. What are you doing? And give me my phone back." She approached Mimi, who turned abruptly to keep her from grabbing them. "What is going on? What are you two doing?"

"Austin, sit down on the porch. We need to talk."

"I don't want to talk. Just give me my things."

Peter insisted, "We are going to talk. Sit down."

Austin moved over to the steps and sat down.

"Sweetheart," Peter opened, "we love you. And we only want what's best for you. We don't think you're set up for success right now. We want you to take some time off and come back to Atlanta, and then you'll head back to school in September."

"No, I'm not coming back to Atlanta. I'm going back to school, with Jack."

Her father tried to take charge. "Austin, there is no more school. You're not welcome back. You failed out. But they're willing to let you come back if you get some help."

"Help? What kind of help?"

"For addiction. They've never offered this to anyone else. But given your story, they are willing to make an exception for you. It's an incredible gift."

"That's no fucking gift."

"Austin, have you ever heard anyone in this family use that kind of language?"

"Shut up. I don't need this shit."

"Austin—" Mimi started but was quickly interrupted.

"No, Mom. You're behind all of this. I know Dad would never do this. You've made him do this."

Peter stood up for his wife. "No one has made me do anything, Austin. And I know this feels like punishment to you. But everyone is doing this out of love."

"You're all just a bunch of fucking assholes. Give me my things. I'm going back to Jack."

"Actually, you're not doing that."

"I can do whatever I want."

Peter hesitated. He didn't want to head down this path, but it was clear he had no choice. "Young lady, you don't turn eighteen for another forty-three days. You don't have a legal say in the matter."

"You can't make me do anything."

"Actually, we can," Mimi interjected.

Peter quickly added on to that before Austin could verbally go after her mother. "But having said that, we are going to give you a choice. If you go into a ninety-day program and get clean, after that, we will get you a place in a sober community that will offer you lots of flexibility. We will pay your bills until you head back to school. We will also continue to pay for your education until you finish school. You'll still be on your own. You won't have to come back to live with us unless you want to. But if you decide that you don't want to do any of that, then you are free to go."

"That's easy; I'm gone. Give me the keys and my things."

"Let me finish," Peter continued. "If you decide you don't want to be well, then we cannot support anything you choose to do next."

"Fine, give me the keys. I don't want your support anyway. You've never supported me. You've always hated me. I don't belong in this family."

"You absolutely belong in this family," Mimi stated emphatically.

"Mom, I'm not listening to anything you say. You're the reason my life is ruined."

Peter immediately stepped in. "*We* are the reason. And your life is not ruined. We are offering you a path to everything you wanted."

"Fuck you. Fuck you both. Give me the keys."

"Apparently you weren't listening, Austin. That car is my car, this phone is my phone, and everything in your purse belongs to me except the drugs, of course, which will be in the river in the next ten minutes. If you leave, you leave with nothing."

"And just how in the hell am I supposed to get back to school?"

"Sounds like a good question," Peter said as calmly as he could.

Austin's head was spinning. She knew she could call Jack to come get her. But his number was on her speed dial; she hadn't needed to memorize it. She thought about walking or hitchhiking, but it was ten miles to the highway. She had only one option, and it caught everyone by surprise. Feeling trapped, she started breathing very heavily, charged Mimi, and started throwing punches until her mother dropped her things. Austin grabbed her purse and snatched back her phone. Peter was too far away to stop it, and he saw both the purse and phone hit the ground. It was the phone that concerned Peter the most. The purse, no doubt, had her drugs, but her phone was a viable option for her. Once Jack got wind of what was happening, he'd be here in a few hours. He knew where this house was located, and that would be the end of all of this.

Peter ran over to Austin and tried to grab the phone. Austin reached up and took her nails to his face, creating four deep gashes down his left cheek. Peter stepped back, surprised by the violence of it all. He held his hand to his face, which was starting to bleed severely. Austin took off across the yard and flipped open her phone. She had Jack on speed dial in the number-one location.

The phone started to ring, but she could only keep it up to her ear intermittently because she was running so fast. "Come on, pick up!" she screamed into the phone. She could hear her father getting closer.

"Pick up, damn it, pick up!" She was now running as fast as she could. Austin could hear Jack pick up the phone just as her father caught her and swatted it out of her hands. She could hear Jack just barely as his voice came from the phone now lying on the ground. "Hello? Baby is that you?"

Peter could hear it too. They both went for the phone, and he could tell she had the better angle to get to it first. He had no choice. Instead of going for the phone, he pushed his daughter hard onto the ground.

"Hello, baby, hello? What's going on?" Jack was now screaming on the other end of the line.

Austin lay on the ground crying and holding her arm. "You bastard, you fucking bastard."

"Baby? Who's a bastard? Why are you saying that to me?" Jack's voice now sounded urgent and upset.

Peter grabbed the phone and flipped it shut. Jack called back several times, but with Peter in control of the phone, there was no way Jack was going to reach Austin now. Peter turned around and threw it as hard as he could. It landed, with a plop, in the river behind the house.

"You asshole! What have you done? What have you done?"

With his adrenaline now slowing, Peter started to feel the pain in his cheek. He put his hand up to his face and could see that his bleeding had intensified. The blood was all over his shirt and dripping onto his pants. She had cut him deeply.

Feeling that the worst of the moment had passed, he walked back to Mimi, who was crying on the steps of the porch.

"You okay?" he asked her.

"I will be. You, on the other hand, are going to need some serious stitches for that."

Austin got up from the ground, brushed herself off, and walked back to them. Apparently, she was not as done as they thought. "I'll never go with you anywhere. Ever. You can just leave me here to die. I hate you! You've ruined my life. Things will never be the same. I'll never trust you again!"

She picked up some rocks and started bashing in all the windows of her car. Peter went to stop her, but Mimi grabbed him and motioned for him to sit down. Together they watched their daughter destroy the car she had once so loved—the car that once represented her path to freedom, the car that once meant independence, the car that once made her feel like maybe there was hope she could someday be a normal human being.

YEAR 23

Peter looked at his reflection in the rearview mirror. His scars were still visible, but not so much that he had to explain what happened to him to every person he met. He told people he'd been mugged, but that only led to a web of lies so intricate that he could no longer remember all of them.

He looked away from his own reflection and glanced at the vacant back seat where Austin and Gracie used to sit. Since having children, this was the first time Mimi and Peter had planned a trip to River Soul on their own. It felt like a very lonely, very empty car, even with his wife sitting beside him.

Gracie was off on a mission trip with her school friends, and Austin was somewhere in the state of Florida, where she'd been for the last three months. The only time he heard from her was when she'd call for money. Her calls for cash grew increasingly more urgent and uglier the more Peter refused. He hesitated even to answer her calls but always did. He never stopped hoping that one day she might reach bottom and finally ask to come home.

The person on the other end of the phone was no one he recognized. There was a time, even while her changing appearance screamed "addict," that he could still hear her voice. But now, even that was gone. Every time he thought she had reached a new low, she managed to redefine what bottom looked like.

Just six months earlier, he had thought they might have a chance to reclaim her after she successfully completed the ninety-day program. They saw glimpses of the real Austin the further she got away from her last fix. Her skin cleared up, she gained some much-needed weight, and they even shared a few moments of laughter during their frequent family counseling sessions.

The counselor had warned them that it would take time for her to heal and for them to heal. "She's fried her brain," he said. "All the synapses need to reconnect, and your family needs to reconnect. But she will become herself again, and eventually, you will once again become a family."

And to some degree, she did become herself, although the drug-free Austin had some issues her parents did not understand. She was deeply ashamed of what she had done and who she had become. But while most people would use that shame to become a better person, Austin's shame became a trigger to use even more drugs.

At the end of one of their family sessions, Peter stood up and moved toward Austin to create a physical closeness to match the inner closeness he was feeling for the first time in a long time. Although he always loved his daughter, he hadn't felt connected to her for a while.

"We love you," Peter said as he moved in for a hug.

"I love you too," she said as she hugged both of them tightly. "Goodbye. Thank you for getting me help."

The word "goodbye" seemed so final to them. And yet her comment about getting help seemed so encouraging. They weren't sure how to respond. "See you next time," Mimi said to change the tone.

Austin hesitated and just said, "Okay."

One week later when they showed up for their next appointment, Austin was not there. Peter drove over to the apartment Austin had been sharing with some rehab friends, only to find that she had moved out in the middle of the night a few days earlier. When Peter asked how she left with no car and no money, the girls said that someone from Florida had come to get her, someone with a description matching Jack.

It was a month after that before they got the next call.

"Dad?"

"Austin. Is that you?"

"Yes. Dad, I need some money."

"Where are you, Austin?"

"I'm in Florida."

"How did you get to Florida?"

"A friend came and got me. Dad, send me money."

"And where would you like me to send it?"

"Western Union. Here's my number."

"Where are you, Austin?"

"Dad, I'm in Florida. Just send me some fucking money. You're swimming in cash."

"I'm not sending you any money."

"Why not?"

"I've already told you, Austin. If you choose a life of drugs and drug addicts, then you are on your own. Any money I've ever given you, you've used for drugs. Anything of value I've ever given you, you've sold for drugs."

"Dad, I need money for a place to stay. For food."

"If you need money, then get a job."

"Jack's father has paid for everything for the last six weeks. Why won't you pay for anything? Why don't you ever support me?"

"So now we know it's Jack who came to get you. Perfect."

"He loves me. And I love him."

"Neither of you knows what love is, Austin."

"Are you going to give me any money or not?"

"If you choose to do drugs, you'll never get anything from me ever again. And if—"

A loud click signaled that the call had been terminated.

Peter didn't hear from Austin again for another full week.

"Dad, don't give me any fucking lectures," came the greeting. "I need money. Jack's dad paid for another week, but he won't pay it again."

"Austin, I don't think Jack's father should be paying for anything."

Another click.

But the calls kept coming, ever more urgent. Austin claimed they were now sleeping outside and that Jack had been arrested, that she was on her own and was scared.

"Dad, please send me money. I've never been more scared in my life. I'm all by myself at night. And these people are freaking me out."

"I'll come get you, Austin, and bring you back to the program."

"Just send me money, Dad. I am not going back to the program."

"I won't send you money, Austin. But I will fly down to get you right now. I can be there in a few hours. Tell me where you are."

"Dad, just send me money. I'll take care of things here."

"Austin . . ."

"Look, you asshole," came a male voice. "Just send her the damn money."

"Well, hello, Jack. Glad to finally flush you out."

"I'm not going to keep paying for this shit."

"Perfect. I'll come get her and take her off your hands."

"She's not going anywhere. You say you love your daughter, but you clearly don't. We're living on the street."

"And it's because I love my daughter that I'm not going to contribute to your habits. And I'm sure as hell not going to give her any money that will support you in any way. If you need money, get a job!"

"Fuck you, asshole." *Click.*

With that final hang-up, Peter's mind raced, conjuring up images of the life Austin and Jack were leading. The thought made him physically ill. If he knew where she was, he would fly out that night, kidnap her, and bring her back home. But even if he could find her, what good would that do? Even if she agreed to come with him, she'd only stay long enough to rest up before she headed back out. She was eighteen now, and he had no legal right to force her to do anything.

He felt helpless and hopeless. He started to pray, but he had no more words to say to a God who had gone silent. He'd poured his heart out over and over again, but things only got worse. No matter how much he believed, no matter how much faith he had in her healing, nothing changed for the better. So, what was the use now?

Gracie was a blessing to the entire family, but everything else was crumbling around him. Austin's addiction was dragging the family down in ever-tightening concentric circles of grief. No one talked much of anything else, and certainly no one thought of anything else. She was an all-consuming force.

Even as they sat in the car on the way to South Carolina, Peter's every thought centered on Austin. His mind and his heart drifted from one Florida town to the next, searching for a daughter who did not want to be found.

And Mimi, sitting next to him, knew he was far away, searching as much for himself as for anyone else. Peter viewed Austin's plight as his failure as a father, and his failure as a Christian. But Mimi viewed it as the utter rebelliousness of an impertinent child, bent only on meeting her most selfish desires. She had long since given up on her daughter and was now determined to keep the rest of her family together. Austin had become a cancer that needed to be cut off.

But Peter could not let it go. His obsession kept the whole family locked in a cage no one could open. No matter how much he tried, the thought of his daughter living in constant danger ate away at whatever moments of peace a normal man could hope to find.

Mimi was busy at the end of the pier as she waited for Peter, who was preparing the nets and fishing gear for a day on the water. She readied the crab trap and placed some raw chicken inside the metallic rectangular contraption. As Peter came into view, she carefully positioned the trap up on the pier railing and then lowered it down into the water via a rope.

She wanted the traps in the water before Peter got there. Even though he was still hesitant about the whole thing, he had grown more accustomed to fishing and shrimping. He participated now, reluctantly, but still did not want any part of boiling things alive, as was the fate of the crabs she hoped to find scurrying around this trap by the end of the day.

"You about ready?" Peter asked as he got close enough to speak.

"I am. Let's go catch our dinner."

"You know, I've discovered a more humane way to cook the crab," Peter offered as they pulled away from the dock.

"And what is that, Mr. Stewart?"

"You put them in the freezer to slow their metabolism so that they are unconscious before you boil them."

"So rather than boil them to death quickly, I should freeze them to death slowly instead. Do I have that right?"

"Well, now that you say it out loud . . ."

"I'll give it a try tonight, Dr. Dolittle, and you can ask them later which way they prefer."

"Yeah, yeah, yeah."

Once on the boat, they found their usual shrimping spot. "Pull in over there. Let me cast the net," Mimi directed.

They had gotten quite good at a team catch. Peter would slowly approach the shallow water, and Mimi would cast the net off the bow. When the net landed, he would gently throw it in reverse to keep from beaching the boat, while Mimi pulled in the net. By the end of the first day, they had a five-gallon bucket of shrimp filled halfway to the top, which took care of the entire week's menu.

Their fishing for the day proved uneventful, but they rejoiced in the time alone. Mimi had always loved this place, but being alone with Peter made it all feel new again.

"It's almost as though we never left from our first trip here, Peter. I always feel younger when we are here, except that some of the stuff up here," she said, pointing at her chest, "is now drifting down there."

"You still look awesome to me."

"Thanks for saying it."

"No, I mean it, Mimi. You still look awesome to me."

Mimi moved in close, and they kissed a little. And then they kissed some more. Peter looked up and was grateful to find that there were no other boats anywhere in sight. He moved Mimi down onto the cushion and began to unclasp her bathing suit. She worked to do the same with him, and before long they were both naked and aroused. He rose on top of her but, in the process, became entangled in the lines of the boat.

Not wanting to ruin the moment, he tried to stay focused on Mimi while moving his leg around to get untangled. But that only made things worse. Mimi tried to cooperate by moving out of the way but instead pushed Peter from the narrow seat onto the deck of the boat.

On the way down, Peter's leg caught the shrimp bucket, which turned over on top of Peter's naked body. Hundreds of live shrimp started scrambling for their lives on Peter, near Peter, and across the rest of the boat. He jumped up, frantically trying to swat away the shrimp that had made their way to his private parts.

Once convinced he no longer had shrimp in his crotch, he turned around to see Mimi on the seat staring up at him.

"Well, I guess that moment has passed," she said as best she could while almost choking with laughter.

Peter, realizing his shame, made light of it and held out his arms. "Come to me, baby."

"How about we just move on, and I'll try my best not to come up with about fifty different shrimp jokes about your masculinity right now."

"All right. But I'll clean up, and man up, a bit later. Deal?"

"Deal."

As they motored back, Mimi moved up front and dangled her legs off the front of the boat. It was not the safest place to be on a fast-moving boat, but it gave a person the sensation that they were skimming across the water on their own power. The sun was making its descent in the west over their final destination for the evening. He sat back in the captain's chair and thanked God for this moment.

And just as he prayed that, he realized that he had not thought of Austin for the entire afternoon. He had been absorbed in his marriage. He had been focused on Mimi, and the water, and the shrimp, and the sun.

He was relaxed and at peace. Was that wrong? Was he selfish to have forgotten his daughter? Had she needed him in those hours?

They pulled up to River Soul, and it was one of those rare days when the tides and winds worked in their favor. Both pushed the boat gently into the dock, making the process flow without effort.

They spent the next hour pulling the heads off the shrimp, which they had collected, one by one, back into the bucket after the great naked shrimping debacle.

"This doesn't seem to bother you anymore," Mimi said to Peter after he'd ripped the heads off at least fifty shrimp.

"I guess the world has shown me there are worse things in life."

"Very philosophical."

"I'm sorry."

"No, I didn't mean that as a slam. I meant it as a compliment. It's one of the things I love about you, Peter—most of the time."

"It doesn't always feel that way."

"I know."

"We're about done here. Want to get the trap up?"

"Sure."

Peter placed his hands on her shoulder before Mimi could lift the trap. She backed away, and Peter pulled on the line. It was heavy, signaling good news about its contents.

As Peter pulled the trap over the railing, about fifteen crabs scurried inside.

"Watch your fingers," Mimi said. And then she reached around and touched his upper thigh. "And watch your privates. Those claws could do a bit more damage than the shrimp."

Mimi was outside by the fire pit when Peter came out from his shower in jeans and a white shirt, which accented his tan.

"Hmm," was all Mimi said, and that sounded good to him. Peter poured a couple of glasses of wine and placed them out on the table.

While Peter pulled a couple of Adirondack chairs up close, Mimi poured some spices into the boiling pot. "It just needs a little more kick. This ought to do it."

"That was fun today," he said.

Mimi simply smiled and kept about her work. The sun was now in full setting mode with colors starting to pop. Peter got up to light a couple of candles to keep the bugs away but also to set the mood. Mimi finished what she was doing and sat down beside him.

It was a moment that did not require words. They sat there for five minutes in silence, when Mimi finally got up. "Help me with this."

Peter grabbed the potholders and ushered the boil into the kitchen where Mimi went to work with final preparations. Peter went back to sit outside just as his phone rang. It was a Florida number he did not recognize.

His heart sank. He was too relaxed to have a fight with Austin. He stared at the phone and watched it as it vibrated across the wooden table by the fire pit. For the first time, he did not take the call. It stopped ringing, and he sat back in his chair.

"I have to let this go," he said to himself.

But when the phone rang again a few minutes later, Peter couldn't refuse her twice.

"Hello?"

"Is this Peter Stewart?" asked an older female voice.

"Yes."

"And is your daughter Austin Stewart?"

"Yes. Who is this?"

"I cannot tell you who this is. I shouldn't be making this call."

Peter stood up anxiously. "What's going on? Who are you and what do you want?"

"I'm a nurse at Franklin Memorial Hospital. Your daughter is here."

His facial expression became severe. "Why? Why is she there?"

"She's overdosed on heroin and cocaine."

Peter held his breath. "Is she alive?"

"Barely. But that's not all of it."

"Just tell me!"

"If your daughter survives the night, we're going to have to amputate her leg."

"Amputate? Her leg? Why?"

"She's been injecting heroin in the same spot in her upper thigh, and it's become so infected that it's eaten into her bone. We're about to transfer her to Gainesville General. We don't handle amputations here."

"Let me speak to her."

"I can't do that."

"Why not?"

"Because there's a man in her room. He won't let her speak to you. And because she's eighteen, we're not legally allowed to contact you."

"How did you find me?" Peter asked, still in a state of shock.

"I took her phone when they were both distracted. You're listed under Dad in her directory."

"Thank you for calling. If I drive all night, I could be there before morning."

"You'll have to hurry. If we don't take the leg by noon tomorrow, she may not make it."

As the phone call ended, Peter found himself out on the pier. During the intensity of the call, he had gotten up and paced without even realizing it. He looked back at the house and could see Mimi bringing two plates out to the table. She waved at him, smiling, and making a "come back" motion with her hands.

As he walked back, Mimi put the final touches on a meal that would never be eaten. She thought about lovemaking that would never happen. And she enjoyed a moment of peaceful ignorance that would be shattered as soon as her husband could form the words to explain just how much worse their lives had become.

By the time Peter and Mimi arrived at Franklin Memorial, Austin's hospital room had been placed on lockdown. The night before, Jack, blitzed on drugs, had taken siege in the room. He barricaded himself at the door so as to block entrance to anyone not bringing pain medication.

Eventually, the police dragged a handcuffed Jack screaming and swearing from the room. Austin, hysterical, had to be sedated and strapped to her bed.

"We can't let you up on the floor," the receptionist said as they inquired about Austin's room number. "Your daughter has specifically listed you as those without permission to visit."

"My daughter, or that creep she's with?" Mimi asked.

"I couldn't say," was the only reply.

"In that case, could we speak with her doctor?"

"We are not allowed to disclose any information about an adult patient."

"She's being transferred today. We are beside ourselves. Can you at least let us know when her transfer is going to happen?" Peter asked.

The receptionist looked around. "Look, I shouldn't be telling you this. But it's a very small hospital in a very small town. And you seem like nice people. Your daughter and her friend have created quite a stir around here. He's been thrown in jail, and your daughter has finally calmed down now that he's out of the room."

"And what about the transfer?"

"Well, that's also been a hot topic of conversation. She's not being transferred."

"Wait. Why?"

"Because they're no longer going to amputate. Her massive infection has cleared up faster than anything they've ever seen before. No one can say for sure, but they think she'll recover."

"Thank God," Peter said out loud.

"And antibiotics," Mimi said.

The receptionist looked at Peter. "We've had a prayer chain going. All night."

Peter spontaneously dropped his head and closed his eyes. "Thank you, Jesus." After a few moments, he opened his eyes back up and looked at the receptionist. "And thank you. And your friends."

"You're welcome. It's been a source of encouragement for us too." She looked at both of them. "Look, go home. No one will talk to you here. And we cannot let you see her given her instructions. She's fine. She'll be here for a few more days. There's nothing more you can do."

On the trip back, Peter was deep in prayer for at least the first hour. He finally turned to Mimi and said, "Well, He's saved her again. He must have big plans for that girl."

Mimi was incredulous. "You really think she's saved, Peter? The only reason she's calm is because they have her drugged and strapped down. The animal is in the cage after being hit by a drug-laced dart. Let her out and she'll be right back at it."

"One thing at a time, Mimi. Yesterday, they were going to amputate her leg. Today, she's had a miraculous recovery."

"Until she starts it all over again."

"Maybe this is it. Maybe this will wake her up."

"How many wake-up calls do you think she'll get in a lifetime?"

"I guess exactly the number she needs."

"Or maybe one less than she needs. She wouldn't be the first addict to overdose for good."

Trying to change the subject, Peter brought up something he'd been trying to figure out how to say to Mimi for a week. "You know, she called me last Thursday. She says she wants to go back to school."

"Well, that will never happen."

"That's what I told her at the time. But then I started thinking. She needs something to be proud of. She needs something to work for. She needs something to think about other than drugs. And she needs someone other than Jack in her life. We're not doing her any service by cutting her off from everyone and everything she loves."

"Maybe she needs to be sober before showing up to calculus."

"We told her that if she did the ninety days, she could go back to school. We promised her."

"And do you think we actually had to say when we promised that this assumes you won't go do so many drugs that your leg will be amputated! *Promised?* Really, Peter? What promise has she ever made and lived up to? Not one. Ever!"

"I said she could go back. I've already called her advisor. It's all set for January."

"You did that without asking me? Without talking about it first?"

"I knew this would be the conversation with you. I knew you'd only see the bad in her. I knew you'd assume that she could never make it, that you'd never even give her a chance."

"I feel like I've heard this somewhere before. Oh, yeah, it was during her first year at school, and then again at rehab."

"We promised her she could go back to school. She may lie to us all the time, but I can no more lie to her than I could lie to you."

"Isn't that what you just did, Peter? Lie to me? By going behind my back, you lied to me by default."

Peter was silent. He knew she was right. They were quiet for the rest of the drive.

The moment they arrived back at River Soul, Mimi started packing up her things. Even though they were only a few days into their week together, she knew that rest wouldn't be found, even in the place that had, for nearly two decades, brought her comfort. There was no use in staying. It would only be a reminder that the reality of their life had overtaken them once again and destroyed whatever peace they could conjure in their sanctuary.

Without saying a word, Peter walked out onto the back deck and watched the last of the colors fade from the sky. He sat down at the table that just twenty-four hours earlier was going to be the beginning of a wonderful night with his wife. He smiled at the memory, but then, without warning, he started to cry. He didn't intend to cry. He hadn't thought about crying. The tears just came.

He wasn't sure why he was crying. Was it the pressure on his marriage? Was it Austin's descent into a life he never could have imagined for her? Was it what his family had become? This place used to remind him of all the happy years filled with laughing children and a joy-filled wife. But now it was just sadness and loss.

Mimi tapped on the back sliding glass door, startling Peter out of his funk. She could see he had been crying, but without speaking, she handed him all the food she could not pack for the trip home to Atlanta. Peter took it from her and walked out back toward the river, where he tossed it into the marshy water. By low tide, every raccoon in Okatie would feast on a week's worth of meals intended for a romantic couple on their first vacation alone in twenty years.

They drove away in the darkness, and Mimi was asleep before they hit the highway. Eventually, in the silence, Peter realized he had not eaten in more than twenty-four hours. He reached back into the cooler to see what Mimi had packed for the trip home. But the only thing she had saved was a large block of frozen shrimp they had caught together in a boat called *It's All Good.*

YEAR 24

Mimi sat on the back deck of River Soul, but the river held nothing special for her anymore. Nothing did. She felt dead inside. Two decades of pain had finally taken their toll. She wished she could feel at least sadness, because that implied there was also its opposite, joy, somewhere inside her. But instead, she felt nothing.

She was alone at the house, but did not intend to stay long. She told Peter that she was heading out for a long weekend with her friends, but that was a lie. She was here for something Peter would never agree to and would try to stop if he could. She was disgusted with him for putting her in this position.

A couple of months earlier, Austin had gone back to school at Peter's insistence. Mimi did everything she could to change his mind, but he was absolutely convinced that Austin would rise to the occasion. "As soon as she has something to live for, she will start thriving again." The words became a mantra for Peter anytime he and Mimi fought over the subject. But she knew that was crap. Austin had more to live for than anyone else on the planet, and yet she chose self-destruction every time.

"Peter, you just don't get it. With all she's been through, Austin isn't afraid of death. She's afraid of life. She's not going to start living for anything or anyone. She's doing everything she can to avoid living at all."

But Peter would not be moved. "Trust me. She'll step up."

It took only a week before her advisor called. "She's not come to any classes yet," he said. "Is there a problem? I see that she registered on time." Peter called Austin every day for the next week, but there was never a returned call. Finally, one day, Jack answered her phone.

"Hello," came a sleepy, drugged-up voice.

"Jack?"

"Yeah. What the hell do you want?"

"Austin."

"She's sleeping."

"It's two p.m. Her classes started four hours ago."

"And?"

"And? She's supposed to be in school. What's going on down there, boy?"

"Boy? Who are you calling *boy*?"

"Look, just give me my daughter."

"Not gonna happen."

"Then tell her to call me as soon as she gets up. She's going to fail out of school before she even starts."

Jack just chuckled.

"What arc you laughing at, boy?"

"You, sucker." *Click.*

Jack had taken her books, computer, bicycle, and meal card and sold them all before school even started. He had locked Austin in a room inside a house, which his father was paying for, so he could keep her from the few people who wanted to help her. Austin had been showing some signs of remorse lately, and he knew that if she ever got her act together, she would lcavc him for surc.

School was a threat to their relationship. Peter was a threat to their relationship. Her father believed in her, and that was dangerous. Austin had been responding emotionally to Peter's outreach recently more than Jack liked. He had kept them apart, but he wasn't sure how much longer he could maintain that distance.

He had kept her supplied with plenty of drugs to keep her sedated. But as the drugs would wear off, Austin would complain that he was holding her captive. Gradually, he had become more violent to keep her compliant. At first, it was some gentle pushing, but that turned into shoving, which turned into slapping, until one day he finally hit her hard.

Austin had only reevaluated her circumstances after Jack grabbed his shotgun and placed it up against her temple when she tried to break out a back window. But in a mindset most people could never understand, her final straw did not involve leaving Jack. Instead, she had hardened her heart, fully believing she was so far gone into a despicable life that she could never recover. It was in that moment that she came to believe she was an addict and embraced all that that life implied.

She never tried to escape again. In fact, she just dug deeper in. No longer was she a passive addict, allowing others to do all the messy work. Now, she got her hands dirty—she did her own deals and used violence as necessary. She did whatever she had to do, including playing on her father's heartstrings to get whatever cash she could.

Mimi had seen the truth and was determined to put an end to it. One day, she had answered Peter's phone, and she learned from Austin's class advisor that Austin had not shown up for class for the first month. They were closing out her file, and she was no longer welcome at the school. This was Mimi's only indication there was a problem. Peter had not kept her up to speed.

She researched Florida law and found something that allowed concerned friends and family to have loved ones arrested for potential harm to their own well-being. She had worked with a lawyer to file all the necessary paperwork and now needed to sign, in person, some documents for the final arrest to take place.

After making the trip from Okatie, she lured Austin to a public location under the guise of delivering some tough news about her father's health. Austin reluctantly agreed only if Mimi promised to give her a couple hundred bucks to cover "groceries." Mimi had arranged for the officer to approach when she handed her the money, which he did.

Austin was confused at first, thinking that this was a delayed arrest from some undercover operation on a deal that she had done previously. But when she realized that she was being arrested based on a warrant her mother had arranged, a handcuffed Austin became enraged. She lashed out violently, swinging her body around toward her mother until the officer could get her back under control. Still, Austin lashed out while in the grasp of the police officer.

"You bitch. You fucking bitch! You have never loved me. Ever! You've always hated me. You've finally done it. They'll put me away and your life will be so much easier without me. Are you happy? Are you fucking happy?"

The police officer pushed Austin into the car and made sure Mimi was okay. He handed Mimi a card noting which court and which rehab Austin would be placed into for the next week. Mimi accepted the card but didn't look at it. Instead, she just stared into the back seat of the police car, where Austin was screaming at her mother from behind the glass and banging her head up against the window.

As the car drove away and Austin looked back at Mimi with a hateful glare, all her mother could think of was the day the entire Stewart family thought that Austin had taken her last breath. If she had known back then what she knew now, Mimi would have welcomed the death of her daughter as sweet relief from a life neither she nor Austin could have ever imagined.

ACT III

I suppose I could end the story there. It would be easier to stop now than to tell the rest. But every story must have a beginning, middle, and end, so as painful as it may be to continue, I must. For it is in the end that the worst—and the best—are found.

Dad would often tell the story of the little boy found digging in a pile of horse manure. When asked why he was so happy digging away amid the horror of the mess, the little boy responded that with all this crap, there must be a pony hiding in there somewhere.

I often feel like that little boy, digging through the mess to find the pony. Yet I was raised to believe the best in everyone and to find the best in everything. "Everything," Dad said, "is a gift from God, even if it doesn't feel like it." With all he had put up with for so long, his advice was credible. He remained optimistic and grateful no matter what happened to our family.

Until he didn't.

The years that followed the arrest were turbulent at best. Austin returned to the Stewart home reluctantly, and Mimi allowed her back reluctantly. Their relationship was cold most of the time until it launched into fiery hot.

But despite the turbulence, Dad had cause for his optimism. Austin started attending a local community college, and it turned out that with a clear head, she was an intelligent woman.

He would tell Austin over and over again how proud he was of her, that she was making great progress. He encouraged her to find nice, safe girlfriends and to stay away from men altogether. "Bad company corrupts good character," he would quote from the Bible. "Find people who are better, smarter, and faster than you, and aspire to be like them. Learn from them. Be like them . . ."

Austin listened to her father but rarely took his advice for long. She knew he was right, and she knew he wanted the best for her. But "good" people held no appeal for her. They were boring and only made her feel bad about herself because she was so far behind them in so many ways. She was comfortable only around people who struggled to fit in. So she looked for "less-than" when seeking the company of others.

And women, in her mind, were catty and cliquish. She preferred the company of one boy to a pod full of girls, even as a child. As she grew older and discovered how her beauty could alienate women and attract men, it only solidified her preferences. She could manipulate men, but with women, she had to actually be a good friend. She had no interest in being a good friend.

The excitement of school seemed to distract her from men for a time, but eventually, she succumbed to the constant attention she received while on campus. She started with Seth, who was replaced with Robert, who was replaced with John. Each one was progressively worse than the last. Austin could feel the tug of her old life as each boyfriend brought her deeper back into the party scene. Before long, she was using as much as before.

The final boyfriend that year, Thelonius Vess, was not much different from the others, but he was more willing than the rest to allow drugs to be Austin's true love. Austin was way out of his league, and if that meant he had her attention only some of the time, that was better than 100 percent of most women he could attract.

Theo, as he was called, was nice and polite in company but behind the scenes was depressed and sedated. He was a pothead, alcoholic, and Xanax abuser. He was moody and sometimes violent, but the drugs kept most of his issues at bay. While not attractive, Theo provided a steady stream of pills, weed, and alcohol, which Austin now needed in ever-larger quantities. Theo filled that need, which attracted her more than looks ever could.

Theo finally met the Stewarts about three months into the relationship. While not perfect, he was a saint compared to Jack. Mimi, on the other hand, had no interest in any of Austin's boyfriends. She assumed that the only reason any man was with Austin was for the sex and the only reason Austin was with any man was for the drugs.

To keep the family together, Dad invited Theo to River Soul one year, and they had a relatively good experience early on. But Theo could not suppress his moods and addictions for the entire week, and he began to act out in ways that made it clear he was not well. Although they survived the trip, Dad no longer allowed Theo in the house and told Austin that she could no longer use their car to be with him.

This, of course, only made Theo more appealing, and Austin secretly started to spend more and more time at his place until she barely showed up at the Stewart house at all. She invented a series of girlfriends that she said she would be visiting, and even brought some fake friends home to help add an ounce of truth to the ruse. She had become an expert in manipulation and knew what she had to do to use the family car, to keep some cash in her pocket, and to maintain her party lifestyle.

Dad and Mimi knew things weren't as they appeared, but they eventually just allowed the deception because it became too tiresome to constantly disprove her claims. And with every challenge to her integrity, Austin became harder and harder to be around. She made sure to punish her parents every time they dared question her plans. And she smiled inside each time they apologized for thinking she was not telling the truth, which, of course, she was not. She wasn't sure why she so enjoyed lying to the people who loved her, but she did.

If truth be told, it was a relief to have her out of the house. As Austin became more withdrawn, Dad and Mimi grew closer. Austin always had been what caused distance between them, and so her absence made their hearts grow fonder. The further she retreated out of their lives, the more Mimi relaxed into their marriage. Dad felt guilty for allowing himself to be both deceived and happy while his daughter fell to pieces yet again. Mimi did not. She was grateful to finally have at least some of her husband back.

In their quiet moments, both Dad and Mimi, each in their own way, prepared themselves for the inevitable call that their child either had been arrested or was dead from an overdose. But the one thing they never expected—ever—was what happened next.

YEAR 27

Peter and Gracie traveled down the river, casually fishing along the muddy banks of the Okatee. Gracie had developed a skill for fishing that Peter never understood. He paddled their canoe while Gracie silently searched out the best places to cast her line. She saw a perfect spot and landed her fly exactly where she wanted.

"You do that well," her father said proudly.

"I learned from the best," she smiled back.

"Yeah, right. Clearly, you've been hanging around different company."

"I know some people."

"You're a fine young woman, Gracie. I'm very proud of you."

"Thanks, Dad. I'm proud of you too."

Peter went to respond, but Gracie got a bite and set the line. She battled with a red drum for the next six minutes until she finally reeled it in, and Peter scooped it up in a net. She gracefully removed the hook and placed the fish back in the water, where it swam quickly away.

"Live a good life, little fish," Peter said as it disappeared from view.

Grace shook her head and giggled. "Still such a softie."

"That's me. You going again?"

"No, I think I'll just enjoy you taking me around for a while. Ride on, Mr. Stewart."

"Perfect."

They paddled in silence, enjoying the scenery for a while, until Gracie asked her father, "Dad, what do you believe?"

"Believe? About what?"

"About life. About God. About what's happened to our family."

"That's a very deep question for such a lazy day. Do you really want to go there?"

"I do. With Austin out of our lives, I've been able to relax a bit. But now I miss our family, our whole family. The way we used to be. When we were young. I don't understand why God tore us apart."

"Do you want the complex Peter answer or the quick and easy Dad answer?"

"We have time. I'd really like to know."

"Okay, then." Peter was introspective for a moment. He took a few strokes with the paddle and gazed at the beauty all around him. He turned around so as to face his daughter. "For starters, I believe that Jesus of Nazareth is the Son of God. Through His grace, we are saved. Not because of what we do, but because of what He did."

"I got that. I know that. But that all sounds very churchy. Why are you so on fire for Him given how hard our life has been?"

Peter thought for a moment, his countenance still peaceful. "Let's look at it this way. I can sit in my chair at home and read about loving unconditionally, even loving my enemies. And I can agree with that from the comfort of my cozy room. But then put me with someone who is a pain to be around or someone who is actually trying to hurt me, and I'm probably not going to respond in a loving way. So then I ask you, do I agree with the Word of God or not?"

"Probably not."

"Exactly. You don't know what you believe in until you're given the opportunity to act on it. It's God's way of helping you see things about yourself that you could never know when life is moving along easily.

A belief is nothing until you claim it through your own experience, until you hold firm to it through suffering. I can observe someone else's suffering and contemplate how I'd respond in the same situation. But until I actually suffer, I don't really know who I am."

"What about a man like Jack? Do you forgive him?"

Peter's expression tightened. "That's probably the hardest and most important question you could ask me. I pray about that all the time. I have two answers, and I'll give you both. The first is that the Bible tells me I'm no better than Jack."

"Dad, you are *way* better than Jack."

"Well, thank you, Gracie, but actually, I'm not. By God's standards, I'm just as bad as he is."

"How could that be?"

"Sin is sin. It's all bad."

"But you're a good person. And he is not a good person."

"Good people don't necessarily go to heaven. Saved people do. And God puts people in our path that He wants to save. God has put Jack in my path."

"But, Dad, he almost killed your daughter. And now there are other men just like him who are also killing your daughter. How can you love people like that?"

"And now comes the harder answer, my real answer to your question." Peter hung his head and hesitated to go on. But then he picked up his head and spoke with a viciousness that Gracie had never, ever seen in her father.

"I want to kill them all."

He paused for a moment more and then went on.

"I want them to die slowly. I want them to feel all the pain our family has felt. I want them to feel every moment of hope that was crushed when they sucked Austin back into that lifestyle. I want them to know the pain of not knowing if their child is alive or dead.

"I want them to know what it feels like to spend decades in a hospital room praying that your daughter will survive the night, only to have her throw her life away because of what they've done to her. I want them to know what it feels like to have their families torn apart over the lack of trust, lack of respect, and utter selfishness. I want them not to sleep for weeks on end, living on the edge financially, emotionally, and spiritually.

"I want them to know what it's like to have to put deadbolts on your bedroom door because you can't trust your own child. And I want to have them watch their own life fade away slowly, just as they made me do with Austin."

Peter was staring so intently into Gracie's eyes that he was looking right through her. He wasn't really speaking to her. He was letting go of deep, suppressed pain. She just happened to be in the same area.

"And that, Gracie, is why I am not a good person. I'm just as bad as Jack. I'm just as bad as Austin. My lies, my sins, are just more subtle than theirs. But God views it all the same. In fact, mine might be worse because I hide it. At least Austin and all her cohorts don't pretend to be something else. They are addicts for all it's worth. They know they're lost, but I can trick myself into thinking that I'm not lost. And that's a dangerous place to be."

"Do you feel the same way about Austin?"

"Sometimes. But she's my daughter. I told you as children that I would love you no matter what. It's still true. Now I actually get to live those words, rather than just say them. Another opportunity to show myself what I believe."

Eventually, Peter turned the canoe around and pointed the boat back toward the house. He was ashamed for expressing his true feelings. He had let her down. Yet another failure.

Gracie understood why he felt the way he did, but she had something to say. "Dad?"

Peter answered without turning around. "Yes?"

"You know it would be very selfish to do something bad to Jack, or any one of them. You might feel better for taking revenge, but you'd only end up in jail and then we'd lose you and Austin both. I can't live with that."

"You're right, Gracie. I'm sorry I lost control there for a while."

"Actually, I am happy to know what you really think for a change. We might not be so torn apart if you expressed your true feelings more. If Mom knew how angry you actually are, it would make her feel better. She thinks you don't care. She thinks you are too soft. That you're in denial."

Peter stopped rowing and turned back to look at his daughter.

"Gracie, I'm a man like any other man. I have very raw, very hard views. But I'm not called to be like every other man. I'm called to something different. We are not called to overcome evil with more evil. We're called to overcome evil with good. It wouldn't do me or the family any good if I unloaded with hate every time I felt like it, even if that's what you or Mom want from me. If you think less of me because I'm *too soft*, then that makes me sad, but I don't intend to change. I'm trying to please God, even if the world thinks I'm not living up to my manly responsibilities.

"Please don't confuse my attempts to rise above our circumstances as indifference. God's ways are not our ways. But that doesn't change my desire to lash out. It's a battle that rages inside me every day. Faith would not be faith if the ride was trouble-free."

Peter reached out his hand and held on to his daughter. "I love you, Gracie. More than you could ever know."

"I love you too, Dad."

Peter turned around and started paddling, a little less aggressively than before.

"Dad?" came Gracie's voice behind him.

"Yes?"

"If Jesus could save a man like Jack, he could also save a man like you."

Peter simply nodded in the affirmative as the profundity of that comment washed over him.

"And, Dad?"

"Yes?"

"You're a good man and a good father, even if you do have one mean, nasty, hidden fire burning inside of you."

Peter chuckled and paddled back to the dock of a home, where his wife waited with news that would make his outburst on the canoe seem tame.

As the dock came into view, Peter found himself in a rhythm that put him at peace. He had unloaded something he'd been hiding deep inside him for a long while. It felt good to get it out. With each stroke, his heart rate slowed. He became aware of his breathing and started to time each breath with every pull of the paddle.

He thought of nothing else but the water and the sound of the canoe slicing through the shifting tide. Just for the moment, there was no sickness, no addiction, and no strife. He was just Peter. He was not a father, a husband, or a boss. He just *was.*

His moment passed when he noticed that Mimi was sitting in one of the chairs on the dock. As they pulled in, Mimi stood up and brought the line to Peter. He handed her the paddles and tied down the canoe.

"Good morning," Mimi said. "Catch anything?"

"I did," Gracie responded. "But it's afternoon now."

"Oh, I lost track of time. I've been out here for a while, collecting my thoughts."

"And did you find them all?" Gracie teased.

"Not yet. Hey, do you mind if I catch up with your father for a moment?"

"Sure. He scares me anyway." Gracie turned and winked at Peter.

"What?"

"Inside joke. I'll see you both inside."

Gracie walked the ramp toward the pier, while Peter took care of the last of his duties as captain of the Stewart canoe.

"Peter, sit down. We need to talk."

"What did I do now?" he asked in jest.

"Nothing—yet. Sit down."

Peter moved the other chair to face Mimi and sat down across from her.

"What's up?"

"You know how you're always saying that people need to become completely neutral about things? That we need to hear from God before we make judgments about things?"

"Yeah."

"Well, I need you to take your own advice. I need you to stay neutral."

Peter looked puzzled. "Mimi, what's up?"

"Austin's here."

Peter was incredulous. "Austin? Here? Now?"

"Yes."

He sat more upright in his chair and his voice started to rise. "She goes on a four-month bender, doesn't answer any of our calls, doesn't let us know she's okay, and now she's here? In Okatie?"

"Yes."

Peter went to get up and go to the house, but Mimi stopped him. "But wait, there's more."

"Great. Let me guess, she brought some loser with her?"

"Theo."

"I thought they broke up. That was the trigger that caused her latest descent into wherever it is that she goes."

"They did. But there's more to the story."

"What else could there be?"

Mimi paused.

Peter was becoming animated and agitated. "Stop dancing around this, Mimi. What else?"

"She's pregnant."

"What? That can't be. She's . . . she's not capable. All those years of chemotherapy, they said she couldn't have children."

"Actually, what they said was that it was highly unlikely she could get pregnant. Apparently, she beat those odds too."

Peter disappeared into his own mind for a while. Mimi allowed him the time, until she saw a flash of fear come across his face.

"But she can't have a baby. She won't survive it. Her spleen is too big from all the liver failure. Her belly is literally held together with wire from her transplants. How's that going to hold together when she gets bigger? How will it all hold together when she has to push during delivery? This will kill her!"

Mimi tried to stay calm and rational. "I've heard that before. And yet she's still here."

"But what about her illness? She'll pass it along to the baby. And with all the drugs she and Theo have done, only God knows what kind of baby that will be."

Mimi threw up her hands and turned away. "Well, I'm glad you've stayed so neutral about this."

"But this is her life we're talking about. And now . . . another little life inside of her. Both of them are at risk here!"

She turned back toward him and spoke with strength in her voice to snap him out of his downward spiral. "Unless this is the miracle you keep hoping for. Maybe this is what God had planned for her."

Peter calmed down just a little bit to think. "Why are you okay with this? Usually, I'm the one talking *you* off the ledge with her. Why are you in her corner?"

"Peter, a baby changes everything."

"A baby changes nothing! Those two are addicts. It just puts a small, innocent life in the crosshairs of their destructive lifestyle."

"You just don't understand a mother's love. It overcomes all. This will be the thing that sets her straight."

Peter fired back up again. "Overcomes all? *Really?* You wrote her off years ago. Where was your mother's love back then? I've had to drag you kicking and screaming into every intervention, into every reconciliation. And now you're telling me a mother's love conquers all?"

Mimi's face darkened. "Fair enough. That's what I've been thinking about out here, while I was waiting for you. I haven't been there for her, not emotionally at least. But now we'll have motherhood in common. This will be the thing that brings us back together. Isn't that what you've been praying for?"

"You're using my faith, again, to shut me down."

"Well, is it working?"

"A little."

"It will be okay, Peter."

"And what about Theo? Is he in for the ride?"

"Who can say? He's hardly said three words since they walked in just after you and Gracie launched this morning."

"Are they sober?"

"Austin looks clean. She says she's clean. Theo looks the same as ever."

Peter stood up to walk to the house, but he stopped himself. "May I leave, Mrs. Stewart?"

"I'm not sure. Are you ready?"

"I'm ready."

"Then you may go . . . Grandpa."

By the time Peter reached the house, he had prayed three times that God might allow him to respond in a loving, faithful manner. But when he saw Theo leaning up against the house with his head down, hair draped over his face, and smoking, it got Peter's blood boiling all over again.

Theo made no gesture toward Peter. He never changed his posture or even looked up to acknowledge him. He kept staring in Peter's general direction, but not directly at Peter. He just kept lifting up his hand to take another puff, with his thumb and middle finger clasping the last little bit of the cigarette as though it were some precious possession.

Peter hated the culture of addiction, the constant need for something to calm the nerves. If it wasn't this drug or that drug, it was booze or a cigarette. But always something. They had more in common with what they held in their hands than they did with the normal world around them.

He despised their weakness and their constant attempts to avoid dealing with reality. If they put as much energy into life as they did into finding their next fix, they'd all be wealthy and happy contributing members of society. Instead, they sucked the life out of anyone they touched with their pitiful presence. *Vampires*, Peter thought. *Authors of lies.*

All the addicts he had come to know were the same, as though there was some father of addiction that just cranked out one clone after the other. They looked the same, they thought the same, they believed the same, they talked the same, and they were all so utterly and predictably selfish and self-absorbed. Most could manipulate you at first, make you believe you were talking to a normal person. Theo had done that with him for a time. But once you came to know the look—too thin, pasty complexion, dirty clothes—you could identify the lies as quickly as they rolled off their tongues.

Peter could feel the hatred rising as he grew closer. This punk, this stupid punk who had been so selfish, had no problem putting Peter's daughter at risk. He wanted to go slap him and tell him to stand up straight, take a shower, get a job, and get help. *Get off the Xanax, and stop sleeping through life. Wake up! Do the hard work! Set a good example! Take care of my daughter.* But instead, he barked directions about his smoking. "You'll have to stop doing that before the baby comes."

Seeing that Peter was going to engage, Theo took a last puff and flicked the butt into the yard. "I got a while. She's only five months."

"Four months left? Do you know how much needs to be done between now and then? What plans do you have to provide a place for the baby? Do you have money to pay for all the doctor bills that are coming? Do you have baby clothes, a crib, a car seat, or a playpen? Do you have toys, baby food, diapers, and blankets? And what about my daughter? What about her health? What about what this baby might do to her? Have you thought of that?"

"She'll be fine."

"Fine? *Fine?* So says the man who doesn't have a clue about what she's been through for the last twenty-two years. You don't even know how to take care of yourself. How are you going to take care of my daughter? How are you going to take care of a baby?"

"Austin knew you would react like this. That's why she made me come. To protect her from you."

Just take him down, Peter said inside his head. *Just take him now.* Peter clenched his fists and approached Theo, who never moved. His complete lack of response gave Peter enough time to think twice about physical violence. He turned to walk inside instead, but his anger at Theo carried into the room as he slammed the sliding door open so fast and hard that it came off the tracks. Gracie was holding Austin's belly until they were startled by their father's sudden appearance. Still angry, he aggressively approached his daughters. Gracie took a subtle step in front of Austin and said, "Dad, isn't this wonderful?"

Peter felt trapped between his emotions and the person he wanted to be. He had blown his cool with Theo, and now, he obviously had expressed his anger without even saying a word. On his walk up the pier, he had prayed to be loving—to *be* love—but that proved impossible in the few minutes that had followed. Despite all that disappointment in himself, his anger continued to win the battle.

"Is it wonderful, Gracie? Is it wonderful that two addicts have reproduced? Is it wonderful that two people who can't even care for themselves will now be responsible for a completely dependent human being? Is it wonderful that two people who aren't even able to love each other, let alone be married to each other, will now need to be a representation of love to a child? Is it wonderful that Austin may not be able to survive this pregnancy?"

Peter went to continue, but both Austin and Gracie interrupted in unison, "*Dad, stop!*"

Peter paused only for a moment and stared into Gracie's eyes almost as intently as he had done out on the canoe. For years, he had begged her to give Austin a chance—to be a big sister. He had pleaded with her to spend more time with Austin, to be an example for her, to love her back into sobriety. But now that she was actually doing just that, he felt strangely betrayed.

In just a matter of minutes, the entire family dynamic had shifted. Both Gracie and Mimi were on Austin's side, and he was the one furious with his daughter. He liked being the only positive voice in the crowd. He hated being the only negative one. And yet he could not stop his feelings or his tone.

"What have you done, Austin?"

"Dad, nothing. And everything."

"You've spent the last five years running from your life, destroying your life intentionally. And now you want to create a new one? What were you thinking?"

"I wasn't. I didn't plan this. I didn't want this. But now that it's here, what am I supposed to do?"

"A little late to be asking yourself that question, don't you think? Now the consequences of your actions are no longer your own. They belong to that baby growing inside of you. Do you get that?"

"Dad, yes."

"Have you been to the doctor?"

"Yes, liver clinic and my OB. They're talking to each other about it."

"And what do they say?"

"I'm a high-risk pregnancy. Very high risk."

"Of course you are."

"Of course I am." Austin let out a little smile. It was a gallows humor the entire family had developed over the years when Austin's condition always moved toward unique and severe. If the worst-case scenario was possible, Austin had it—and lived through it. They had come to joke about it as a way to mask the pain of their reality.

"And the drugs?"

"I'm clean. Ever since I found out."

"You have to be. It's not fair to the baby."

"I know, Dad, I know."

Peter relaxed just a bit. He turned to see if anyone else had joined the room. Mimi had, but Theo had not. He looked at his wife. He looked at his three girls—Mimi, Gracie, and Austin—and knew he was on the wrong side of this issue. A baby from anyone, especially from Austin, was a miracle. Peter let out the last of his disappointment as a way to move back toward neutral.

"Theo? Really? You had to choose Theo?"

Austin rolled her eyes. "Ugh. I know. What a putz. Now that I'm clean and he's not, I see him for what he is. Addicts are a real downer!"

Peter couldn't help but chuckle.

"But he's the father. We have to make something work. We have to be civil."

Austin's words reminded him that he had been anything but civil on the way inside. It embarrassed him to think about it.

"I love you, Dad."

Peter pulled her in for a hug. "I love you, Austin." Mimi and Gracie joined in the huddle, and they shared a moment Peter could have only dreamed of, even just that morning.

The casual observer would have thought that was the happy ending to our story. The Stewarts had finally reached a peace that had been so long in the making. And for a time, it almost felt that way. They laughed and hugged the way most families do when they hear wonderful news. They dreamed of the future, and it seemed from the outside as though nothing had ever gone wrong.

It was the family of old, an answered prayer in the midst of a family's pain and turmoil. But this happy family now had two new members. One, yet to be born. And the other, a depressed pothead who stood outside, propped up against the wall of a house where he did not feel welcome.

Peter sat in his captain's chair while the dock of River Soul faded from view. With nothing but the marsh and the river out ahead, he was as happy as he'd been in a long time. His family was reconciled, a dream once so distant that even he had given up on it. Up on the bow of the boat were all his girls, chatting like old times. The wind from the boat's acceleration made it impossible to hear their words, but he could "see" their conversation, and it was beautiful.

He watched them for so long that he had forgotten about Theo. Peter turned to see him sitting aft, facing back toward the wake. He knew he should engage him, but he just couldn't stand to deal with such depression when his girls were making him so happy. He determined to engage Theo once they got to the sandbar and they could share some quiet time together. He was family now, whether Peter liked it or not.

Once he reached his intended destination, Peter slowed the boat to get into position. Thinking he was being a good sport, Peter asked Theo for some help to drop anchor.

"Theo, could you go up front and help me secure this thing?"

Theo simply nodded. He got up slowly and moved to the front of the boat, stepping over all the Stewart women without so much as an "excuse me." He pulled out the anchor and threw it overboard, not waiting for Peter to give him the word to drop it. The boat was still moving forward, and the anchor line quickly slipped under the boat and was heading toward the prop. Peter slammed the boat into reverse to keep from entangling the line, which sent Theo tumbling on top of Mimi.

Thinking Peter had done that on purpose, Theo pushed off of Mimi so hard she let out a yelp. Peter started to move in that direction to prevent further problems, but Theo simply jumped in the water, which was only waist deep, and walked to the sandbar. The Stewarts looked at each other in disbelief. Austin just shook her head.

Peter pulled back the line to regroup. He thought for a moment about leaving Theo on the sandbar and going somewhere else altogether. The sandbar would be gone in a couple of hours, and he knew that Theo was not a great swimmer. Casting aside the temptation, Peter got the boat back into position and finished the job of setting the anchor into the marshy peat of the pluff mud.

The rest of the Stewarts went to work getting all the supplies to the front of the boat. Theo never once offered to help. In fact, he had walked away from them and was sulking on the opposite side about thirty yards away. Everyone looked at Austin, who said, "Don't look at me. The boy's on Xanax. There's no dealing with him."

"Let's take a walk," Mimi said.

Peter looked at the boat. "I'm not sure that anchor is set fully into the mud yet."

"Theo can keep an eye on it," Austin said. "I can promise you he's not going to want to walk with us." She screamed over to him. "Theo, we're going for a walk. Want to come?"

He shook his head. "No."

"Told you," she said to the rest of the group. She turned back to scream in his direction. "Then watch the boat. Make sure it doesn't drift away." Theo nodded in the affirmative, and the group started down toward Hilton Head Island. The hard-packed surface felt good as they walked, since the sand had settled into wavy patterns that massaged their feet along the way. They lost their sense of time and location as they dove into conversations about all the promise and joy that a baby would bring.

Seeing they were far down the sandbar, Theo went back to the boat to get a joint he had put in his jacket pocket. It would be fun to smoke it so close to Peter, knowing how much he bitterly disapproved of his drug use. He climbed back on the boat and fished it out of his pocket, along with his lighter. As he jumped back into the water, the weight of his body pushing against the boat dislodged the anchor from the mud, just gradually enough that Theo didn't notice it.

He walked back onto the sandbar and stared down at the family in the distance. He faced them directly as he lit up. Even if Peter turned around, he'd just think he was smoking a cigarette. "In your face, you S-O-B," he screamed into the wind. Peter heard something and turned around, but Theo just smiled and waved. Peter waved back half-heartedly and turned back to chat with the girls.

Theo sat back down on the other side of the sandbar and stared across to Palm Island. He contemplated the shape of the trees and wondered how these little islands were created in the first place. No human development could be seen. He felt at peace for the first time since arriving in Okatie.

No one in this family accepted him for who he was. And everyone blamed him for the pregnancy. But, to his own defense, Austin had told him she could not get pregnant. He was only stupid for not contemplating that her claim might not be true.

He was both overwhelmed and excited about the baby. He loved the thought of having a child. And as much as he hated to admit it, he knew Peter was right. He had no plan, he had no money, and he was not the most reliable person. He couldn't even count on himself, and now Austin was looking to him all the time for answers. He knew her questions would only get more intense as they got closer to the delivery. But instead of stepping up to that pressure, he retreated into his pot and pharmaceuticals so that he could forget his many shortcomings.

As a slight buzz settled in on him, Theo remembered back to his own childhood. His father had left him when he was only four. He could remember the moment he walked out and never came back. He didn't make a scene or explain where he was going. He just left. From that moment on, Theo had made a promise to himself that he would never do that to his own children. And yet he had no earthly idea how he was going to support a family.

He couldn't even fathom what it would mean to be sober all the time, or what it would take to be up all night feeding, rocking, or changing diapers. He loved being an addict. He loved the complete irresponsibility of it all. And he was good at it. He was not at all confident he would be as good a father as he was an addict.

While lost in his thoughts, the boat started to drift away behind him. As it slowly made its way out, Peter turned around from a half mile away as if he was psychically connected to the boat.

"Does the boat look farther away from shore?" he said half to himself and half to the girls.

But they were too caught up in their conversation to hear him. Peter just stared at the boat for a couple of minutes. "Hey," he shouted, "is the boat drifting?"

Each of them looked in that direction until Gracie said, "No, Dad. It just looks like that from this angle."

"And Theo's got it," Austin said.

Peter looked and could see that Theo was on the opposite side, although he was too far away to know for sure which way he was facing. "Okay, I guess," Peter said. "But let's turn around just in case."

As they walked back, Peter kept studying the position of the boat. About ten minutes later, the tide had started to come in full force, and with each passing minute, the boat inched farther away from its original mooring. Although it was dragging an anchor, the tide was powerful enough to push the boat into deeper water, where the anchor would be less of a factor.

"Peter, you may be right," Mimi said with some hesitation in her voice. "It's not the angle; I think that thing is getting farther away."

Peter picked up the pace, and before long, he was running fast. The wavy sand that once felt so good on his feet now hurt as he was pounding the bumpy surface with all his weight. As he got to where Theo was sitting, where the boat used to be, he could see that it was drifting into the middle of the channel and picking up speed back toward Lemon Island.

Peter contemplated his options. He had just over an hour before they'd all be underwater. He realized all the phones were on the boat, so calling for help was not possible. He thought about whether his family could swim to the opposite shore, but that was a long way. He looked at pregnant Austin and then at Mimi and Gracie, and he knew what he had to do.

Peter looked to see how much of the sandbar was left heading back into the river. He could run faster than he could swim, so he took off down in the other direction as fast as he could. He sprinted until he ran out of sand and then dove into the water without breaking stride. Peter was a good swimmer, but he wasn't sure if there was any real possibility he could make it to the boat before it outpaced him. His only hope was that the anchor would slow it down just enough that he could catch up.

He had swum a good ten minutes before he found himself in a fast-moving school of fish. One hit him. Then another. Within seconds, he was getting pelted on his right side by more fish than he could count. Peter kept swimming but suddenly wondered why the fish were swimming so fast, and all in one direction. Were they being chased by a bigger fish? Or something worse?

He stopped swimming for just a moment, in part to see where he was in relation to the boat and in part to see how far he was from shore, just in case something terrible was about to happen. He was about six hundred yards from shore, and going back to the sandbar at this point would be against the current. It would take him at least fifteen minutes to get back.

The boat, on the other hand, was about two hundred yards away down current. So he decided to make his move and get to the boat as quickly as he could. It hardly felt possible, but he was now swimming even harder and faster than he was before, nudged on by a new fear. Besides the boat, he also worried about what might lurk beneath.

The fish pelting seemed to go on forever. But even worse than the pounding was when it ended. In its place came an eerie, sudden stillness. The fish had made their escape, and the quiet of their absence screamed loud in his head. He had that terrible feeling when you know something is there, but you can't see it or hear it.

He looked up to see the boat one more time. Even though it was moving quickly in the current, so was he. And with the anchor still weighing the boat down, he was gaining on it. *I can make it*, he thought. He put his head down and swam. He focused on the rhythm of his strokes as a way to calm his mind. Stroke. *You can do this.* Stroke. *It will be okay.*

But then it happened. He got bumped hard by something big. Peter let out a scream into the water and sat up quickly. But as his feet dropped down into the water, he became panicked about what might swim by to take his legs off. He got back into a horizontal position and started swimming again. *Don't panic.* Stroke. *Don't pound the water too hard. Don't splash too much.* Stroke. *Just get to the boat.* Stroke.

He got bumped again, harder this time. Stroke. *God protect me.* Stroke. *Please, God, my family needs me right now.* Stroke. *My family! The sandbar will be gone soon and then they will have to deal with this thing.* Stroke. Bump. *Oh, God. Oh, my God!* This time he got bumped closer to his head. He pushed his hands into whatever this thing was, and it pulled away quickly. He looked up and was very close to the boat now. Stroke. *Almost there now.* Stroke. *Get your body up onto the swim deck quickly. Don't dangle your legs.* Stroke. Stroke. Stroke. *It's in reach now. That's it!*

Peter reached up and grabbed the boat. In an instant he hoisted himself onto the swim deck and leapt into the seated section so that no part of his body was in reach of whatever was after him. He laid down on the hard surface to catch his breath and recover. He looked up into the sky, where gentle winds moved big white clouds across the blue background. He watched them intently, so much so that he almost forgot where he was.

He turned his face into the sun and felt the warmth on his skin. He found himself in a twilight state, and oddly enough, he had no thoughts at all. It was as though someone had sucked all the brain matter out of his head and the only thing left was his actual being. It was an awesome feeling, and he was not sure how long he lay there reveling in the nothingness.

But soon he remembered where he was and how he had come to be there in the first place. He stood up and took note of where the boat was headed. Then, as he looked back toward the sandbar, he could see small figures facing his direction. He was so far away now that he could not see their expressions.

He wondered if they had seen what he had just been through, or if all of it was below the surface. But that didn't matter now, as he had more work to do.

He pulled anchor and then walked over to the console and fished the key out of the cup holder. He went to put it into the ignition when something surfaced just off to his right. It was murky at first, but soon the dorsal fin of a shark came into view. It circled the boat a few times and then lashed its tail up against the boat as if to say, "You escaped this time, but I'll be waiting for you."

The reality of what he had fled put a pit in Peter's stomach. He motored back to the sandbar where everyone, including Theo, waited for him. The sandbar was starting to disappear, which was clearly disconcerting to the man who couldn't swim.

Theo got on first and sat down. Mimi and the girls handed the supplies up to Peter, who loaded them into the back. He pulled all three of his girls up into the boat.

"Well, that was fun," Mimi said. "Did you have a nice swim?" Peter looked at their expressions. It was clear that they did not know what had happened to him along the way.

"Lovely," he replied. "It was a great day to be out on the water." Peter pulled back from the sandbar and turned the boat back to Okatie. Theo never said a word. He never apologized or even acknowledged that he had fallen asleep while on watch. And like all addicts, he lacked any awareness of the consequences he had caused.

Mimi and Gracie took off for the store while Peter was still asleep. He had been up all night and had not fallen asleep until after 4 a.m. While grateful for his family's restoration, he spent the night worried about Austin's health as she entered the latter months of her pregnancy. He worried about the baby's future. He worried that this new life might mean the end of his daughter's life.

All night, he second-guessed himself about things he should have said to his daughter years ago. Had Austin followed the proper order of things, Peter would have had a talk with her about how dangerous it would be for her to get pregnant. She and her future husband could adopt. There were plenty of children in desperate need of a mother.

After hours of tossing, he finally got out of bed and down on his knees to pray. He pleaded for Austin's health. But the more he prayed, the more agitated he became. With each prayer, in his mind, the problem was growing bigger than the God he was praying to. He knew that his fears were a statement of unbelief about God's goodness and His ability to make miracles happen. But he could not stop himself.

Finally, he simply gave up on both prayer and sleep and walked out the back door, which Peter hadn't gotten around to fixing. When he shut it behind him, the door jammed completely. He'd have to get to that before the trip ended. In the meantime, he fumbled in complete darkness toward the backyard, guided only by the dim lights of the pier ahead. He could see his destination, but the steps between here and there were treacherous.

By the time he got to the dock, he was grateful for the distraction of a rising blood moon, one that turns coppery-red during a rare total lunar eclipse. The spectacular moon rose over the oaks across Pinckney Colony and then reflected off the water where his feet dangled over the side of the dock. The warmth of the water, the cool of the night air, and this incredible vision before him temporarily overwhelmed his senses. He welcomed the few moments of peace that had evaded him since he had turned off the lights.

As soon as his overly analytical mind kicked back in, he began to think about what he was seeing. Blood moons happened so infrequently. They appeared in the Bible as a sign of the end times. Peter wondered if this was an omen about his own family. Why had God brought him out to this place to see this rare event in such solitary conditions? Was this the end of his family?

He stayed there for an hour, until he finally was able to slow both his breathing and his mind. Maybe now he could actually sleep. He made his way back toward the house and was thankful that the moonlight, however muted, provided a clearer path to the backdoor. But when he reached the door, he remembered that it was jammed, and he had no path inside. All the other doors were locked, and he would wake the entire house if he rang the bell or knocked on the doors.

He spent time trying to loosen the jammed door with little success. He thought about breaking the glass, but that would be louder than a knock on the door. He gave the door one last try, but to no avail. He placed his head down against the glass door and contemplated where he would spend the next several hours. He decided on a kayak and hoped that he had left a tarp on the boat to help fend off the mosquitoes.

As he pulled his face back from the glass, he was aghast to find another man's face staring at him from inside the house. He leapt back in a panic.

"Holy crap," he shouted without any breath left to make much of an audible sound. His body launched into full attack mode until he realized that the other man was Theo.

"Theo! What the hell are you doing?"

Theo did not respond. He simply pointed to the right, indicating that Peter should move to a side door where he could let him in.

Theo opened the door but still did not say anything. Peter simply said, "Thank you," and walked past him into the house.

When they came inside, Peter noticed that Theo had a beer in his hand. Knowing that Peter disapproved, Theo thought that the best defense was a good offense. "Want one?" he asked Peter, lifting up his beer to show what he meant.

The night seemed shot already, so Peter decided not to protest and simply said, "Sure."

Theo grabbed him one and twisted off the top, handing Peter the bottle. Theo held his bottle up to clink Peter's. Peter hesitated, but eventually did the same. It was the first friendly gesture either had made toward the other since arriving in Okatie.

They both sat down in the living room and looked out the back. "Blood moon," was all Theo said.

"You know of them?" Peter asked.

"My grandfather was an elder in our church. Fire and brimstone kind of guy. The world was always coming to an end in his mind."

"You have a church?"

"You sound surprised."

"Well, actually I am. Do you go?"

"With family, occasionally."

"Do you get anything out of it?"

"Not much. But it's important to my mom. So it's important to me."

"And your father?"

"Not much to say about him. He left when I was young. I hear he lives close by, but I never see him."

"And your mother?"

"She did what she could. But she was never home. She was either working or looking for a new man. She never really got much out of either. Not the happiest person."

Peter softened a bit. He realized that he had judged Theo harshly, without taking the time to understand his background.

There was a pause, until Theo broke the silence. "You know, I don't like being a screw-up. I had different dreams for myself than this."

Peter was surprised at the depth of feeling coming from a man who couldn't say two words without sounding like an idiot.

"So why do you do what you do?"

"Habit, I guess."

"So break the habit."

"Not quite so easy as that."

"Maybe it is, and you just don't believe that you can."

"I've tried to believe it."

"And?"

"You see me, don't you?"

Peter said something more harshly than he intended. "Oh, I see you."

Theo thought for a moment and decided to say something with as much respect as he could, one man to another. "You know, Mr. Stewart, you're pretty good at judging the sins you don't commit. I wonder how good you are at judging the sins you do commit." Theo pressed on. "None of us has it as together as you do. All of us want to be like you, but it's so far out in front of us that none of us feels like we can get there from where we are. So we don't even try. And yet I know there are things that are hidden from our sight, things you'd never want us to know about you."

Peter started to listen intently as Theo expressed himself in ways Peter never would have expected from him.

"And I'm guessing that the things that bother you don't bother me at all. So should I judge you about those things I don't struggle with but you do?" Theo paused for a moment.

Peter got up and walked away. But just as Theo went to lash into him for running, he realized that Peter was walking into the kitchen. He opened the refrigerator, grabbed two more beers, and came back to sit next to Theo. Peter opened Theo's beer and handed it to him. Neither man said anything. Peter looked over at Theo and raised his beer. Theo smiled just a bit and raised his beer to Peter's.

The two men drank until about 3:30 a.m. when both of them ventured back to their beds. They would never again refer to that time, and yet something changed in both of them that night. In a small part of his heart, Theo desired Peter to be the father he never had. In Peter's mind, Theo was not as lost as he thought. They were never actually friends after that, but neither were they enemies.

As Peter got back to bed, he had consumed just enough alcohol to ensure that he would get at least a couple of hours of sleep. He didn't drink much, so when he did, it hit him hard. He dreamed vividly of the water, made red by the reflection of a blood moon that did indeed signal the end of his family as he knew it. His family had been reborn. But reborn into what?

As Peter sat by the water in his dream, his dolphin friend's head surfaced right next to the dock, but not in a way that startled Peter at all. It was comforting. They looked at each other for a time until the dolphin moved his head to look beside Peter. When he turned, there was someone sitting beside him. Someone Peter did not recognize.

The man was unremarkable and not at all threatening. He smiled at Peter in a way that made him feel safe. And then he said, "Peter, if Austin had followed the proper order of things, you would have filled her head with your fears, and she never would have had the baby that now grows inside of her. I couldn't let that happen. I've got this. She's not afraid, and neither am I."

He reached out to place his hand on Peter's shoulder. And when he touched the dreaming man, Peter's eyes slowly opened. He was in his room, in bed, alone. The sun was shining brightly. Peter could not remember a time when he had awoken to sunshine. He looked over to the clock; it was 12:16 p.m. Was that even possible?

Peter gathered himself together and walked out into the family room. Across the way at the kitchen table was his entire family, and Theo, eating the lunch that Mimi and Gracie had purchased while at the store. They looked to see Peter emerging from his room at such a late hour. They stopped their chatter and looked at this amazing sight.

Their man of the house, for the first time ever, was catching up to where the family already was.

Austin was the first to chuckle and then the entire table burst out laughing. They went back to talking among themselves as Peter walked toward the table. Without looking back at Peter, Theo simply pulled out the empty chair beside him to make a place for the man who helped create a family he had never before experienced, and never would again.

YEAR 28

No one would blame me if I chose to dwell on the happiest twelve months in the Stewart family history. After all, everyone knows that a baby can bring unimaginable joy. What made it so remarkable for the Stewarts, though, was how it stood in contrast to all the pain that had come before it. The scales had fallen from their eyes, and they were seeing each other for the first time in a very long time.

They had a depth about them that had not existed before. Pain they had always known, but happiness had never been a part of who they were together. They were always the yin and never the yang. Now the darkness had finally been defined, not by itself, but by its opposite—the light.

Grayson Peter Stewart was born on a sunny day in the South. According to Mimi, he was the first of the Stewart children to be born in the proper part of the country. He was born after only three hours of labor, in one of the easiest deliveries on record. Both mother and baby were tired but well.

Peter, Mimi, and Gracie were all present, except for during the actual delivery, when Peter thought it best to step into the waiting area. The only one absent was Thelonius Vess. Theo had made his exit sometime during the eighth month of pregnancy and then disappeared from the scene altogether. And so the "Father's Name" on the birth certificate remained blank, and Grayson carried the Stewart name into the next generation.

Austin chose Peter as Grayson's middle name, in part to honor her father and in part to keep Peter engaged financially. In her heart, Austin had hoped that the prospect of a child would cause Theo to rise to the occasion, but he was incapable of caring for a child in any sense of the word. Peter was going to have to pay for Austin's mistakes yet again, only now it was for a child's lifetime.

Yet despite all of that, the family flourished. Austin again went back to school part-time and worked toward her degree. Gracie moved closer to Atlanta to be near her nephew, and Peter seemed to find more time than usual to linger around the house, especially when Grayson was awake. Mimi was thrilled to help out as Austin studied and focused on her recovery.

And so it made Austin's next move all the more curious. During an NA meeting, she met someone who had a mutual acquaintance from her very first rehab, so many years ago. She asked for his contact information and reached out. They reconnected a couple of days later, and within a few weeks, they were dating.

His name was Frederick, but he went by the name Santana because he thought Fred just wasn't cool enough to suit his lifestyle. Austin hid the fact that they were dating as long as she could because she knew her parents would not approve. A recovering heroin addict unable to hold onto a job, Santana was still very active in a methadone program and bore all the marks of an addict.

There was nothing about him that her parents would respect, like, or admire. And he carried the stain of multiple arrests and a lifestyle that even Austin knew ran the risk of bringing her right back into hardcore addiction. And yet she was more comfortable with him than she was with her own family. The novelty of her year of normalcy had grown tired, and her insecurities were multiplied tenfold with the prospect of being a lifelong single mother.

Within a week of her dating Santana, Austin found herself sitting before a table in a dark room lit only by candles. There in front of her were ten tinfoil wrappings of black tar heroin and a needle she knew had to have been used before. Santana pulled out a spoon and a lighter to liquefy the heroin.

Once complete, he picked up the syringe and placed it into the spoon where he sucked the heroin into the needle. He pulled Austin closer and began to look for her veins, which barely existed because of all her medical issues and drug use. As he went to inject the needle, Austin pulled back. Santana stopped.

"What's wrong," he asked.

"This. This is wrong. I have a son now."

"You can't be a good mother as stressed as you are. And I can't take another moment on this stupid methadone program. Do this with me."

"I can't."

"Okay. Then maybe it's time you head home to Mommy and Daddy."

"Stop."

"Well, isn't that what's bothering you? Let me guess, they hover around you every minute, wondering what you're doing. They won't give you a car or anything that gives you access to the outside world. Do I have this right?"

Austin hung her head. "Yes."

"And you're going to put up with that shit?"

"I have to."

"You don't have to do anything they want you to."

"But I'm a mother now."

"And so what's it going to hurt, you doing this right now? Your parents have him, don't they?"

"Yes."

"So he's safe, and you're free to be free."

Santana's comment brought back the memory of something her father had told her one day, several rehabs ago. She was at her most rebellious teenage stage, and she'd yelled out during a family session that she just wanted to be free to do anything she wanted to do. She was tired of being told what to do, by her parents, by her therapists, and by this "fucking rehab."

Peter knew by then that she used language to provoke him and had learned not to react to her every time she cursed. He simply sat there and let her rant until she had it all out. When she had exhausted herself, Peter reached over and held Mimi's hand. He stood up and pulled Mimi with him to a standing position.

"Freedom. You want freedom, Austin?"

"Yes, Dad. That's what I'm saying. I want total freedom. And I want it now!"

"Are you free from your addiction?"

"What?"

"I'm asking you, as the one who wants total and complete freedom, are you free to walk out that door and really do whatever it is you want? Could you go for a walk, or sit by a lake, or play a video game? Or would every ounce of your being be driven toward stealing the money you need, to finding the dealer closest to you, to paying for a fix that will get you through the next couple of hours until you have to steal more money to pay the dealer again?"

Austin had no response.

"Are you free to get a job that will give you the money you need to do the things you want to do? Are you free to walk next to a police officer and not wonder if he's suspicious of what you look like? Are you free to have friendships with people who aren't trying to take you for everything you're worth? Are you free to enjoy your family, or is every meeting we have laced with tension and mistrust?"

Again, no response.

"You're not free, Austin. You are enslaved. You're just so blitzed, so brainwashed, so out of control that you can't see it. Or maybe you do see it and you're trying to numb yourself to the reality of the life you've chained yourself to. Or maybe you just don't care. But the truth is, Miss Stewart, it's one of those three things. There are no other options.

I used to think it was the Devil doing this to you. But I don't think so anymore. Maybe he was the one to give you the initial idea. But he's not the one putting the needle in your arm. You are."

With that, Peter left the room, holding hands with Mimi the entire way. He did so both because he needed his wife's support to walk out on his daughter and also as a symbolic gesture that Austin's parents were united, and there would be no playing one against the other.

Austin complained to her counselor for an hour after they left. But she knew in her heart that her father was right. And with no drugs to numb that truth, she had no choice but to attack every position that did not validate her own beliefs.

But here, now, with Santana in front of her, coaxing her to put the needle in, she wondered if her father was wrong. Maybe it was Satan putting the needle in after all. Maybe it never was her all this time. It was a force greater than herself. Who could withstand that?

Santana's suggestion grew in her mind until her want for the drug was greater than the fear of falling back into the chains that awaited her. She extended her arm and closed her eyes. She could not watch the beginning of the end.

YEAR 29

It did not take long for things to change. It was only two weeks from her first meeting with Santana that Austin's addictive behavior again made itself known. At first, it was a very bad attitude that worked its way into every interaction with her parents. Then it was the constant sleeping—eighteen or more hours a day. But eventually, it was her scabbed complexion and alarming weight loss that were the telltale signs she could no longer hide.

Mimi and Peter's concern started slowly at first. Things had been going so well for so long, the thought of her relapsing never even entered their minds. But as the days strung together, they both started wondering separately if something terrible had happened. It was in the fifth week that Mimi first spoke the words that Peter himself hadn't yet communicated.

By the seventh week, Austin was rarely at the house. She claimed that she was spending extra time at school, but her grades did not reflect all the extra help she was supposedly getting. While at home, she spent her time in another part of the house, always away from her family. She rarely interacted with her son, let alone took care of him. The few times she actually engaged with him, she lost interest quickly as one text after another stole her attention.

She dyed her hair black, which replaced her naturally blonde hair. She applied a quarter inch of makeup to hide the scabs now obvious on her face. Her now ghostly white complexion accentuated bright purple lipstick and eyeliner. She came home one day with tattoos on her arms, and later on her shoulders, back, and legs. She knew this would be a direct assault on her parents as they were both anti-tattoo—Peter for his faith and Mimi for Austin's health.

When her parents confronted her about this behavior in particular, she went into her usual tirade of obscenities, claiming that all these choices were simply artistic expression and that she could not believe that they did not trust her after all this time of sobriety. She claimed she could do nothing right in her parents' eyes, so she might as well do whatever she wanted.

Peter first discovered her relationship with Santana when he followed Austin one night as she went to "take a walk." Around the block was Santana in his car, waiting for her. When Austin got in the car and Santana pulled forward, Peter stood in front of the car. Santana was forced to slam on the brakes. Austin got out of the car and went into a fit while Santana just sat there saying nothing at all.

But once their relationship was out in the open, Santana started coming to collect Austin right in front of the Stewart family. He showed up whenever he liked to collect his "baby," sometimes for days. Peter found himself in another kind of hellish predicament: trying to push back on Austin, hard, while also trying not to upset the entire family—including Grayson. Austin caused such a scene that sometimes it was just easier to let her leave.

As the family's yearly week in Okatie was forthcoming, Austin surprisingly seemed excited to go—even though Peter had indicated that Santana was not welcome. But the scheming plan became clear when, on the morning of their departure, Austin claimed that she was not well enough to go and that she'd decided to stay in Atlanta. Peter forced the issue, to the point of escorting Austin into the car and standing outside the door until everyone else was ready to go, including getting her son locked into his car seat. She could at least be a mother to him temporarily while with the family on vacation. He was only a child, but he seemed to be picking up on all the tension around the house and was starting to act out in his own way.

During the five-hour trip to River Soul, Austin became increasingly anxious and needed to pull over every thirty minutes or so. Her stomach was cramping as she went into withdrawal. Her minor discomfort turned into outright pain, nausea, vomiting, and diarrhea. By the end of the trip, Peter was pulling over every ten minutes as Austin had an increasing sense of urgency to vacate her bowels.

On the last stop, Austin ran out without grabbing her purse because she knew she was about to mess her pants. When Mimi noticed it on the back seat, she turned to Peter.

"Keep your eyes out. I'm looking in her purse."

"No, don't do that. You know how she gets."

"I'll do it," Gracie said as she grabbed the purse.

"No, give it to me. I'll do it." Mimi grabbed the purse and started rummaging through it. "Let me know if you see her coming."

It didn't take long for Mimi to find three bottles of pain meds prescribed to Santana. She also found several different loose pills that she could not identify.

"Mom, she's coming back," Gracie said urgently.

Mimi kept the pills and closed Austin's purse, throwing it on the back seat.

When Austin returned, she said very little, resting her head against the car window. But suddenly, she realized that she had left her purse behind and picked it up to make sure that no one had gone through it during her time in the bathroom. Peter watched her in the rearview mirror as she opened and closed every compartment three times, until she realized what had happened.

She was screwed.

To complain about it would mean that she'd have to admit to her addiction. To not ask would mean that they might throw the pills away, which would send her body into convulsions so bad she would surely die. They did not understand how desperately her body needed those drugs.

Peter could see her mind go into overdrive as she shifted back and forth in the seat. She did not know what to do, but in the meantime decided to be very sweet and very compliant so that when she needed the drugs later, she'd have more power to negotiate.

By the time they sat down to dinner, Austin was noticeably shaking, but still determined not to reveal her poorly kept secret. She figured she could create a distraction later that evening and steal her pills back.

Peter started the meal with a blessing. "Heavenly Father, thank You for allowing us to be in this place. We thank You that You give us the strength to deal with all things and the grace to find our way through them. It is in Jesus's name we pray."

And they all said, "Amen."

As they started to gather their food, Gracie gasped as she grabbed the potatoes from her father. "Dad, you have blood all over your shirt."

"Oh, so I do. It's nothing."

Mimi chimed in. "Peter, it's not nothing."

"Really, it's nothing. I'll just go change this shirt. I shouldn't have put on this white one. I wasn't thinking."

"Dad, the color of your shirt isn't the problem. It's the blood on it. What's happening?" Gracie's eyes were wide with concern.

Peter stood up from the table. "Well, I was hoping to surprise you later in the week, when we went out on the boat, but I guess this shirt ruined that plan."

"Peter, what is it?"

Peter started to unbutton his shirt. He looked over at Austin.

"I know we've given you a hard time about your tattoos. I thought maybe this might make you feel more at home."

As Peter took his shirt off, it revealed a large Christian cross taking up almost all of the left side of his chest. It was still swollen and bleeding as he'd done it only a couple of days before, in preparation for this trip. He was looking for anything to connect with Austin, to bring her back into the family.

"Dad, what have you done?" Austin asked, with a smile. "Don't you think tattoos are evil?"

"Well, I figure if God's going to be upset about it, He'll at least give me credit for inking a cross."

His entire family was smiling. Even Mimi was surprised at her husband. Although she wasn't wild about the fact he'd gotten a tattoo, she was happy to see him step so far out of his comfort zone.

"Look at you," was all she said, but in such a way as to convey approval.

Austin moved her eyes up from the cross on Peter's chest and stared into his face. She knew her father had done this for her, and she was grateful for it. But she was really searching his soul, desperate not for a connection based on an inked cross, but for what he and Mimi had hidden somewhere in the house. This house once provided her shelter from a life of illness. But now it hid something that caused her nothing but pain.

It was 1:43 a.m. when Austin first started knocking on the door of her parents' bedroom. Mimi had fallen asleep, but Peter had never closed his eyes. When the family went to bed around 10:30 p.m., Peter could hear an agitated but muffled conversation coming from Austin's room. He assumed she was talking to Santana on the phone, walking through her predicament.

By midnight, he could hear her walking around in the dark in the kitchen and family room, opening every cabinet and drawer, looking for her stolen stash. As the movement grew more agitated, Peter got up and turned the deadbolt he had installed on the bedroom door when Austin's stealing had grown so pervasive. He knew this would force her to knock on the door eventually.

The master bedroom door handle started to move, slowly and quietly, but Austin soon realized it was locked. The knock came gently at first, and he deliberately chose not to respond. As the knocking turned into pounding, he finally called out, "Yes, what do you want?"

"You know what I want," came the voice from the other side of the door.

"I can't imagine what you want."

"I want what you took from me in the car earlier today. Dad, open this fucking door."

Peter got up. When he unlocked the door, Austin opened it quickly.

"Give it to me!"

"Give you what?"

"Stop playing games."

"Say the words, Austin. Say what you've been lying to us about all this time."

"All right, all right. Give me the pills you took."

"What pills?"

"The Xanax and Roxies."

By now, Mimi was awake and chimed in. "What do you need those for?"

"Shut up, Mom. I'm not talking to you."

Peter continued. "Say it, Austin. Say what your problem is."

"I hate you fucking people. I hate you."

"Say it, Austin."

"All right, I'm using again. There, happy?"

"How could we be happy about that?"

"Just give me the pills. I'll go crazy without them."

"You're getting help when we get back home."

"I'm not going anywhere with you or for you."

"You're not going for *me*. You're going for yourself. And for your son."

"Just give me the pills and give them to me now. I'll go to your stupid rehab."

Peter walked over to his bed and pulled a bag out from under his pillow. He walked back to Austin and started to hand them over. But as she reached out, he pulled them away partially and looked at her.

He held up the bag. "Is this what freedom looks like to you?"

Austin reached out and grabbed it. As she marched out into the darkness of the rest of the house, she hollered back, "You are all horrible people. Fucking horrible people."

Peter stayed there long enough to make sure that she had truly retreated to her room. As Austin slammed her door, Gracie peered out from her bedroom, which Peter had built the year before.

"Are you okay?" he asked her.

"Yes, I'm fine."

"Lock the deadbolt," he called back.

"You can count on that," she said. As she closed the door, Peter could hear the deadbolt click. He closed his own door and turned on a light.

Mimi looked up at him. "Happy vacation."

"Yeah," he came back. "Happy vacation."

Peter moved over to his walk-in closet and opened the door. There inside was a playpen and his precious grandson still sleeping.

"He okay?" Mimi asked.

"He's fine," Peter reassured her.

He turned out the light and went back to bed. Through the walls, he could hear Austin back on the phone upstairs. After some very loud updates to Santana, her countenance mellowed as the pills took away the awful cravings. Gradually, her voice slowed to the point where he could just barely hear that she was talking at all. And before long, there was silence.

In some strange way, Peter was more relaxed than he'd been all day. His daughter was numb to her pain, and he was grateful that her battered body had found some rest. But he was starting to wonder if that would be all the peace she would ever know.

YEAR 30

By the end of the thirtieth year, Austin had been in and out of rehab three times. Each time, she showed signs of promise. She would genuinely repent and seem ready to make the final step back toward her family and her life. But eventually, she forsook all the love and forgiveness of her family and her few sober friends and traded them for the filthy rags of drugs and people who would only use her until she held no more value to them.

Santana didn't want to wait for Austin to "do rehab," and so he would come in and out of her life with each wave of relapse. With Santana absent, Austin jumped from one rehabbing boyfriend to the other until they all relapsed. Peter and Mimi blamed each one for her problems but silently began to question who the real problem actually was. Austin was the only common denominator with them all.

The dynamic around the Atlanta house evolved from uncomfortable to dangerous. Austin moved into the basement and, unbeknownst to Peter, began doing drug deals from there. She'd meet people on the Internet and bring them through a basement window to do God knows what in the darkness and stillness of their house.

On occasion, Peter would hear noises, but he assumed it was Austin on the phone, or going outside to smoke. It wasn't until he was out walking late one sleepless night that he saw someone crawling through the window of his house. Not knowing that Austin had invited him in, Peter ran down and pulled the man from the window, and they got into a struggle. But the man got the better of him and put a gun to Peter's head.

When Austin figured out what was happening, she ran outside and told the man that it was her father.

"Not cool," was all he said to Austin as he ran off into the darkness.

From that night forward, Peter was never the same. For starters, he kicked Austin out of the house the next morning and did not speak to her for months. He purchased a security system that wired every window and door, with ten cameras surrounding the property.

Three days later, he purchased two shotguns and three handguns, one for every room that would give him quick access if someone broke in. And he signed up for martial arts classes, focusing specifically on those techniques that were built on aggression rather than style. He didn't want to dance. He wanted to protect his family.

All of this came as a complete shock to his family. Peter had been the most anti-gun, anti-violence advocate anyone knew. He would claim that without God's protection, no weapon would help him. And with God's protection, no weapon was needed.

At first, the training he took repulsed him. The guns were loud and terribly destructive. It made him sick to his stomach to think that he might ever cause the kind of physical violence that a single bullet would inflict on a human being. And the fighting classes were no better. He came back bruised and bloodied from every session.

He dreaded every class, but he dreaded the thought of not protecting his family even more. But within a couple of months, something started to evolve in Peter's personality. The more violence he was exposed to, the more he embraced it. And the more he liked it, the better he became at it. And the more he excelled at it, the more he began to identify with it.

By the end of that year, Peter had become a fighter both inside and out. His physique had changed from a bit soft to rock hard, and his mind was always focused on learning new techniques. He found himself enjoying the mock confrontations on the shooting range, and he gravitated toward the more aggressive partners while sparring during classes.

While his family saw the outward changes, they were less aware of what was happening inside of Peter. As best they could tell, Peter was as faithful and loving as ever. They were more intrigued by his dalliance with his new hobbies than they were concerned about them. They appreciated his efforts to man up but never thought he actually would. He was too soft to ever act on anything other than saving someone's soul.

More than anything, they were amazed at how he completely cut Austin out of his life. He had always been the one to reach out to her no matter what she had done. But now, he no longer called her, and he no longer received her calls. Mimi and Gracie assumed he would break down and reach out, but he never did.

Since Peter was the only one talking to Austin through most of her rebelliousness, his refusal to speak with her left no channel of communication in Austin's direction. And Austin eventually became too ashamed to reach out to her family. Too much time had passed, and too much distance had built up between them. It wasn't until many months later that a chance encounter brought them into the same place at the same time.

Peter had taken a different route to work than usual because of an accident on the main highway. He was sitting at a stoplight when he noticed a young woman on the opposite corner. She was holding a sign, begging for money. He didn't recognize her at first because she was, in fact, unrecognizable as his daughter. For some reason, though, he felt an unusual compassion for her and found himself drawn into her situation. This lasted only a moment as he was distracted by a male panhandler knocking on the windows of the cars in front of him.

Peter searched his wallet for some money but found none. Mimi had emptied him out the night before to pay for groceries. He looked in his briefcase and through the car for some emergency cash and lost track of the beggar who now startled him as he banged on Peter's car. Peter rolled down his window to give him some of the loose coins he found in the ashtray.

As the man leaned down to take the money, his face came into view for the first time. It was Santana, who was just as startled to see Peter as Peter was to see him. It was then that Peter realized the young woman on the other side of the street might be Austin. Peter threw his car in park and hurried to get out. Santana pushed the door shut, trapping Peter half in and half out of the car.

"Baby, run!" Santana shouted across the street. Austin, not knowing what it was about, took off before Peter could extract himself from the vise Santana had created. Peter leaned back against the car and used his now-considerable strength to push the door off of him. Santana backed off, and Peter approached him until he was nose to nose with this man who had destroyed his daughter.

As the light turned green, several angry drivers began honking their horns, aggravated by Peter's stopped car. While they could see two men about to get into something, they had no time for whatever was going on between them. Several drivers shouted obscenities, but Peter was too agitated to care.

Peter looked around, but Austin was gone. "Was that my daughter?"

Santana smiled, revealing a rotted-out mouth. His face was filthy, and his clothes were just as black. "Your daughter? *Your* daughter? Your daughter's as good as dead. She's my bank now. She's my servant. She's my mule. She screws for me! Hell, she screws with me! You raised a great lay, even though she ain't much to look at anymore."

The cars behind them began honking aggressively, and the people nearby were screaming out of their windows for them to get out of the way. But Peter heard none of it. The rage that had been building inside him all these years consumed him. While in the past, Peter had begged God to take this kind of anger from him, this time there were no prayers to make it stop. There was no call for help to a God that had dragged him into a life he could no longer tolerate.

For a time, Peter thought he had been called to love the unlovable. He thought that no matter how bad things got, he was an ambassador for Christ, the One who came to love the sinner, even if the sinner did not want to be loved. Jesus died for the people who killed Him and did so with joy in His heart. Surely Peter could spread the Gospel to a few drug addicts. But there was no loving Santana or anyone like Santana. For them, it was like casting pearls to the swine.

The punch that would be Peter's first to ever meet flesh on flesh, started in his right fingers as they closed tightly and carefully. Peter thought through what his instructors had taught him. *Fold the fingers over and squeeze all the air out of your hand. Wrap your thumb around your fingers. Punch with the two biggest knuckles for the greatest impact and to avoid breaking your hand. When you punch, don't wind up, signaling your movement. Push off the right foot and turn your chest to the left to put all your weight into the punch.*

Peter held onto his fist for only a moment, but during those few seconds, he questioned over and over again what he was about to do. Was Gracie right? Was it selfish to lash out? Would these few moments of anger result in a lifetime of sorrow and pain? Would the next few seconds be what would define his life? Would he lose his witness to others as to what a Christian life should look like?

He studied Santana's face and the scheming grin that had not left his lips since making his point about Austin. It infuriated him, but Santana was right. Peter had long ago lost his daughter's innocence to a life of drugs. She was dead, even though she lived. She was no longer his daughter. Somebody else had stepped inside her soul and stripped her of everything lovely and joyful.

Peter thought he could bring her back. He thought he would be her savior, the only one never to give up. But you can't save someone who does not want to be saved. You cannot force someone to love herself or anyone else. You can only offer her the path, the encouragement, and the means by which to take those difficult first steps.

Austin had taken those steps so many times, hand in hand with Peter and her family. Yet each time, the likes of Santana would coax her back in. These men were pure, unadulterated evil. How many more lives would they ruin? How many other little girls would they lure into their trap? There could be only one solution. Kill them all.

Then he let it go. His fist hit Santana between the upper lip and the bottom of his nose, a particularly soft and sensitive part of the face. Peter's training had been effective. He delivered the punch so fast that no one watching saw it coming, let alone Santana, who flew backward onto the pavement, bouncing his head off the street.

The crowd around him that had once been so loud went quiet. There was no honking and no shouting. It was, in fact, the overwhelming silence that finally retrieved Peter's attention and woke him out of his trance. It was as if all of heaven stopped in that moment of violence for a man who claimed to be a child of God.

He looked around. Many of the men got out of their cars, but Peter's expression was one of crazed hysteria, and they all raised their hands and backed away. No delay in traffic was worth dealing with a man who just knocked out a helpless homeless guy.

Santana lay on his back. The bridge of his nose was split, raised, and bleeding, indicating that his nose had been broken completely. There was also blood coming from the back of his head where he had hit the pavement.

A woman was the only person brave enough to approach the scene. She walked slowly toward the two men until she caught Peter's attention. She stopped fifteen feet away, looked him in the eye, and spoke softly.

"I just want to check on him. Would that be okay?"

Peter looked at her and then at Santana. He nodded in the affirmative.

As she got down to assess Santana's injuries, he regained consciousness and pushed her away. "Get off of me, bitch."

"Look, I just want to get you some help."

"I don't need any damn help, woman. Get away from me."

"You're delirious," she said. "I'm calling 911."

Santana was a wanted man and had no desire to draw attention from the cops. "Do that and I'll kill you, lady. Just walk away."

Confounded, she turned to the people in the other cars who all shrugged their shoulders in amazement at his lack of gratitude.

Peter started to collect himself and wiped off his shirt, now spattered with Santana's blood. He looked at the people around him who were still quiet and waiting for the next move. After staring down Santana one more time, Peter turned to get back into his car. As he opened the car door, Santana started laughing behind him, with blood spurting out of his mouth while he did.

"You *are* delirious," Peter said as he got into the driver's seat.

"No, man, not delirious. Just happy to see the real you after all this time. You ain't no man of God. You're just like me. You just dress fancier and drive a nicer car. But deep down, you're no better. No wonder Austin turned out the way she did. She's her father's daughter."

Peter put the car back in drive and looked over at his victim one more time. Then he looked across the street where Austin had been. With everyone stopped in all directions, scrutinizing the unfolding scene, Peter took advantage of the opening and cut across four lanes of traffic through the intersection to head down the street where Austin had run. But she was long gone.

He finally pulled over and parked the car. He thought he'd feel bad about what had just happened. At least, he thought he *should* feel bad. But there was no remorse. He looked down at his hand, which was swelling up. It wasn't broken, but it hurt. The skin that hit Santana's mouth was split open where it had caught his teeth. He grabbed a napkin and wiped up the blood that would signal the beginning of the end for a man once filled with hope and optimism.

Gracie dove into the water off the dock. It was early morning, but it was already hot, and she knew the water would be the perfect temperature. She allowed the current to sweep her upriver, away from the dock. The tide would turn soon but she had grown strong enough in her swimming to make her way back to the dock in any event. She was strong and athletic without being ostentatious about it.

She rolled onto her back and just let the river take her. The sky had turned from red to blue, and the water had turned from the blackish tones of the early morning to the mix of colors reflected from the bright sky above.

As she allowed the current to pull her along, she could see the sun begin to highlight the oaks that framed the home they called River Soul. While she always loved this place as a child, she had taken for granted what the home meant. As she grew older, she had begun to appreciate what this place meant to her family and what it meant, in particular, to her mother. This place *was* her mother.

While the house was built by her father, it was her mother who brought the home to life. But it was more than the house. It was this entire place. It was the water, the wildlife, and the warmth of the South that nurtured her. Gracie wondered if her mother created this place or if this place created her mother. They had become so intertwined that it was impossible to tell the difference between the two.

Gracie was happy when her mother was here. It was a brief bit of rest in between all the pain that her sister had caused the family. From the day she was born, Austin had brought drama into the household. As a child, Gracie felt bad that her sister had been through so much undeserved pain. But now she wondered if maybe God knew what was coming and the pain had been deserved after all. God could just see it before the family could.

Gracie had gone from a loving sister then to a bitter one now. She had no relationship with Austin; nor did she desire one. Austin had hijacked her childhood, and now she had taken the family hostage once more. Even with her absence, the air was thick with her presence. Every word, every expression, every muted laugh that came from both her parents expressed what she already knew; their every thought was tied to a sister who hadn't thought of any of them in months.

Her initial pity for a difficult childhood had morphed into an outright hatred for the most selfish, most evil girl she knew. And so it made the dream she had had the night before all the more curious, all the more disturbing. Why would Austin even come to her mind when Gracie had perfected the art of keeping her out of her life?

And yet the dream was so vivid, she couldn't let it fade from memory. As she had faded off to sleep the night before, an image had come to her as though she was walking down a dirt road lined with oaks that formed a perfect canopy above her head. The sunlight peered through the branches, but it was filled with some of the most vibrant colors she had ever seen.

As she focused more intently, she heard a familiar voice that sounded almost as though it came from the trees.

"Grace Elizabeth."

She turned around but saw no one.

"Grace Elizabeth."

Again, no one. She started to walk down the road, and she heard the voice again, this time as though just over her shoulder.

"Gracie."

She turned around and her father was there next to her, although it was not her father exactly. But it looked like him. He smiled in a way that made her feel comfortable, until it was clear that he was looking at something in the distance. Gracie turned around to see Austin there in the middle of the dirt road. It was the young Austin in a hospital bed, hooked up to several IV pumps.

Next to her in bed was her son, Grayson Peter. They were the same age. Grayson was tending to her many needs, and they were playing together while he did. It was the happiest Gracie had ever seen Austin. Gracie turned to the father figure and said, "I don't get it. They look so happy together. And yet Austin hasn't even spoken to Grayson in a year."

The man did not reply. His eyes continued to focus on the bed. When Gracie turned around, the scene had changed. This time it was the adult, addicted Austin, all alone in the bed. She was asleep, but clearly very restless. A nurse approached and placed her hands on Austin, causing her to go still and into a very deep sleep.

The father prodded Gracie to move closer, and as she did, she could see that the nurse was Austin herself. But this Austin looked like the healthiest, happiest person Gracie had ever seen in her life. Even the hairs on her head seemed alive.

As Gracie moved closer, the nurse turned around and spoke.

"Hello, Grace Elizabeth."

"Austin?"

"Sort of. Yes."

"What are you doing here? What are we doing here?"

The nurse continued to care for the young woman in the bed, while only casually looking back at Gracie. "This girl in this bed, she's very conflicted, you know. She's fulfilled her purpose. And now she's not sure if she should stay or go."

"Her purpose?"

"Grayson. He's something she could never be. He's something she was never meant to be. Such a glorious purpose. Don't you think?"

Gracie looked at the person in the bed and back at the other Austin. Pointing to the nurse, Gracie asked, "Austin, is this who you really are?"

The nurse smiled. "This is how God sees me." The nurse looked down in the bed. "That . . . that is how you see me." Then she looked back at Gracie. "So you tell me, Gracie, is this the real me, or is that the real me?"

Gracie started to cry. "I don't know."

"Well, then," the nurse continued. "I guess you have some work to do too."

"Huh?"

The nurse nodded at Austin. "This one here. She is obedient only to her body. She stopped listening to her soul a long time ago. Such a miserable existence. It's so sad. She has traded everything God has to offer her in return for nothing but pain—for her and for you."

"Exactly," Gracie said with emphasis.

"Be careful, Gracie. You judge Austin because she only sees her body. And yet that's all you see of Austin too. You see her body and everything she's done to it. Your soul has been trying to show you more than that. But you've been so focused on how unlovable she is that you have been just as deaf to your own soul as Austin has been to hers."

Gracie was quiet, absorbing the conversation.

The nurse made one last attempt to have it all sink in. "You have been a marvelous aunt to Grayson. He thinks of you as his mother because that's all he's really known. And your spirit lights up around him. I've seen the way you two are together. It's—"

"Miraculous," Gracie interrupted but spoke mostly to herself as she began to catch on to what the nurse was trying to communicate to her.

The nurse smiled brightly. "Yes, Gracie, miraculous. And who is responsible for bringing that miracle into your life?"

"Jesus?"

"Well, yes. That is true of everything. But think a little closer to home."

Gracie looked over to the addict in the bed. "Austin."

"Yes, Austin. And in some respects, me. So I'll ask you again, Gracie. Is this the real me, or is that the real me?"

Gracie looked back and forth between the two of them. "I guess it's . . . both of you."

"Ah, now that's progress. We'll save the rest for another day."

The nurse made some final adjustments to Austin's IVs and looked back to Gracie. "My shift is almost over. I need to file my paperwork. Is there anything I can do for you?"

"I don't want you to go!" She looked at Austin in the bed. "And if that's you, I don't want her to go either."

"How sweet. But it's not for you to decide. Only she can."

"You mean, only you can."

"Not really how it all works. But I'll see you again, Gracie, regardless of what happens when this one makes up her mind."

The nurse leaned over to give her a hug, and when Gracie woke from the dream, she was holding her pillow tightly, as though the hug were real. It was early, but there was no going back to sleep, and so she walked down to the dock, where she now had returned from her swim.

It was a feeling Gracie held on to for days. With no druggie Austin in front of her, she was able to see her sister in a different light, and it felt good. But all visions ultimately intersect with reality, and Gracie would soon forget the Austin she met that day on a dirt road under an oak canopy in Okatie.

As Mimi came out of the bedroom for coffee, Peter was at the dining room table with blueprints spread from one end to the other. He was so deep in concentration that he did not hear his wife approach from behind. When she placed her hands on his neck, he was startled and readied himself for one of his self-defense moves.

Mimi leaned back. "Hold on there, Rambo."

"Sorry. Just force of habit."

"What are you working on?"

"A room for Grayson. He's fine in Austin's room for now. But he'll need a place of his own by the time he's four or five."

"I think that's nice. Where's it going?"

"Not completely sure yet. But I'm thinking off the side here. On the ground floor near our bedroom, so we can hear him when he tries to creep out at night."

"He's got a few years yet before that hits."

"I know. Just planning for it now. I think this is the right design."

"Do you plan to get some help this time around with the building?"

"Are you implying that I need some help?"

"You're not as young as you used to be, Grandpa."

Peter lifted up his arms and flexed his biceps. "As young and as strong as ever."

Mimi touched one of his flexed arms and pretended to fawn.

Peter wrapped his arm around her body and pulled her in close. He was still sitting, and so he rested his head on her stomach. Mimi wrapped her arms around his neck with her left hand and caressed his head with her right.

"I love you, Mimi," Peter said softly and affectionately.

Gracie came out of her room toward the bathroom and could see her parents embraced below, beyond the loft banister. "All right, you two. Break it up down there." She continued into the bathroom and shut the door.

"She's a good daughter," Peter said as they broke their embrace.

"Pretty much always has been. Never given us any trouble. Not like somebody else I know."

"Let's not go there so early in the morning."

Grayson started talking to himself in his crib, which they could hear on the baby monitor.

Mimi started to talk to the monitor as if Grayson were sitting right in the room. "He's so sweet. So innocent. So happy. So totally unaware of what his life is really like."

"And let's keep it that way as long as we can. Ignorance is bliss."

"He'll ask questions someday."

"And we'll answer them someday."

Gracie came out of the bathroom and down the stairs. "I'll go get the big boy."

As Gracie entered the room, Peter and Mimi could hear the conversation over the monitor.

"Hey, baby Gray. Let's go change that diaper and get you dressed."

The banter continued, and Gracie's parents listened with a mix of laughter and hidden sadness that their other daughter was missing out on all that Grayson's childhood had to offer.

Mimi looked to Peter. "All I ever wanted was to be a grandma. I never expected to be a mother again."

"Not quite what I envisioned for our empty nest. But families do what families need to do."

With that, Grayson came running around the corner and leapt into Peter's arms. He looked over at Mimi and said, "Morning, Mimi!"

Mimi went over to tickle him. "Morning, little one! I'm grateful for you!"

Gracie turned the corner, and Peter checked in with her. "Hey, we were thinking about making a day of it on the boat. How's that sound?"

"Perfect! Let's give Grayson his first ride on the tube today."

After breakfast, Gracie took Grayson out back to play in the yard. As Gracie chased Grayson around the yard, Mimi watched from the back deck, capturing every movement as they ran through the grass. As the moments passed, she was able to see beyond them as the herons and storks flew from their roosts and made their way to their solitary hiding places for the day ahead.

It seemed like things slowed down into a rhythm in Mimi's heart that had been missing for some time. The faster Grayson ran, the slower Mimi saw it in her mind. This had been what she had imagined for herself thirty years earlier. Children. Grandchildren. Fun. Laughter. Family in the midst of natural beauty. It could only be more perfect if Austin's entire life hadn't cast a veil across what she had seen so clearly when she first stepped onto the soil of this land.

The dilapidated house they had purchased decades ago once lessened the beauty of this place to the casual observer. But Mimi could see beyond what others saw. So many before her had focused only on the house, with all its shortcomings. Mimi focused on the dream. She could see what Peter had since built before he ever broke ground.

But now, in reverse fashion, Austin's life marred the perfect scene before her. In the time before Austin's fall, Mimi could see beauty in what was not yet created. Now, after seeing the worst of what humanity had to offer, Mimi could see despair where it was not immediately evident. She had a bad feeling.

As if right on cue, Peter's phone rang.

"Who is it?" Mimi asked.

"I don't know. It's a number I don't recognize. I'll just let it go into voicemail."

"I think you should take it."

"Who are you, and what have you done with my wife?"

"Take it, Peter, before it goes to voicemail."

"Okay, okay." He picked up the phone. "Hello?"

Mimi could hear an automated voice on the other side.

Peter continued. "Yes, I'll accept the charges."

"Dad?"

"Austin? What are you doing in DeKalb County?"

"Never mind that. I need you to come bail me out."

"Bail you out? You're in jail? For what?"

Austin paused, knowing what her dad would think. But she was beyond shame at this point, and so she just came out with it. "Heroin and cocaine possession. But it's not my fault. It was Jack's car and—"

"Jack? *Jack?* What are you doing with Jack?"

"Don't worry about that. Just come and get me."

"I'm not even in the state, Austin. We're in South Carolina."

"Dad, I'm in jail. It's scary in here. I need you to come get me. Now."

"Why doesn't Jack bail you out?"

"He's in jail too. His father is posting his bail. But he can't afford to post mine. It's five thousand dollars."

"Five thousand dollars? I don't have that kind of cash with me. I don't even know where to begin bailing someone out."

"Here, this lady can tell you." Austin passed the phone.

"No, don't hand it over. We have more—"

"Hello, Mr. Stewart? This is Officer Green. You can go to our website, and it will tell you what you need to do."

Peter wrote down her instructions. "Thank you. Could you please put my daughter back on the phone?"

"She left to go back to holding."

"Ah. Well, I guess we're done then. Thank you for your help."

Peter hung up and put down the phone. While Mimi had only heard parts of the conversation, she could glean the essence. "So, what are you going to do?"

"I guess I'm going to go bail her out of jail."

"Peter, it's our one week a year in this place."

"I think Austin in jail is a bit more important."

Mimi became instantly agitated. Her emotions on this subject had evolved to the point where she flew into a rage the second Austin's choices interrupted her life. "Everything about Austin has always been more important. When she was sick, it was just what we had to do. But she's done this to herself. We are forever dropping everything to clean up her messes. I'm just tired of it."

"Just moments ago, you knew something was wrong, and you seemed concerned for her at the time. Now it seems like you don't care."

"I thought she was dead."

"So, if she's dead, I should take the call. But if she's about to be murdered in jail, I just let it go. Do I have that right?"

"You know we've talked about this for years. It was only a matter of time before she got arrested."

"And?"

"Leaving her in jail just might be exactly what she needs. It could save her life."

Peter's voice finally started to rise. "I can't do that, Mimi. She could be killed in there, before I even make it back to Atlanta."

"And she could be killed out in the streets, Peter. Did you say that Jack was involved somehow?"

"Yes. Hard to believe, but yes."

"How could anything be as dangerous as that? Her with Jack? That's bad news any way you look at it. You'll know she'll go right back to him as soon as she's out."

"Look. I admit that's bad. But that's hypothetical bad. Her in jail, that's bad right now."

"Hypothetical bad? Really? That man is the worst of them all. He started this curse, and every time she uses, his curse pulses through her veins. At least in jail, he can't hurt her."

Peter's tone became sarcastic and patronizing. "How sad that you view Austin being in jail as a good thing."

Gracie could see that her parents were arguing, which stood in stark contrast to how they had been just moments earlier. "What's up?"

Mimi chimed right in. "Austin's in jail for drug possession."

"Good."

Peter looked at her, incredulous. "Good? You really think that's good?"

"Dad, she needs to learn the consequences of her actions."

"These consequences are too severe, Gracie."

"You can't save her. She doesn't want to be saved."

"How can you say that? How do you know her heart?"

"Maybe I don't know her heart, but I know yours. You're mourning."

"Mourning what?"

"The loss of your child's innocence. The dream of your perfect family."

Peter's voice started to crack. "She's had such a miserable life. I just can't leave her to suffer anymore without someone to love her. Even if she's done all this to herself."

"I know. But don't you always say that God breaks our hard heart by putting us through suffering? Maybe this suffering is what Austin needs. Maybe you are getting in the way. You're trying to fix her, but this is between her and God."

"God wants us to help people. To visit them in prison."

"Yes, visit them in prison. It doesn't say to get them out of prison."

"That's not unconditional love."

"I think it is. I think it's a trust in her and in God."

"I can't just leave her there. You'd understand if that were your child."

Mimi couldn't hold back, even though Gracie was doing such a great job. "She's my child. And I think Gracie is right."

Peter was now completely silent. He wasn't sure what to do.

"Dad, I love you. But you think that by rescuing her from jail, providing her with money, caving into her manipulative behavior, and picking her up every time she falls that you're being a good Christian man. But even God left Jesus in a desert for forty days. How is she supposed to take responsibility for her life when you are there every time with love and money?"

"Gracie, if you were ever in trouble, I'd be there for you in an instant. Austin's in trouble, and I'll be there for her too. Now."

Peter got up and walked away before there would be further conversation. Mimi reached out to grab his hand but missed it as he yanked it back. "I'll be back here tomorrow."

But that was just another untruth among a long list of untruths where Austin's life was concerned. As with so many things with Austin, it was far more complicated than that. It took almost two days to post bail over the holiday weekend, and another eighteen hours for her to be released after that.

Peter lived on the lobby floor of the massive jail for almost three full days. A jail big enough to house most of Atlanta's criminals proved to be a complex web of bureaucracy and government workers who could care less about his schedule. He was robbed of his spare clothes while he slept, he went hungry from no food for three days, and he was crazy from the boredom

When Austin finally came down, she looked horrific, still in county-issued garb.

Her hair was matted to her face and her complexion pale and ghost-like. She had very little to say except, "I need food."

On the way to eat, Austin texted away with the phone they had returned to her upon her release. She texted all the way through the meal and then asked to go to Walmart to get some clothes. She told Peter to give her some room to spend time buying what she needed to buy, but every time Peter went to find out where she was, she was on the phone.

"Dad, stop bothering me. They're going to take my phone in detox. I'm just letting people know where I'm going, so they'll know I'm okay."

"How about you get moving, Austin? I'd like to get back to South Carolina."

"Just give me a minute, Dad. Back off."

When she finally finished, Peter shelled out over $400 for a cart full of supplies, without getting even a thank-you. As they went outside, Austin said she needed to smoke.

"You'll probably want to go to the car, Dad. I know you hate the smell."

"Okay, I'll take the cart."

"No, thanks. I want to organize my stuff so you can just drop me off once we get there."

Peter went to the car and called Mimi to say he'd get Austin to the court-ordered detox and then be on his way back south.

"Just make sure she gets there. She needs it, and we don't want to lose the bail money."

"Oh, she's going. I'll make sure of that."

With that, Peter looked up to see if Austin was ready. She wasn't in his line of sight, so he said his goodbyes to Mimi and got out of the car to find her. The cart she had been using was still where he had left her, but it was empty. He went inside the Walmart and searched the entire store. Nothing. He came out and spent the next half hour walking the property, back in the alleys and by the loading docks.

She was gone.

Peter drove back to Okatie in the darkness after spending most of the day in his Atlanta home. He had reported Austin missing, but it was clear that no one much cared, and a search party wouldn't be forthcoming. The courts would issue a bench warrant if she missed her preliminary court date, but in the meantime, she was one of hundreds of junkies who skipped bail every week and left the courts to wallow in mounds of paperwork.

He was deep in thought for most of the trip. He called Mimi only to give her an update on the fact that he'd arrive late. Their conversation was brief and to the point. It was clear that Peter had a lot on his mind, and his wife realized he'd been through quite an ordeal. She gave him some breathing room to relax. But Peter was anything but relaxed. He was consumed with hatred over men like Jack and Santana.

Once again, they had robbed his daughter of any chance at happiness, and they made it virtually impossible for Peter to reconnect his daughter with the rest of their family. This latest move ensured that she'd wind up in jail, and that was only if the police found her alive first.

He felt a hardening of his heart as his every thought moved him further and further away from God. He tried to convince himself that he was well intentioned in his hatred; after all, these men were harming his daughter. Surely he had the right to harbor bad intentions toward them. Surely that was his responsibility, his right as a father.

To outsiders, Peter guessed that his heart appeared as rocky, thorny soil, consumed with the cares of this world. The reality, though, for those who looked closely, was that his heart had become very fertile soil. Soil will grow a weed with just as much veracity as it will grow a fruit-producing tree. What matters is the kind of seed that is planted.

Peter had been planting seeds of hate and revenge, cloaked in a shell of self-righteousness. And he had been watering those seeds from the moment he awoke until the last moments of the day. He no longer prayed, and his identity in Christ had been replaced with thoughts of himself as avenger of all the wrongs done to his family. He was, after all, now equipped with weapons and a body trained to fight.

Surely God had sent him down this path to give him the skills necessary to take care of the mess created by all the evil around him. "Vengeance is mine, sayeth the Lord. I will repay," he once read in the Bible. Peter decided that if there was a God, he was called to be His avenging angel. Mimi was right all along. He had been cowardly with men like Jack, and he needed to man up.

By the time Peter arrived in Okatie, Gracie and Mimi were asleep. He moved throughout the house in the dark with great precision. He knew everything he needed to do and how long it would take to do it. It was sometime after 3 a.m. when he finished all of his task list. He allowed himself to sit down, if only for a moment. He had one thing left to do, but he couldn't start until after 4 a.m., when the tides would be just right.

He rested his head on the back of the chair and contemplated the next twenty-four hours. He had never been so sure about what he had to do, and yet never so conflicted about how his actions would affect the family. At this point, he couldn't care less about his life. But his family meant everything to him, and they would feel the weight of his actions for the rest of their lives.

He had been the dominant figure in the household for years. And yet he decided his presence had done them no good. Nothing he did worked. Austin was the unhappiest person he had ever known, and his wife had to hide a sadness that grew inside her with every disappointment. He had not been the husband or father they needed him to be to keep them from harm's way, both physically and emotionally.

Gracie was the only saving grace. She was faithful to the family in spite of who he was. In spite of who they were. She had been the true rock of the family. He was the figurehead, but she was the one who turned out to be what they all had wanted to be. He was counting on her to fill the void once he did what he was about to do.

He checked his watch and rose from his chair. He walked over to the kitchen table and pulled out a piece of paper to write a note. "Got back from Atlanta late. Was wired from the trip, so I decided to take an early morning cruise on the river. The tides won't get me back until after sunrise, so I didn't want you to worry if you got up early. But my guess is that I'll be back before you're up, so I'll have breakfast waiting. Pancakes and bacon on me. I love you all so very much."

He walked over to the kitchen and made preparations for the pancakes. He set the table and placed the note where it would be obvious. He scanned the house, which was now illuminated with a nearly full moon on the rise behind him. He took an inventory of everything he could see, pausing in particular on a picture of him and his three girls when they were all so much younger.

This was the family he would remember, the one filled with innocence and hope. Not the twisted mess his life had become. This is the vision he would hold in his heart for the rest of his life.

He walked toward the back door and picked up two backpacks he had ready on the floor nearby. He opened the sliding door that had never worked quite right since he broke it back in the Santana days. He had tried to fix it, but never could get the alignment where it needed to be. Yet one more broken thing he would leave behind.

He turned around and scanned the family room one last time, and then he walked out the back door of the house he and Mimi had created from virtually nothing. He walked down onto the pier and never looked back. Whatever last bits of softness and grace that still lived in his heart were gone. And so was he.

When Gracie awoke that morning, she noticed immediately an unfamiliar bag sitting by her bed. It was 10 a.m., and they didn't plan to leave for their Atlanta home until noon. Why would someone leave a bag in her room and not out by the front door?

She slid her legs over the side of the bed and let herself wake up just a bit before moving. She heard voices downstairs that were slightly elevated, and she assumed that her mother and father were arguing about Austin, as usual.

Instead of going downstairs to get in on the drama, she succumbed to her curiosity and unzipped the bag. What? Was she still dreaming? She sat up and looked around, not sure what to think. She kept looking down at the bag and then up again. Down at the bag and then up.

After several minutes, she reached in and pulled out a wrapped stack of $100 bills. She quietly counted and found that the stack had twenty bills for $2,000 total. Inside, she found four more stacks just like it. One by one, she set the stacks beside her on the bed.

Her amazement turned into a bit of nervous laughter, and then into outright laughter. She had never seen this much money in her life. Ten thousand dollars in cash. What in the world? Where did it come from? Why was it here?

Back in the bag, she saw something she had not noticed before. She reached in to find the hard, cold steel of her father's 9mm M&P handgun. She pulled it out and found two more items—magazines loaded with sixteen hollow-point bullets in each. Her father had taught her how to handle a weapon and had taken her to the shooting range several times. She took one of the magazines and loaded it into the Smith and Wesson until she heard it click. Then via instinct, she pulled back the slide and loaded a bullet into the chamber.

She stood up, took a firing position, and started pointing the gun around the room, until she heard her mother call up from downstairs. "Gracie, I need you to come down to the kitchen, please. I have someone here I need you to talk to."

Grace looked around as if she were caught red-handed. Ten thousand dollars in cash and a loaded weapon in her hands. How was she going to explain that? She quickly removed the magazine and cocked the slide one last time to eject the bullet in the chamber.

She followed the safety measures her father had shown her to make sure that the gun was no longer loaded and placed it and the cash back into the bag. Searching quickly, she zeroed in on a good hiding spot under some blankets on the top shelf of her closet.

After a quick primp, she took a breath and opened the door. As she walked out onto the loft landing and looked over the banister, she could see her mother with a Beaufort County Sheriff standing in the kitchen.

"Oh, this is classic," she said to herself. "I wake up with guns and money, and now the police are in my house. What has Austin done this time?" As Gracie turned the corner down the stairs and into the kitchen, she tried to act as calm as she could.

"What's up?"

Her mother clearly had been crying but tried to put on her best mom face and the fake calm voice that all parents use when they're trying not to be hysterical in front of their kids.

"Did you by any chance get up earlier and see your father?"

Gracie immediately became concerned by the question. "No, I just woke up. We stayed up so late waiting for Dad that I slept in a bit. What's going on?" she asked with a voice that sounded suddenly desperate.

The sheriff interrupted. "It's probably nothing at all. I know your dad knows this area very well. So I'm sure he's fine."

"Mom, what's going on?"

"Dad got back from Atlanta very late last night and went out on his kayak, like he always does when he needs to relax. He was supposed to be back a while ago. I just haven't seen him. I'm sure it's nothing, but in the unlikely chance he needed help, I just wanted to get people looking for him."

The sheriff looked at Gracie. "Did your father say anything to you last night?"

Gracie started to put the pieces together. Something clearly was not right. But not knowing what her dad was up to, she decided to say little. "No, nothing. He's been in Atlanta for the last few days. I haven't even spoken to him on the phone."

Mimi stepped in for her daughter. "But I have. He seemed perfectly normal when I spoke to him last night. He told me he'd be late. He doesn't sleep much, so he spends a lot of time on the river."

The sheriff made some notes. "Okay, thank you. Based on the tides last night, I have my men looking mostly toward the Colleton River—and one man a little farther back here in case he missed his mark with the tide coming back in. But that doesn't sound like him. So I'm sure we'll find him perfectly well, just stranded and embarrassed somewhere out there."

Mimi absorbed his comment, wishing it to be true. "Thank you, Sheriff. We really appreciate your help."

After showing him out the door, Mimi broke down as she turned to find her daughter waiting there for a hug. She sobbed into her daughter's shoulder for several minutes until there were no more tears left.

As they both gently let each other go, Gracie said to her mother, "Mom, I'm sure it's fine. You know Dad knows what he's doing."

"I know. That's what concerns me, Gracie. He'd never be late like this. You know he plans everything perfectly."

"I know. But stuff happens. Let's stay positive."

Mimi just nodded her head up and down, like a woman in shock.

Gracie continued, "Come on. Let's make some breakfast. Looks like you were ready to make some pancakes."

Mimi broke down crying again and said through her tears, "No, your dad was going to make us pancakes."

Gracie moved in and put her hands to each shoulder. "It will be okay. I'm sure it's nothing. He's just upset over Austin, so he's gone longer than usual. That's all."

Gracie sat her mother down and then went into the kitchen to get things ready. Her mind was racing, and she needed time to think. What was her father up to? What was going on?

After forty-eight hours, an official missing person's report was filed, triggering an entirely new set of visits by the police. Most of the questions were routine. "What was your husband wearing when you last saw him? Where does he normally go on the river? Does he know these waters? When was the last time he kayaked at night?"

But there were two questions that were difficult to answer. The first of which should have been easy. "Did Peter do anything unusual before he disappeared?"

For Mimi, the answer was indeed easy. "No, not at all."

But for Gracie, that question launched her into inner turmoil. There was something that was very unusual. And she wasn't sure how to answer. The thought that her father might really be in trouble made her physically ill. If she didn't talk to the police about the cash and the gun and her father needed help, she might be causing him harm.

But the more overriding thought was the conversation she had had with her father out on the river about how much hate he had inside. Had he finally snapped and done something stupid? If she told the police about what she had found, that might put her further at risk too. But if he was somewhere out there on the water, her story would only keep them from looking for him with all of their resources.

She hesitated and said, "No, nothing."

The deputy looked at her. "Are you sure, young lady?"

She hesitated again. "Yes, I'm sure. I'm trying to think of any small detail, but nothing is coming to me."

The deputy relaxed just a bit. "That's very understandable. This would be an upsetting situation for anyone."

The second question is what launched them into a three-hour discussion. "Is there anyone who would want to hurt your husband?"

Mimi responded immediately, "No, absolutely not. He's one of the most reliable, most kind people I know."

But this time Gracie spoke up. "Mom, really? What about Jack, or Santana, or any of the bevy of other creeps that Austin knows?"

Mimi sat back in her chair. "Oh, yes, of course. I hadn't even thought of that."

She turned to the police officer and began to recount the entire history of Austin's addiction, all her boyfriends, all the arrests, all the tension. The deputy took pages of notes. After Mimi stopped, it still took him a couple of minutes to catch up. "I assume they only know your Georgia address. Correct?"

Mimi started to cry. "No, they've all been here. Peter always tried to find the best in everyone. He was convinced that if he could just love them enough and show them what a stable family looked like, he could turn them around. He didn't trust any of them, but he still reached out to see if he could find something good to hold on to."

The deputy hesitated. "I'm sorry, but I have to ask this question too. Would your daughter want to harm your husband?"

Mimi and Gracie both said, "No!" in unison. They said it so strongly that the officer flinched.

Mimi noticed the reaction and said, "He's the only one in our family who believes in her. The rest of us wrote her off years ago. He has never given up on her, and Austin knows that. She would never intentionally hurt him."

The deputy made some further notations and then looked up. "Okay, thank you. I think that's what I need for now. If you think of anything else, here's my card. Call me day or night. And I'll do the same if I find anything out."

As the deputy left the house, Mimi and Gracie sat back down. Gracie's mother looked over to her and said, "Gracie, is there anything you're not telling me?"

"No, Mom."

"I saw how you hesitated. Did your father say anything to you I should know about?"

"No. Nothing."

Mimi's voice started to crack. "Okay. I'm sorry. I'm just looking for anything to hold on to. I just can't imagine a life without your father."

"I know. Me neither."

Three days later, Mimi's phone rang in the middle of the night. She answered it quickly, hoping it was news of Peter being found alive.

"Hello?"

"Mom?"

"Austin?"

"Yes, it's me."

"Where are you, Austin?"

"Never mind that. Why do the police keep calling my phone? And why are they trying to track down Jack?"

Mimi sat up in bed and turned on a light, wiping away the fresh tears she had shed in the darkness of her room. "Austin, I have some potentially very bad news."

"What?"

"Your father is missing. He went out for a midnight kayak ride and never came back."

"What? No way. I just saw him in Atlanta last week. And he knows the river so well. It's not possible."

"I'm still trying to get my head wrapped around it myself. It's hard to believe."

"Well, I don't believe it! You're both just trying to trick me to get me into rehab."

"No, honey, I'm not."

"Yes, you are."

Austin hung up the phone. Seconds later, Gracie's phone rang. Gracie was still awake on the bed with the light on, just staring at the bag on the floor. It was a number she did not recognize, and she picked it up hoping it was her father.

"Dad?"

"See, I knew it. You're trying to trick me."

"Austin? Is that you?"

"Yes, it is. What's all this about Dad missing?"

"I was going to ask you the same thing!"

"What are you even talking about?"

"Austin, swear to me that you've not done anything stupid."

"I haven't even thought of you all in a week, let alone done anything."

"You better not have. Nor any one of your druggie boyfriends. I swear, if they did something to him, there will be hell to pay. Dad only ever wanted to help them."

"Yeah, some help. He hated them."

"And yet he welcomed them into his home anyway."

"Only to try to change them. Not everyone wants to be like Dad. Some of us are happy just as we are."

"And you all have so much to be proud of."

Austin ignored the sarcasm. "Where's Grayson?"

"He's in his crib, safe, asleep."

"If Dad's gone, then how will Mom care for him?"

"I'll help her, which is more than I can say for you."

"Well, you won't have to. Jack and I will come get him."

Gracie's eyes got wide; her heart started racing. That thought had never occurred to her. After a few seconds to collect herself, she replied,

"You two can't take care of yourselves. How are you going to care for a child?"

"We'll figure it out."

"Do you know how many times you've said that before—that you'll figure it out? And yet you never, ever do!"

"Look, Gracie, you're not his mother. I am."

"And how would I know that, Austin? You haven't acted like a mother once since he was six months old. You chose drugs over your son. Mom and Dad gave you so many chances to choose him over your druggie life. And you threw away every one."

"I'm coming down there to get him."

"You're doing that out of spite. Not out of love for Grayson. Not out of his best interest."

"Whatever. I know my rights." With that, Austin hung up the phone.

Gracie got up from her bed and started pacing. How would she deal with this? How would her father have dealt with this? She kept pacing until a thought came to her. She immediately looked over at the bag on the floor. Her father had anticipated this very scenario. She ran over and pulled out the cash and the gun.

She looked at it for a while. But she wasn't really looking at it. She was thinking intently about her next move. She shoved it back in the bag and started grabbing anything she thought she might need.

It was 6 a.m. when Gracie knocked on her mother's door, gently at first, and then more loudly when she realized her mother was still asleep. She walked into the room and sat down on the side of the bed and stroked the hair on her mother's head back off her face. She rubbed her arm for a while until Mimi started to wake up. Her mother turned over on her back and smiled.

"Hi, girl."

"Hi, Mom. Did you sleep?"

"Not really. Maybe a little bit. I finally took a pill a couple of hours ago."

"Good. You need your rest."

"How about you?"

"I'm fine. Hey, I had a thought. With all that's going on around here, I was thinking maybe I'd take Grayson back to Atlanta. He senses the tension here, and I think it would be best if I got him out of this environment. What do you think?"

"I'm not sure. I think I'd like you both here, with me."

"I know. But I'm thinking of Grayson. I think it's best for him."

Mimi paused for a moment. "You're probably right. Let me get up and get him ready."

Gracie put her hand on her mother to keep her from getting up. It surprised Mimi just a bit in how forceful it was. But she was still a bit dazed from the sleeping pill and didn't have much resistance in her after several days of no sleep.

"Well, okay then, if you have it handled."

"I've got it."

Mimi smiled. She lifted her hand up to stroke her daughter's face. "You always have, Gracie. From the time you were very little. You're a good girl. Always dependable. I appreciate that now more than ever."

"Thanks, Mom. I love you. Now rest. Sleep. You've got plenty of time to worry later."

Mimi put her head back on the pillow. "Okay, thanks, hon. Call me when you get to Atlanta. Love you."

Gracie stayed until her mother fell back to sleep. She stood up and looked down at her one last time. "I love you, Mommy. Goodbye."

Gracie walked out of the room and headed out the front door toward her car. She already had moved the car seat from her parents' car into her own. She got into the driver's side and looked back. Grayson was already in the car, still asleep.

All her bags and his bags were packed into the back of her small SUV. She looked over into the passenger seat at the bag that had been left in her room. She put the car in drive and pulled down the path for what she believed would be the last time. Once she carried out her plan, she knew she would never be able to return to the home that was built with her in mind.

Later that night, Mimi finally got the call she was both hoping for and dreading. It was news of Peter's whereabouts.

"Mrs. Stewart?"

"Yes."

"I have some news for you. Can I come over and visit with you for a moment?"

"Yes. No. Wait. If you have news, I want to hear it now."

"I'd rather come by, if that's okay with you."

"It's not okay. Please tell me now. Where's Peter?"

"Well, ma'am, I'm not totally sure. But we did find his kayak in the Port Royal Sound, almost out to the Atlantic. We're not sure if it floated there, or if it's where it actually happened."

"It?"

"Yes, ma'am. I have some disturbing news to share with you."

"What news?"

"Well, Mrs. Stewart. This won't be easy to hear. We actually found your husband's kayak a couple of days ago."

"Why didn't you call me then?"

"Well, ma'am. It was covered in blood, and we didn't want to alarm you. Especially since we didn't know if it was his blood or not."

"Oh my God!"

"Yes, ma'am. I'm sorry to say that the samples we took do match with the DNA we took from the toothbrush you gave us."

Mimi started to sob, and the officer gave her time.

"I'm afraid there's more."

"What else could there be?"

"There's a backpack he must have taken with him. Does that make sense?"

"Yes, he always took emergency supplies with him. Just in case something like this happened."

"Well, that makes sense based on what was left."

"What was left? What do you mean, 'what was left'?"

"The backpack. Well, it was all tore up."

"Torn up?"

"Yes, ma'am. Tore up. Like a gator or a shark or something like that got to it. We're not sure if he had pulled over to seek shelter and was out of the kayak or what. But either way, we weren't happy with what we found."

Mimi was in shock. No words formed in her mouth. Her mind was blank. Finally, the only thing that came to her mind seemed so unimportant.

"How could it be a gator? They don't like saltwater."

"Unless it's mating season, ma'am. And it is. They'll cross anything to find a mate. Our crew has run across a couple of them during our search."

"Oh . . . I see," she said softly, staring at the floor.

"But there's still some hope, ma'am. We didn't find a body or any parts of a body." The deputy was sorry he said that as soon as the words came out of his mouth.

Mimi started crying once more, and the officer waited a few minutes. "I'm very sorry, Mrs. Stewart. We'll still have some people out looking for him. There's always hope."

Mimi had no reply.

"Mrs. Stewart?"

Mimi didn't want to speak. She had nothing for him, except, "Thank you, officer. I'll wait to hear more news from you." With that, she hung up the phone and slowly lowered herself onto the floor, where she stayed until dawn.

Gracie had no intention of going back to Atlanta. She had plotted a course up to Cleveland, Georgia. She had heard about Cleveland years ago when her parents bought her a Cabbage Patch doll. They were made in Cleveland, and they also had a hospital for dolls in need of repair. It was the only place she'd ever heard of that was tucked away in the mountains.

She had turned off her cell phone to avoid detection and got lost several times along the way without a GPS. She finally pulled into a hotel off the side of the road, but there was a police car there, so she drove another twenty minutes to the next one. She knew it would be old and dirty, but she hoped there would be no security cameras, given how dated the construction was. Still, she made a trip back to the car to get a hoodie and a hat. She put the hat on first and then pulled the hoodie over on top of the hat to add an additional level of caution. She did the same for Grayson.

As she checked in, she tried hard not to make eye contact with the clerk, who really could not care less. Other than a few truckers and some stray travelers, there was no one remarkable that came through his place, and this seemed to be just one more of a long line of strange people to rent a room. He was just happy to have some business.

As Gracie made her way with Grayson back to the room, she figured she was probably fine for the next few days. No one would really report her missing any time soon. With all the focus on Peter, and with her cover story, she should be okay for about seventy-two hours. But with the police involved, and with Austin's pending arrival in Okatie, she could never be sure just when it would become obvious that she had kidnapped her nephew. After getting Grayson to sleep, she allowed herself a few tears but then sat down in a chair and scanned the room. It was as old, as dirty, and as creepy as she had imagined.

Was this her new life? And what about Grayson? Where would he go to school? What medical care could she afford? How would she get a job as a fugitive? And what would happen to Grayson when she was finally found out and brought to jail? She really had not thought this through when she left. It had seemed like such a good idea at the time.

Austin looked down at her wrists, which were handcuffed to the table. She was alone in a sterile eight-by-eight interrogation room in a downtown Atlanta police department. They'd left her alone in that room for over an hour. She had to pee, she was hungry, and she was starting to go into withdrawal. She hated the games that the cops played with people like her.

But they had her now, and there was nothing she could do about it. It was times like these when her father's words about the life she had chosen blared in her ears. He had always been right, but she could pretend he wasn't until she found herself like this, in deep trouble. There was no escaping his words then.

She contemplated whether her father was really gone, or whether he was going to one more extreme to save her. He was always trying something, which she both loved and hated. She recalled a conversation with him one day down in Okatie when he told her he would never give up on her. "Why?" was her only response. She had long ago given up on herself. Why would he hang on when she had let go years before?

He had given her a Bible once, written in modern language so she could understand it. One of the pages she flipped to was in Ecclesiastes, whatever that means. She found a sentence there that explained her entire life. It said something like, "Who can straighten what God has made crooked?" Crooked. Her whole life was crooked, and God had made it that way. No man or woman, not even she could open the doors He had shut or close the doors He had opened. None of this was her fault. God was to blame.

That might make some people angry. But for Austin, it was the first thing that gave her life meaning. God had scrambled her brains and turned her into something He would use for whatever purposes. If there were a God, then He would have made her this way. And if God is all-powerful, then she was supposed to be this way. Instead of making her angry, it gave her an odd sense of peace.

But here, now, all she could think about was using the bathroom. She started pulling at her handcuffs, shaking them up and down on the table. "I've got to pee in here." She stared into the two-way mirror. She assumed someone was watching her, but maybe not. Maybe they were out drinking coffee and laughing at her, waiting until she was completely undone before they asked her questions.

Finally, someone walked into the room.

"Good evening, Miss Stewart. I'm Sergeant Hall. How are you tonight?"

"Ha, like you give a damn. What am I doing here?"

He looked down at his clipboard and spoke using a dismissive, bureaucratic voice. "Says here that you have quite a background on you. Right now, we're holding you for skipping out on your court-ordered rehab."

Austin went to make an exaggerated arm motion but was stopped by the cuffs. "Really? All this, for that? I am sure you don't really care that I am not in rehab."

Seargent Hall gave her direct eye contact for the first time. "Truthfully, no. You can do with your life whatever you want as far as I'm concerned. I couldn't give two shits about you. But your father, he seems like someone I might care about."

A slight smile came over her face. Now she knew what this whole thing was about. "He's not missing. He's just trying to find me and get me sober," she said somewhat flippantly.

"Do you have any evidence of that?"

"No, but I know him."

"Tell me about him."

"Look, let's not play any games. Stop with the bullshit. What do you want?"

"I want to know if you or any of your friends had anything to do with his disappearance."

"I've been in Atlanta the entire time. And so have they."

"Do you have any proof of that?"

"No."

Sergeant Hall made some notes. He flipped the pages on his clipboard back and forth, back and forth.

"Stop playing with your fucking papers and get me to a bathroom. Or I'm going to pee right here on the floor."

"I'll get you a female officer in a minute to do just that. In the meantime, tell me about Jack."

"I'm not going to tell you anything about Jack or anyone else."

"Do you know where he was five days ago?"

"He was with me."

"Where?"

"Fifth Avenue, asshole. We're homeless."

"How nice for you. And Santana?"

"Haven't seen him for months."

"When was the last time you were down in South Carolina?"

"It's been a very long time. Maybe a year. Look, you going to get me to a bathroom or not?"

"In a minute. You saw your father just last week. He bailed you out of jail. Tell me what happened there?"

"Nothing."

"Clearly something happened. He reported you missing."

"Of course, he did."

"Based on what I'm reading here, he was very concerned about you."

"He's always concerned about me."

"Sounds like a loving father."

Austin softened for the first time. Her voice slightly cracked, and she said gently, "He is. . . . Or he was."

Austin started to cry. She realized for the first time that the police would not be asking this many questions if her father was just playing a game. The thought that he might actually be gone was starting to hit her and hit her hard. If he was gone, then the only man who ever actually believed in her might no longer be there to do so.

She felt herself starting to soften, starting to feel vulnerable. She hated that feeling, and so she did what she always did when placed in that position. She hardened. She became mean and defiant.

Austin spoke almost with a growl. "Get me out of here. Get me out of here, now."

Sergeant Hall matched her tone and directness. "Where's your father?"

"I don't know where he is!"

"What did you do to him?" he asked with force and authority.

Austin started to move aggressively in her seat, frustrated that she could not walk off her agitation. Still yelling, she barked back, "I did nothing to him. And neither did my friends."

"How can you be so sure of that?"

"Because I love him, damn it! I love him. I'd never do anything to him. And I'd never let them do anything to him either. I'd kill them if they touched him."

Sergeant Hall looked at her intently. He read her face, and he read her emotion. It was clear to him that she knew nothing. And so he wrapped things up.

"I'll get someone in here to process your paperwork. We'll transfer you to the Salvation Army for detox."

"I'm not going to detox."

"Well, Miss Stewart. The courts say otherwise."

Austin sat back in her chair, exasperated. Then, with one last act of defiance, she started pulling at her cuffs violently. Sergeant Hall moved back to keep out of her way. She pulled and thrashed until she had no more energy.

"Are you done, young lady?" was all he asked.

She paused for a moment and then stood up as straight as she could with her hands still attached to the table. She leaned forward and stared him right in the eye.

"Not yet," was all she said.

A few seconds passed until Sergeant Hall heard something below the table. He pushed his chair back and looked underneath, where a puddle of urine was forming under Austin's feet.

Gracie spent the next two days moving from one place to the next, never sure when she'd be found out for what she'd done. Little did she know that Mimi was so distraught over the news of her husband's possible demise that she had thought of little else. And once Austin was sent back to detox, her focus, as usual, became completely centered on herself. The only one thinking of Grayson was Gracie, and he was all she thought about.

The more she considered what life would be like on the run, the more she second-guessed her decision. What was worse, life with Austin or life in the shadows? Was there any difference between the two? At least with her, Grayson would see what true love was—unselfish, unconditional love. With Austin, he would never feel a mother's love. He'd be constantly passed over for Austin's latest need for men or drugs. And yet this thing Gracie had done did not feel right.

She packed her things and got Grayson back in the car. She was still unsure what to do, but she was leaning toward heading back to Okatie. She decided that Charleston would be a good spot to lay low for a while. It was close enough that she could get to River Soul in a couple of hours. And it was far enough away from Atlanta that no one would think to look there.

She traveled east on I-20 and then turned onto I-26 east until she hit Charleston. She found a mid-range hotel near several downtown hospitals and took advantage of the first set of clean towels she'd seen in days to get them both cleaned up and presentable. Grayson was restless, so she got him in a stroller and merged out onto the very busy streets, packed with tourists.

She moved down Market Street and walked down the center shops, filled with local merchants selling their wares at the best price they could negotiate. It was hard to maneuver the stroller with all the people traffic, but it was nice to be out and about. She also felt safe amid all the people. No one would recognize her in the crowd. For the first time since she left, she took the hat off her head and turned into the sun. It felt good.

After several hours of walking, she found a nice restaurant on a side street. She had she-crab soup and shrimp and grits, both Lowcountry favorites and something she missed while in Atlanta. And it was certainly better than the fast food she'd been eating while on the road.

After paying in cash, she gathered Grayson's things and moved outside the restaurant. She was halfway down the street when she heard from behind her, "Ma'am?"

She turned around, and there was a police officer trying to get her attention.

"Please, hold on," he said as he walked toward her with a sense of purpose. Gracie was not sure what to do. In the back of her stroller was the bag with all the cash and the gun. She had not been comfortable leaving it in the hotel room. She was prepared to do what she had to do if Austin or Jack found her, but she was not prepared to hurt an innocent person, let alone a police officer.

As he got closer, he put his hand on his side. Gracie assumed he was going for his gun, and in that brief moment, she decided she was prepared to go to jail or die for the momentary privilege and responsibility of caring for the vulnerable child who sat just inches away from her. If she had done everything she could do, then so be it. She was prepared to live with the consequences or die with them if that was her fate.

The officer came within a few feet, and the hand that had come down to his side went into his pocket. He smiled and pulled out a toy.

"Your little boy dropped this back there. I didn't want him to melt down when he figured that out later today. I've got a couple of kids back home. I know how that can be!" He laughed. "But I don't know what I'd do without them. They mean everything to me."

Gracie was still breathing a bit heavily about what just happened but managed to get out, "Oh, thank you so much. They're very special, aren't they?"

"Yes, they are. Have a nice day, ma'am."

"Thanks. You too."

As the police officer left, Gracie stayed frozen on the sidewalk as hundreds of tourists made their way around her. Her mind was racing as an internal dialogue played out in her head.

I can't do this for the rest of my life. There's no way I can do this to Grayson. He'll never understand it. I can't keep Grayson from people forever. I can't keep him from his family. We have to take the life we're given. And if God can't fix this, I certainly can't fix this.

She finally started to move, this time very deliberately, back toward the hotel. She looked down at the stroller and said to her nephew, "We're going home, boy."

As Austin was finished with her mandatory five-day, lock-down detox, she grabbed her phone and told Jack to come get her. She had a mandatory month-long rehab awaiting her, but there were no facilities with open beds, so she was set free on her own recognizance. She had been told that she was required to keep calling until a bed opened, but that was a call she would never make.

As she sat on the curb smoking a cigarette, she could see a car she did not recognize parked off in the distance. She could tell there was someone in the car, but the reflection off the windshield kept her from seeing who it was. Just another faceless creep, probably looking to score something she either didn't have or didn't want to give, at least not right now. She'd been clean for five days, and she wanted to get high.

Eventually, Jack pulled up, and they started driving back to the hotel where they'd been staying. Austin had been bankrolling their temporary accommodations by stripping, and Jack let her know they were going to be kicked out the next day if she didn't come up with some cash soon.

"You'll need to go work the streets tonight," he said unapologetically.

"How about you, Jack? What are you going to do to pay for something once in a while?"

Jack leaned over and punched her in the face. "Don't talk to me that way, bitch."

Austin put her arms up to protect herself from further harm. "All right, all right. Just let me get high first. Can I at least have that?"

"I'll get you something, but then I want you out there."

Austin stared out the window, more to keep her face away from Jack than anything else. She was sick about what her life had become but still felt that a normal life was even worse than this. She'd never felt comfortable in that life.

She looked at the cityscape as it went by, transforming from upscale to ghetto as they approached their current residence. When Jack pulled into the hotel, she noticed that the same car she had seen before drove past the entrance, but very slowly. Was that a coincidence?

"Jack, I think we're being followed."

"What? By who?"

"I don't know. But I noticed that car back at detox. And it just pulled by here."

"Let me see." Jack got out of the car and went out to the entrance to look up and down the road. Nothing matched the description Austin had given him. He got back in the car. "I don't see anything."

"I'm telling you. It was there."

"Well, who would be following you?"

"Me? Nobody. I've already been found, remember?" She held up her wrists that still showed the marks from where the handcuffs had bruised her. "The cops know where I've been. They must be after you."

"Great! Just great!" He started bashing both hands on the steering wheel until he ran out of steam. He thought for a moment and looked over to Austin. "Go in and get cleaned up. Pack your things and let's get out of here. I've got a deal I need to do down in Miami anyway. We're going to take a road trip. I can't get anything done here if I'm being watched." Austin got out of the car and did as she was told.

Around the corner, tucked into an alley, was a stolen 1972 Ford Falcon. The man inside was simply waiting for an opportunity to walk away and steal another car before his victim made his next move. While he waited, he looked down onto his forearm where a three-inch gash was crudely sewn back together. The wound was healing, but it wasn't pretty.

Gracie got her things together and pulled Grayson out of his stroller and into the car seat. She got into the driver's side and pulled out her phone, which she still hadn't turned on to keep from being located. She thought about turning it on and telling her mother that she was coming back, but she decided that she wanted one last chance to check things out before she came out into the open, in case Austin had made the trip south.

She tucked the phone away and pulled out the paper map she had purchased at a gas station. She had never used paper maps before but had gotten used to them over the last week or so while she had to navigate on her own. She was somewhat impressed with the skills she was developing, however bad the reason might be for needing them.

She got onto Highway 17 heading south toward Beaufort. Although she didn't much remember the drive, she knew from her parents that this was the same way they used to come when they lived in Chicago and flew into Charleston. As anxious as she was with her entry back into her sister's reality, knowing that she was on the same road that her family traveled in happier days gave her a sense of peace she hadn't felt in a while.

And it was a beautiful stretch of road after all, often lined with majestic oak trees and marsh on each side of the road, a road where you wouldn't see another car for miles. She looked back at Grayson, who was occupying himself with the same toy the police officer had found back in Charleston. He looked up and made a silly face, which made Gracie laugh. He laughed as well.

He was so sweet, so innocent. His joyful countenance made it so hard to feel anything but happiness. Despite all that Austin had done to destroy everyone around her, she also had delivered into the family the greatest gift Gracie had ever known.

Gracie studied Grayson's face. His little teeth, so white and tiny. His nose, which he would often wrinkle to make a silly face. His shaggy blond hair that fell down on his beautiful face, covering his ears and curling into locks that would make any woman jealous. Would he be taken away as soon as she got back? Would Austin take this gift from her like she'd taken everything else precious to the family?

She looked at him one last time and decided she should probably keep her eyes on the road. As she turned around to get her bearings, she saw that a family of deer had leapt up onto the highway. She veered to the right but found herself heading straight for the marsh, only a few feet off the road. She overcorrected to the left, and the car began spinning in circles down the middle of the road.

Gracie found herself spontaneously praying for help, which she thought she received when the car slowed down. But in the final rotation, the car caught the end of the road and started to slide down into the marsh. She tried to get out of her seatbelt, but it had locked in place during the spinning, and she could not get it loosened enough to unlock.

As the car rolled deeper into the rising high tide, water started coming into the windows that were open from before the accident. Gracie worked harder and harder to free herself, but she could not. Her distress turned into panic as the water levels rose to the point where it was above her chest. She turned around to see Grayson crying, still in his car seat. As the car sunk deeper into the marsh and spartina grass, it shifted nose down, placing Grayson almost directly above her.

She tried to say something encouraging, but she wasn't sure if that last call for hope was meant for him or herself. "It will be okay, baby Gray. I'll be out of here in no time, and I'll get you too."

But that was one more untruth spoken by a Stewart. The seatbelt had locked for good. She struggled to reach back over her head to free

Grayson from his car seat as the water rose up to her mouth. But the angle of her shoulder strapped into the belt would not allow her to do so. She thought if she could free him, he could crawl out and hold onto something to save himself. But she could not fix this, no matter how hard she tried.

As the water rose above her mouth and then her head, Gracie looked back to Grayson. The sunshine shone through the water and created a halo around the little boy's body. She could see his head and his arms thrashing about, and it was the saddest thing she had ever seen. Her last vision, she thought, would be the terrifying death of her favorite person in the world.

But as she started to lose consciousness, she felt a sense of calm come over her person. The image of her nephew silhouetted by the sun was replaced simply with light playing through the water. The light seemed to move in unison as though it were alive. And then came the same colors she had seen in her dream. Colors all around her, surrounding her like a warm blanket on a cool fall day.

She gave herself one last half-hearted attempt at freedom, but it was not to be. She was gone. Gracie's lifeless body lay only one foot below the surface of the water. But it might as well have been a mile deep, at least for her.

It is said that the sins of the father carry on to the next generation, but who can ever know that for sure? The only certainty that the Stewarts could ever know was that Gracie was her father's daughter.

Who is the cause of suffering? Is it man? Is it the Devil? Is it God? In the valley of despair, every man or woman eventually asks this question. "Who is it that rains down this terror called my life? It cannot be God, for surely no loving being could possibly bring this much pain upon me."

Philosophers attribute suffering to a fallen world. God, they say, offered us the garden, heaven on earth. But man's sin created the chaos all around us. We pay the price of our rebellion as a loving God looks on in tears over the mess we've made. Still others say that surely the Devil delights in our suffering and is the cause of our affliction.

But look deep and you just might find God at the center of it all. Our lives are but a breath of smoke in His eternal plan, all weaved together in His majesty. We are but a whisper in His chorus, a candle lost in the blazing light emanating from billions of suns throughout His universe. We are nothing when compared to His everything. Our striving makes Him laugh, and our pride puffs up an imaginary self—the people we think we are based on our own merits.

He twists and turns our circumstances, bringing us to the end of the confidence we might have in anything we say, think, or do. In the end, we have nowhere else to turn but to Him. His power stands in greatest contrast to our contemptible weakness. His grace abounds all the more as we fall deeper into the pit.

And so it was with Mimi when the call came in to interrupt the little sleep she had known. But she was anxious for that call, whatever news it might bring. She sat up quickly and grabbed the phone.

"Hello?"

"Is this Mary Stewart?"

"Yes. Yes, it is."

"Mrs. Stewart, I need you to go to your front door. A Beaufort County sheriff is standing outside. His blue lights are on so you can see that he's one of us."

"Wait, what?"

"It's the middle of the night, Mrs. Stewart. He didn't want to alarm you by banging on the door. It's Sheriff Matthews. You two have spoken before."

"Yes, yes, I know him."

"Ma'am, I will stay on the line until you two have connected. Can you go to your front door, please?"

As Mimi opened her bedroom door, she could see blue lights revolving around her living room, coming from the patrol car.

"I see the lights," Mimi said to the dispatcher.

"Very good, ma'am. Let me know when you have opened the door." Mimi looked through the glass side panel and could see him. She turned on the living room lights and unlatched the door.

"Mrs. Stewart, have you two connected?" came a question from the phone.

But Mimi was too focused to answer. She opened the door to see the sheriff looking quite stern. Behind him, at the car, was his partner. The sheriff tipped his hat in a formal show of respect. "Mrs. Stewart. I'm sorry to disturb you so late, but this is quite important. May I come in?" Mimi hesitated, if only to absorb the serious tone of his request. "Yes, yes, of course."

The phone was in her hand, but down by her side. The voice of the dispatcher asking for confirmation got louder and louder, but Mimi did not hear it.

Sheriff Matthews extended out his hand. "May I speak to the dispatcher?" Mimi handed him the phone.

"Hi, Sandra, it's Mitch."

"Okay, thank you."

The dispatcher hung up the phone, and he handed it back to Mimi. She reached out and took it, moving with uncertainty around this seemingly delicate situation.

"May we sit down over here, ma'am?"

Mimi extended her arm to indicate her agreement, but her head lowered as she made her way to the couch. She was certain she was about to hear about Peter's body being found, and she was bracing herself for that news. "Is it Peter?" she asked. "Did you find him?"

With a somber expression, Sheriff Matthews shook his head. "No, ma'am. No news on that front."

"I don't understand then. Why are you here?"

"Mrs. Stewart, do you know where your daughter is?"

"No. I told you, we haven't spoken to Austin in weeks."

He shook his head again. "Actually, I'm asking about Grace. Grace Elizabeth."

"Oh, yes, she's in Atlanta with my grandson, Grayson."

"If I told you that she wasn't actually there, would that make any sense to you?"

Mimi thought for a moment. "No, not really. She took him back there to give me a break for a while. To give me some room to process all of this."

"Have you spoken to her since she left?"

"Well, no, now that I think about it. I haven't spoken to her."

The deputy pulled out a bag that was heavy and wet, and it was inside a much larger, clear plastic bag. "Do you recognize this bag?"

Mimi was confused, but she looked at the bag. "I'm not sure. I don't think so."

"What if I told you that it was your daughter's?" He paused. "Grace Elizabeth, that is."

"Gracie is an adult. I don't know what things she buys. What is this all about?"

"We found this in Grace's car."

"Really? Wait, why would you be looking in Gracie's car? And do you cover Atlanta from here?"

"No, ma'am. We don't. And we don't cover the Charleston area either."

"Charleston?"

"Your daughter has been in Charleston, at least recently."

"Why would she be there?"

"That's what we're trying to figure out."

"I'm sorry, but I don't understand."

"Ma'am, the contents of this bag included almost ninety-five-hundred dollars in cash."

"Where would she get that? She's a teacher and can just barely make ends meet."

"That's also a good question. But there's something even more curious. There was a gun in this bag. A loaded gun."

"All right, what the devil is going on here? What are you talking about? You're talking in riddles."

Sheriff Matthews had been assessing Mimi's reaction, to see if she knew anything. When it was clear that she was as confused by all of this as he was, his tone changed, and he prepared to break the news to her.

"Mrs. Stewart. I don't know why, but I seem to be the bearer of very bad news for you as of late."

"Yes, it's been a rough couple of days."

"No, ma'am. Not just that. There is more I have to tell you."

"More what?"

"Your daughter. Um . . . Gracie. She . . . she . . ."

"What about Gracie?"

"Well, ma'am, for some reason your daughter was in Charleston. It appears she was headed this way when . . ."

"You must be confused. She's in Atlanta. I'll call her right now and you can see."

"Okay, Mrs. Stewart. That sounds like a good idea."

Mimi picked up her cell phone and dialed. There was a brief pause until the sound of a ringing phone filled the room. The sheriff reached into his pocket and pulled out a phone. He pointed it to Mimi, showing her the call identifier as "Mom."

"Is this your daughter's phone, Mrs. Stewart?"

Mimi looked completely confused. "Yes, it is."

"We extracted this from her car near Edisto Beach. It's been underwater for a while. It's a miracle that it still works."

"Underwater?"

"Yes, ma'am. Underwater."

There was a long pause, until the sheriff continued. "You see, as I said, it appeared that your daughter was driving this way. We're not sure what happened, or exactly when it happened, but there was an accident. Your daughter's car veered off the road—"

Mimi stood up. "Oh, my God! Gracie! Where is she? We have to go see her now. I'll go get dressed."

"Well, we do have to go see her, but it's not good, ma'am. I'm very sorry to tell you that your daughter died in that accident. And as hard as this is, we need you to identify the body when it gets here tomorrow."

Mimi said nothing. She simply sat down on the couch, looking as though she'd just been punched. She held her arms in a self-embrace, and she started rubbing her shoulders. She rocked back and forth like she was holding a child.

The tears did not come then. It was just all too much to absorb. The only thing that did come was the nausea. It hit her suddenly, and she leapt up and ran to the bathroom where she vomited violently.

Sheriff Matthews sat on the couch, not sure what to do. Not sure how to help. He waited until she returned.

"Is there anything I can do?"

Mimi simply shook her head and then finally asked after a long silence, "So how does this work? Where do we go?"

"Her body is being transported here. Given the suspicious contents of this bag, it's an active investigation. When they called up Grace's name in the computer, they saw my involvement with your family. And given all that has happened recently with your husband, well, this just doesn't look very good."

"Not good, how?"

"Well, Mrs. Stewart, your husband's missing and likely dead, and we found your daughter with cash and a gun. It seems quite unusual, don't you think?"

"I think nothing of the sort! Neither my husband nor Gracie had a suspicious bone in their body."

"Well, ma'am, I hear that, but you have to admit, it just all seems kind of strange."

Mimi did not reply, as it was indeed just so strange. She sat thinking through it all and then, as if in denial, said, "She was just in Atlanta. None of this makes sense."

They both sat in quiet stillness, until Mimi's eyes got wide in a hurry. She stood up and shouted, "Grayson! Where is my grandson?"

"He was in the car, too, but—"

"Not him too! No!" And that is when the tears came, so much and so fast that the sheriff could not get her attention. She sobbed for several minutes until he got up and sat next to her.

"No, ma'am, not him too. Grayson is okay."

Mimi looked up with hope for the first time since she opened the door. "He's okay?"

"Yes, he's fine. We treated him for some hypothermia. He'd been in the marsh for a very long time, until someone finally saw the car behind the spartina grass."

"In the marsh? What do you mean? What marsh?"

Sheriff Matthews started to explain with his hands the picture of what happened. "The car slid into the marsh off the road and went headfirst to the bottom, like this. As the water filled the car, the front seat was completely submerged. But the back end rose up into the air, and the tide never reached his face. Since he was strapped into his car seat, he was suspended over top of the water. It was cold last night out there, but not so cold as to cause damage. He was bitten by some bugs, but that appears to be the worst of it."

"Where is he?"

"Well, ma'am, he's out in the car with my partner. We weren't quite sure how this would go or what you might know. But it's clear to me this has all caught you by surprise. If you are well enough, we'd like you to—"

Mimi got up and rushed out to the car, where Grayson was in the back seat. He was calm until he saw Mimi, when he immediately started to cry and reach out his hands to her. She removed him from the car seat and held on to him as tightly as she could.

She carried him into the house and held him while the deputies finished their paperwork. As they drove away, Mimi rocked Grayson to sleep, all the while whispering in his ear that everything would be okay. And for him, it would be okay. But for Mimi, she was not so sure. She had lost everything else in the world that she once held so dear. First, her youngest daughter to a life she would never understand. Then her husband. And now, her firstborn. Only this young Southern boy had survived, and she would hold on to him for as long as she could.

As she rocked him until dawn, Mimi lived through the darkest night of her soul, even while holding a glimpse of heaven in her hands. In the silence that night, she came to realize that her life was no longer her own. She would spend the rest of her days raising this boy. But more than that, there was nothing about this new life that even closely resembled the dream she once held so dearly, so clearly. She was no longer who she once was, and she would never be what she dreamed she would be.

She came to know that despite what most people think, in the face of unimaginable loss, men and women never actually ask the question "Why?" That question is asked only when the mind is still engaged, when there is still fight left in the body. But when the deepest pain comes, the mind gives up, and the body is drained to the point of utter exhaustion. There is nothing left to ask. And that is when God can finally have His way.

In the midst of our sorrows, we walk down a tightrope strung across an endless chasm. To fall to the left leads to an ongoing cycle of one event after the other with no meaning behind any of it. It is hell on earth. To fall to the right, one flings into the unknown, confident only in the One who can save. Some would call it heaven, but it is only a reflection of heaven. It is a life of utter helplessness, completely dependent on a God who calls Himself love.

While some might see that as a prison, others experience it as total freedom. To trust completely in a God who only wants you to experience His love is just like a child who depends on the largesse and loving embrace of his mother and father. This child feels no sense of responsibility, no sense of worry, and total confidence in an expected end.

This truth will set man free.

It is not man. It is not sin. It is not the Devil who places us on the tightrope. It is God. The rope is a frustrating and scary place to be. It's where all lukewarm and double-minded people reside. It is filled with worry and fear of falling. We were never meant to reside on the rope. Ultimately, our only choice is to fall left into the hell we know or fall right into the loving unknown.

And on that night, Mimi traded the person she imagined for the person she was meant to be. She looked down and jumped.

YEAR 31

Austin reclothed after a long night of stripping at a rundown club north of Miami. Her body could no longer be showcased at the more upscale clubs. Heroin chic only looked good to a point. Sooner or later, even the creeps found the skeletal, emaciated look unappealing. The tips dried up first, and then before long, the general manager kicked her out. She bounced from one club to the next, each one bringing her further into the cesspool of humanity.

She was tired of this place and wanted to head back to Atlanta. They'd been down here for five months now after what was supposed to be only a couple of days. But word was that people were still looking for Jack back in Georgia, so South Florida would have to be home for a while longer.

She had no network here, and while Jack had promised they would get married, he had long since lost interest. He kept her around only while she was useful.

Her life was no longer her own. She was at Jack's mercy for everything she needed. She traded all her dignity, all her peace, and all her money for his assurance that he'd keep the drugs coming. It was the only currency he had with her, but it was all he needed to keep her wherever he wanted.

But these few moments out of each day, while she waited for Jack to come pick her up, were her own. She loved this time of night. The normal people were not up yet, and most of the wild crowd had finally crashed or were too drunk to be out and about. It was one of the few times she felt at peace.

Austin walked out into the night air and lit up a cigarette. She sat down on the sidewalk, knowing that it would be another ten minutes before Jack would arrive, if he did show up at all. He only came to get her about half the time, but if she ever took a cab home on the days he actually did show up, he'd slap her around for wasting his time. So more often than not, she'd be on her own for a long while, sitting comfortably in the warm Florida breezes.

She looked up at the night sky. She contemplated the stars and thought back to a time when she would sit in the backyard of River Soul, watching the reflection of the moon ripple in the current of the Okatee. As confining as her family was to her, she still loved that place. She felt more at home there than anywhere else.

She was startled when one of her fellow strippers stumbled out from the door behind her with the manager, who had stayed after closing to be with her. Austin sat up quickly, and the couple both giggled that they'd been caught together. They stumbled off in a drunken stupor without saying a word. There were no friendships at clubs like these. Only fellow travelers, running from one thing or another.

Austin's heart was still racing as they finally walked out of sight. She had been on edge lately. She couldn't shake the feeling that she was being watched—all the time. Jack had said the same thing, but he was always paranoid some cop was going to jump out of the bushes and haul him away. But she felt pretty certain at times that someone was nearby, watching her every step.

She had that feeling again now. It freaked her out, so she stood up and started looking around.

"Is anyone there?" she screamed out into the stillness.

No reply.

"I've got a gun, and I know how to use it."

Nothing.

She supposed that it was just her nerves, and she pulled out her phone to call Jack. He did not answer. As she went to dial the number for a cab, she heard a sound around the corner.

"Hey, I know someone's there. What do you want?"

Silence.

"Where are you, asshole?" she said under her breath to Jack, wherever he was.

She did not have a gun, but she did have pepper spray, and she pulled it out of her purse. She looked around and decided that it was better to walk headfirst into trouble than to sit back and wait for it to come. She mustered up her courage and started walking in the direction of the sound.

She extended out her arm with the spray pointed in that direction and turned the corner, prepared for whatever might come her way. Just as she turned the corner, a car turned on its headlights, blinding her to the point where she had to put her head down. But she would not go down without a fight, and she sprayed in the direction of the car until the canister was completely empty.

She heard nothing and started to panic. Whatever protection she possessed had just been sprayed into the air with no effect. She was about to turn and run when she heard laughing. Whoever was in that car was headed straight toward her. She knew she could not outrun anyone while wearing stiletto heels, so she held her ground.

As he came closer to her, she got down in a crouch, ready to fight. It was impossible to see who it was with the lights still shining behind him and into her eyes. When he was close enough, she mustered all her strength and then finally took a swing.

The man grabbed her arm in midair and stopped the momentum of her punch. Again, he started to laugh.

"Well, look at you! You sure gave my windshield a piece of your mind."

The voice sounded familiar, and she looked up. Jack. Austin was temporarily relieved and all at once very angry again.

"You son of a bitch," she screamed at him with as much anger as she'd felt in a long while. "Do you know what you just put me through?"

He laughed again. "Whoa, doggie. Feisty girl!"

"Why did you do that to me? You gave me a heart attack."

"I just wondered what you did while you were waiting for me. Thought I'd come a little early to check it out."

"I'm not doing anything but waiting for your sorry ass each night!"

Jack chuckled, but less enthusiastically. His face turned sour, and he grabbed her arm. "Now get in the car before I kill you for real."

Austin looked at him with intensity and then pulled her arm away. She stormed over to the car and slammed the passenger side door as she got inside. Jack laughed again, got in the car, and turned on his wipers to clear the pepper spray. He pulled out of the lot and drove off toward their hotel room for the night.

As the taillights faded away, a muscular man with long hair came out of the shadows and watched intently as the car drove out of sight. He looked down at his watch and pulled out a pad and pen he kept in his back pocket. He made a few notes and placed them back into his jeans.

He started punching the air, and his anger grew with each swing. He looked down and saw a bottle on the street. He picked it up and flung it into the darkness, waiting to hear the sound of broken glass in the distance. He took a few more swings at nothing, bouncing around on his feet like a boxer. Eventually, his anger dissipated, and he calmed down. He took a few breaths and then walked off down the street into the darkness.

As night descended on Miami, Jack got in his car and headed to his usual spot. Austin had already left for work, and it was time for him to go to work as well. Austin's tip money was no longer supporting them, and he needed to get out on the streets to deal. He had found a corner not owned by any particular gang and had set up shop a few weeks ago.

His car was known to the locals, and they would approach him on a regular basis. He dealt mostly in heroin but had added a little bit of everything else as customers expressed a need for this or that. He was amazed at how easy it was to source and to deal. No matter where he was, there was always a part of the population that would require his services.

He was earlier than usual tonight. He wanted a few moments to relax before the busiest time kicked in, usually around 1 a.m. By then, the day's supply had run out for most of his customers, and they were looking to score something to get them through the night. He was only too happy to oblige.

He drove around the corner and into an alley, pulling out a joint. He put his head back on the seat and thought he might catch a few moments of sleep before he had to kick into high gear. The pot would relax him.

Despite the stress of living on the street, he loved this life. He was not a big-time dealer, which suited him just fine. There was too much stress in that role, always defending your turf against rival gangs. Although that meant he had to move constantly from one place to the next, it also offered the freedom of working when he wanted, and it reduced the violence to a minimum.

While he was not king of the hill, he had enough power over the people in his life to feel like he was in charge. Austin, and all the people like her, were weak enough to control and manipulate without much effort. The combination of manic insecurity and physical addiction made them fodder for his threats and domination.

After rubbing out the joint, he sat back in his chair. Before closing his eyes again, he could see someone in his side view mirror approaching from the back. He was annoyed and shouted out his open window.

"Not open for business. Beat it!"

The man paid no attention.

"I said that I'm not open for business!"

The man approached even more deliberately. To make his point more forcefully, Jack reached under a newspaper on the other car seat and pulled out a .45 pistol. He liked a .45, even though it was bulkier than a .38, because he could use it as a striking weapon rather than a shooting weapon. A shooting would be investigated by the police, but a beating was rarely ever reported.

Jack pointed the gun out his window, assuming the man would back off. He actually got closer and leaned into the car. Sensing that this was no ordinary customer, Jack put the gun to the man's forehead.

"Look, asshole. I told you to back off. You want some of this?"

The man smiled, which was not Jack's intended reaction. In one swift motion, he took the gun from Jack by lowering his head and grabbing the barrel of the gun with both hands. He thrust it up, smashing Jack's hand against the top of the door. After weakening Jack's grip, the man twisted the gun to the side, breaking Jack's trigger finger with a loud crack. In a circular motion, he moved the gun up again until it was pointed backward at Jack. Then he simply pulled it from Jack's hands. It all took less than three seconds.

In horrific pain, Jack began to scream as he grabbed at his hand and pleaded.

"Dude, okay, okay. I'll give you whatever you want. Everything is in my trunk. Here are the keys."

The man took the keys but did not stop. He pushed the gun into Jack's cheek, breaking off a couple of molars inside his mouth. Again, Jack screamed in pain.

"Shut up or I'll shoot," said the man in a very authoritative, husky voice.

"Dude, I told you, take whatever you want. I won't fight you."

The man pulled the gun back only enough to open the door, and then he thrust it back in Jack's face, buried deep in his cheekbone. He knew that simply holding a gun to a person's face could be easily defended, as he had just proven with Jack. But to press his head backward with the gun not only kept the defender off balance but ensured that any defense would be more difficult to execute.

The man pulled him out of the car. As Jack got partially to his feet, the attacker slammed Jack's head into the top of the car, which broke his nose. Now bleeding profusely, Jack could not keep his balance as the man dragged him across the car toward the back, never once letting him get both feet on the ground at the same time. At the end of the car, he slammed Jack's face against the back window. The pain caused him to pass out.

Jack's attacker dropped him to the concrete where he hit face-first, breaking off all his front teeth. While Jack lay unconscious, the man grabbed a bag he had brought with him. Inside the backpack was a roll of duct tape, rope, and scissors.

The first thing he did was adhere the tape across Jack's excessively bloody mouth. He taped his legs together and then his arms behind his back. Then, like Jack was a steer in a rodeo, he placed the rope in between Jack's bound hands and his bound feet and pulled tight, causing his feet to rise behind him toward his hands.

The man took the keys and opened the trunk of Jack's junker. Inside were boxes and bags of all kinds of drugs. He grabbed them and dumped them as quickly as he could in the alley. He picked Jack up like a child and threw him into the trunk, banging his head along the way. He stared down at his prey and took great pleasure in watching him bleed.

He closed the trunk and turned around to get into the driver's side door but found himself looking at four junkies watching the entire scene. He went to grab the gun, but before he could, all four of them raised their hands to show they were no threat. The four men stayed perfectly still for a few seconds, focused on the attacker, until one of the four broke his gaze and looked down at the drugs scattered across the ground. He lowered his hands only slightly and pointed at the bounty.

The attacker nodded his head. After all they had just witnessed, all they cared about was what was in it for them. The man relaxed his attack position and waved them on. All four of them grabbed as much as they could, stuffing them in every pocket until the drugs were gone.

After collecting all the loot, the four men stood up and looked at the gunman, asking permission with their eyes to walk away. He simply nodded. They turned around slowly at first but then ran off with excitement about their good fortune.

"What scum," he said, partially out loud to no one but himself.

He got into the car and scanned his body. He was amazed that he had not a scrape or a bruise to speak of. His training had served him well. He turned on the motor and looked to the rearview mirror before backing out. Knocked around in the struggle, the mirror was pointing directly at him.

He looked at his reflection and paused. His hair was very long now, and he had grown some facial hair to disguise his appearance. His face was thinner but more muscular than it ever had been in the last thirty years. No one else would have recognized him. But he knew who he was. There was no hiding from himself.

He looked into his own eyes, the windows to his soul, and he spoke. "What have you become, Peter Stewart? What have you become?"

When Jack awoke, he found himself strapped to a chair, with his hands tied behind his back. He was in a darkened room in a house he did not know. He was very confused. If this had been about the drugs, his attacker would have taken them when offered. If this had been a gang hit, he'd be dead by now. But this? This made no sense.

Every part of his body hurt. His arms were sore from being tied behind his back, but much more than that, his injuries were severe. His vision was blurred, and he had a banging headache. He was having trouble seeing or thinking. He was too disoriented and too severely beaten to be afraid, but he knew he had to clear his head for whatever was coming his way. As he moved his body around to assess the damage, he was startled to hear a voice come from directly behind him.

"Good morning, sunshine."

Jack tried to swivel his head around, but he could not turn enough to see who it was. His mouth was so swollen it was hard to speak, and his words almost whistled through his broken teeth.

"Who the fuck are you?"

"Such language from a little child."

Peter reached down and twisted Jack's broken finger, eliciting a scream.

Once Peter let go, Jack stopped screaming, but he was still breathing hard from the pain.

"How about we talk in a more civilized manner?"

"Just let me out of here. Let me out now!"

"I'd say you are in no position to tell me what to do."

Jack kept trying to swivel around to see who was talking to him.

After taunting him with the mystery, Peter finally got up and walked around in front of him. Jack could not see well, and he tried to wipe away the blood dripping down over his eyes by moving his face down onto his shoulders. He was able to clear enough away so as to make out shapes and features.

He looked at the man, trying to assess who had done this to him. But there was nothing Jack could register.

"What is it that you want?"

"You."

"I'm flattered," Jack said sarcastically, "but I'm taken."

"Yes, both literally and figuratively."

"Stop talking in riddles. You obviously want something, so tell me what it is."

Peter sent a left hook across Jack's face, causing what was left of a few teeth to fly out onto the floor.

Jack closed his eyes and tried to summon all his courage. Weakness on the street was death. But after a few minutes, he could not take the pain any longer, and he started to cry, spewing blood out of his mouth as he sobbed uncontrollably.

Jack's original defiance had spurred Peter's anger forward, but seeing this young man break down because of Peter's brutality made him ill.

He made his way to the bathroom and stood there for a few moments, until he threw up all over the floor. He fell against the back wall of the bathroom and sunk down to the ground where he tried to absorb all that he had just done. He leaned over and heaved again.

Eventually, he got up to wash his face. His goatee was dripping with vomit, but more than that, his shirt was covered in blood. He put his finger up to touch the blood, as if that would somehow explain what he was now doing.

For the first time in six months, he started to have doubts about the plan he had been obsessed with implementing. With just a day of revenge under his belt, his anger had dissipated long enough for the second-guessing to creep in.

The sight of Jack's blood on his shirt wasn't helping his courage, so he pulled it off, exposing the giant cross on his chest. He didn't want to look down at the tattoo. Somewhere deep inside, he knew that God was watching all of this, and he would be called to account for what he was doing.

But he was in too deep, so he hardened his heart, washed off his face, and returned to the room where Jack was sitting.

This defiant little creep had become more compliant after his sobbing episode. With weakness already displayed, he might as well go all the way.

"Dude, I don't even know you. What do you want from me? I'm begging you to stop. Tell me what to do and I'll do it. I swear I don't know you. What do you want from me?"

"You know me, but I meant nothing to you at the time. You had your sights set on something else—something very precious to me."

"Dude, I swear to you, I don't know you. You have me confused with someone else."

Peter's comment about his precious daughter enraged him all over again. He remembered why he was here, to avenge his daughter's abuse.

He pulled out the hunting knife strapped to his belt and approached Jack. With his conscience seared, Peter went in for the kill.

Jack noticed the big cross on Peter's chest and searched his memory for anything that might save him. But seeing Peter's eyes, Jack knew this was it. He was done for. In one, last desperate measure, he screamed out into the room, "Help, somebody, please help me!"

Peter took delight in his fear and added to it by letting him know he was hopeless. "No one can hear you, boy."

Jack noticed something about the word, "boy." This man said boy with such emphasis that it sounded familiar. And then it hit him. This was Austin's father. He was both excited that he finally knew what this was all about and fearful that he knew where this anger was coming from.

He scanned Peter very quickly. He had to act fast if he had any hope for survival. The cross on Peter's chest gave him an idea. He looked up at Peter and said, "I know no one else can hear me, but you can."

It was the only thing that could have stopped Peter. Jack knew that Peter held himself accountable to a self-righteous standard no one could live up to. He knew by Peter's actions that he no longer cared what Jack thought of him. But he knew Peter still cared about what he thought of himself. Or so he hoped.

"You know this isn't who you are."

"You don't know anything about me, boy."

"Yes, I am just a boy. And you are my spiritual father."

It sounded like such crap coming out of Jack's mouth that it jarred Peter back into the reality that this was a conniving, manipulative man sitting in front of him. So Peter sent a right cross across Jack's chin.

"You don't care anything about spiritual things in your life," Peter yelled at him.

After recoiling from the punch and moving his jaw around to make sure it wasn't broken, Jack started to laugh.

"Ah, there he is, the hypocritical bastard who wants to save me. Is this what Jesus would do? I always wondered."

Peter was infuriated and punched him again.

"This is why I never listened to all your preaching. Because I knew this is who you really are. You stand there and judge me for the very things you are doing to me right now. If God does exist, just imagine how he's judging you at this very moment. You're going to hell right along with me." Jack could see him thinking. "That's right, buddy boy. You know I'm right."

Peter stepped back and lowered his arms, which made Jack laugh again. "You Christians are all the same. You can't even follow through on your darkest ambitions. It's no wonder your daughter is dead."

"My daughter is not dead. I saw her walk into the club, right before I came to get you."

Jack stopped and scanned Peter's eyes, back and forth. And then he started to smile. "You don't know, do you?"

"Know what?"

"Oh, this is so good. So ironic. I get to be the one to break the news to you. How wonderful!"

"Shut up and tell me what you are talking about."

"Oh, now the shoe's on the other foot, isn't it?"

Peter raised his hands for another punch, but Jack recoiled his face and said, "All right, all right, I'll tell you."

Peter lowered his fists, and Jack continued. "First of all, bravo. Everyone thinks you are dead. Well done."

Peter took a step forward, annoyed with the delay, and Jack sped up to keep the next punch from coming. "After you left, your special little Gracie took off with Grayson to keep him away from my Austin."

"She's not *your Austin*."

"Oh, I think you'll find that she is. But anyway, back to our little story. After you left, and Gracie left with the baby, she got in a car accident and got wet, very wet. Thanks to you, Daddy, your daughter drowned just a foot underwater. Can you just see her, lifting her head up trying to breathe? So close and yet so far." Jack mimicked a person trying to gasp for air just above his head.

Peter sat down on the floor against the wall. Delighting in his misery, Jack continued.

"But wait, there's more. In the car, they found a gun and a bag of cash. After months of investigation, the police had no choice but to conclude that she killed you. They can't figure out why, but they closed the case anyway. It made a bad situation so much worse. Your hottie wife now has to live with the death of her husband and child, while her favorite daughter was accused of a crime most people would have thought Austin would have committed. Isn't it just precious?"

Peter's entire body slouched down to the ground. Without even touching him, Jack had delivered the worst blow between them. Peter's mind raced through the consequences of what he had done. He had placed too much responsibility on his daughter. Expecting her to care for Grayson while being a fugitive was too much to ask.

He was the one responsible for her accident. The wheels he had set in motion killed her as surely as if he held her underwater himself. He was a failure. He was condemned for all that he had done.

Peter was a captive to the life he had created, but he had also put his entire family at risk in the process. Now Mimi was alone. Or was she? Peter looked up. "And Grayson?"

Jack just looked at him, keeping him in suspense. Infuriated, Peter leapt up and held the knife to Jack's face. "And Grayson?" he asked much more forcefully.

"Don't you worry, Papa, little Grayson is just fine. Austin and I will be collecting him any day now. You surely can't care for him. You're dead, after all."

Peter looked down at Jack and knew what he was going to do. What he had to do. With the weapon held up to the left side of Jack's face, Peter stuck the knife in. It took a few seconds, but the blood rose to surface and started pouring down Jack's cheek and onto his shoulders. Peter dug deeper and pulled the knife down the side of his face, opening up a gash as wide as his finger.

Mimi untied the boat from the dock and pushed the throttle down gently to pull out into the falling tide. After a few disastrous trial trips on the boat, she had learned how to drive it and dock it while keeping a three-year-old sitting still long enough for her to do what needed to be done.

Peter had always taken care of these things, so she had to learn it all from scratch. She was proud of herself for taking charge and learning it on her own. She was now a woman of the river, in both body and soul.

Grayson loved the water. He would shriek with excitement each time Mimi recommended they head down to the boat. It became one of so many things they would do together throughout his childhood, things that only a family living on the banks of the Okatee could understand and appreciate. Or at least, that's what Mimi would say. Grayson only knew that he was happy and loved. Nothing else mattered.

As Mimi sped up to get the boat on plane, Grayson perched himself in the front seating area, leaning into the wind and laughing with a joyful sound that Mimi found delightful. She watched him from the helm with so much joy in her heart that she found herself overflowing with love.

It would sound so cliché to say that he filled a hole in her heart. He did that, too, but it was so much more than that.

She knew that this was her destiny, to raise up a man of character and decency who might just change the world. Whereas she once felt stressed at the thought of starting over with a baby at her age, she now felt perfectly at peace with it. It just seemed the right—and easy—thing to do.

It is said that God has a way of giving us the desires of our hearts. Mimi just knew that her entire life had prepared her for this moment. If there was a God, and if He were love, then He was present with them in the boat that day. And if that's who God was, then she was all in.

She was learning to take what was handed to her and find meaning in all of it, even the bad bits. Everything in her life had brought her to this river on this boat with this boy. Her dreams had taken her only so far. But her reality had brought her to *this* place, right now. She had moments of sadness, when Peter or Gracie or Austin would cross her mind. And yet they were part of her story. They are part of this story. Mimi's story.

Shakespeare once said, through Hamlet, "There is nothing either good or bad, but thinking makes it so." Experiences come and go with the wind, but thoughts shape a life. It is not the things that happen to us from the outside that create us; it's the thoughts that come from the inside that make us either tender or brittle, moldable clay or broken pottery.

As Mimi watched Grayson play with the salty spray coming over the bow of the boat, she contemplated that without Austin and her tragic life, there would be no Grayson. Without Gracie's death, she would not live so passionately for each moment as she did today. And without Peter's disappearance, she would not have become the woman who stood confidently there in the boat, in her favorite place in the world.

She had no destination that morning on the water. They just motored around and took in whatever God handed them at that particular moment. They would discover their day as it unfolded one step at a time. They would take what they were handed and be all the better for it.

As the clock approached noon, Mimi anchored near Lemon Island. They shared some apples and crackers while sipping playfully on some juice boxes. Grayson thought it was funny to see Mimi sip from such a small straw, and he laughed each time she put her lips to the box to take a sip.

In the midst of their fun, Grayson walked over and sat in Mimi's lap, which was unusual for such an energetic boy who rarely sat still. He pointed at himself and said, "Grayson happy." Then he placed his hand on Mimi's heart and asked, "Mimi happy?"

It was, after all, the right question. He had watched her go through so much. He had heard the tone in her voice, he had seen the unintended tears, and he had noticed the oppressive silence in the house as the presence of his family disappeared one person at a time.

Mimi collected him into her arms. "Yes, Grayson. Mimi happy. Mimi is very happy."

There is nothing either good or bad, but thinking makes it so.

Austin made the bed and started cleaning up their hotel room. She was going into withdrawal and needed a distraction to keep her mind off her physical symptoms. She was angry with Jack for a lot of things, but leaving her alone like this for two days was just too much for her to bear.

It was dark now, and she was going to have to burn up the little bit of money she had on a cab ride to work and then pay retail prices for her drugs as soon as she made enough tip money.

She had gathered her things to leave when she heard a knock on the door. A male voice said, "Housekeeping."

Jack had instructed Austin never to let the cleaning crew into the room because they would either steal their drugs or report them to the manager. So she gave their standard reply.

"It says 'Do Not Disturb' on the door. Please go away."

But there was no response.

"Did you hear me?"

Still no reply. Austin realized that it was almost 9 p.m. What housekeeper would be stopping by at that time of night? This was, no doubt, Jack playing a trick on her, testing her to see if she'd open the door. "Jack, get in here. I need you to take me to work."

Still nothing.

"Jack, this isn't funny. Get your ass in here."

Silence. She contemplated going over to open the door anyway, but then a wide range of possible scenarios started to enter her mind. Had someone tracked them down? Was it the police or a rival drug dealer? She froze perfectly still in the middle of the room. She had already given away her presence. They knew she was there. So now what?

She looked around the room and tried to guess where the gunshots would eventually come from if the gangs were involved. There was only one part of the room that might be safe. She got down on the floor and crawled over to a back corner, where she stayed for the next hour.

She had been cheating death since she was a child, and so this moment held no particular difference for a woman who had hardened herself to the worst that life could bring her. And what she could not harden she had numbed. Yet there was something about this time, this day, that just seemed to get to her.

In that hour on the floor, she saw her life for what it was. Her entire existence had been a rejection of the reality all around her. As a child, she had rejected her illness. As an adult, she had rejected her health and her sobriety. Then she had rejected her parents, and now she rejected her child.

She had spent her entire life being defined by what she didn't want to be. Knowing what you are not is not the same as knowing what you are. It was so much harder to be something than it was to reject what other people wanted for you. And now she had no idea who she was or what she stood for. She only knew that something had to change. She could not spend the rest of her days running away from what was. She would start running toward something, and she would begin by walking over to the door and seeing who was there.

She stood up and walked with determination toward the front of the room. She thought about looking out the window first but decided that would only demonstrate fear. She prepared herself, turned the handle, and opened the door with confidence. But what she saw sitting on the ground was worse than anything she had imagined.

Outside the door was Jack. Or at least it might be Jack. His face was so distorted it was hard to tell. His hands were wrapped in dock line, and his mouth was taped shut. He was tied to the balcony banister, lying on the concrete with his hands stretched up over his head to where they were tied down.

Sitting on his lap, neatly placed, was a pair of scissors, which Austin used to cut his hands loose. She pulled the tape off his mouth as gently as she could and was horrified to see his lips split in five different places and all his teeth gone. But worst of all were four deep gashes down the left side of his face, crudely sewn together with regular thread.

It took Jack a few moments to gather himself, and he pulled himself up and into the room. He sat down on the bed, and Austin tried to attend to him. He pushed her away.

"Get out," he shouted at her as best he could utter the words through his badly injured mouth. "Just get out of here."

"Jack, you need help."

"Yes, I do. But not from you."

Austin surprised herself. With all this man had done to her, she cared about how badly he was beaten. "You're delirious. I need to get you to a hospital."

"You'll do no such thing. I just need you to leave, now. I only have ten minutes before—" He hesitated.

Austin leaned in, confused about what was really happening here. "Before what?"

"Nothing." He took a breath and sighed. And then he made eye contact with her for the first time and said with resignation, "I just need you to go."

"Jack, please. I need to care for you right now."

"Get out!" His shouting became more insistent.

"Okay, okay. I'll leave. I'll be back in the morning. I'll help you then."

"No, I mean get out. Forever. Don't ever come back here."

"Jack, what are you saying?"

"I'm saying that we're done. How can that be so hard to understand?"

"Why would you say that? I have nowhere else to go."

Jack reached into his pocket. "I'm supposed to give you this."

He reached out and handed her an envelope. She looked in it, and there was $2,000 in cash.

"What do you mean you're supposed to give this to me?"

He looked down at his broken body. "Nothing. It's like you say. I'm delirious. Just go."

"I don't understand what's happening."

"You don't need to understand. Just *go. Go now!*"

Austin went over and placed her hand on him, which he pushed away again. She grew angry, pulled it back, grabbed her things, and walked out.

After a few minutes on the bed, Jack got up and went into the bathroom to try to clean up some of the mess that was his entire body. He tried not to look in the mirror, but he had to assess just how bad it was. He looked. It was worse than he thought, and he wasn't sure how he could ever recover.

He held up his hands to feel the gashes on the side of his face. As painful as the cutting was, it was even worse to have the multiple pricks of the needle as Peter had sewed him up. The broken bones and bruises he could understand, but these cuts were just bizarre. And then to be sewn back together, even stranger.

Peter had made it clear to Jack that if he did not follow his instructions, he would be back, and it would be so much worse for him. The forty-eight hours they had spent together would only be a preview of the anguish he would feel if Peter ever had to come back and finish the job.

Outside, Peter watched as Austin left with her things. He followed her to the dealer on the corner as she bought some of the best heroin she would ever have. And he followed her to the nice hotel, where she would spend the next several days in a drug-induced slumber. While not perfect, at least she was away from Jack and once again numb to her pain.

Peter pulled out his list and crossed off Jack's name. And then he planned where he would go next. Santana—and all the men like him—would have their own time with Peter. Each one would walk away sure that they would do whatever they had to do to keep Austin out of their lives.

Not that she didn't try to make her way back. She approached them all and found it more than a little bit odd that each one had the same four cuts down the left side of his face. What she would never know, and they would never know, is why the four cuts.

But Peter knew. He saw the reason every day when he would shave his beard back into a goatee. There on his face were the remnants of the scars that Austin had left so many years ago in Okatie. These men had left scars on his family that could never heal. And now, every day they looked in the mirror, they would remember just an ounce of the pain that lived in his heart forever.

Only Thelonius Vess would escape Peter's wrath, for Peter remembered how he had humbled himself that night in South Carolina. And Theo had given Peter one of the greatest gifts of his lifetime, a child who now bore his name.

Mimi placed the last of her things in the truck and looked back at her Atlanta home. When she had come back a few days earlier to pack up and sell the house, she had felt completely disconnected, as though no part of their lives ever happened in this place. She had dreaded coming here. It would only remind her of Peter. She could not fathom going through his clothes and getting his affairs in order.

But she found Peter's things particularly easy to manage. He was always neat and organized, so she just assumed that he had gone through one of his typical "purges" just before he left for vacation. Most of his clothes were gone, and what remained was neatly placed into piles in the closet. They were easily packed into boxes and donated.

In his office, virtually all of his files had been discarded, except for everything Mimi needed to know to pay the bills and sell the house. The wills were out on top of his desk, as were the names of their attorneys, financial advisors, and bankers. A folder marked "Important" was placed on top. In it were three different life insurance policies totaling more than $5 million.

She opened the drawers to his desk, and everything was gone except for one leather-bound journal. She opened the book and started reading about their family through his eyes. It was a love letter written across decades, and she found herself in tears as she read through his entries, starting as far back as when Gracie was just a baby. She grabbed a bottle of wine and consumed it along with every page Peter had written. In the early morning hours, she came to his final entry, which was dated just a day before he disappeared.

> What is it to love your family? When does a child stop being a child? Does God ever look at me and say that He no longer is my Father? Can I ever look at Gracie or Austin and claim that I no longer own their suffering? Or their safety?
>
> We are told to live as if everything depended on God and work as though everything depended on us. I am no longer able to discern between the two. I don't know where God leaves off and I begin. If I am His hands and feet for love, am I also His hands and feet for wrath?
>
> What God has made crooked, no man can make straight. But what if we are the ones who made it crooked? Can we fix the mess we ourselves created?
>
> I love you all more than you could ever know.

Mimi closed the journal and looked out at the sun rising through the trees in the backyard. There was no river here, but this place had its own beauty. Rather than live oaks, there were pines and poplars and pear trees, which were just starting to turn colors for the fall.

She noticed an owl staring back at her, so majestic and so confident in his place. She remembered how Austin would name all the birds she saw in this yard and how joyful she would be each time a new one would fly into their lives. Mimi missed those times, even knowing how difficult Austin's childhood had been. At least then, there had been love and trust between them. At least then, Mimi had seen her as an innocent.

Mimi couldn't decide what was worse—knowing that an innocent child had been punished unjustly or knowing that a guilty adult was now throwing away every chance she had ever been given. Was it worse to witness her baby tortured by illness or to never see her child and not know what hell she might be going through right at that very moment?

She looked down and stroked the journal. It was times like these when she missed Peter the most, when he would help give her perspective. But apparently, he was as lost as she was. He just had a way of hiding it better than she did. Or perhaps his faith had held off the anguish long enough for him to figure it out, until it didn't. Without him there, she could only conclude that it mattered not who Austin had become. She was her daughter. She was the little girl who sat in the same chair and beheld the majesty of God, one bird at a time, outside a picture window in Atlanta.

She could hear Grayson start to stir on the monitor. No matter what had happened in her past, she had this boy to care for now. And that is where her attention would lie. She wished that Peter had been able to see what God had placed right before him within Grayson. He would have been able to see that whatever God had taken from him was paid back in full in the unconditionally loving eyes of his grandson. Maybe that would have given his confused soul some clarity.

Mimi had had a dream once—two boys in the South on the beach. Maybe one boy on the river was all she ever needed. She got into the truck, looked back at Grayson and smiled, and then drove away from the life that was no more. She would leave this world with all its problems to all the people who didn't know where heaven really was.

YEAR 32

When Austin arrived back in Atlanta, she was excited and filled with hope. She was home and determined to create a life based on the newfound courage she had summoned in Miami. But as with most decisions to repent, the days and months that followed were filled with weakness and second-guessing. The dream to be reborn meant that sooner or later Austin would have to wake up to reality, and Austin just didn't do reality. She had spent the last decade trying to avoid it.

She entered detox, but detox always led to rehab, and rehab required a level of introspection that was missing in the addictive personality. She became an addict to escape reality, not to analyze it. *It's an oxymoron*, she thought. For her to rise above her addiction, she would first have to define herself as an addict every day for the rest of her life. And to heal relationships, she would first have to explore how deeply she had damaged relationships. It just didn't make sense.

But you can't rise above something until you are willing to face the demon that has grabbed hold of you. Jonah could not be saved until he spent three nights in the belly of the big fish. He was not set free until he finally went to Nineveh. Austin spent many nights in isolated darkness but never once went to Nineveh. She had to learn her life lessons over and over again, never recognizing that if she only did the work to see what she had become, she would be free at last to rise above it.

So far, though, the best she could ever muster in almost ten years was to get to step five in the twelve-step program. Back then, she had written letters to members of her family and admitted to most of her deeds. There were tearful family sessions that gave Mimi and Peter hope. But Austin had an endless capacity to disappoint.

She would stay in a program, it seemed, just long enough to break through the walls her parents had put up to protect themselves. And as soon as those walls were down, she stormed the gates and trampled on their hearts with such disdain that it seemed supernaturally ordained. It just couldn't be that bad unless God wanted it to be that bad.

With each relapse, she had driven the spear deeper into her family. She remembered the day her father finally said that he couldn't take it anymore. He had been the only one to claim that he "would never give up," and yet the day came when he finally did, at least, leave her to herself. She was all at once relieved and saddened when he, like all the others, finally left her in the pit.

He was the only marker she could look back on and know how far lost she really was. But if her father didn't believe in her anymore, then why should she? And now he was dead anyway. There was no chance to ever recover in his eyes.

And so Austin sought to reconnect with each of her old boyfriends, the only people who understood her, the only people she could look at and not feel bad about herself. Yet one by one, they all ignored her outreach, or literally ran from her when they saw her coming. It all seemed too strange.

Every man Austin ever knew had used her and then abandoned her. And now, they were all pushing her away so fast that Atlanta no longer felt like home. So Austin did what she always did—she left to find herself somewhere out there, never realizing that her salvation could not be found anywhere beyond her very own soul.

Austin used the last of the cash she had from the $2,000 and caught a bus to South Carolina.

YEAR 33

Peter always sat in the back pew when he went to church. After all he had done, he wasn't sure if he was welcome in God's house. Surely, he would be thrown out into the darkness, where there would be weeping and gnashing of teeth. He was a condemned man, if not in this life, then in the next.

In the months that followed the last of his violent outbursts, Peter moved from place to place and finally settled in Key West. Everyone was strange in Key West, and he did his best to blend into the crowd long enough to figure out how he would live the rest of his life as a dead man. He wandered the streets by day and came to churches like this at night to see if reconnection to the man he used to be was even possible. While he was dead to everyone else, he was not yet dead to himself.

While there was a certain freedom in his invisibility, he mostly felt trapped. He had the whole world to roam, yet he could not go back to the one place he wanted to be. But he was the one who had built this prison, one act of revenge at a time. His cell walls could only be seen by the one trapped inside them.

As church broke, Peter walked out onto Duval Street and later found himself turning down Whitehead Street where he stopped before the Key

West home of Ernest Hemingway. The author had lived there before he committed suicide later in life. Peter once thought his writing was inspired. But now he found the machismo of man versus beast distasteful.

It was all vanity and chasing after the wind. It left people empty. Once they faced death, his characters no longer feared it. But they also lost all meaning. Apparently, so did Hemingway. Adventure can only take a man so far. Sooner or later, he must remove the distractions of the body and come to peace with his spirit.

The only thing Hemingway's writing got right was the benevolent influence of nature. His books were as much about the place as they were about the people in the place. God's creation had a way of stirring a sense of awe, connection, and peace all at the same time. Nature humbled Peter and inspired him. He wanted to go home to the only place that gave him peace.

Still on the street, he closed his eyes and pictured himself on the river outside River Soul. He found himself sensing the flow of the water beneath his canoe and the feel of the paddle in his hands. In his vision, the sun reflected off the water and temporarily blinded him. He shielded his eyes from the flash of light, and when his eyes finally adjusted, he was startled to see Gracie facing back at him from the bow. He started to cry.

"Oh, Gracie, I'm so sorry for what I did to you."

"It's okay, Dad. I did it to myself."

"Forgive me."

"I forgive you. But can you forgive yourself?"

"I don't think I can. I've gone too far."

"You can never go too far. Do you really think God cannot undo anything you've done?"

"I've turned my back on Him."

"But He's never turned His back on you."

"It's too late."

Gracie looked up at the sky and started moving her arms in a circular motion. As she did, the rays from the sun collected in a sphere just off the side of the canoe. After forming a magnificent mass of swirling light, she held out her cupped hands and the ball moved over into Gracie's palms. She smiled at Peter, took a breath, and blew the orb of light at him, blinding him once again.

When he regained his sight, Gracie was gone. But her presence was replaced with a wave of love that washed over his body. For the first time in his life, he felt completely forgiven, completely free.

As he sat back in his daydream, he heard Gracie's voice surround him in a way that was unlike anything he had ever heard in the real world. Her voice had substance and power, and her words wrapped around him.

"Daddy, if God can forgive a man like Jack, he can surely forgive a man like you."

He walked the streets of Key West for the rest of the night hours and watched the sunrise on the beach the next morning. Peter knew what he had to do. He packed his bags and caught a bus to South Carolina.

YEAR 34

Most people know that the Civil War started in South Carolina. What they don't know is that it wasn't in Charleston. Twenty years before the first shots were fired by the Confederacy to claim Fort Sumter from the Union garrison, the call to secede was proclaimed by US Representative Robert Barnwell Rhett under a seventy-five-foot oak tree in Bluffton, South Carolina. The tree later came to be known as the Secession Tree, and Rhett's followers came to be known as the Bluffton Boys.

But to Austin, the term "Bluffton Boys" had a whole different meaning. These were the men she serviced in a variety of ways in exchange for drugs, money, and lodging. They were her customers, her suppliers, and her abusers all wrapped into one. But they needed each other in a sad and twisted way. Criminals have the same need for connection that normal people do. They just show it in ways that good people could never understand.

Austin came to Bluffton on her way back to Okatie. She had intended to go right to her mother, beg forgiveness, and ask to be taken back into the family. But she had lost her courage along the way and decided to stay in Bluffton for just a few days after the bus dropped her off. A few days stretched into a few months, which then stretched into two years.

She had been so close to her only remaining family for all this time but never made the twenty-minute drive over to her South Carolina home. She was so close to reconnecting, and yet River Soul might as well have been a thousand miles away. She had burned all the bridges that had been rebuilt by her parents at least a hundred times. How would she even begin to apologize?

And how would she explain herself to her son? He'd be six now. She justified that Grayson was better off without a mother like her; she had put herself first with her every action since the day he was born. There came a time when benign neglect was no longer well-intentioned avoidance.

Living so close was both a comfort and a constant reminder that she had walked away from everyone who loved her, everyone who actually cared for her. She knew her parents were right about her and right about what she really needed. And yet, along the way, she felt that she had a right to be whoever she wanted to be, no matter who got hurt in the process. Now she was finally seeing what the consequences of claiming a right to rebellion really were.

It had been a long night, and she had been unsuccessful in finding someone to crash with. It was fall, and the normal tourist traffic from nearby Hilton Head was long gone. People didn't have as much spending money, and that meant less business for her and fewer people to latch on to for a bed to sleep in.

Now she was going to have to rest in her usual spot by the grocery store off State Route 46. She could find something to eat there and then sleep back behind the restaurants on the town square. It was almost 9 a.m., so the food from the morning would already be tossed, and she was certain she could steal a few things from the breakfast crowd before she crashed until nightfall.

By the time she reached her spot, she began to feel the normal pangs from withdrawal. She stared across at the brick wall in front of her and contemplated how she would survive the next twelve hours without something to tide her over. She was so tired of the constant need to hunt for survival. She longed for the days when everything had been handed to her.

Her mind began to wander, and she noticed how poorly these bricks had been laid. She and her father had done a far better job when they built a garden retaining wall together at River Soul. He had taught her so many things . . . back before she stopped listening to anyone except her druggie friends. If only he were still around to teach her now. She would listen this time.

As her withdrawal symptoms grew, she put her head back and closed her eyes to try to concentrate on something else. She could smell the wood burning from the outside fire pits, and it reminded her of Christmas in Chicago, when her father would light a fire and put on some music before they were allowed to open presents. It built a level of anticipation that her father loved but she and Gracie found stressful. If only that were her sole anxiety now.

As her mind started to clear a little from all the drinking she had done just a few hours before, she remembered that she kept a small dose of heroin hidden in her purse for exactly this purpose. She sat up quickly, pulled it out, and went to work. She wrapped an elastic band around her bicep and looked for a vein for the next five minutes. Nothing. She pulled off the band and tried her other arm. Nothing again. She repeated that routine until she found a vein in her foot that still had some life in it. She injected and finally began to relax.

She leaned back on her purse, which she used as a pillow. As her physical symptoms started to fade, her mind came back to notice all the things that were happening around her. She could hear the chatter and laughter from the nearby coffee shop as the more civilized people of the world enjoyed their addiction-free lifestyles. She envied them in so many ways, but Austin assumed that while they may not be trapped by drugs, they were probably trapped by greed, or lust, or ignorance of what was really important. We all have our idols. Hers just happened to be something the world judged more harshly.

As the heroin began to do its work, her mind went numb, and she started to drift off. As her body grew frailer from all the damage she had done to it, it wouldn't be long before one of these doses would put her to sleep for good. It was something she hoped for. She didn't have the courage to do it intentionally, but she prayed that someday it would happen accidentally.

But at least without the pain, she could sleep. In a half-awake state, she heard the laughter of a child off in the distance. She thought of Grayson and what his laughter would sound like at this age. The more she thought about it, the closer the laughter sounded until it seemed to her that the sound was right above her body.

Austin opened her eyes and could see a little boy at the end of the alley. He had stopped laughing and was looking down at her. He was still too far away to see well, but he started to walk slowly down the alley toward her. Austin was not happy. For wherever there was a kid on his own, an adult was not far behind. She was in no condition to be dealing with adults at the moment.

She tried to shoo him off, but she was still so drunk and high that she could just barely form words or move her hand. He kept approaching, which forced Austin to try to regain some sense of clarity to deal with the situation. As she opened her eyes more, she found the boy's face close enough to see. He was beautiful. She looked into his eyes, and he smiled.

She was only half conscious, and she wondered if this were another one of her lucid dreams, until she could see a woman run down the road past the alley calling out frantically for this child. The woman doubled back after she saw him out of the corner of her eye and came running down the alley.

She yanked the boy's hand back and pulled him away from Austin. "I told you not to run off like that," she yelled at him. "And I told you never to approach a stranger."

The woman looked down at the pitiful wretch in front of her and did her best to show the boy good manners.

"I'm sorry he bothered you."

She pulled the boy away, but he would not be moved.

"Come on, let's go now."

But still he would not be moved.

Finally, she shouted, "Grayson, I said let's go."

Austin heard the name, but it was the last thing she heard. She passed out, and when she next awoke, she would no longer be in the state of South Carolina.

Mimi sat on the windowsill of a high-rise hospital in downtown Chicago. She had spent way too much time at the children's hospital just down the street while Austin was young. Sitting there, looking out at one gray building after the next, reminded her of how dull the world was outside of the South.

It wasn't even Halloween yet, but already it was snowing outside. The flurries came from a washed-out sky and fell to the ground twenty stories below. She could not see where they were coming from or where they were going to. And yet they affected her spirit. How was it possible that something so fragile and so temporary could change her mood so dramatically?

She turned around and looked at her daughter. The view was no better looking inside the room than out. Austin lay on the bed, ventilated and hooked up to more machines than she could count. The incessant beeping drove Mimi insane. As soon as one machine stopped alarming, another one started.

She had seen her daughter near death before, but when Mimi came to realize it was Austin in the alley that day, she knew there was only one place to go. Her combination of illnesses was so rare that only a few doctors knew what to do. They all just happened to be in Chicago. Mimi had Austin airlifted in a medical aircraft directly to Midway Airport. The flight wasn't cheap, but Peter had left her with plenty.

She swung her legs around from the sill and looked at Austin.

Although her eyes revealed someone who didn't even resemble the daughter she once knew, Mimi had learned to see beyond what was in front of her.

The only thing she could see right now was her daughter, so innocent and fragile, just like when she was a child. It no longer mattered to her what her daughter had become. Regardless of what this world had done to define this child, Mimi was a mother and Austin was her daughter. That was the only definition she would accept. Everything else was secondary.

She decided that day to stop thinking of Austin as an addict, or a failure, or a disappointment. Whatever Austin's life had become, it could never change what God had created her to be. Austin's life was a far cry from what Mimi had hoped it would be, what she dreamed it would be. But that would never be a reason to stop loving her, to stop believing in her.

Sometimes dreams define the person. Sometimes the person defines the dream. Austin's life had created a very different Mimi from the one who would have lived on the banks of the Okatee if everything had gone according to plan. Although the life she dreamed may have seemed a happier life, it would not have been as full or as deep.

And so she thanked God for all she had been given. She thanked God for the child who lay in the bed before her. In that moment, she stopped mourning the life that could have been and became grateful for the life that was.

As Mimi watched over her prayerfully, a young man walked in the room with a bouquet of flowers. He was neatly groomed and nicely dressed in slacks and a white button-down shirt. He walked over and placed the flowers next to Austin's bedside.

"Hello, Mrs. Stewart."

Mimi assumed he worked for the hospital and replied politely. "Hello."

The young man looked over at Austin. "How is she?"

"Perfect."

The man smiled. "Yes, she is." He adjusted his tone and rephrased his question. "How is her health?"

"Not so perfect. She's been in a coma for a couple of weeks now. They don't hold out much hope."

"I'm sorry."

"Me too."

"No, I mean, I'm sorry for what I did. Or maybe for what I didn't do, more like it."

Mimi was confused. "Excuse me?"

"I wasn't the man she needed when she needed me."

Mimi looked at him, puzzled. "I'm sorry, I don't understand what you're talking about."

The young man came over and sat next to Mimi. "Mrs. Stewart, it's me. Theo."

Mimi looked at him with amazement. The last time she had seen Theo, he had hair down to his shoulders that covered most of his face.

"Theo?"

He chuckled a little bit. "Yes, it's me. People tell me I look a little different these days."

"What happened to you? I mean, in a good way."

"I guess I happened to me. I decided that I didn't want to be that man anymore, the one that you knew. I saw what you and Mr. Stewart had together and decided that's what I wanted out of life. I chose differently."

She reached over and touched his arm. "How wonderful."

"I'm sorry about Mr. Stewart."

Mimi simply nodded. This was all a bit much to absorb. But then she realized where they were, and a natural question arose. "How in the world did you find us here?"

"I stopped by the house in South Carolina, looking for Austin. I couldn't find her anywhere else. Your neighbor was there, watching Grayson. She told me where you were."

"Did you see Grayson?"

"No, he was napping, which is probably for the best. I didn't want to confuse him. No matter who I might be now, I cannot hide from my past. I don't ever want him to think that my old life lives inside him. He'll have a better chance that way."

She held his hand in silence, until Austin's machines started to change the rhythm of their beeping. They both got up and moved quickly to her bedside. They stood together, not sure what was happening, but they assumed this was it, the end.

And in some ways, it was the end. But in others, it was the beginning. For it was in that moment that Austin opened her eyes and turned to look at the man who may have been just exactly what she needed after all.

YEAR 35

Peter stood at the helm of a boat making its way through the Savannah River, heading out past Tybee Island. He had a family, not unlike his own, gathered in the bow, giggling with excitement over the prospect of making a big catch for the day. He watched them as they spoke and laughed the way normal families do, and he was jealous of their closeness.

His route for the day would be to head north, past Daufuskie Island, just off the southern part of Hilton Head. For lunch, he would take them into Harbor Town, where they would dine underneath the famous lighthouse in the resort plantation called Sea Pines. He used to take his family to the very same spot. One year, they had come on the Fourth of July, and they picnicked on the beach off the famous golf course. The explosions from the fireworks were so close they had to dodge the embers that fell from the sky.

Peter now worked for a fishing guide company that catered mostly to the tourist trade visiting in Savannah. Usually, his customers were bored men who couldn't stand another stroll through the courtyards and squares in the historic part of town, where women gathered for tea and luncheons.

Savannah was beautiful, but people who didn't live in the South didn't know how to appreciate what it stood for, or slow down long enough to enjoy all it had to offer.

But occasionally, and delightfully, he would get families that were there for the adventure of a day on the water. They were excited about the fish, but it was more about the time together and the pictures they would treasure in the years to come. The day was temporary, but the memories lasted a lifetime.

Peter found the irony of his new profession amusing. If Gracie could only see him now. The man who purposefully would not fish, now taught others how to fish. He became known as a capable guide and a seaworthy captain who knew the waters well and was patient with his guests. Most people thought of him as a simple Southern man, which was amusing to a slick Chicago boy.

There was a time when Peter had led a multibillion-dollar business with tens of thousands of employees. But here, it took him over a year to work his way up to be trusted enough to take a boat out on his own. And now, the most challenging decision he had to make was how much beer to pack for his guests.

Peter loved the simplicity of it all. His work was tangible. He and his guests either caught fish or didn't. There were no politics, sales presentations, or speaking engagements. There were no budgets, forecasts, or board meetings. On the boat, if a customer wanted to talk, he talked. But mostly, Peter gratefully worked behind the scenes, making other people happy.

He had come to Savannah only because that was the closest he could get to Okatie on the bus from Key West. He had fully intended to make the twenty-minute trip up Route 17 to approach Mimi, but on the long ride through Florida, he reconsidered because he was fearful he might put his family at risk. The police would surely put him in jail for faking his death, the insurance company would sue for the spent insurance money, and then the county might take Grayson out of a seemingly unstable home.

And he could not contemplate how to explain to his widow that he had never died in the first place. It would scare her and upset her that he would have put her through that emotional trauma. She had already grieved his loss and moved on. How could he put her through the shock of his resurrection? As desperately as he wanted to be with his wife, he thought it would be selfish to do so. So he stayed where he was and built a life in a place that was far enough away to elude being discovered but close enough to watch over his wife and grandson.

During his days off, he would boat up the intercoastal waterway on the west side of Hilton Head and into the Colleton River, where he'd make his way back into the Okatee. He'd pretend to fish on the opposite bank from River Soul, but mostly he just wanted to be close to his memories. It wasn't long before he came to realize that Mimi had moved into the area full time, which pleased him greatly but also made it that much harder to stay away. He craved the chance to see them but also dreaded the feeling of separation that it created in his soul every time he was nearby.

He usually was successful at avoiding direct contact, but there was one late afternoon when he was pulling into the area just as Mimi and Grayson were pulling away from the dock. He thought he had been caught. He hoped he had been caught. But they were far enough away that Mimi simply waved the standard boating wave and kept moving.

He did not wave back. He could not wave back. The sight of his wife undid him. Her smile was always enough to touch his spirit, but to see her in such control and so happy with Grayson by her side was more than he could absorb in the few seconds he was given to process their encounter. He slowed the boat to a complete stop and reveled in the moment. His wife had acknowledged his presence.

In that moment, he realized just how invisible he had become. A simple wave was enough to validate his existence. For all of his money and power during the height of his career, he now valued more than anything else the simple acknowledgment from the person he loved most in the world. He thought about following them, but he knew at this time of day, she was just out for a sunset cruise.

As they returned, Mimi deftly managed the tides and the winds, pulling the boat up perfectly to their dock. Grayson jumped off and tied down the bow, while Mimi tied down the stern. She handed Grayson a boat bag and then got up onto the dock. They both moved in such synchronicity that it was clear they had done this together many times before.

She took Grayson's hand and started to walk toward the ramp. But suddenly, she stopped and turned around, looking exactly in his direction. Peter held his breath, both at the sight of her and with the anticipation of having been found out. She smiled, looked up at the sky, and turned back around, playfully chasing Grayson up the ramp. She had not seen him at all. She had only taken a last look at the water as the reflective colors of the sky faded to black.

He stayed out on the river for hours that night, watching the lights of the house turn on, and then eventually off, light by light. He could see his bride move from room to room as she first made dinner, then put Grayson to bed, and ultimately made her way into their old bedroom. He saw her undress and then turn off the light.

He wanted to walk up the pier and into the house and lie down next to his wife. To hold her. To make love to her. What he wouldn't do to take back all the mistakes he had made. His temporary satisfaction for having taken revenge had forever changed his destiny.

They say fate is not what happens to you, but rather the cumulative effect of all the choices you make. He had chosen poorly.

YEAR 46

Mimi responded to the doorbell, greeting the florist, who was waiting with a dozen yellow tulips.

"Hello, Samuel. Good to see you again."

"Surprise!" He handed her the vase.

"Lovely." Mimi took the tulips and instinctively held them up to her nose, even though they had no scent. "I love yellow tulips. They are my favorite!" She had said that same thing every week for over a year now.

"Imagine that," he said with a smile. "I'm glad you're enjoying them."

Mimi handed him his usual five-dollar tip and was about to close the door when it became obvious that Samuel wanted to say something. Mimi opened the door wider and gave him an expression that invited his comment.

"Mrs. Stewart, I don't mean to pry, but I've been delivering these for a long time now. Do you know who is sending these to you? We're desperately curious about the cards. We got a year of them in advance. What do they say?"

Mimi smiled. "How big is the pot?"

Samuel blushed. "It's up over two hundred now."

"If I tell you, will you share the money with me?"

"Most people say it's a secret admirer. But a few of us think it's an old boyfriend. How else would he know about the yellow tulips?"

"Hmm. Maybe. But I can't help you, Samuel. Your guess is as good as mine. It's a mystery."

"Yes, ma'am. I'll see you next week. We just got a batch of new cards and an order for another month."

"Just a month?"

"Yes, one month. And four new cards, including the one in your hand now."

He tipped his hat and started walking down the path back to his truck. Mimi looked at the flowers and then up at Samuel and said, "Nothing."

He turned around. "Ma'am?"

"Nothing. The cards don't say anything."

"I see. Well then, the mystery deepens."

Mimi took the card off the plastic holder with her free hand. She replied with a polite smile. "Yes, indeed. Thank you."

"Yes, ma'am."

She went inside and set the flowers down but held onto the card, which she brought over to the chair overlooking the back deck. She studied the card for a few minutes, unsure as to whether she should open it. Just four more cards? What was that about?

What she didn't tell Samuel was that while the cards didn't "say" anything, they weren't exactly blank either. Each week, for the last year, there was a hand-drawn picture of the entrance to the house. But it wasn't the current way the entrance looked. It was the way she had found it forty-six years ago.

The trees were smaller, like they were back then, the driveway was still just a dirt road, and the old mailbox was there, tilting to one side.

She opened the card and started to unfold the picture just as Grayson walked down the stairs with all his bags in hand.

"Another batch of tulips, I see."

Mimi folded the picture back up before she looked at it. "Yes, aren't they beautiful?"

"Anyone claim them yet?"

"Not yet."

Grayson sat down beside her. He was eighteen now and had grown into a powerfully handsome and caring boy. He placed his hand on her arm. "You know, Pops would be okay if you dated again. He'd want you to be happy."

Mimi laughed to hold back a cry. "Ah, I could never go there. I'm too old and set in my ways."

"Mimi, you know I'll always be there for you. But you're going to be alone here, a lot. It's okay to have some company once in a while. I'd feel better if I knew you were happy, if you had someone to be with while I'm gone all the time."

She smiled and, in a mom-like tone of voice, said, "I know. Thank you."

"That's your dismissive voice. You're avoiding this."

"Speaking of avoiding things, I'd really rather you not leave today."

"I'll be ten minutes away. Parris Island is right around the corner."

"Somehow I don't think the Marines are going to let you take time off to see your Mimi."

"Maybe not. But I'll be home every chance I get."

"I'll never understand why you're not going to the Naval Academy instead. You're brilliant, young man. You could write your own ticket."

"I'll go. Someday. I just don't think I can lead men if I haven't been through what they've been through. I have to learn how to follow before I can learn how to lead."

"Yeah, yeah. Your Pops said that all the time."

"He was right."

"But now, I'm sorry I taught you that."

"I'm not. This is right for me. It's what I need to do."

"Okay, okay, I give." Mimi stood up, and Grayson stood up beside her out of respect. He towered over her, and his rugged youth stood in such contrast to her elegant feminine maturity.

"I love you, boy. I'm so grateful that we had all the time we had. You were a bonus round for me. I'm such a blessed woman."

"You sound like we'll never see each other again."

"I learned a long time ago to savor every moment. To care for what God's given me while I still have it."

They hugged, and Mimi walked him out to the car.

Grayson packed his things in the car and then came back for one more hug. "I love you, Mimi. Pops would be very proud of you."

"I'm sorry you never got to know him."

"I did, through you."

"You remind me of him."

Grayson smiled, saluted, and left for basic training. He had been accepted to four Ivy League schools and all three of the military academies. And yet he chose a path that anyone who just barely graduated could have taken. But that was Grayson. He was different, in an incredibly special way.

Mimi went back into the house. The silence and emptiness were tangible. To keep from feeling such an incredible sense of aloneness, she looked for something to do. She walked over to where she had been sitting, picking up the folded piece of paper she had taken out of the card. She held it briefly and closed her eyes, speaking words of faith over her grandson and the journey he was about to take.

She opened her eyes and looked over at the river that had sustained her for more than four decades. She whispered a word of gratitude over all that she had been given. Looking down, she opened the paper and found the same picture she had received more than fifty-two times over the past year. Only this time, there was a sign propped up against the tilted post of the mailbox. On the sign were the simple words "What if?"

Peter walked along the banks of the river on a trail only known to the locals. It had been created not by hands but by the feet of explorers over the centuries. Well-worn paths weaved along the bends of the Okatee underneath a canopy of oaks that stretched out over the marsh. The mighty oak branches that hung down almost to the water shielded the late-day sun, but the light that filtered through was magical.

Above him, raccoons scurried from branch to branch, using the overhanging trees to gain easy access to the marsh where they hunted for fish and shrimp trapped in pools of water made isolated by the ebb tide. They deftly moved about the pluff mud and used their five-fingered paws to rip apart their prey as easily as any human might use a knife to slice a tomato.

He came to a rock by a lake where he and Mimi used to sit for hours, dreaming about all the possibilities that young families imagine. But as the years passed, they would dream more about what could have been if their lives had turned out differently. They wondered what normal families thought about. Did they dream, too, or did they simply talk about how good they had it?

It was evening, so all the life around him was in transition. The diurnal animals were making their way toward their dens and roosts while the nocturnal animals were preparing for nighttime hunting. He watched as thirty or forty storks gathered each evening to claim their spot on the tree they had chosen as a roost.

The long, circular path each stork took before coming to rest on a branch put him in a meditative state. He leaned back and relaxed until a young stork fell out of the tree and landed down by the lake. It stood all by itself in the shallow water, and Peter wondered how it would make it through the night on its own. So many dangers lurked in the dark for something so young and innocent.

It wasn't long before Peter noticed the bulky head of an alligator surface in the center of the lake. Someone foreign to the Lowcountry would not recognize the danger, as only the eyes and traces of the snout appeared on the surface. To a casual observer, it could be mistaken for a floating bit of debris. But to the locals, it was an unmistakable sight.

Peter saw the gator move very slowly but intentionally toward the young stork on the edge of the lake. He wondered how long it would be until the little bird's life would come to a swift and unexpected end. But as the predator came within twenty yards, a female stork left its roost and flew down to stand beside the young stork. She stood tall beside him, knowing what was coming. The young stork was blissfully unaware and seemed unchanged by her presence.

The alligator stopped and lay still for a long time. Nature is remarkably patient. But perhaps happier to have two meals instead of one, he began his approach once more. Peter estimated the gator to be at least twelve feet long based on the bit of head he could see. It was a formidable foe, but neither stork moved or even seemed all that concerned. One was oblivious to the danger, the other resigned to it.

Peter knew that while the gator's approach was slow and stealthy, the eventual strike would be very fast and very violent. He watched with anticipation of all the harm that would come to this mother and child, when Peter saw a huge male stork suddenly swoop down from above and stand on the opposite side of the young stork. Each parent moved close to the young one, making all three together look like one very large object.

The gator observed this growing white puff of feathers and contemplated his next move. Most predators look for easy prey—the small, the isolated, and the weak. This gator was no different. He sank to the bottom of the lake, perhaps not quite prepared for a fight on this particular night. It was remarkable to Peter how casual this entire encounter had been, despite the desperate nature of the situation. The storks made only those moves that were necessary, when they were necessary. Nothing more, nothing less.

As the sun set, Peter knew he needed to get back to his boat before it became too dark to see the path. He walked along the trail and noticed how different the trees looked with the sun below the horizon. While he could still see the dim light and colors of the sky through their branches, the path below had become very dark and eerie. He was well aware of how much life surrounded him, but he could not see any of it.

As he reached his boat, he looked toward River Soul. No lights, no Mimi, no Grayson. His trip here had been unfruitful. He turned on his navigation lights and GPS, but they were unnecessary. He'd been making this trip in the dark for more than ten years. He was willing to do anything to be close to his family. Even from a distance, he could get some sense of the man Grayson was growing into, and some peace being near his wife as she grew older and more graceful.

He pulled anchor and turned the boat upriver. When he made his way past Hilton Head down toward Savannah, he knew the water around him was vast and deep, but the darkness made it feel empty and small. These hours on the ocean left him alone with his thoughts, feeling as though he'd been cast out onto the sea to contemplate his life and all the choices he had made. He should have been a better father and a better husband. He never should have let his anger get the better of him.

From the moment Peter had walked down the dock of River Soul for the last time so many years ago and set adrift onto the Okatee, it was as though he had walked away from everything he had ever known about himself. He was no longer a CEO, husband, father, or Christian. He couldn't even claim to be a decent man. He was invisible, a nobody, a curse to his family. He had become, in his own mind, unredeemable.

But after more than a decade on the water, he had begun to put some distance between the man he was now and the man he was before, or, perhaps better said, as the men he was before. He had lived two lives—one as the man in the suit and the other as the man with the knife. Both of them were lost. One just looked more acceptable on the outside.

And so it was with Austin, and all the other addicts he had been exposed to. He was just as lost as they were. They relied on drugs, and he relied on himself. Neither were dependable choices to make. He had judged them harshly and, in the process, judged himself. He had done worse things than they had ever done. He was no better—maybe worse.

He thought he had been the savior. Instead, he came to realize that he had become the alligator in the lake.

But at least the lost know they are lost. Peter had spent decades thinking he was found. It was not until his life as the savior had passed away that he could see it for what it was—empty, shallow, and confused. Peter knew there was only one Savior, and he was not it. But sometimes you have to go through a thing before you can rise above it. He had to spend his time in the world before the wind and the waves could gently wear away at his callous outer shell.

He decided that it's no harder for God to forgive the sin of pride than it is to forgive the sin of addiction or vengeance. It's all sin. It matters not how bad our language is or how often we throw away all that God has given us; He still pursues us. He still sees us as He created us. He still loves us perfectly. If we deny Him three times, He'll give us three chances to tell Him how much we love Him.

Peter had had it right all along. Jesus was the answer. It just turned out to be a different Jesus than he had ever imagined. And Peter turned out to be a very different Christian than he ever could have been if Austin had been born happy and healthy.

Mimi sat back and contemplated the envelope she held in her hands. It was the fourth and final card. She was afraid to open it. Over the course of the last month, questions had been flooding through her mind. Who could be sending these flowers, and how did this person know so well the intimate details of their family?

The picture, to start with, was so strange. The entrance to the house. Why the entrance? And why did it look the way it looked back when they first found the place? Who would know that? There were a few neighbors who lived nearby back then, but none of them seemed like the kind to send flowers and cryptic notes.

And what about the notes? She had received three of them, each with a different message.

What if . . .
Taking life as is
Was always the plan?

The first message, "What if," was a simple enough question. Millions of people ask it every day. But to Mimi, "what if" was something more, a game that she and Peter would play for hours on end.

The game started seriously enough, where they would contemplate their lives "if" Austin had not been so sick. But after years of thinking about what might have been "if" things had been different, it had become a joke between them. One person would make up outrageous scenarios starting with the question "What if," and the other person had to finish the story in some fanciful way.

The second card also was potentially harmless. "Taking life as is" is a common phrase. But what made the message so interesting is that the picture changed just slightly. At the entrance to the driveway was a "For Sale" sign that looked exactly like the sign that was out front when she and Peter first found the place.

At first, she was focused on the change to the picture. Again, who could possibly have known what that sign looked like back then? Was this the realtor they had used when they bought the place? She thought about the sign for days. But then, about midweek, she sat up in bed in the middle of the night when she remembered that she had told Peter to take the house "as is," forcing him to repeat the words out loud.

Who could possibly know this much, and why would they play on her emotions about her late husband? It was starting to feel creepy as the intrigue was turning into anger at whomever was doing this to her. But then again, these were also common phrases. Was she reading too much into it?

The third card was also commonplace, and yet still potentially too close to home. "Was always the plan?" To anyone else, a very common thought. But to Mimi, the words "the plan" hit her deeply in her soul.

Peter always joked about "her plan." She was always making plans, plans that never worked out. Peter and the family were the only ones who ever used that phrase with her.

And along with the third card, the hand-drawn picture changed completely. Instead of the entrance, it was a complete layout of their home. In bold lines were all the parts of the house that had existed when they bought the place. And with dotted lines, were all the additions and changes they had made to the house over the years. Was the house "plan" what the card was referring to?

But if that wasn't enough, even more bizarre were all three comments together. "What if taking life 'as is' was always the plan?" Throughout their marriage, Peter was far too serious—about everything. The whole family continually had to tell him to calm down and have some fun. Be spontaneous. Take life as it is. Roll with it.

Mimi couldn't think of a time when she had been more upset, and she had been through plenty. She had grown comfortable with the flowers spread over the last year. Intrigue had turned into a fun diversion, which had turned into a pleasant curiosity. But these last three cards had turned disturbing, and she thought about it every minute of every day.

She decided there were only two possibilities: Someone was playing a horrible joke on her, or the impossible was, in fact, possible. It seemed too unreal to even contemplate. It was too much to hope for a simply outrageous notion. And yet it could be the most wonderful thing that had ever happened.

So, when she held the fourth card in her hands, it was so much more than just a card. And the flowers were so much more than just flowers. She was too apprehensive to read it and yet had been waiting for this moment for days. When Samuel the florist had come to the door, she tried to appear nonchalant.

"Oh, hello, Samuel."

"Hi, Mrs. Stewart."

"So is this it, or were more ordered?"

"I can't believe it, but this is it. I'm going to miss our little get-togethers."

Mimi smiled. She handed him a $50 tip.

"Oh, Mrs. Stewart. I can't accept that."

"Samuel, I'm going to miss you too. Please take it. I appreciate all that you've done."

"Well, thank you. Until the next admirer."

Again, she smiled. "Until then."

She took the flowers and set them on the table like always. She took the card outside on the deck and watched the river for a few moments. What was said in that card could change the rest of her life, and it could also upset her beyond her ability to withstand it.

She reached down and peeled back the seal on the envelope. The first thing she did was to open the folded picture. This time, the drawing was of the river, which looked mostly the same. But the pier heading down to the dock was the old, twisted mess of splintered boards that looked the way it did before Peter had it torn down and then put it back together. At the bottom of the page were the words, "A River's Soul was where it all began."

She put the card down and stared at the river, even though she didn't actually see anything. She was too deep inside her thoughts to process anything around her. Tears welled up within her, and her heart was both sick and excited all at the same time. To calm herself, she picked up the drawing again and held it up in front of her, comparing the landscape as it was then to how it appeared now.

As her heart rate slowed a bit, she looked down at the writing on the card. "River Soul" was nothing anyone else would have known. Only the family called the place River Soul. And yet this message didn't exactly call it River Soul either. It said "A River's Soul." Was this all just an amazing coincidence? How could it be? There was too much that was too close. It couldn't be, and yet it had to be.

Mimi pulled all four cards out together and read the message over and over again.

What if
Taking life as is
Was always the plan?
A River's Soul was where it all began.

It was the next day when Mimi got an unexpected visit from Grayson, who showed up on a one-day pass. She was so grateful that she latched on to him and held tightly.

"Mimi. Mimi. Let go so I can see you."

Mimi still hugged him for a few more seconds until she finally released her grip. "Give your old grandma a break. I've missed you."

She kept holding his hand. While it seemed normal to Grayson, what he could not know was how much she needed something comfortable, something tangible to hold on to. With all the mystery and the thought of ghosts flooding her memories, she needed to be in the now, in the moment with someone she could physically see and touch.

"So," she continued, "how is it in the Marines? If it's possible, you're even more handsome than when you left. Are they feeding you? Are they being too hard on you?"

Grayson laughed. "You're being such a mother hen right now."

"Yeah, yeah. So tell me."

"It's good. It's hard. It's brutally hard."

"So why don't you go to the Academy instead?"

"They don't take quitters there, Mimi. I've committed to this. I have to finish."

She playfully tapped the little bit of hair he had on his head. "Such a hard mass of stubbornness up there."

"But I have some news for you."

"Well, that sounds ominous."

"Not so bad, but it is news. They're transferring me out to the San Diego Recruit Depot in California."

"Why would they do that? Are you in trouble? Is something wrong?"

"No, Mimi. I'm not in trouble."

She shook her fist. "You better not be." And they both smiled.

"They called me into the sergeant's office and told me they think that Parris Island is too easy for me since I grew up here. I know the terrain, and I'm okay with the heat. I guess I'm not suffering enough. They want to see me in a different environment."

Mimi laughed out loud. "So the United States Marines told you that boot camp was too easy for you?"

Grayson tried not to smile. "Yes, ma'am."

"Grayson Peter Stewart. You are just too much. When do you leave?"

"Tomorrow. That's why they let me come see you today. I fly out in the morning."

Mimi's face dampened. "Oh, I see. Of course."

"If I do well there, they want to ship me overseas to train with some elite units in the Middle East."

Mimi started to sound a bit distressed. "So when will I see you again?"

"You can come out for graduation, but then I'm off right away, at least if I do well."

Not wanting to appear needy or to make him feel bad, Mimi tried not to let her emotions rise to the surface.

"Grayson, you've always been a special young man. I'm not surprised they have seen that in you. I'm just not sure why it took them a whole month to figure it out."

They both laughed. "Now," she said, "go up and get a nice warm shower, and I'll cook us up some dinner."

As Grayson made his way up the stairs, Mimi watched him ascend. She knew that her purpose in life had been to raise this boy into a man, a special man. She had done just that. But she knew in that moment that she couldn't keep him to herself any longer. Now that the world could see him for what he was, it would want him for all he was worth.

Mimi busied herself around the house, and then out in the garden, and then back in the house again. She kayaked and boated and fished until she couldn't do those things anymore. It was not so much that she was bored, but she was agitated with the thought that Grayson was now mostly out of her life. And the mystery of the flowers was still completely unresolved.

It was Friday afternoon. For the last fifty-six weeks, Samuel had shown up at about this time. Knowing that he was not coming today left her feeling a void that she could not explain. While she was relieved that the cards had stopped, the fact that it was over was a surprising disappointment. Why would this person wind her up so much just to leave her wondering what it was all about?

She thought about calling the florist to see if anything had changed, but that just seemed needy and pathetic. She looked out the window a few times to see if Samuel's truck was coming up the drive. But it was just more of the same. Silence. Deafening silence.

She walked out to the back and watched as the tide rushed in. It would be a full moon tonight, so the water would be especially high. She sat down and wondered if her life, if their life, had really begun on this river. They had lived in Chicago before they ever came here. So didn't their life begin there? And they had only come here one week out of each year, so their life together really existed elsewhere.

And yet this place always called them. They were at their happiest here.

Maybe everything out there was not life. Maybe life as it was meant to be lived was here, in this place. But was it right to hide in heaven, or was she supposed to take heaven out to the world? Maybe everyone else would only ever know happiness if they'd just let her tell her story.

As the sun began to set in the west, the moon began to crest on the horizon in the east. It was still light out, but it was always spectacular to see the moon rise over the mighty oaks of the Okatee. To have both the moon and the sun in the same sky was particularly wonderful. Soon the sky would be dark, but for now, it was a remarkable combination of the night and the day all mixed into one.

As she leaned back to take in the scenery, she heard a knock on the door. Except for Samuel, no one ever knocked on her door. She looked down at her watch. It was almost 8 p.m., too late for any deliveries.

She got up somewhat apprehensively and moved carefully inside so as not to give away her presence. She could see in the side window panels next to the door a dozen yellow tulips extending over the shoulder of a man looking away, out to the setting sun. She found herself smiling and said to herself, "I guess Samuel got another order after all."

She walked more confidently toward the door, although along the way, the mystery of what the newest card might say flooded her thoughts. She had finally let it go, thinking it was over, and now that tension returned. She opened the door to greet the florist, but found herself staring right into the setting sun, which created a halo of colors around the man, who still was turned away from her. Before she could clearly see him, she spoke.

"Well, it looks like we meet again."

But as the man turned around, it was not Samuel. And when Mimi could finally see, her hands went first to her mouth and then to her heart. As it turned out, this was where her life began after all.

YEAR 56

Grayson placed his bags down on the front porch and knocked on a door that appeared unusually worn. He waited for a response and then knocked again. He'd been gone almost four years now and hadn't been able to reach Mimi to let her know he was coming. While he waited, he looked around the rest of the outer buildings. The paint was starting to peel, and some of the boards were starting to split. A few of the shutters were askew, and the yard was slightly overgrown. Not at all up to Mimi's standards.

No one answered on his third knock, so he used his key and pushed open the door.

"Mimi? Mimi? It's Grayson."

He noticed the house smelled musty, as though no one had been in it for a while, so he opened some windows to let the fresh air inside. He walked gingerly over to his grandmother's bedroom and knocked.

"Mimi, are you here?"

Nothing. He grabbed his bags, threw them into his room, and made his way out back to see if she was somewhere on the water. As he walked down to the dock, he noticed that a number of the boards on the pier were warped and buckling. But he continued toward the water, where he could see the boat up on its lift and the kayak and canoe in their proper place.

"Hmm."

He returned to the house and unpacked. He had been thinking he'd be eating a wonderful home-cooked meal tonight, but instead, he rifled through his backpack for some granola and a can of soda. He'd lived off far less during his deployments overseas, but it was not what he was hoping for today. He knew he should have called, but his orders were always so last minute that he did not have a dependable schedule to arrange with her.

Mimi also had grown strangely unavailable over the years. She had come to his graduation from boot camp, and then again from Annapolis, but then she had stopped reaching out to come see him when he was in the country. Whenever he would get her on the phone to arrange a visit in Okatie, she'd ask very specific questions around when he'd be coming and for how long. It seemed odd to him, but he just assumed she was getting particular in her old age. She was almost eighty after all.

She always made him feel like the most important person in the world when they were together, but he began to sense that her mind was elsewhere, like she had something else to do. And yet she also seemed happier and more at peace than he'd ever seen her. When he'd ask her why, she'd just say that living in the South had that effect on her.

He had hoped she was out running errands, but after a few hours, he realized that she was not coming home. He sat down on the deck out back and contemplated all that this place had meant to him. Like most kids, he had taken it for granted growing up. But he was beginning to see what Mimi had seen all along.

He went inside and started going through the house. He looked at the pictures and the books and the trophies. He came to an odd-looking box on a shelf, and he opened it up to find a dozen dried flowers. He was about to close the box when he noticed a card inside. He pulled it out and sat down. On the envelope was simply the name Mary. He opened the card and on the inside it read, "Fragrance clings to the hand that gives the flower."

It was a Chinese proverb that his grandfather had used many times according to Mimi, when trying to show his family that it was better to give than to receive. Grayson assumed that she had kept these flowers as a way to remember her dead husband.

He moved around the house some more until he came to Mimi's desk. There on top of her work area were a few organized files. One contained the utilities required to keep River Soul running. He could see that all the bills and taxes on the house had been pre-paid for five years. Another file contained the title to the property with a sticky note pointing to the name on the title. To his amazement, the document showed that he was now the owner of their family home.

A final file was marked "Important." He opened it to find a letter with his name on the envelope. He picked it up and sat down at the seat where he had seen his Mimi sit so many times before. He peeled back the seal and pulled out the paper inside.

> Grayson,
>
> You are the most wonderful spirit that any family could ever hope for. I would call you my grandson, but you are so much more than that. You are my joy, you are my heart, and you are my soul. It seemed that after losing both my daughters to one life or another, there would be nothing left to sustain me. But the child left behind turned out to be everything I needed.
>
> You were my second chance. My redemption. I found myself in you. I could not tell you that because it was too much responsibility to put on a child. But I want you to know that you were the strength I needed before I could find that strength in myself and in the One who strengthens all of us. You were the bridge that took me where I needed to go.

And now the man that you have become belongs not only to me but to the world. You are strong. You are the kind of person that other people want to be. Never be afraid to be yourself. Never hide your strength. This world needs people who know who they are and Whose they are.

When you face struggles, for we all face struggles, remember that the people who are the most tormented are the ones God wants to use the most. Turn whatever you may go through into tenderness for what other people are going through themselves.

I am sorry that I'm not here to say goodbye in person. But I've done what I came here to do. I've come to rely too much on this place for my happiness. I need to take what God has given me here into the rest of the world.

This house is now yours. But you know that this is so much more than a house. This is our family. Someday, you will bring your family here, and I hope they can experience what we found together. For in this place, we discovered our true selves. And there is no greater gift that God could give us than to know Him and to know who we really are.

I love you. You are my rock.

Love,
Your Mimi

Grayson put down the letter, but his attention immediately shifted at the sound of a text on his cell phone. He was being ordered to report for duty as soon as possible.

He sat there for a few minutes more. The naval air station was only twenty minutes away in Beaufort. He held Mimi's letter in his hands and took it with him while he repacked. As he headed out the door, he turned around and took in the house one last time. He closed the door and wondered if he'd ever be back. He was never sure if he'd be back.

As Grayson drove out of sight, the water began to withdraw from the banks of the river, where it would spend the night flowing out to the Port Royal Sound. The insects began their chorus of sounds while some raccoons finally broke back into the attic of a house they once owned.

We are but a whisper in the wind. And yet we shout, and cry, and strain to leave a mark that others will remember. We claim a truth that we'll never understand and profess our virtues as right and just. But we know not where the wind comes from or where it goes. We only know that it carries away our striving.

A river is just a river. A house is just a house. A life is just a life. Nothing is either good or bad, but thinking makes it so.

EPILOGUE

My dad used to say that Austin dated enough fools to fill the acre on which River Soul was created. But in the end, the only real fools were the ones who lived there. God uses the foolish of this world to confound the wise. And so I proudly call my family an acre of fools. They laid themselves low so that I might rise high.

And so I come to this river to remind myself of who I really am. Twenty years out in the world stripped me of my soul. I can only reclaim it on this river, where my mom and dad did the best they could with a life that most would have called a curse. Instead, they did what they had to do and stayed positive as long as they could. In the end, only Mimi found her true self, and she helped me find mine, right here on the river.

I'm not sure where my dad is. No one really is. But sometimes when I'm here on the river, fishing the marshy banks of the Okatee, I think I see him watching over me. I know he protected me from harm, as did the one he named Grace Elizabeth. Both of them gave their lives so that I might lead a life different from what I was destined for on my own.

You know my dad as Peter Stewart, my grandfather. I never knew Theo. I never really knew Peter either, as he left before I was old enough to remember much. But Peter lived on in the stories Mimi would tell me and in the pictures she would show. He lives in my room at River Soul, the one that he designed but never built. It's the only room in the house he did not create through the work of his hands. It was only his spirit and his soul that made my place here.

My natural mother has never contacted me. Mimi would say that it's because she was too ashamed of what she did. I think it's because she loved me too much to bring me into her world. She didn't want me to live her life. I choose what I want to believe and love the way I want to be loved.

You know my mother as Mimi, Mary Stewart, my grandmother. Her story is the true tale of redemption. This was always her story. We simply played bit parts in her play. And now I tell others, in the hopes that they might find joy in the midst of whatever struggles they find themselves. We all have a purpose in life. And we find that purpose not in spite of the pain but because of it.

My name is Grayson Peter Stewart, a name I wear proudly, a name that now hangs on the governor's mansion for the state of South Carolina and on the ballot for president of the United States. Mimi would be so proud. Finally, a man of the South to carry on where she left off.

But that is another story.

Our faith must be exercised in the realities of everyday life. We will be scattered, not into service but into the emptiness of our lives where we will see ruin and barrenness, to know what internal death to God's blessings means. . . . It is certainly not of our own choosing, but God engineers our circumstances to take us there.

—**OSWALD CHAMBERS**, *My Utmost for His Highest*

AUTHOR'S NOTE

I was in an Al-Anon meeting many years ago and was listening to one father speak of his drug-addicted, alcoholic son. It was Christmastime, and all of us were getting cards and letters from friends and family—the ones where we learn about how miraculous everyone else's children are.

This particular father was the comedian in our group, always having something funny to say. When it came his time to share, he read aloud to our group one of those letters. And then he showed us a copy of what he did when he returned the letter. In red marker, he replied, "That's terrific news. You must be so proud. My son's in prison."

Most of us laughed. The only ones who were silent were the first-time parents, the ones who had not yet worked through the shame and the utter disappointment the rest of us were used to feeling.

There is a journey that every parent, every child, every sibling of an addict takes—a journey from the life that we dreamed for our family and the life they actually chose for themselves.

For some people, the ones who write the Christmas letters, that journey is short. Their family members grew into wonderful people who may have even exceeded expectations. But for those of us with addicts in our midst, that journey between the life we dreamed and the life actually lived is a rocky and steep path spread across thousands of miles of treacherous terrain.

On the face of it, it might seem that the shorter path is the better path. But for those of us who have made the difficult journey, we have discovered a depth of understanding about ourselves that we would never have come to know without the pain we had to suffer along the way.

The journey is not one of love, but of acceptance. Few of us ever stop loving our children, spouses, or parents. But many of us reject, sometimes aggressively, the life they have chosen. And so we sit on a self-righteous high horse, pouring out our love conditions with our every comment, every threat, and every glance of disapproval.

This is a difficult, almost impossible place to be—not wanting to validate the drug use, the abhorrent lifestyle, the destructive behavior—but also not wanting to invalidate the souls of the people we have loved, in part, for who they were before the addiction came.

As with so many things, it may be that the old dream must die before the new dream can emerge. But dreams die hard.

I remember sitting across from my once beautiful daughter in a restaurant. I hadn't seen her in months, and the image before me was disturbing. She wore dirty sweatpants and an oversized sweatshirt. She smelled bad and obviously had not washed her hair in weeks. And the scabs on her face from the drug use were bloody and dripping with pus.

I was judging her with every fiber of my being. I couldn't hear a word she was saying because she couldn't have been further away from the person she used to be.

But then, unexpectedly, a vivid thought entered my head. *Don't judge her for the next five minutes. Just love her.* It was the best five minutes I'd had with her in ten years. I allowed myself to love her for the pure joy of seeing my daughter and knowing that for these few minutes, she was safe, well fed, and cared for. I listened to her intently, and I think for the first time in a long while, she felt listened to.

But then the time came when she once again rejected an offer of help, and I needed to send her back into the life I had come to dread. The sadness returned as my dream for her died all over again. I dropped her off at the hotel room I had once again paid for to keep her off the street for at least a couple of nights. As she walked back into the abyss, likely into the arms of the real-life Jack, I drove away completely broken, a feeling I had come to know as a regular part of my everyday existence.

My son is in prison. My daughter is in prison. Can you ever say that and be okay?

If you had asked me forty years ago if I would have chosen this version of my family, my answer would have been a predictable "No way!" But if you were to ask me that same question today, I would tell you that addiction has both destroyed and rebuilt my family into something that none of us would ever trade away.

I love her for who she is, what she is, and how she has shaped me into the person I am today. The shame I feel today is not for what she became, but for who I was when she became that person. Maybe this is a journey of true love after all. May God bless you and your family and give you the true desires of your heart.

ACKNOWLEDGMENTS

Everything I know I have learned from my family, current addicts, former addicts, friends, pastors, mentors, work associates, and a myriad of people who interjected hope and encouragement into our lives along the way.

More specifically, I thank my family—the real-life Mimi, Gracie, and Austin who have taught me more about love and compassion than I ever could have learned by reading Scripture alone. I am reminded of how lucky I am to be your husband and father every day. And to my parents and sister, who gave me the foundation and strength I needed to survive the journey that has become our life, I say thank you for your unconditional love and grace. And to my grandsons, I can only hope that the fools you call your family have given you the courage you need to be strong and kind all of your days.

I also thank my first-edition editor, Anna McHargue. This book is better written and richer for your input along the way. You made it fun to write about something so painful. Your encouragement and guidance were the added boost I needed. I am thankful for your presence. It lives in this book too.

And to the Greenleaf team, I say thank you as well, especially to Jeanette, my copyeditor. I am grateful to all of you.

ABOUT THE AUTHOR

SCOTT MACLELLAN lives in the Lowcountry of South Carolina, where he enjoys the outdoors with his wife, daughters, and grandsons. He is the author of seven books and is also an executive producer of the upcoming streaming TV series based on *An Acre of Fools*.

A percentage of the profits of this book will be donated by the author to causes focused on addiction, human trafficking, and family restoration. In addition, Scott has partnered with Mission 17, a nonprofit organization, to create short-form video experiences to equip addicts and families of addicts. For more information on this mission, called the River Soul Project, please scan the QR code below.

Join the movement. Read the book. Watch the series. Help change lives.